Close to You

NISSA RENZO

Bloom books

Published by Bloom Books, an imprint of Sourcebooks
1935 Brookdale RD, Naperville, IL 60563-2773
(630) 961-3900
sourcebooks.com

Originally self-published in 2026 by Nissa Renzo.

Cataloging-in-Publication data is on file with the Library of Congress.

Printed and bound in the United States of America.
PAH 10 9 8 7 6 5 4 3 2 1

To A.

Author's Note

I want to start by saying that *Close to You* is not an easy read if you've been a victim of bullying. I contemplated writing this book for a long time before finally going for it. While the book is purely fictional, the bullying scenes and (some) characters are very real.

It's a very personal book, and I know many readers will feel connected to Milow and what she goes through.

Close to You is a slow burn with no spice, is character-driven, and tackles topics that may be upsetting. For a full list of triggers, please check out my Instagram post on @authornissarenzo.

Because the FMC is mute and communicates in sign language, whenever she or another character signs, it will be indicated with brackets [ ]. Spoken dialogue will be as normal.

Content Warnings

Anxiety and panic attacks
Skin picking disorder
Bullying
Childhood trauma
Child SA/abuse
Mental abuse
Physical abuse

Playlist

Chasing Cars—Snow Patrol
The Best Day—Taylor Swift
We're Going to Be Friends—The White Stripes
Arms Open—The Script
Seventeen Going Under—Sam Fender
They Don't Know About Us—One Direction
seven—Taylor Swift
Fall—Justin Bieber
Look After You—The Fray
Fix You—Coldplay
Keep Holding On—Avril Lavigne
Shadow of the Day—Linkin Park
If I Die Young—The Band Perry
I Love You Always Forever—Donna Lewis
Close to You—Gracie Abrams

PART 1

1

Milow

Friday, January 2nd
6 years old

Every morning, I woke up before Daddy because getting up first meant I could slip out of my room and go to the kitchen without him stopping me. I liked knowing I had a small chance to pour a big bowl of cereal since he always said I should only eat a little. When he served the cereal, the amount barely covered the bottom, and when I signed for more, he always shook his head. Daddy always said that I shouldn't eat too much because girls weren't supposed to eat a lot. That's why he never filled my plate like he filled his, and why I was always so hungry and snuck into the kitchen when he wasn't watching. So I waited on my bed until I was sure he was still asleep and hoped today would be one of those days when I could eat until I felt full.

My belly growled as I pushed open my bedroom door. I paused and looked toward Daddy's door and waited to see if the knob moved or if I heard him shifting around in his room. Nothing happened. The door stayed closed, and the house stayed still, which meant he was still asleep, and I still had time.

I walked down the stairs slowly and as silently as a mouse to not make noise. I had gotten good at being quiet. Very good, actually. Even when I tried to speak, I couldn't. Daddy said it was because obedient girls were only supposed to nod, and since I was an obedient girl, my voice magically disappeared.

The kitchen was bigger without Daddy standing in it. Daddy always took up a lot of space. I moved a chair to the counter and climbed onto it, gripping the edge so I wouldn't fall. The cereal box was in its usual spot, and I reached for it until I could grab it. With my knees on the counter, I scooted over to the cupboard with the bowls inside, and after grabbing one, I turned around to sit and poured the cereal until the bowl looked full the way I always wanted it to look. I used my fingers to eat, and I chewed each bite long enough to savor it because I couldn't be sure when I'd get another chance to eat as much as I wanted.

I kept glancing toward the stairs while I ate. Daddy usually came down by now, and the second I'd hear his footsteps, I'd put everything away and go to sit on the couch. Daddy always checked on me. He always watched what I was doing. But today, minutes passed, and the house stayed quiet. I finished the cereal and kept listening because the stillness made me feel strange inside. Daddy never stayed asleep this long. Not ever.

Still sitting on the counter, I turned toward the sink and rinsed the bowl before placing it back into the cupboard so Daddy wouldn't notice I had eaten from it without him knowing. I put the cereal box away, then jumped off the counter and pushed the chair back to the table. I wiped my mouth with the back of my hand to ensure there was no evidence of the cereal, then I walked out of the kitchen and toward the stairs. Something felt different about today, but I didn't know what. I climbed back up holding the railing, and when I reached the hallway, Daddy's door was still closed. And there was still no sound coming from his room.

I stopped in front of the door but didn't step too close. Stepping any closer made my stomach twist. Only bad things ever happened in there.

I stood there for a long moment before lifting my hand and bravely opened the door a little. The room was dark, and I saw Daddy on the bed with his back facing me. He wasn't making the noises he usually made when he slept.

I walked closer so slowly that my feet barely left the floor and stopped beside the bed with my breath stuck in my throat. I waited for him to turn or sit up or say something.

But he didn't do anything at all.

I was glad, in a way. Because if Daddy saw me standing here, watching him, he would get angry. I thought about poking him, even if I was scared. But something wasn't right.

I looked at the bed and frowned because I didn't like the things Daddy did to me on it. Every time he brought me in here, I ended up crying and in pain, but he always promised me that he was supposed to make me cry because it meant he truly loved me. Daddy always said I still had a lot to learn, and that when I got older, I would understand better. He said that everything he did to me would prepare me to one day go outside.

I was only six, and Daddy said I had to stay in the house for twelve more years.

When I looked at Daddy's back again, I thought that maybe he was just very tired, and that he needed more sleep than usual. It had happened once before, him telling me not to bother him because he needed to sleep for longer one morning. Back then, there was a strange smell coming from him. Something strong, like the smell that came out of his soda cans. It was soda I wasn't supposed to drink because it was for grown-ups, but I didn't even want to drink his soda. It was stinky.

I scrunched my nose at the thought of it and took a step back because I didn't want to wake him. I didn't want to bother him when he was this tired.

Maybe, with him being this tired, he wouldn't put the owie-stick inside of me.

I took a slow step out of the room and closed the door without making it click too loudly, then I walked downstairs and turned on the TV because I didn't know what else to do. Daddy was okay with me watching TV all day. There wasn't really anything else I could do, and he said that as long as I sat still and didn't bother him, watching TV was fine.

I watched cartoons for hours, until my stomach growled, and until it started to get dark outside. I looked toward the stairs to make sure Daddy wouldn't suddenly appear, and when he didn't, I got up and went to the fridge to grab the first thing I could reach.

For the rest of the late afternoon, I sat on the couch and kept listening for his footsteps. But there was still no sound.

When the sun had fully disappeared, the bad feeling in

my belly became heavier. I hugged my knees to my chest and stared at the staircase, and I kept telling myself that Daddy was just tired. That maybe he just needed a long nap, and that he would come down when he felt better. He wouldn't go a day without seeing me.

He loved me.

He was my Daddy.

But he didn't come downstairs.

I started to feel so confused that I couldn't keep sitting on the couch. I walked back upstairs, and when I reached Daddy's door, I stood there in the same spot as this morning, taking a deep breath before I reached out and pushed the door open.

Daddy's body lay in a different position now. His head was turned toward me, but I couldn't really see his expression in the darkness. I took a step closer, and when his face became clearer, I noticed something strange about it.

His eyes were closed, but there was white foam on his mouth.

I froze, and hot tingles ran from the very tips of my toes all the way up to my head. Then my hands went cold, and my heart started to go *boom boom boom* so very fast. I didn't know what the foam meant, but it scared me because I had never seen Daddy look like that. His body didn't move, and the longer I stared at him, the scarier Daddy became.

I wanted to poke him, but I was too scared to. My heart thumped even harder in my chest, and I stepped back until my shoulder hit the doorframe.

Daddy was sick. But Daddy was also a doctor. Why didn't he make himself better like he always made me better?

My hands shook as I backed out of the room. I kept my eyes on him until the darkness swallowed him. I ran down the hallway and stopped at the top of the stairs, unsure what to do.

I wanted to hide under my blanket. Maybe a monster got to him. Maybe it got inside him and made that foam come out of his mouth. Would the monster get to me, too? If there was a monster in the house, was it watching me? I was scared. I wanted Daddy to sit up. I wanted him to look at me, even if he was never happy to see me.

I ran down the steps before I knew it. My bare feet slapped against the wood, and my breathing was so fast that my chest hurt. I didn't know where to go, but I knew I had to get away from Daddy's room. The house wasn't safe anymore, and it felt like the walls were moving in on me.

At the bottom of the stairs, I stopped in the hallway and looked around. Everything looked normal, but it didn't feel normal. I felt like something bad was moving around me and wanted to get me like it got Daddy.

I didn't want foam to come out of my mouth. I didn't want to not move or nap for so long.

My eyes darted to the front door.

I needed to go outside where the monsters couldn't get to me.

But Daddy always said I couldn't go outside for twelve more years. He said it was dangerous. He said the world would hurt me. But Daddy was lying on his bed, and he didn't move, and there was foam on his mouth, and monsters didn't stay in rooms forever.

I ran to the coatrack. Daddy's big snow boots sat under it. They were heavy and too big, and I had never put them on before, but I had to if I wanted to go outside. Daddy always put them on when he left the house. My hands shook as I grabbed them and sat on the floor. I shoved my feet into them. My toes didn't reach the ends. They felt like giant buckets around my legs. Daddy also put on his big coat and gloves when he went outside, but I couldn't reach the coat. It was too far up. The gloves were shoved into the coat's pockets, and I grabbed them and put them on. They were thick and way too big for my hands, but they were soft and warm, and I didn't have any of my own. Daddy had never given me any because he said I didn't need them.

I stood up, wobbling in the giant boots, and looked at the door again. My breath was shaky, and my heart still thumped too fast. Maybe the monster in Daddy's room wanted me next. Maybe it hid in the walls. Maybe it waited for me to go back upstairs.

I grabbed the doorknob with both hands and turned it hard. The door opened, and the cold gust of wind startled me. Snowflakes blew inside and touched my face, and I blinked at the brightness outside. The front yard was all white, and it was way brighter out there than inside the house.

Holding my breath, I dared to step outside.

The snow reached almost to the top of the boots, and my legs sank with each step. The cold bit at my skin through my pajamas, but I kept walking because the house scared me more than whatever waited for me out here.

Daddy was inside with foam on his mouth, and I didn't know if he would ever move again because the monster got to him.

I didn't know where I was going. I only knew I had

to go somewhere to find someone who could help me get Daddy to wake up. Or make the monster and the foam go away.

My teeth started to hurt from the cold, but I kept moving bravely, one giant-boot step at a time, because staying in the house felt scarier than walking into the white world I had never seen before.

The air was sharp in my nose, and my fingers hurt inside the gloves even though they were supposed to keep me warm. My pajamas stuck to my legs, and the snow kept getting inside the boots, but I tried not to think about it. I just kept walking.

I followed the road. Daddy always told me the world outside was dangerous, but the road didn't look dangerous. It looked empty. Where would monsters hide? There were no walls.

After a long time, I saw something red in the distance. A big building at the end of the road. At first, I didn't know what it was, but then I saw the tall doors and the big trucks behind the windows. I stopped and stared because I had seen places like this on TV before.

It was a fire station.

I remembered the people on TV wearing big coats and helmets. They carried hoses. They rescued people from burning houses and helped them when they were hurt. I didn't know if they helped with monsters or foam on people's mouths, but they helped with a lot of things on TV, so maybe they could help me too.

The snow crunched louder as I walked faster, and my feet slipped a little in Daddy's boots. My legs hurt, but I didn't stop. The red building got bigger and bigger with each step, and when I finally reached the driveway, the snow there wasn't as deep. I shuffled forward until I stood right in front of the big doors, and I looked around for someone.

There were lights on inside the fire station, but after I lifted one giant glove and knocked on the door, nobody came to open it. I knocked harder, as hard as my heart beat, and I waited again. I hoped someone inside would hear me. Hoped that someone would know what to do about Daddy and the foam and the monster in the house.

2

Milow

A man with a funny mustache opened the door. For a second, he stared at me like I was something strange. I stood there shivering in Daddy's boots and wondered why he looked at me that way. I was just a little girl, not a monster at all.

The man blinked and muttered something I couldn't understand, then lowered himself until his face was close to mine. His blue eyes moved over my cheeks, hair, and pajamas like he was trying to figure out what I was.

"Hey, sweetheart," he said softly. "What are you doing out here?"

I frowned at him. That was a very silly question. If I could speak, I would've told him right away. I'd tell him I came because Daddy had foam on his mouth, and there was a monster in my house, and I needed help.

"You must be freezing," he said. "Come in, sweetheart. Let's get you warmed up." He smiled, but his mustache covered most of it. It made him look like he had a furry little animal stuck to his face. Maybe a squirrel.

For a moment, I almost grinned. It would be silly to have a squirrel on your face.

I was unsure at first, but then I let the funny-looking man lead me inside because Daddy needed help. The fire station was warm and big, and the lights overhead were so very bright that I had to blink to adjust. The man pulled a chair over and helped me sit. As soon as I lifted my legs, Daddy's boots slid right off my feet and thumped onto the floor. My toes curled from the cold, and I pulled them up onto the chair.

The man turned and grabbed a thick blanket from a shelf, wrapping it around my shoulders. "There you go," he said, crouching again so he could look at me. His mustache wiggled a little when he talked. "Let's get you warm first. My name's August, but everyone calls me Gus. What's your name, sweetheart?"

He waited for me to speak and say my name back, but I couldn't. Because I was an obedient girl, and obedient girls didn't speak. I stayed still, and my hands fisted in the gloves.

Gus glanced down at my pajamas, then at the giant gloves swallowing my hands. "You came out in this? All by yourself?" His voice sounded worried now.

I nodded once.

Gus let out a slow breath. He rubbed a hand over his face, then stood and called out for someone else in the building. Another man appeared from behind the fire trucks, and their voices filled the space.

I kept sitting there, trying to stay brave while Gus spoke to the other man in a low, serious voice. Every few seconds, they looked over at me, and each time they did, I wondered if they really knew how to help me at all. On TV, firefighters always knew exactly what to do. They saved people all the time. Firefighters were brave and confident. But Gus and the other man looked unsure, and they didn't know that I needed help.

I frowned and waited and waited. When my patience ran out, I slid off the chair and pushed my feet back into Daddy's boots. I took two steps toward Gus, grabbed his hand with both of mine, and pulled as hard as I could.

He looked down at me again and smiled with that silly squirrel mustache of his. But the smile didn't fix anything, and it didn't help Daddy.

I tugged harder, my frown growing deeper.

"Can you tell us your name, sweetheart?" Gus asked, crouching in front of me again.

I shook my head and tugged at his hand once more, more desperate this time.

"What's your name?" the other man asked. He didn't have a silly mustache, just a serious face with lines on his forehead. He looked older and grumpier, almost like Daddy.

I shook my head again. I didn't know how else to answer. I couldn't give them something I couldn't say.

"Where did you come from? Where do you live?" the grumpy man asked.

I looked at Gus instead, because I liked him better. He was nicer. Then I lifted one hand and pointed toward the door.

"I think she wants to show you," the grumpy man said.

I nodded quickly, relieved that at least one of them understood what I was trying to tell them.

But Gus sighed and shook his head. "You can't go back out there, sweetheart. It's freezing."

But Daddy is that way. Daddy isn't moving. Daddy needs help!

"Might have to call the cops," the grump said as he turned away.

Gus guided me back to the chair again.

Why did they have to call the police when firefighters were already helping people too? Why didn't they want to help me get Daddy?

I took off the gloves and pointed at the door again, then lifted my hands and made the scariest face I could, hoping Gus would finally understand. My fingers curled like claws. My eyes went wide, and my mouth stretched open.

His eyebrows lifted. "What's that? A bear?"

I shook my head and did the face again.

"A monster?" he guessed.

I nodded so fast my head spun.

"There's a monster? Where?"

I pointed at the door again.

"Outside? In the snow?"

I shook my head. I didn't know what was in the snow, but I knew the monster that made the foam come out of Daddy's mouth wasn't out there. I would've seen it otherwise. It was at my house.

I pointed again.

"At your house?" Gus asked.

I nodded hard, then made the scary face again and pointed at Gus, because he was a grown man, and Daddy was a grown man, and maybe that would make him understand better.

But Gus's eyes only narrowed in confusion. He didn't get it. He didn't see what I was trying to show him.

He placed his warm hands on my arms and rubbed gently with his thumbs. "I'm trying, sweetheart. I really am. But I need you to tell me where you live. Do you know the name of your street?"

I stared at him. That was silly. Streets didn't have names. Streets weren't people. Why would they need names?

Frustration overcame me, and before I could do anything else, the grumpy man came back, holding a phone in his hand.

"The police are on their way," he said, glancing between Gus and me. "Won't be long now."

———

When two police officers arrived, one of them asked me the same questions Gus had. He kept answering for me. He sounded calm, and he kept holding my hand, which made me feel safe. The officers wrote things down, but they didn't smile the way Gus did. They looked serious.

The one asking the questions sighed heavily and told Gus that they'd have to take me to the police station. My stomach tightened. I didn't want to leave Gus. I needed them to take me home, where Daddy needed help.

I looked up at Gus and squeezed his hand, not wanting him to let me go.

"You'll be all right," he told me with a smile as he fixed the blanket around my shoulders again. "They'll take care of you."

I shook my head and scooted closer to him on the chair, wrapping one hand around his arm while keeping the other in his.

Gus looked at the police officers. "I'll go with her."

"Fine with us," one officer said.

His hand slid out of mine, and I quickly reached up to him so he would pick me up. My feet were too cold, and I didn't want to walk anymore. Gus smiled and hooked his hands under my arms, lifting me until I could wrap my arms and legs around him.

We followed the officers outside. The police car looked exactly like the ones on TV, but it was scary to get inside. Normally, only bad people get put in the back of police cars for doing bad things. I didn't do anything bad. I was trying to help Daddy.

Gus carefully sat me inside, and I grabbed his sleeve to make sure he didn't leave me here. He smiled again and moved in next to me. "I'm here, kiddo. Don't you worry."

I looked up at him wide-eyed and hoped that he would soon understand what I needed. The car started moving, and I stared out the window. Houses passed by slowly, and my chest felt strange. I kept thinking about Daddy and the foam on his mouth, and the monster in the house.

The street we drove on looked familiar. It was the same street I had just walked along before reaching the fire station.

Then I saw my house.

They knew where it was, and they were finally coming to help.

My eyes widened, and I followed the house with my eyes as we got closer.

But the car didn't slow down.

I started to panic, hitting the window with my hands.

The officer in the front turned. "What's wrong—"

I hit the window harder, both palms smacking the glass.

"Stop," Gus said, and the car immediately stopped.

I tried to open the door, but it was locked.

"The house, over there," Gus said, pointing past me toward my house. "The one with the open door."

"That's not good," the driver said before getting out. The other one twisted around to look at Gus. "Stay here with her," he said, his voice firm.

"Yeah." Gus cupped the back of my head with his large hand, caressing my hair gently. Daddy never did that. "That your house, sweetheart?"

I nodded quickly, staring at the house again. Daddy was in there. Or, at least, I hoped he still was.

What if the monster took him away?

My whole body shivered as I watched the officers walk up to the house, and as they went inside, I hoped that the monster wouldn't get them too. A lot of time went by, and I kept my eyes on the house. The lights turned on upstairs, and I could see the police officer's shadow in the window.

Gus kept stroking my hair. His hand moved slowly as he said things under his breath, but I didn't hear any of it. I wanted to run inside and see Daddy. I wanted everything to stop being strange and scary. But the door stayed locked, and the car kept me in place.

"Shit..."

I snapped my head toward Gus. That was a bad word. Daddy always said grown-ups shouldn't say bad words, and that kids shouldn't repeat them. Not that I was able to, anyway. Gus had said it out loud, and if I had a voice, I'd scold him for it.

Red and blue lights flashed across his face, and I turned my head back around to see an ambulance rolling to a stop at the front of the house. Two people stepped out and moved quickly through the snow, carrying a bag and pulling a folded stretcher. One of the police officers pointed toward the door, and they rushed inside without slowing down.

My eyes stayed glued to the doorway, and I leaned forward as far as the seat belt let me. My heartbeat throbbed so fast I could hear it in my ears.

Gus shifted beside me. "Kiddo…" His voice sounded careful, but I didn't turn.

I kept waiting and waiting until, finally, the two ambulance people came out again. This time, they were pushing the stretcher with someone on it.

They got the monster!

I smiled widely as relief washed over me.

They caught the thing that hurt Daddy!

They caught it, and now they're taking it away.

I looked at Gus, expecting him to smile and look happy too.

But Gus wasn't smiling.

His mouth pressed together tightly under the silly mustache, and his eyebrows pulled low. He looked like he didn't want me to see his face at all.

I turned back to the stretcher as they rolled it through the snow.

The monster didn't move.

It didn't fight.

The monster's arm hung off the side for a moment before they lifted it.

Why did his arm look like Daddy's?

My heart tightened. The closer they brought the stretcher to the ambulance, the clearer the shape of the monster under the blanket became.

It didn't look like a monster.

A monster was big.

I looked at Gus again, wanting him to tell me why the monster didn't look like one. But he wouldn't look at me.

My smile disappeared, and my fingers curled into the blanket.

That wasn't a monster.

That was Daddy.

And that was the last time I ever saw him.

3

Milow

Monday, February 23rd

I missed Daddy, but I didn't miss the owie-stick. I didn't miss the pain, and I didn't miss the way he made me cry, even when he said he only did it because he loved me.

Since the last day I saw him, I have been living in a big house with many children. Boys lived on one side, girls on the other, but most times, they were all just running around in the whole house. The girls talked all the time. They didn't lose their voices the way I did. That meant they weren't obedient. I was the only one who was obedient here.

I had to share a bedroom with five girls. Their voices never stopped. At night, I stayed awake because I wasn't used to noise. Back home, everything stayed quiet, and I never shared my room with anyone because I was the only child.

When they brought me to the big house, the kids crowded around me. They asked me many questions. They always asked why I didn't speak. I wanted to explain that good girls didn't talk, and talking wasn't allowed because it made you bad. But I couldn't tell them that.

They kept laughing and asking things I couldn't answer, and I kept frowning because they didn't understand why silence made me a good girl.

Maybe one day their voices would disappear too, the way mine had when the magic took it. Then they would finally understand.

For now, I stayed proud that I was the only obedient girl in the whole house.

There was a woman named Jensen who played with us almost every day. She was very pretty, almost like a princess, and I wished my hair looked like hers. She had shiny golden curls that bounced when she walked. My hair was dark brown and straight like uncooked spaghetti. If I slept on it the wrong way, it pointed in every direction and never listened to me, even when I brushed it every day.

But Jensen and I shared the same brown eyes. Well, only one of my eyes was brown, and the other was brown and blue. Daddy said it was because he had blue eyes, and by having both colors in one eye, I'd have him with me forever.

One day, Jensen leaned close and whispered a secret. She told me I was her favorite to play with because I learned faster than the other kids in the house. She said I understood things quickly, especially when we played number games. She taught me to count, and she showed me how to solve Sudoku puzzles. I loved them. I did three every day. Jensen said she had never met a six-year-old who could solve them as fast as I could.

After numbers, she taught me something new. She sat beside me and held up her hand in a shape I didn't understand. Then she moved her fingers into another shape, and another. She said it was the alphabet, and that each hand shape was a letter. She took my hands in hers and helped me copy the shapes until my fingers got tired. But I liked learning a secret language that only smart kids knew.

Soon I could spell my name with my hands. Then I could spell Jensen's name. Then I could spell the names of the loud girls in my room, even if they didn't deserve it because they talked too much. And then I learned other words: animals, foods, and anything I liked.

Jensen said that if I kept practicing, I would be able to communicate anything with my hands. I liked that idea, because this would be the way I could finally get people to understand me.

Today, after eating breakfast in the big room with all the long tables, I went back to the bedroom because I was tired. I didn't want to play outside with the other boys and girls. They were always loud and wild, running in circles and shouting for no reason. They never wanted to play with me anyway. I liked it better when the room was quiet, and I could sit on my bed and move my fingers through the alphabet Jensen had taught me.

I sat with my legs crossed, watching my hands form the different letters and signs I had learned. I liked how calm it made me feel. There was no yelling. No stomping. No laughing.

The door opened softly, and I looked up. Jensen stepped inside with her bright smile, which always made me smile too.

"Hey, sweetheart," she said, walking over to me. "How are you doing?"

[Good.]

"Did you have a big breakfast?" she asked, sitting beside me.

I nodded. Since living here, I always had a big breakfast. I was allowed to eat as much as I wanted to, until I felt sick to my stomach.

"That's good." Her smile softened as she sat beside me. "Do you remember how to sign breakfast?"

I watched her for a moment, then nodded again. [Breakfast.]

"Very good!" She brushed a bit of messy hair out of my face. "I'm glad you're doing okay today."

I smiled at her. [Play with me?]

"I would love to play with you, Milow, but there is something special happening today."

I tilted my head and frowned. [What?]

Jensen's face grew more serious. It didn't get smaller, but it got more serious. "You have visitors today, Milow."

Visitors? I blinked fast.

I didn't know anyone who would visit me. Daddy was taken away by the ambulance.

Other kids got visitors sometimes, and sometimes those kids didn't come back. The visitors took them away, and no one explained where they went. I didn't know if I wanted that. Even if the other children were too loud, even if they made my head hurt when they shouted, I didn't want to leave Jensen.

I shook my head fast, hard enough to make me dizzy.

Jensen rubbed my back gently. "It's a good thing, you know?" she told me, her voice warm. "You've learned a lot here, and I'm proud of you. Every new thing you do, you do it so bravely."

I stared at her. My fingers twitched, wanting to ask something, but I didn't know what shape the question had. She had taught me a lot, but not everything yet. How would I keep learning without her?

Jensen took my hand and squeezed gently. "The people who are coming today…they want to meet you." She brushed another strand of hair from my cheek. "And if everything goes well, you might get to go to a forever home."

I blinked, not understanding. Was that where the kids disappeared to? To a forever home?

"A home with good people," she continued. "People who will take care of you. People who will love you."

Like Daddy?

I didn't want them to hurt me. I didn't want to feel pain or cry again.

Jensen watched my face and saw how scared I was, and she was quick to calm me down. "Nobody will hurt you, okay? They're good people, and you have already met one of them before."

I did? So it was Daddy. It had to be.

My hopes were high, so I nodded.

"Are you ready, sweetheart?" she asked, her smile soft again.

I didn't really feel ready, but Jensen wouldn't let me meet bad people, right? Jensen never let anything bad happen to me. I looked at her hand, then up at her face, and nodded slowly.

I grabbed her hand when she stood. My fingers wrapped around hers tightly. "It's okay," she whispered. "You can hold on."

We walked together down the hallway, and the house

became louder the closer we got to the downstairs. Kids were shouting, but Jensen led me to the other side of the house where it was quieter.

I held her hand all the way down, gripping tighter whenever a sound made me jump. She squeezed back each time to calm me.

At the bottom of the stairs, she guided me to a big living room where we kids weren't allowed to play. The door was closed, but I knew what was inside. The room had big windows, soft chairs, and shelves filled with books no one was supposed to touch.

Jensen stopped in front of the door, and she crouched down to meet my eyes. "They're right inside," she told me, giving my hand one more squeeze. "And I'll stay with you the whole time, okay?"

I nodded, watching her with wide eyes.

She smiled tightly, speaking softly now. "I know this is a new situation for you, but you're super brave. You've learned so much, and the people waiting for you in there will see just how smart and strong you are."

Her words made my heart beat faster. They were nice words, and ones I never heard Daddy say to me.

I lifted my other hand to sign. [Okay.]

"Okay," Jensen said, smiling brighter now. "I'm right here."

She stood again and pushed open the door, and I braced myself for whoever was waiting for me in there.

I couldn't see who was sitting in the room because I stayed hidden behind Jensen. I only saw shoes on the floor. Two pairs. One was a pair of white sneakers. The other was brown boots. The boots were smaller than the sneakers, which meant they belonged to a woman and the other to a man. The sneakers didn't belong to Daddy, though. It meant Daddy wasn't here, unless he had gotten new shoes.

"Milow," Jensen said gently, reaching back to cup the back of my head. "Let's sit down."

She guided me toward the couch, and I climbed up onto it while keeping my eyes down, not looking at the people across from me. My fingers curled into the fabric of the cushion, and when curiosity took over, I finally looked up. I was a brave girl, and with Jensen next to me, I didn't have to be afraid.

My eyes widened when I saw the man sitting there.

It was the firefighter.

He sat forward on the couch, elbows on his knees, looking at me with the same kind eyes he'd had that night. The big, silly mustache was still on his face.

"Hi, Milow," he said softly. "It's Gus. Remember me?"

I did remember him. I remembered the fire station. I remembered every detail of the night I went to get help because Daddy wouldn't wake up.

I studied his face, then lifted my hands and moved my fingers across my upper lip.

[Mustache.]

Jensen laughed quietly beside me. Gus glanced at her with a raised brow.

"She's signing 'mustache,'" Jensen said.

Gus chuckled and reached up to touch it. "My mustache, huh? It's still there. Still silly-looking."

I nodded once, then lifted my hands again.

[Squirrel.]

Gus looked at Jensen again.

Jensen did the same sign and explained, "That means squirrel."

Gus laughed louder this time. "You think my mustache looks like a squirrel?"

I nodded, biting the inside of my cheek to not smile, even though I wanted to.

"I've heard that before," he admitted, grinning widely. He shifted and wrapped an arm around the woman next to him. "Milow, this is Iris, my wife."

My eyes flicked to the woman beside him as she leaned forward. Her boots shifted on the rug, and her smile grew bigger. She looked careful, like she didn't want to scare me. But I wasn't scared. I was brave, and Iris looked like a princess, too. Just like Jensen, only with brown hair like mine.

"Hi, Milow. It's nice to meet you," she said. Her voice was so soft and soothing.

I looked at her hair, then at her face. She had kind and gentle blue eyes. I didn't lift my hands this time. I just watched her quietly, trying to understand why they were both here.

At first, I thought they were only here to visit. Just one time, to see how I was doing. But why would Gus bring his wife when she had nothing to do with the night Gus sat next to me as the ambulance took Daddy away? There had been other visitors before. People came, sat in this room with the kids, and then left again. Kids whispered about it afterward. Sometimes those kids disappeared. Sometimes they didn't. I didn't know which kind of visit this was.

But I soon learned that Gus and Iris had come back.

I wasn't excited to see them again when they came to visit a second time. Gus smiled brightly, and Iris looked like she was happy to see me again too. They sat on the floor with me instead of the couch, showing me books they had brought, and Iris even baked chocolate cupcakes for me, which we ate together.

Then, they came a third time.

That time, Iris brought paper and crayons. She drew with me for a little bit while Gus talked to Jensen, and later, it was Iris's turn to talk to Jensen, and Gus came to draw with me. That day, they stayed longer than before. They even ate dinner with me, and I overheard Jensen tell Gus and Iris that I had something called mutism. I didn't know what that was, but Jensen said I would talk one day again. I wasn't so sure about that. I was an obedient girl, and I lost my voice to magic. My voice surely wouldn't come back unless I started to be as wild as all the other kids.

When they left, Iris hugged me tightly and said she'd see me soon. She made it sound like a promise, and I started to wait for them again.

When the fourth visit came, Jensen helped me brush my hair extra carefully. She put out the nicest pants and sweater, and she even had my boots cleaned so they would shine, just like Iris's did.

Gus and Iris smiled when they saw me, but their smiles looked different this time. Bigger and nervous.

They talked to Jensen for a long time while I sat on the couch and looked at one of the books Iris had gifted to me. Then Jensen knelt in front of me and took my hands. She looked sad, and I didn't understand why.

"You're going with them today," she said softly.

Going where? And for how long?

But I didn't ask. I was a brave and obedient girl, so I just nodded and let Gus and Iris take me away.

4

Milow

Thursday, March 26th

We drove for a long time. The houses became fewer, and the trees grew closer together. More snow covered the road, and I watched with my forehead pressed to the window as it kept falling. I watched everything pass by, and I tried to remember it all. I didn't know where we were going, but Gus and Iris seemed excited. They had a secret, but they hadn't told me.

I leaned closer to the middle seat to look between them. Gus drove with one hand on the wheel, and Iris sat beside him, turned slightly toward him. Gus's other hand rested on her thigh, and her hand held his. I had noticed that they held hands a lot. I liked holding hands too. I used to hold Jensen's hand because it made me feel safe. Thinking about that made my chest ache. I didn't know when I would ever hold her hand again, but maybe Iris and Gus would let me hold theirs.

Before we left, Jensen had hugged me tight. She told me I would have my own room, and lots of toys, and quiet whenever I wanted it. She smiled like she was happy for me, even though her eyes had tears in them.

I didn't care about rooms or toys or quiet. I only cared that Jensen wasn't coming with me.

Iris turned around in her seat and smiled at me. "We're almost there, darling," she said. "Only five more minutes."

I nodded because there wasn't anything else I could do. Five minutes wasn't very long. It was only five times sixty seconds.

I started counting in my head and on my fingers. I watched the snow blur past the window while I counted. I was only at thirty-nine seconds into the third minute when the car slowed.

We turned onto a long driveway, and at the end of it stood a big house with leaves climbing up its walls like they were hugging it. I frowned, trying to understand how plants could grow on a house in the snow.

"We're here," Gus said as he parked the car.

I turned to look at him.

Iris twisted in her seat again, her smile trembling a little. "This is where you live now, Milow," she said softly. "With us."

I stared at her because I still couldn't quite understand what this meant.

Gus nodded, glancing back at me too. "This is your home now," he said. "Forever."

Forever was a very big word. Bigger than five minutes. Bigger than a whole day.

Iris reached out and touched my knee. Her hand was warm and gentle. She wanted to say something, but no words came out. Instead, tears stung her eyes, and she quickly turned away.

Gus reached over to brush her cheek, and I watched in awe as they looked at each other lovingly.

When he looked at me again, I frowned and lifted my hands to sign. [She's sad.]

Gus smiled at me again. Even if he hadn't understood me at first when I signed, he seemed to have learned a few things because he didn't need Jensen to tell him what I signed anymore. "No, she's not sad, sweetheart. She's happy, and so am I."

My confusion eased a little when I looked at Iris. She laughed softly and wiped her tears away, then nodded and reached back to touch my knee again. "I'm happy. These are happy tears."

I studied her face to figure out if she was being honest, and I decided that she was. [Happy!]

"Yes, that's right." She pressed her lips together and lifted her hands to sign the way I had while saying, "Happy."

Gus got out of the car and came around to open my door. I hesitated before taking his hand, but when I did, he held it like he didn't want to let go. Iris waited for us to move, but before I did, I slid my hand into hers. They both gave me a sense of safety, and I was finally ready to go with them.

The inside of the house was big, and even with all the colors on the walls, the pictures and posters everywhere, it didn't feel crowded. There were shelves stacked with books, lined up and piled sideways, and rugs covering the floor, overlapping, as if they couldn't decide which one they liked better.

I stopped walking and looked around, feeling a little overwhelmed.

Gus chuckled. "There's a lot to see," he told me. "We'll take it slow."

Iris squeezed my hand, looking down at me with an encouraging smile. As they showed me around, they told me I was allowed anywhere and could touch anything I wanted, because it was my house now, too. It felt strange to be allowed to do everything when all my life I had to be careful not to touch or do anything without asking for permission.

The living room had two large couches with lots of pillows and blankets, and there were even more shelves with books and décor. The kitchen had dark-green cabinets and drawers, and one wall was covered with many drawings. They looked like kids' drawings.

The next three rooms were a bathroom, an office, and a large bedroom that looked out onto a big garden. The more I saw, the more I was in awe of this place, and I wondered how much prettier it could get when each room was prettier than the next.

They led me up the big stairs, where they showed me two more bedrooms and a big bathroom with a large tub. One of the rooms looked like a kid's bedroom, with trophies and medals on a bookcase, and bedsheets with hockey sticks and ice skates on them, while the other bedroom looked more plain.

I didn't have time to question whose bedrooms those were because Iris and Gus were already guiding me up another flight of stairs. We stood in a smaller hallway, with one door straight ahead and two on either side.

"That's another bathroom," Iris explained, pushing open the door ahead. "And this…" She turned toward the door on the left. "This is your bedroom."

I stepped inside carefully. Jensen had told me that I'd get my own bedroom, but I didn't think it would be this big. The walls were soft, earthy colors, and two large windows let in a lot of light.

There was a large bed on the other side, and a bookshelf that was already half full. There were toys—lots of them—and one large bean bag in a corner.

I took it all in as I stood there, admiring every little detail.

Iris knelt in front of me, her smile soft. "We'll fill it together," she told me. "At your pace."

I studied her for a while before nodding. [Okay.]

"Okay," she repeated with a relieved laugh, fingerspelling the word as I had.

I looked around again, my mind still not fully understanding that I would be staying here forever.

When I moved my gaze back to Iris, I lifted my hands slowly and signed, [Mine?]

"Yes, this is yours," Iris replied, squeezing my arms gently.

My eyes flicked to the window, then the bed, and then back to Iris. [Thank you.]

"Oh, sweetheart." Iris's eyes filled with tears again, and because I didn't want her to be sad, I wrapped my arms around her neck and gave her a big hug.

Her body trembled, and I thought maybe hugging her wasn't a good idea after all. It only seemed to make her cry harder. But just as I wanted to let go, she wrapped her arms around me and held me tightly.

"Happy tears," I heard Gus say, and I looked up to where he was standing. "Those are happy tears."

I nodded slowly and kept my arms around Iris, not letting go until she would.

Later that day, I sat on the couch with my Sudoku book on my lap and a pencil in my left hand.

Since Jensen had gifted me the book, I had already solved half the Sudokus in it, and I'd soon need a new one. I wasn't sure how I'd ask for a new one, though, because Iris and Gus had already given me this house, and asking for more seemed disrespectful, and I didn't want to come off as greedy because I wasn't.

Iris sat next to me, her arm resting along the back of the couch, and her body turned slightly toward me. She was watching me solve the puzzles, and now and then I looked up at her, and she smiled, telling me how good I was at it. I smiled, enjoying the moment with her.

Iris was patient. She wasn't rushing me to do something else, and she also wasn't running around the house like Jensen used to when she didn't have time to hang out with me. Though she still spent the most time with me, teaching me new things. I hoped Iris would teach me new things too. But for now, I liked just sitting here with her.

Earlier, after showing me the whole house, she and Gus had told me two boys were coming.

They said the boys were their sons. One lived in the room next to mine, and the other in the one with the hockey sheets. I wasn't sure if I wanted to live here with two boys. Boys were loud. Boys ran and yelled and didn't listen. But Gus and Iris didn't seem scared of their boys, so maybe their boys were different.

I didn't know if I was supposed to ask questions about them. I was intrigued, but I had also liked the idea of being the only kid in this house. So, I just nodded after they told me. Gus left the house some time ago and told me he would be picking up the boys, and again I nodded.

Sometime later, the front door opened, and cold air rushed in before it closed again.

"Hey, we're home," Gus said.

I looked up from my book, watching Gus shake snow off his shoulders. His hat was covered too, and so was his silly mustache. Behind him came the two boys, stopping next to Gus in the entryway. One was taller, one smaller, and both had snow on their hats and coats too.

Iris smiled right away. "Hello, my loves." She turned toward me again and leaned in close, her voice low so only I could hear it. "Are you ready to meet them?"

I shrugged at first because I didn't really know. Boys had never been good to me before. Boys were loud and rough and didn't listen, and they always laughed at me. I didn't want that again. But then I reminded myself that I was brave. Jensen had said so. Gus and Iris had said so too. I could face my fears.

So I nodded and carefully set my book on the coffee table.

Iris stood and held out her hand. I slid mine into hers and got up too. She led me toward the entryway, where the two boys had already taken off their coats and boots. We stopped right in front of them, and suddenly, there was nowhere to hide.

The taller boy had very light blond hair. It was wavy and stuck in every direction like he hadn't brushed it in days. His eyes were pale blue, and he was smiling at me. Boys usually looked at me funny, but this boy didn't. I decided that maybe he wasn't a loud, annoying boy after all.

My eyes shifted to the shorter boy. Unlike his brother, he *was* looking at me funny. He was staring at me with wide brown eyes and his mouth open. I wanted to scrunch my nose at him. It wasn't polite to stare at someone like that.

The boy had brown hair, though most of it was hidden under a strange blue hat that was too big for his head. It had long flaps on the sides that hung down near his shoulders and a wide furry part across the front. His nose was dotted with freckles, which confused me. I thought people only got freckles when the sun shone, but the sun hadn't shone for a long time. It was always snowing and gray outside. Maybe some kids just had them no matter what. Maybe this boy was different, and that's why he stared at me like that.

"Milow, this is Wesley. He's thirteen," Gus said, resting a hand on the taller boy's shoulder and giving it a small squeeze. Then he put his other hand on the shorter boy's shoulder. "And this is Ashby. He's seven."

"Hi, Milow," Wesley said, his smile growing even wider. "How do you like your room? I helped decorate it."

I tightened my grip on Iris's hand and then wrapped my other hand around it too. Wesley talked a lot, but he wasn't loud. He seemed happy to see me. And he had helped with my room, which was nice of him.

I nodded to let him know that I liked it.

Wesley kept smiling, but Ashby's brows pulled together tight.

I looked at him, feeling the urge to stick out my tongue because he was still staring. But I stopped myself. Obedient girls didn't do that.

When Ashby kept staring, Wesley nudged him with his elbow. "Don't be weird."

Ashby blinked, as if he'd just woken up, then stumbled over his words. "Hi. I'm Ashby."

"She knows that already, you goofball," Wesley said, frowning at him.

Ashby shrugged and shot Wesley a look. "What else am I supposed to say to her?" He looked back at me, thinking very hard before asking, "Do you like our house?"

I nodded.

He tilted his head, studying me like he was trying to solve a puzzle. "Can you not speak?"

I hated the question because it reminded me of everything I couldn't do. But it also made me feel strong, because I knew something he didn't. I lifted my chin and slowly shook my head. [No, I can't.]

Ashby stared at my hands as they lowered, his face changing. For a second, he looked confused. He looked at Gus, then at Iris, and then back at me. His eyes widened, not with fear, but with something bright and curious. Then, a smile spread across his face.

"What does that mean?" he asked. "Is that a secret language?"

My chest felt funny all of a sudden. He was asking a question no kid had ever asked me. Other kids didn't care about my language. They didn't care to learn it so they could understand me.

I nodded slowly, standing a little straighter because I knew my language was special.

"That's so cool," Ashby said quickly. "Will you teach me?"

Teach him? He wanted me to teach him my language?

I tilted my head to the side, wondering if he truly

meant it. His smile stayed glued on his face, and he waited for me to reply.

I nodded again, and this time I smiled too. It was a real smile that reached my eyes, making my face hurt.

Ashby's smile grew even wider when he saw it. "Awesome! And maybe you can teach Wesley too, so we both know your secret language."

His enthusiasm kept me smiling, and it made Gus and Iris chuckle.

"That sounds like a super fun idea," Gus said, placing his hands on top of the boys' heads. "But first, you two need to go shower and clean up."

They both groaned quietly but didn't argue.

"After that," Iris added, looking at all three of us now, "we'll have dinner, and get to know each other a little better."

"Okay, Mom," Wesley said, then he looked at me again. He was still smiling. "See you later, Milow."

"Yeah, see you later, Milow. I can't wait to learn your secret language!" Ashby said, then they both disappeared upstairs with Gus.

I looked up at Iris to see her face. She seemed pleased with that first interaction. She smiled at me and brushed her hand over my hair. "They've been so excited to meet you," she told me. "Would you like to help me prepare dinner?"

I quickly nodded. I never got to help cook, but I've always been intrigued by it because I could use my hands and learn new things.

"Perfect." She took my hand and led me to the kitchen. "We're making chicken with potatoes and spinach. And we'll make a batch of cookies too."

I lifted my free hand and signed, [Yummy!]

She looked at me and smiled. "Sounds delicious, huh?"

She pulled a step stool over to the counter, and I climbed onto it to watch her. She washed the potatoes and handed one to me, then showed me how to peel it.

While the chicken cooked, Iris let me tear the spinach with my fingers and put it into a bowl. It was a lot of spinach, and I wondered if we'd really eat that much, just the five of us.

[This is a lot of spinach.]

Iris studied my hands for a moment, then looked at the spinach. It took her a moment to understand what I meant, but then she asked, "The spinach? You think it's too much?"

I nodded, making the same motion with my hands again. [Too much for all of us.]

She pursed her lips, taking a moment to understand what I signed. I loved how patient she was with me and with herself, because it meant she truly cared. She and Gus had learned a lot of my secret language, which showed me how much they cared.

"Oh, you think this is too much spinach for us?"

I nodded harder this time.

She smiled and looked at the bowl. "It does look like a lot, doesn't it? But you know what?"

[What?]

"When we cook the spinach, it shrinks."

My eyes widened. [Really?]

"Yes." She grabbed the bowl and placed it next to the pan on the stove. "You see, spinach is over 90% water, and when it gets cooked, that water evaporates."

Evapo-what?

I tilted my head, giving her a strange look.

Iris laughed softly. "Here, watch closely."

She put all the spinach into the pan. Some leaves fell out because there were so many that they barely fit into the pan. I kept my eyes on it, and over time, I noticed the pile of spinach getting smaller.

"See?" Iris said, leaning in a bit closer to me, her eyes also fixed on the spinach. "The water inside the spinach is evaporating."

[What is that?]

She looked at me. "Evaporating? That's when water changes into gas. It's chemistry."

I've heard that word before, but I didn't know that spinach had anything to do with it. Pursing my lips, I looked at the pan again, and my eyes widened when I saw that the leaves were now just a small mass.

"Cool, huh?"

I nodded, hoping I could learn more fun things like this in the future.

I heard footsteps and voices getting closer, and I turned my head to see Gus walk into the kitchen, with Wesley and Ashby right behind him. Both of them had damp hair, and they were wearing pajamas now. It was the first time I saw Ashby without his funny hat, and he looked less silly now.

"Something smells really good," Wesley said.

"That's because you're finally clean," Iris replied teasingly.

Wesley grimaced. "Good one, Mom."

Ashby came to stand between us, peeking over the counter to see what we were making. "What's in that pan?"

[Spinach,] I fingerspelled.

Ashby stared at my hand, his eyes wide with wonder again. "Whoa. I have no idea what you just said."

I scrunched my nose, then looked at Iris for help. She smiled softly and looked at Ashby. "It's spinach. And try to say 'signed' instead of 'said,' darling."

Ashby's face twisted into a frown. "Why?"

"Because it's more appropriate. Milow signs."

It was an easy explanation, yet I didn't really understand why it mattered so much.

Ashby thought about his mom's words, then nodded slowly before looking at me again. "You speak with your hands."

I did speak with my hands. It was the easiest way to put it. I nodded, then lifted my hands again. [Chicken and potatoes too.]

The more I signed, the more fascinated he looked, and it made me smile because he still wasn't laughing or making fun of me. He was truly trying to understand me.

"There's chicken and potatoes too, and for dessert, we made…"

[Cookies!]

"Cookies," Iris repeated.

"Yum!"

"All right, boys, help Dad set the table."

Gus carried the plates, Wesley helped with the glasses, and Ashby took care of the cutlery.

When we all sat down, I took the chair closest to Iris. I ate slowly while observing the others. Wesley talked about their Grandma's house and the snow fort he'd built in her backyard. He said he had to keep rebuilding it because Ashby jumped on it. Ashby laughed and didn't even try to deny it.

I wanted to let Ashby know that ruining someone else's snow fort on purpose wasn't nice. But Wesley was smiling when he talked about it, like it was a funny story instead of a bad one. So I kept eating and decided it was okay to let it go.

I listened and watched their faces. No one told me to join the conversation. No one waited for me to lift my hands and sign. I was allowed to be there and take everything in.

A new feeling I couldn't place made itself noticeable in my chest, and I held it there, trying to understand what it meant. They were a family, and even though I had only been here for one day, it felt like I already belonged with them too.

5

Milow

After dinner, we moved into the living room. Gus carried the plate of cookies, and Iris brought the warm milk. We all sat together, me next to Iris and Gus, and their warmth was so comforting. It was nothing I had felt before. Iris pulled a blanket over my legs without asking, and I liked that she just knew what I needed.

Ashby sat on the floor in front of the coffee table, already eating the cookies. He had eaten a lot at dinner already, and it had looked like he hadn't eaten in years. He was a hungry boy, and it made me scrunch my nose. But not because I was disgusted. I was actually fascinated by how much that boy could eat.

Wesley sat on the other couch. His eyes landed on the book lying on the table. He picked it up and flipped through the pages, his brows lifting higher and higher.

"Sudokus?" he asked, looking from the book to me. "Did you solve them?"

I nodded slowly, expecting him to laugh. To call me a "nerd," as some other kids had back at the children's home.

But Wesley's eyes widened as he looked back down, turning another page and letting out a low whistle. "These are hard. Like, really hard." He looked back at me, this time with something new in his eyes. He looked proud. "Only really smart people know how to solve these."

Warmth spread inside me, and I lifted my chin without meaning to. I liked that he said that. I liked that he thought that about me.

"Yeah, super smart," Ashby said with his mouth full. He chewed and swallowed, then added, "Smarter than Wesley because he can't solve them."

Wesley scrunched his nose at his little brother and gently kicked his legs with his foot. "You can't solve them either."

"Boys," Iris said softly, shooting them a serious look.

"I haven't tried to solve one yet," Ashby muttered, looking up at me. "Will you teach me? And you also have to teach me your secret language."

It was overwhelming. Everything I was seeing and hearing made my heart pound loudly in my chest, and everything I was feeling was so intense that I didn't know how to handle it. But I stayed calm, knowing that getting agitated would only cause chaos inside of me.

I looked at Ashby and nodded. [I can teach you.]

As always, he snapped his eyes to Iris, waiting for her to tell him what I signed.

"She'll teach you," she assured him.

"Thanks, Milow!"

"Try this," Gus said, lifting his flat hand to his chin and moving it forward and down. "This means 'thank you.'"

Ashby watched Gus do it again, then he tried it himself, and Wesley did it too.

"Like this?" Wesley asked, and I gave an encouraging nod.

Ashby beamed when he got it right, his hand moving a little too fast and a little too big, but he was close enough.

I watched them both, and my heart felt so full it might have exploded. I had never felt like this. I'd had only had good feelings since Iris and Gus brought me here. That must've meant something. My heart kept beating fast, and I leaned a little closer into Iris without meaning to. Her arm came around me right away, her embrace warm and comforting.

"Are you okay, sweetheart?" she asked quietly.

I nodded, but my eyes were starting to burn. I was getting tired, and my body felt like it was sinking into the couch. I couldn't hold myself up anymore.

Ashby was still watching me closely, waiting for the next sign, his excitement buzzing between his words and movements. "What about another one?" he asked. "What's the sign for…for my name?"

Gus chuckled softly. "That might be a lesson for tomorrow, buddy."

"But—"

"She's tired," Iris said gently, smoothing my hair back from my face. "It's been a long day for her."

I tried to keep my eyes open, but they kept closing on their own. My lashes fluttered and felt too heavy to lift. I rested my head fully against Iris's shoulder, and the room started to feel far away.

"You've both had a long day too," Gus said.

"But I wanted her to teach me more of her secret

language," Ashby said, his voice softer than before. He sounded disappointed but not angry.

"I know," Gus replied. "She will. Tomorrow."

"Okay," he muttered. There was a small pause, then Ashby added, "I like her. I think I'll be her best friend if she wants me to be."

That was the last thing I heard before I fell asleep.

———

Thursday, April 16th

Jensen had told me the truth when she said this would be my forever home. Iris and Gus hadn't taken me back, not even once, and every single day for the past twenty-one days—which I learned was exactly three weeks—they showed me again and again that they wanted me here. They didn't say it all the time. They showed it in small ways, by asking how I was feeling, by hugging me, and no one ever told me I didn't belong.

Most days, it was just Iris and me at home. Gus went out to help people because he was a firefighter, and Ashby and Wesley weren't home either because they were at school. The house was quieter then, but I liked having Iris to myself. She filled the quiet with soft music and her gentle voice, and every day, we did things to pass the time. We baked, played card games, and watched movies. Anything I felt like doing, she said yes to. She even took me to different parks with big playgrounds, and one day, we even went to the shopping mall.

But as much as I loved spending time alone with her, I did miss Gus and the boys a lot. I wanted to go to school too. I told Iris with my hands, and she smiled and said I would, but not yet. I had to wait until summer was over. The thought made my chest flutter in two different ways. I felt excited, because school was where I'd learn a lot. But I also felt nervous, because school meant even more children. Lots of them. And I wasn't sure I would like them. I liked Ashby and Wesley, and they weren't like the kids from before. They were kind, and they were never mean. They talked to me and played with me, but I never got much time with them. Not as much time as I got with Iris.

She told me summer break would come soon for the boys. A few more weeks, and then I'd get to spend every day with them. At that time, I only got to play with Ashby and Wesley in the evenings and on weekends. And sometimes not even then. Wesley had ice hockey every Saturday, and Ashby sometimes went to the aquatic center. He was a swimmer, Iris explained, and she said he was very good for his age. I wondered what it looked like when he swam. I wondered if I'd get to see it one day, and maybe even swim with him.

Today, I waited for them to come home, watching the clock closely. When the front door finally opened, Ashby immediately took off his shoes and jacket, keeping his baseball cap on his head like he always did, before he grabbed my hand. He pulled me upstairs to his room, talking fast about what he wanted to play.

He dragged out his box of superheroes and dumped them onto the floor. He loved them. He loved talking about them and making them do the silliest things. I liked them too, especially because he sometimes let me play with his favorite one: Hulk.

Ashby lined all the action figures up along the edge of his desk, explaining everything while I sat and watched.

"They all have to jump to survive," he said seriously. "The bad guys put explosives up here, and if they don't jump, they'll all die."

My eyes widened, and I tapped his shoulder until he looked at me. When he did, I lifted my hands and signed carefully. [That's dangerous.]

He watched my hands closely, his forehead wrinkling as he tried to follow along. After a moment, his face cleared, and he nodded. "Yeah. It is dangerous." Then he smiled, like he knew something I didn't. "But they're superheroes, remember?"

He turned back to the desk and placed the last four action figures right at the edge, lining them up perfectly. "They won't get hurt," he said with confidence. "They never do."

I scrunched my nose and stared at them. They were only toys. I knew that. But they were Ashby's favorites, and they meant a lot to him. So they meant a lot to me too, and I didn't want them to get hurt.

Before I could figure out how to contain my overwhelming feelings, Ashby suddenly made a loud explosion sound with his mouth and swung his arm across the desk.

All the action figures toppled over at once, tumbling down onto the carpet.

I clapped my hand over my mouth, my eyes going wide. Ashby burst out laughing and made even bigger, louder sounds, with his arms flying through the air. Then he dropped down onto his knees and began setting the action figures upright again, one by one.

"They landed safely," he said in a very serious voice, holding Hulk up in front of me. "See? They're all fine."

I watched the superheroes stand there, but I wasn't

fully convinced. When Ashby looked up and noticed the worry still on my face, his smile softened. He reached out and placed his hand on my shoulder.

"Don't worry about them, Milow," he said gently. "They're all okay."

His hair stuck out in every direction from under his backward hat, and it made him look silly.

"They're strong," he added with a nod, tapping Hulk's chest. "And superheroes always take care of each other. Just like we take care of each other in this family. That means I'll protect you. And Wesley too. And Mom and Dad."

We might have been just kids, but those words seemed big and important. Like something I should remember. I nodded slowly, letting his words sink in as he turned back to his toys, talking them through their next stunt.

I kept watching him. He was having so much fun, and I liked that he wanted me there. He wasn't forcing me to play with him. Instead, he just let me watch.

After a while, Ashby started lining the figures back up on the desk again, humming softly to himself. That was when I heard loud footsteps in the hallway. I turned my head, thinking it was Wesley coming to play with us, but it wasn't.

A boy I had never seen before stopped in the doorway. He was breathing hard from running up the stairs. His hair was black and stuck to his forehead, and his eyes were blue and confused as they met mine. He just stared, and I stared back.

What was this strange boy doing in our house?

His face twisted, like he'd smelled something bad. "Uh, Ashby?" he said, his voice full of disbelief. "Why is there a *girl* in your room?"

I frowned. I wanted to let him know that Ashby asked me to be here. That I was allowed to be here, and I wasn't doing anything wrong. But I already knew he wouldn't understand me. Boys like him didn't know my secret language, and they never cared to learn it. So I tucked my hands behind my back and pressed my lips together, staying very still.

Ashby looked up at him, completely unfazed. He smiled brightly. "Stan," he said happily. "Come play. You can be Iron Man." He held the figure out toward him.

Stan didn't take it. He didn't even look at it. His eyes stayed on me, narrow and suspicious.

"Ashby," he said again, slower this time, "I'm serious. There's a *girl* in your room."

Ashby raised a brow and glanced at me as if he was double-checking. Then he looked back at Stan and nodded. "Yeah. I know."

He pointed at me with a proud smile. "That's Milow. She lives here."

Stan blinked, still not moving.

"She…lives here?" he repeated.

Ashby nodded again. "Yeah. Mom and Dad adopted her."

Adopted. Was that the word for becoming part of a new family and staying forever?

Stan's gaze moved over me again. He was still unconvinced whether I should be there. I stayed very still as he eyed me. Maybe if I didn't move, he wouldn't find anything wrong with me. The look on his face changed. The sharp disgust faded, turning into confusion, then curiosity. I didn't know which one was worse.

"Milow," Ashby said proudly, pointing at me, "this is

my best friend in the whole wide world, Stan. We go to school together."

I looked from Ashby to Stan, then back to Ashby. I didn't know what to do. Waving felt too exposing, and talking wasn't an option. Stan kept watching me as he stepped closer. He stopped right in front of me and tilted his head. "Hello."

My throat tightened the way it always did when people waited for my voice, but I knew nothing would come out, and my silence could spark any reaction. Especially from this boy, I had a feeling his reaction would be bigger than most.

And I was right.

Stan frowned. "Is she broken?"

"She's not broken," Ashby said immediately, his frown deep as he stepped closer. He stood in front of me protectively, as if his body could block the boy's hurtful words. "She's super cool and really smart. And she speaks a secret language."

"No way," Stan said, shaking his head. "I don't believe you."

"But she does!" Ashby insisted, turning to me with a hopeful smile. "Show him, Milow."

My hands felt heavy. I didn't want to. I didn't want to prove myself to someone who already looked at me like I was strange and wrong. But Ashby was smiling so brightly at me, and I didn't want to disappoint him. I'd do this for him, not for the mean boy. Slowly, I lifted one hand.

[Hello.]

Stan squinted, and his nose scrunched up. "That's not a secret language. She just waved." He scoffed. "She's weird."

The same pain I had so often felt back at the children's

home settled inside my chest. I didn't like this one bit. I moved my gaze to Ashby. [I don't like him.]

Ashby's eyes widened. For a second, I thought I had done something bad. Then his face changed, and he looked angry. But he wasn't angry at me.

"She's not weird, Stan!" he snapped. "You can't say mean things like that."

"But she *is* weird!" Stan shot back. "She's just staring at me like a creepy doll."

Ashby's mouth tightened. He looked really upset now. "Stop it, Stanley. That's not nice!"

Before Stan could answer, a deep voice filled the room.

"Boys, what's going on?"

Gus stood in the doorway. Relief rushed through me so fast it made my eyes sting. I jumped up and ran to him without thinking. He had been gone all day at the fire station, and I hadn't realized how much I missed him until he was right there. He lifted me and kissed my cheek.

"Hey, sweetheart."

I wrapped my arms around his neck and leaned into him.

"Dad," Ashby said quickly, "Stan called Milow weird and creepy. Tell him that's not nice."

"But you lied!" Stan argued. "You said she knows a secret language!"

"She does! And she's teaching it to me!"

"Boys," Gus ordered, his voice firmer now. "Sit down on the bed for a moment."

They both groaned but climbed onto the bed. Gus walked over to the desk and sat down on the chair, placing me on his lap. His arm wrapped around me, keeping me close to him.

"Let's settle down," he said, looking between them. "Stanley, has Ashby not told you about Milow?"

Stan crossed his arms and shrugged. "No."

"Okay," Gus said calmly. "Well, this is Milow. She lives here with us now."

Stan shrugged again. "Okay. So?"

"So," Gus repeated with a small, amused chuckle. It sounded like this wasn't his first time dealing with him. "She's family. And I'd like for you to get along since you're Ashby's best friend, and you spend a lot of time together."

Stan opened his mouth, then closed it again. "But… but…" He frowned, searching for the right words. "Why doesn't she talk to me? That's rude."

"She's not rude!" Ashby said immediately. "She just doesn't want to speak."

"But I said hi, and she didn't say it back!"

"Boys," Gus warned again. They both went quiet. When he had their attention, he continued with a gentler voice. "You see, Milow doesn't speak the same way you do," Gus explained. His hand rested on my back as he spoke, giving me the comfort I needed in this moment. "She has something called selective mutism. That means she can speak, but her voice doesn't always feel safe to use. So she chooses not to."

Stan blinked and uncrossed his arms. But he still didn't understand.

"She hasn't chosen to speak yet," Gus went on. "And that's okay. She communicates in other ways. With her hands. With her expressions. With listening. And one day, when she's ready, she might use her voice too."

I pressed my face into Gus's shoulder. I didn't think I ever would. I wanted to stay obedient, and I didn't want my voice to come back because that would mean I was naughty. The magic had taken my voice for a reason, and I wanted to keep it that way.

Stan was quiet for a long moment. I peeked at him from where I sat, my heart tapping nervously in my chest. His face softened.

"Oh," he said finally. "So…she's not being rude to me."

"No," Gus said. "She's just being herself."

Stan nodded slowly. He looked at Ashby, then back at me. "I didn't know," he murmured, a little awkward. "I'm sorry I said you were weird."

I studied him, and I could see the honesty in his eyes. He dangled his feet and played with his fingers, then he lifted one hand in a small wave. "Hi, Milow. It's nice to meet you."

I hesitated. He was trying to start over. No one had ever wanted to try to start over again, because after not understanding me, they just pushed me aside. No one ever wanted to keep up with me because that was much easier. But Stan was different in that way. Maybe he wasn't nec-essarily doing it for me, but for Ashby and Gus instead, but it was enough.

I slowly lifted my hands, forcing myself to be brave.

[It's nice to meet you too.]

Ashby gasped like it was the coolest thing he'd ever seen, as if he hadn't seen me sign before. "See!" he said triumphantly. "I told you!"

Stan's jaw dropped. "Whoa! That's…actually so cool. Can you teach me too?"

"Of course she can," Ashby answered for me.

"Awesome!" Stan exclaimed, throwing his hands into

the air before he looked at me with a more serious expression. "I won't be mean again. I promise."

I knew promises were something big. Daddy always promised to keep me safe and happy, and he always promised never to hurt me. But Daddy broke his promises. I wasn't sure if I could trust Stan when he promised not to be mean to me again, but what choice did I have? He was Ashby's best friend, and Gus seemed to like him too.

Gus pressed his cheek to the side of my head. "All right," he said gently. "I'm glad we talked about this. We're having dinner in a bit, buddy."

Ashby groaned, but he didn't argue. "Can Stan stay for dinner?"

Gus thought about it as he set me back down and got up from the chair. "Fine with me. I'll call Dean and ask."

I assumed Dean was Stan's dad.

"He'll say yes anyway," Stan stated, his attention already on the superheroes scattered all over the carpet.

"I'll still call and ask. Ashby, ten more minutes, okay?"

"Okay."

I was torn between following Gus downstairs and staying up here. Now that Stan was here, I wasn't so sure if Ashby still wanted me to play with him. He was already explaining something to Stan with big arm gestures, and Stan was listening, setting the superheroes up the way Ash wanted.

Gus brushed the back of my head with his hand, then he left, leaving me standing there in the middle of the bedroom. I took in the scene in front of me again, watching as the boys continued to set up the heroes, talking over each other without arguing.

They got along well, and a small part of me wanted to

be part of what they had. Stan was Ashby's friend, and that had to mean something.

So, I told myself I would do my best to be open to Stan—or any other friend of Ashby's I'd get to meet along the way.

I wanted to do it for Ashby. And, maybe, a small part of me wanted to do it for myself too.

6

Milow

Wednesday, April 22nd

Birthdays were a foreign concept to me. I knew people got older. I knew the body changed. But I didn't know there was a day meant only for you—a day where people celebrated you for being born. I didn't know that others lit candles and sang for you on that day.

But they were all singing: Iris, Gus, the boys. My throat tightened, and my eyes stung.

Tears spilled down my cheeks before I understood what was happening. I wasn't used to feeling joy and fear at the same time. It was always either one or the other. I didn't know how to deal with both at the same time.

I saw Iris's eyes widen, and Gus froze with the cake held in midair. Their panic made me panic even more.

Iris moved first. "Oh, sweetheart."

She scooped me out of the chair, and I wrapped my arms around her neck. My face pressed into her shoulder as my body shook.

"Why is she crying?" Ashby asked. I peeked up at him

and saw his hands were still together from clapping. And he was frowning at me. "We're just singing happy birthday to her."

"I know, buddy." Gus put the cake on the table, then he placed one hand on Ashby's shoulder. "It surprised her."

"Maybe we were being too loud," Wesley said, looking concerned. His pale eyes were full of worry.

Ashby scrunched his nose. "Or maybe your singing was so bad it made her cry."

Wesley smacked his arm, and Gus shot them both a look to shut them down. "Boys, be nice."

"You're okay," Iris whispered, her hand rubbing my back gently. The chair creaked as she sat, settling me onto her lap, and I wrapped my legs tight around her waist. My fingers clung to her shirt. I didn't want to let go. Not until this confusion in me disappeared.

I was breathing calmly, with a voice inside my head telling me that I was safe in Iris's arms. Nothing would hurt me here. But the rush still stayed, even if nobody was telling me to stop crying.

I stared at the candles on the cake, and with more time passing, my tears stopped and dried on my cheeks. I lifted my head a little and searched Iris's face. I wanted her to make sense of this. I wanted to know why they had started singing to me, why there was a cake with candles, and why everyone looked so happy that I had been born seven years ago.

My birth never mattered to Daddy. My existence only meant being kept inside, being hurt by his owie-stick, and being punished if I asked for more food.

Iris's eyes shone with tears. There was guilt and sorrow in them, and I didn't like seeing her like that. I didn't want to be the reason for those bad feelings, but it was hard for me to make her feel better when I was drowning in bad feelings myself.

She brushed my hair from my face with a soft smile.

"We're celebrating you," she told me quietly. "We're so happy you're here, Milow."

Gus stepped closer and crouched down next to us, his hand coming up to rest on my lower back. "This is your day," he explained. "Your birthday."

I still just stared, needing more time to understand everything. I had created this mess by crying when all they were trying to do was celebrate me.

Ashby climbed onto his knees on his chair. "Birthdays are really fun," he started to say, his eyes wide and bright. He was trying to cheer me up, and he never once failed. "On birthdays, you get cake and presents. And it's your birthday, so you get all that today."

I wanted to ask why, but I kept my hands to myself.

"That's not what birthdays are all about, Ashby," Wesley said with a frown.

"Yeah, duh! But the presents and cake are the best part."

Wesley rolled his eyes, then he smiled at me. "We're happy you were born and are here with us, and that's why we're celebrating."

I watched him for a moment. I wanted to understand so desperately. I wanted to know why anyone would be happy I was born.

Iris must've sensed the question burning deep inside my mind, and she pulled me closer. "You deserve to be loved."

Gus nodded, his smile gentle and encouraging. "If birthdays feel scary now, that's okay. We'll go slow. We're here with you."

I slowly nodded because I didn't want to ignore them any longer. They deserved more than my silence.

Ashby awkwardly shifted his weight and tapped his fingers on the table impatiently. His eyes constantly flicked to the candles on the cake as the wax dripped.

"Can we help her blow them out?" he asked.

Gus smiled a little. "If she wants."

I looked at the glowing flames and wondered why Daddy never made me blow out candles. Or why he didn't think my birthday was important enough to be celebrated. Maybe he didn't even know we were supposed to celebrate it, because his was never celebrated either.

[Okay.]

Ashby's eyes widened. "Cool!"

Gus pulled the cake closer to us, and Iris whispered, "Make a wish."

I didn't know how to wish. I didn't know what wishes were supposed to do, or what they meant. My mind raced with too many possibilities. What could I ask for that wouldn't be taken away? What was safe to want? Was it okay to wish for my voice back while still staying obedient?

My breath trembled, but I leaned forward anyway, following Ashby's lead. He scooted closer until his arm brushed mine, and he filled his lungs with a dramatic gulp of air. Then, we blew together. Our breaths mixed. The flames bent, then vanished into thin smoke that curled upward.

Ashby cheered loud enough to shake the table, and Wesley clapped his hands with a proud smile.

My chest ached and loosened at the same time. I was still feeling so much, but now, they were mostly good feelings.

I could learn to like my birthdays.

I could learn to celebrate being born.

———

That night, Gus and Iris tucked me under the blanket and read a story out loud. Their voices were calm, and I focused more on them than the words they were saying. They had made the day bearable, without pushing me to play when the boys asked, and giving me time to adjust to the overwhelming feelings I had felt since waking up this morning. When the story ended, they kissed my forehead and whispered that they loved me. Then they turned off the lamp and left, smiling as they closed the door.

Seeing them happy mattered to me more than the candles or the cake.

I curled on my side, hugging my new teddy bear tight against my chest, with its soft fur pressed into my cheek. My eyes were heavy, but my mind still raced, and it would be another difficult night to fall asleep.

My eyes snapped to the door as the doorknob clicked. Fear rushed through me, for a moment thinking that it was Daddy coming to get me. He used to come at night, telling me that it was time to be an obedient girl, and I always went with him without a fight. Because if I fought, the owie-stick would hurt even more.

I tightened my grip on the teddy bear as the door opened slowly, and a small shadow moved across the floor. My heart jumped, and I held my breath as the fear grew. But relief soon followed when I saw Ashby's small frame slip inside.

"Milow?" he whispered into the dark. "Are you sleeping?"

I pushed myself up and shook my head.

He paused and stared at me for a beat. Then he whispered, "Can I come inside?"

He was already in the room. He had crossed the threshold without waiting, but I didn't mind. I nodded slowly. My eyes followed him as he stepped forward, then shut the door softly. He walked to the bed and stopped beside it. The moonlight from the window lit half his face, and he turned on the lamp so I could see him better. I held the teddy bear tight in my lap, arms locked around it, unsure but curious why he had come.

Ashby's mouth tugged upward as a mischievous grin spread across his face. My head tilted on instinct. I waited for him to say something, but he stayed silent. He reached behind him with a quick motion, and when his hand came back around, he was holding a rolled sheet of paper. It must have been tucked into the waistband of his pajama shorts, because I hadn't seen it in his hands before.

"This is for you," he said, his voice filled with excitement as he extended the paper toward me.

I stared at it, my fingers tightening around the bear.

"Take it," he urged, nudging the rolled paper against my hand. "I drew it for you. It's a birthday present I made."

A present. Another one. I had already opened five today. One from each of them, and one they said was from everyone together. Five gifts for me felt like too much already, and now Ashby was offering a sixth.

My fingers loosened around the bear. I reached out slowly to grab it and slid the rubber band off before unrolling the paper.

A bright and colorful drawing appeared.

"This is me. And this is you. And we're superheroes."

He leaned close, pointing at two stick figures wearing capes. He explained each detail with excitement. "We can fly, see? That's us in the sky. And that's the pool where I swim. And this is the backyard with the playground Dad promised to build. And—oh! That's your bean bag with your Sudoku book on it."

His finger tapped each part, and his voice rushed without breathing.

I kept staring at the drawing. My eyes moved across every shape and color.

"And I started another one with Mom and Dad and Wesley," he said. "It's not finished yet, but tomorrow I'm gonna finish it. Then you can hang it up in your room."

He turned to look at the wall above my desk and pointed with certainty.

"Right there. And maybe you can draw something too, so that I can hang it up in my room."

His eyes sparkled at the idea. His voice kept going so fast that I struggled to keep up. My mind lagged behind his words, but it was nothing new.

When he finally fell quiet, waiting for an answer, I nodded slowly.

[Okay.]

He flashed a grin and took the drawing out of my hand to place it on the nightstand, then he climbed onto the bed without warning.

I shifted away a little to make space, and he crawled under the covers, moving with the confidence of someone who had done it a thousand times before. I watched him settle in next to me. I hesitated, unsure whether to stay frozen or move closer. But this was Ashby. If there was anyone I could allow near me, it was him.

So I lay back down and turned to face him, with my teddy bear tight against my chest. The moonlight filtered through the curtains, making the room look pale blue. His messy hair fell over his forehead without his hat holding it back. Only when he slept did he take off his hats. His eyes searched my face, and I looked back.

"Milow," he whispered. "Can you show me how to sign Mom and Dad in your secret language?"

I never used those two signs, but I knew them because Jensen had taught them to me back at the home. I lifted my hands and signed the words, and he repeated them back to me with stiff fingers and a bit of awkwardness. But he tried again until he got it right.

He smiled with pride. "Maybe you can call them Mom and Dad too. It took me a few years before I did. Wesley too. We used to say their names. But now we say 'Mom' and 'Dad' because they are our parents. And they're yours too."

I blinked at him, confused about his words. I thought Iris and Gus had always been their mom and dad. I thought Ashby and Wesley belonged here since they were born. I never imagined they were adopted, too.

So they had come from somewhere else.

Someone else had given them away.

Someone else hadn't wanted them.

Or maybe their daddy had been taken by a monster too, and they were lucky enough to find Gus at the fire station. My heartbeat thudded harder against my ribs as I looked at him. We kept looking into each other's eyes, and I wondered if he knew about the storm he had started inside of me.

7

Milow

The exam room was white and cold, and the paper under me crinkled every time I moved. Iris sat close on a little stool, and Gus was on the chair near the door. They both tried to act calm, but I could tell they were nervous. This was my first visit to the doctor's, ever, and I saw a flash of guilt in their eyes, like taking me here had been hard for them.

I wasn't scared, though. Ashby had told me that doctors were good people who only wanted to make sure you were okay. And Daddy was a doctor too. He had a room just like this back at our house, and I was in it a few times.

When the doctor came in, he talked to me first. He asked me questions, and I either nodded or shook my head because he didn't know my secret language. Then, he checked my ears, eyes, and mouth. I did everything he asked me to, and I sat perfectly still because I always followed directions.

When he asked me to lie back, I did, and I stared

up at the light-blue ceiling, which had big white clouds painted on. The doctor made me lift my shirt so he could look at my belly. He gently pressed down on my stomach, asking me if anything hurt, and I always shook my head. He seemed pleased with my answer, then he reached for a funny-looking thing, telling me it was like a camera that allowed him to look inside my belly.

He turned a small screen toward me and told me to look at it. Something cold touched my skin, then he moved the device around my belly.

"Look at that, Milow," Gus said with excitement. "You know what those are?"

I stared at the screen, only seeing weird gray shapes. [No.]

"Those are your organs."

"Exactly," the doctor said, smiling gently as he kept his eyes on the screen. "And everything looks perfect. Your stomach is full. Did you have a big lunch?"

[Yes, I had pizza!]

The doctor quickly glanced at Gus, waiting for him to translate.

"She had pizza. It's her favorite food."

"Is that so? That's my favorite food too," he told me. "All right. Everything looks fine." He looked at me, his eyes wandering over my face before they dropped to my neck. "Tilt your head back for me."

I didn't know why he wanted me to do that, but I obeyed. Everyone around me seemed more tense, but I kept staring up at the ceiling. The doctor gently placed the device on my throat and slowly moved it up and down. I dropped my gaze to him, seeing his joyful expression changing slowly.

He kept looking at the screen, and the tension in the room grew. Finally, he pulled the device away, placed it back, and cleaned the gel off my throat.

He turned to Gus and Iris, asking them different questions.

"Has she ever talked to you?"

"Has anyone explained anything about her condition?"

"What do you know about her time growing up?"

Iris was frowning, and Gus sat forward, elbows on his knees. They tried to explain that I didn't talk because I chose not to. I had selective mutism, but I wanted to tell them I couldn't speak because the magic had taken my voice away. They wouldn't understand. They'd think I was being silly.

The doctor started to talk about things I didn't understand. He used big words, kept his voice low, and I tried to follow by watching their faces instead. But I couldn't follow.

Then he said something in a clearer voice, but it still didn't make sense to me.

"She doesn't have them."

What did I not have?

The room went quiet, and I saw Gus shift in his seat. His head hung low, and when I moved my gaze to Iris, I caught her wiping away a tear.

The doctor went on, explaining things calmly, but I still didn't understand. I only understood a few things when he started talking about the police, but I had no clue why he would bring them up.

Iris covered her mouth to muffle a sound. Tears rolled down her cheeks. Gus stood up abruptly, making the chair scrape on the floor. His hands curled into fists. He looked shocked, angry, and scared all at once. I had never seen Gus look like that. It frightened me enough that I reached for Iris automatically.

"It's okay, sweetheart," she said quietly, pulling me onto her lap with a smile that didn't reach her eyes. She was upset, and seeing her like that made me upset too.

"This is insane," Gus said through gritted teeth, and I looked up at him to see just how angry he was.

Had I done something? I was clearly the reason for their big, bad feelings. But I hadn't done anything. I had been obedient and let the doctor look at me.

I frowned and lowered my gaze to my hands in my lap, unable to look at their faces anymore. They were hurting, and I was starting to get overwhelmed. The day had started so well, with all five of us sitting happily at the breakfast table. And now, Gus and Iris were upset and angry. And it was because something was wrong with me.

My nails scratched against my thumb until the skin started to loosen.

Iris kept sniffing, her shoulders trembling while she held me tight in her arms. I didn't understand the reason for their reactions. I didn't know why this was such terrible news. I hadn't spoken for a very long time. I thought the silence was part of who I was, and they knew it.

"I'd look into this," I heard the doctor say. "There has been a surgery."

I caught bits of what he was saying, but not enough to make sense of what he really meant. None of them said anything to me directly. They spoke around me, as if the words were too heavy to give to a child. But maybe it was for the best. I held Iris's shirt tightly and leaned against her shoulder, listening to her breathe unevenly. I didn't know what was wrong with me now, but it didn't worry me as much because there was already so much wrong with me.

———

Iris and Gus were still so upset, even after we got home. Iris went straight to the kitchen to cook dinner, and Gus paced a little in the living room. Their worry made the house feel heavy. Iris had told me to play until dinner was ready, but I didn't feel like playing. I looked around for Ashby instead. I wanted him near me because he always talked and made things feel normal. I tugged on Gus's sleeve to get his attention. He stopped moving and looked down at me with tired eyes. "Yes, sweetie?"

I lifted my hands to sign. [Where is Ashby?]

He rubbed the back of his neck and said, "Ashby is at Stan's house. He'll come home soon."

I furrowed my brows but nodded. [Where is Wesley?]

"Wes is upstairs in his room." He smiled and leaned down to kiss my head. "We're okay, sweetheart. Don't you worry about us."

He understood that I had big, confusing feelings and thoughts too, and he was only trying to make me feel better. I wanted to make him feel better too, so I lifted my hands again and signed, [I love you, Dad. And I love Mom. Because you love me too.]

His eyes widened for a split second, then his eyes watered. This time, I was sure that those were happy tears in his eyes. "We do love you, Milow. Now, play a little. Dinner's ready soon."

[Okay.]

I gave his legs a quick squeeze, then headed upstairs to Wesley's room. The door was half open, and I saw him sitting on his bed with a bunch of books in front of him. He looked up when he heard me at the door, and I waved at him.

He smiled a little. "Hey, Milow. What's up?"

[Can you help me?]

He tilted his head like he always did when he watched me sign. All of them had been very interested in learning my secret language, but Wesley was often busy with school, and so he wasn't as good as the others. But he still tried and always wanted to keep learning.

"You want me to help you? With what?"

[Picking flowers.]

He blinked once, then closed the book in front of him. "Picking flowers? From the garden?"

I nodded quickly, happy and proud of him for understanding.

"Yeah. I can do that."

I felt a small bit of relief. I wanted to bring Iris flowers. Flowers always made her smile. I knew because Gus often bought her flowers, which she then placed into a pretty vase. I wanted to be the one to give them flowers this time.

Wesley slid off the bed and followed me downstairs, where we slid through the back door into the yard. Wesley stayed close as I knelt in front of the flower bed. I chose all colors, picking them carefully, and holding the stems tight so they wouldn't fall apart.

Wesley crouched beside me and held out his hand. "I can hold them for you."

I set each flower into his palm so he could hold them in a small bunch. He kept watching me, and I concentrated on choosing the best blossoms.

After a while, he asked softly, "How was it at the doctor, Milow?"

I lifted one shoulder to show it hadn't been that bad. [It didn't hurt.]

"It didn't hurt?" He nodded. "Good. Did the doctor say anything about how healthy you are?"

I straightened and nodded again. I felt proud of that. [I'm healthy and strong.]

"That's good."

I reached for a purple flower and placed it with the others. Then I signed again. [But he said something is missing in me.]

Wesley paused, trying to understand. His eyebrows furrowed. "Missing something? What do you mean?"

I shrugged again. I didn't know how to explain. [Something that made them sad.]

He looked at my hands, then at the bunch of flowers he was holding. His expression softened. "Is that why you wanted to pick flowers? Because Mom and Dad are sad?"

[Yes.]

"That's very sweet, Milow. They're going to love them."

When I was done picking the prettiest flowers, I carried them inside as Wesley followed me. I headed straight to the kitchen, where both Iris and Gus were standing.

"Mom. Dad. Milow has something for you," Wesley told them.

They both turned around, and I held the pretty bundle toward them with a big smile.

"Oh, sweetheart," Iris whispered, taking the flowers from my hands. She pressed them to her chest, then leaned forward and kissed the top of my head. "These are beautiful."

[They make you happy.]

"They do," Gus said, brushing his hand over my hair. "Let's put them in a vase and have them at the dinner table."

I nodded quickly and watched as Iris went to find the perfect vase. As she carefully arranged them, Gus asked Wesley to help set the table. I wanted to help too, and as I placed the last glass down, I heard the front door open.

"I'm home!" Ashby's voice called from the entrance, and I quickly turned around. He was kicking off his shoes and throwing his jacket on the bench before he ran through the living room and toward us. He didn't slow down before he crashed into me, his arms coming around me tightly. His cheek pressed against my hair.

"I missed you," he said.

I froze for a second, then wrapped my arms around him too. His hug made it feel like everything was okay again.

"We missed you too, buddy," Gus said. "Go wash your hands, then come sit. Dinner's ready."

I didn't want to let go, but I wasn't losing him. We'd have dinner with the whole family, and I knew that afterward, we would play until it was time for bed.

8

Milow

Saturday, June 13th

Today was a big day. I had waited a long time to see Ashby swim, and now it was finally happening. I woke up early because I couldn't stop thinking about it. I had wanted to hug Ashby and wish him good luck, but he was already gone. Dad had taken him to the aquatic center first thing in the morning for warm-ups. Mom, Wesley, and I ate breakfast together, and afterward, Mom helped me change into my swimsuit.

I had only worn it once when we bought it two weeks ago. It made me feel athletic and ready to jump into the pool. Mom said I needed to wait until the competition ended before I could get in. Wesley wore his swim shorts too, and he promised to hold me where my feet couldn't touch the bottom. I kept thinking about that—my feet hanging in deep water. I had only ever been in the bathtub, and that had always been safe. The pool would be different, but I wasn't scared.

I wanted to learn to swim. I wanted to feel what Ashby

felt, because I knew swimming was so important to him. But as excited as I was to get into the pool myself, I was more excited to see him swim. Mom and Dad always talked about how strong and fast he was in the water. I wanted to see it with my own eyes, and I just knew that he would win today.

When we reached the aquatic center, I looked around with wide eyes. The pool stretched out in front of us, and the water looked endless. There were long ropes dividing it into long paths, and I was fascinated with everything else in this place. Immediately, I understood why Ashby felt so comfortable here.

I squeezed Mom's hand to make her look down at me, then let go so I could sign.

[Will Ashby swim in here?]

Mom nodded and smiled. "He will."

I stared across the water, then I signed again.

[The lanes are so long!]

"They are, huh," she said, then pointed toward the bleachers. "We'll go sit over there."

We walked across the wet tiles. My bare feet slapped against them, and water sprayed from the other kids who ran past us. Families filled the seats, and I looked at all the faces. Some of them I had already seen around town before. Mom said hi to a couple and waved to a woman further up the bleachers. We sat close to the bottom row, right next to the water, and I leaned forward, peering into the blue. My heart thudded in my chest with anticipation. Mom placed her hand on my shoulder and pointed toward the entrance.

"Look, Milow. Stanley's mom and dad are here."

I followed her finger and saw the couple walking

toward us. Dean had the same dark hair as Stan, and their faces were similar, making it clear they were father and son. Chelsea waved with both hands when she spotted us. When they reached our row, Mom stood and hugged them.

Chelsea crouched down so she could look at me at eye level. Her smile was big and bright.

"Hi, sweetie. How are you today?"

I had met the two before when they once came over for dinner at our place. They were nice and even brought cake for dessert. I liked Dean and Chelsea, but I still had trouble fully accepting Stan as my friend. He could be too loud, and he liked to push every game into chaos. Still, he always included me. He shared his toys and snacks, even if he yelled too much while doing it. Ashby never seemed to mind, so I tried not to mind, either.

I smiled and raised my hands to sign.

[I'm okay.]

Chelsea watched carefully, making sure she understood. Then she nodded.

"That's good. Are you excited to watch the boys swim?"

I nodded hard. My excitement was for Ashby. Stan would be in the water too, but I didn't care as much about watching him swim. I liked him, even when he annoyed me sometimes. But it was different with Ashby. I wanted him to win. I wanted everyone to cheer for him.

As Chelsea and Mom sat down, I saw Dad walk over to us. I waved and waited for him to reach me, then let him pick me up. "Hey, sweetheart. Wow, look at you!" He poked my belly. "I like your swimsuit."

[Thank you.]

Dad smiled and kissed my cheek, then put me back down to greet Mom and Wesley before he sat next to Dean.

The adults started talking about the race schedule and when the boys would be starting. Their voices blended with the noise of the pool. When Mom leaned closer to me, she pointed toward a smaller pool on the other side of the big one. Several kids stood at the edge while coaches talked to them.

"See Ashby?" Mom asked. "That's where they warm up before the race."

I scanned the crowd of swimmers, spotting his dark-blue swim cap as he jogged toward the edge of the pool.

"There's our boy," Dad said proudly.

I watched as he jumped into the water, with the other kids following behind, and I held my breath as Ashby pushed off the wall and kicked hard. His arms sliced through the water, and his legs kicked fast. He looked focused, and I tried to imagine swimming myself. I wouldn't be as good as him—or any of the kids. But I was willing to learn.

Ashby reached the other side and lifted his head. I leaned forward and raised my hand, waving again and again.

His head turned toward us, and for a moment, I wasn't sure he would recognize us from there. But then he grinned and lifted one arm out of the water and waved back before the coach shouted something at him. He ducked into the water again and pushed off the wall.

I sat back and felt warmth spread in my belly as I kept my eyes on Ashby.

After a while, Wesley leaned closer to us, with his pale eyes on Mom and Dad.

"Can I get ice cream while we wait for the race to start?"

Dad pulled out his wallet without hesitation and handed Wesley a few bills. "Take Milow with you."

I loved ice cream, especially on warm days like today. Wesley stood up and held out his hand. "Come on, Milow. Let's get ice cream."

I slipped my fingers into his palm, and he held my hand tightly as we stepped down the bleachers carefully. I watched the water shimmer as we passed, getting more and more excited to jump in.

The kiosk sat near the entrance, and a small line formed in front of it. A fan buzzed behind the counter, blowing the cool air toward us. There was a glass case filled with different-colored ice creams in tubs, and when it was our turn, I pressed both hands against the edge to peer inside.

Wesley leaned in beside me. "What flavor do you want?" He pointed at the tubs one by one. "They have chocolate, vanilla, strawberry, mint chip, and lemon."

I stared hard at each color, trying to imagine how each tasted. I wished I could get all the flavors, but I wouldn't be able to eat that much. Wesley waited patiently, giving me all the time I needed to make a choice I wouldn't regret.

[Chocolate, please.]

Wesley nodded, then looked at the woman behind the counter. "Chocolate for my sister, and vanilla for me, please."

He paid with the money Dad had given us. When he handed me the cone, I held it carefully with one hand while taking Wesley's hand with the other. We walked back toward the bleachers. People moved around us carrying towels and inflatables, and I licked the ice cream so it wouldn't drip. Ahead of us, a girl stepped out from a group of kids. She had long red-blond hair in a braid and wore a purple swimsuit. She looked about Wesley's age.

"Hi, Wesley," she said, smiling shyly.

He froze and stopped, his face turning bright red. He straightened his posture a little and wiped his mouth with the back of his hand.

"Oh—hey, Evie," he answered.

I stopped beside him, looking up with intent. I had never seen Wesley this flushed and nervous. He was usually cool and relaxed, but this girl seemed to change that about him. Wesley still held my hand, but his grip tightened.

Evie glanced down at me with a smile.

"Is this your sister?"

Wesley nodded quickly. "Yeah. This is Milow."

Evie bent down a little so she could look at me better. "Nice to meet you, Milow."

I smiled. She didn't frown or scrunch her nose because I didn't use my voice. She just kept smiling. "She's cute."

Wesley cleared his throat and shifted his weight from one foot to the other. "Uh, are you swimming today?"

Evie moved her gaze back to Wesley. "Yeah. Breaststroke. I'm a little nervous, but I know I can do it. You?"

Wesley shook his head and glanced away. "No. Just watching Ashby."

"Oh." She hesitated, then smiled again. "Well… maybe I'll see you later?"

"Yeah," Wesley said quickly. "Okay."

She waved and walked off toward her group, and Wesley let out a slow breath through his nose, still holding my hand tighter than before. His face stayed red, and when he looked down at me, he tried to act normal.

I raised a brow at him, amused by the way he had reacted to Evie.

"Come on," he whispered. "We should get back before the race starts."

We continued walking toward our seats, and I kept watching Wesley's face as he licked his ice cream, pretending nothing had happened.

Did he like Evie? Evie definitely liked him. I could see it in her eyes. It was the same way I looked at Ashby, and Ashby looked at me the same too. And we really liked each other a lot.

When we reached our seats, Iris smiled and said, "Hurry and sit. Ashby's heat is up next."

We squeezed in beside Mom and Dad, and I looked at the far end of the pool where swimmers lined up behind the blocks. I had almost finished my ice cream already as I listened to the voice coming through the speakers, calling out names one by one.

"On lane number four…Ashby Statler!"

Dad punched the air. "That's my boy!" His voice boomed across the bleachers, and a few people chuckled.

Iris clapped. "Go Ashby!"

Wesley leaned forward, cupping his free hand around his mouth. "You got this, buddy!"

I wished I could've called out to him too. Sometimes I wished that in situations like these, the magic would give me back my voice. Just for a second, to cheer for Ashby. Instead, I just smiled brightly with my heart pounding hard in my chest.

The announcer continued.

"And on lane five we have Stanley Whitt!"

Chelsea and Dean stood and clapped loudly. "You can do this, Stan!" Dean called.

Stan climbed up on his block. His goggles hid his eyes, but I could tell he was scared and nervous. Ashby looked over at his best friend and gave him a thumbs-up. Stan tried to smile, but he just shrugged instead before shifting on the block nervously. They were racing against each other, and Ashby still tried to make his friend comfortable by showing his support.

The swimmers crouched into a start position, and I held my breath, staring at Ashby's frame bent forward, toes curled over the edge.

A loud horn blasted, and they all dove in headfirst. Well, all but Stan, who jumped in feetfirst.

Water splashed high, and Ashby shot forward with smooth, strong strokes. He was in the lead, while Stan kicked hard but wobbled off rhythm.

Everybody was cheering them on, and I forgot about my ice cream as Ashby came closer to the other end of the pool. My eyes followed him, then drifted to Stan for just a moment. He fell behind quickly, his head jerking up for breath every few strokes.

"Maybe we should let him take up karate like he asked," Dean muttered. "Swimming isn't for everyone."

Chelsea sighed but nodded, eyes worried as Stan splashed toward the halfway mark.

I felt a sting in my chest as I watched Stan struggle. He looked helpless in the water, but I knew he hadn't been forced to swim. I bet his parents just wanted him to try everything once, just like Mom and Dad had let the boys try everything before Ashby chose swimming and Wesley ice hockey.

Ashby glided ahead, reaching the wall first in what seemed like no time. Dad stood up, cheering loudly.

Stan touched the wall long after the others, lifting his head and gasping. He was coughing and looked exhausted, but Chelsea clapped anyway, her voice trembling but proud. "Good job, Stan! Proud of you!"

My eyes went back to Ashby. He got out of the pool and pulled off his goggles and cap, and after getting a high five and a hug from his coach, he turned toward the bleachers. We all waved, and he jogged around the pool with water dripping from his hair and shoulders. His grin never faded. When he reached us, Dad grabbed him into a tight hug and ruffled his hair. Iris kissed his cheek, and Wesley slapped his back.

"You're a champ," Wesley told him proudly. "You were insanely fast."

"We're proud of you, kiddo," Dad added.

Ashby thanked them, and when Dad put him back down, he looked at me. His arms wrapped around me, lifting my feet from the ground. Cold water soaked into my swimsuit, but I didn't care. I clung to him, holding on tight. He pulled back just enough to look at my face. He was still breathing fast from the race, and his eyes shone with pride.

"I won because you were here," he said, his voice filled with certainty. "I saw you, and it made me swim faster."

I wasn't so sure if that was true, but I liked to believe it. My chest tightened the way it always did when he said or did something so sweet. I smiled and pressed my forehead against his shoulder, wishing more than anything I could tell him with words how happy I was.

"All right, kids," Mom said, smiling down at us. "We'll set up the towels over there on the grass, and you can go play in the pool."

I had been so excited for Ashby that I had forgotten about getting to go into the pool for the first time. For the rest of the afternoon, Ashby and Wesley stayed close to me in the shallow water, showing me how to kick and move my arms while they kept their hands under me so I wouldn't sink.

9

Ashby

I was only seven, but I understood a lot. I wasn't super smart like Milow, because she was a pro with numbers and her secret language. But I knew someone had done something bad to her before she came here. Something that made her stop wanting to talk. I didn't know what happened. I didn't want to ask and make her sad. Wesley once said that some kids stopped talking when they got hurt badly, and the idea scared me. It made my stomach feel sick every time I pictured someone hurting Milow.

But Milow was safe here with us, and I protected her from anything and anyone.

After dinner, we sat at the kitchen table, coloring with our markers spread everywhere. Mom washed dishes at the sink, and Dad dried them. Wesley sat across from me, working on a math worksheet. Milow sat beside me, legs tucked up on the chair. Her hair was falling around her face while she drew a big blue sky, and I watched her for a while. I liked watching her draw. She always focused so hard that her brows furrowed, and her hand moved slowly and carefully.

"What are you drawing?" I asked, leaning in a bit closer.

She lifted her head and looked at me. [A jungle with lots of animals.]

"Oh, cool! You can draw a snake and spiders and a jaguar and lizards!"

She watched me wide-eyed. She always did when I talked so fast, but I couldn't help myself.

"Slow down, buddy," Dad said with a chuckle.

"Sorry! I know her drawing will be awesome. You want to know what I'm drawing?" I asked Milow with a grin, and when she nodded, I continued. "I'm drawing the pool and us swimming."

She looked at my paper, then smiled at me and signed, [That's amazing.]

I grinned proudly and picked my next color to continue my drawing.

After a while, when they were done with the dishes, Mom turned around and smiled at us. "You two could open a gallery. I bet people would pay millions for these."

My eyes widened. "You think? Oh, boy! I have, like a hundred drawings upstairs."

Dad hung the towel and came to stand behind us. "We can talk business tomorrow. You should get ready for bed. It's late."

"Aww." I slumped in my chair. "Just five more minutes?"

Mom smiled and stood up straight again. "Five minutes. Then teeth and pajamas."

The five minutes passed too quickly, and after saying

good night to Wesley, Milow and I ran upstairs to get ready for bed.

We brushed our teeth fast, then went to our rooms. I got into bed, but I wouldn't stay here long. As soon as Mom and Dad tucked me in, I would slide out of bed and sneak into Milow's room. That's what I did most nights.

After a long moment of staring at the ceiling, listening closely until I heard them walk downstairs, I jumped up and moved quickly but silently.

I tiptoed across the hallway, reaching Milow's door. Without knocking, I slowly opened the door and peered inside. "Milow?"

She was sitting up in her bed, already waiting for me. I smiled and went inside, closing the door behind me, before walking over and climbing onto the bed. She scooted over, and we lay down facing each other.

"Milow, you know Mom was just joking when she said we could put our drawings in a gallery, right?"

She nodded. [I know.]

"Okay, good. Because I would never want my drawings to hang anywhere else than your room," I told her. "I drew them for you, not for anyone else."

She watched me with a pleased smile in the moonlit room. She looked over at the wall above her desk. [Okay.]

"Okay," I repeated with a grin. I wanted to say the next words out loud, but I decided to use my hands instead. With focus and precision, I signed, [You're my best friend.]

Her eyes widened slightly, then she signed it right back to me. [You're my best friend too.]

My heart skipped a beat. It always did in moments like these. I placed my hand on the mattress between us, and her gaze dropped to my fingers as she moved her hand to mine. Her fingers wrapped around mine, and I gave them a little squeeze.

She squeezed right back, then she closed her eyes, without ever letting go. Our eyelids grew heavy, and I listened to her breathing evening out until I fell asleep too.

———

Milow

I opened my eyes at the sound of footsteps coming from the hallway, and I sat up immediately, knowing who was about to open the bedroom door. My eyes stayed locked on the door as my skin prickled, and my stomach twisted.

The door cracked open, flooding the room with a harsh light from the hall. He filled the doorway, his face unreadable and his voice flat as he told me to get up. His tone left no room for hesitation or argument.

My hands curled into the blankets, and when he stepped toward me, he reached down, his fingers wrapping around my arm with a grip that was hard and urgent. He pulled me out of bed, guiding me through the hallway and down the staircase. The house was silent, and each step was cold under my bare feet. I had thought he'd take me to his bedroom again, but we went down another flight of stairs, then another.

He pushed open the basement door, and the blinding white light hit my eyes hard. The room was so bright and sterile that it hurt, making me squint as fear crawled higher inside me, choking my voice before I could even think of using it.

He led me into a room I didn't know existed. It was a long rectangular space with white walls and a metal table waiting in the center beneath a bright lamp. The smell of alcohol burned my nose while my legs trembled uncontrollably.

He told me to lie down, and although every part of me screamed to run away, I climbed onto the table. His hand pressed between my shoulder blades and kept me there, holding me in place as the cold surface shocked my skin.

The world narrowed to the light above me as something punctured my wrist. Sudden sleep came over me, and I tried to open my mouth to speak, but nothing came out. The room buzzed, and my heartbeat thudded louder in my ears as I fought with every inch of my body to stay awake. But I couldn't. I was too weak.

"Let yourself go," I heard him say, feeling his hands run along my thighs. "Let go, princess. Daddy will make you all better."

10

Milow

Summer break started about three weeks ago, and since then, Ashby and Wesley have been home the whole time. We played from morning until the sun went down, and when Mom and Dad weren't working, they took us to the pool. I could swim now, and that made me proud, but Ashby still moved through the water faster and more smoothly than I ever could.

Stan had slept over last night—which he had done at least twice every week so far—and this morning, he was still bursting with energy. He tore around the house, grabbed every toy within reach, and laughed at everything. He never pushed us aside or was mean. He was just being wild, like always. Stan was simply being Stan, and while his loud energy never really bothered me, I still wondered what it would be like to see him calm for once.

We were outside in the backyard playing tag. The wooden playground Dad built stood in the middle of the grass, and we chased each other between the swings and the sandbox. Stan was the catcher, and as fast as he was, he hadn't tagged me yet. I knew he was after me because he never went after Ashby, which I thought was unfair, but I was too fast for him anyway.

Suddenly, Stan stopped running, his eyes widening as he spun around and sprinted back toward the porch. He was yelling at the top of his lungs, with his arms flaring in the air. I froze halfway up the steps, and my hands curled around the railing as I followed his gaze. The hedge rustled, and my mind searched for a reason. Maybe he saw a snake or something bigger. A monster, I thought, but Wesley always said monsters weren't real, and I trusted him, so I stayed where I was and waited for whatever would come out.

"What are you running from?" Ashby called from the bridge of the playground, his voice confused but also a little amused as he leaned over the railing. "Stan, what is it now?"

"A monster!" Stan shouted back. His voice was loud and dramatic, filled with pure horror as he slapped both hands to the sides of his head. "It's over there! It's coming right at us!"

A monster.

My face went cold, and my stomach dropped all at once as I turned to look at Ashby with wide, panicked eyes. When he noticed me staring, I lifted my hands quickly. [Is it really a monster?]

Ashby didn't even hesitate. He shook his head firmly and frowned, like the answer should have been obvious. "Of course not, Milow. Monsters aren't real."

"Yes, they are!" Stan yelled again, pointing wildly toward the hedges. "And it's right there! Aah—there it is!"

I didn't want to look. Every part of me told me not to, but the fear felt too big to ignore. My heart thudded hard in my chest as I slowly turned my head, bracing myself for something terrible. But the fear drained away almost instantly when I saw her.

It was just a girl.

She stood there with her dirty-blond hair pulled into a messy ponytail, her hands planted firmly on her hips as she glared at Stan like she'd had enough of him already.

"I'm not a monster, Stanley," she said sharply.

"Are too! You're scary and ugly!" Stan yelled back, not even thinking before the words came out of his mouth.

But the girl was far from ugly. She looked like a princess, even with strands of hair sticking to her sweaty forehead, and her cheeks as red as tomatoes.

"And you're a baby!" the girl shot back immediately, her voice sharp and fearless. She started walking straight toward the playground like she wasn't scared of him at all.

Stan took one look at the girl coming closer and decided running was his best option. He turned on his heel and sprinted across the grass. I stayed where I was, watching with wide eyes as the girl chased after him without slowing down even a little. Ashby burst out laughing, with his arms crossed over his stomach.

The girl was fast. Much faster than Stan. I didn't even realize how fast until she caught up to him in seconds and tackled him to the ground like a football player, sending both of them rolling across the grass. They wrestled for a moment, arms and legs everywhere as Stan yelled dramatically. Ashby laughed even harder, and I found myself smiling just a little too.

In the end, she won, and she climbed on top of Stan's

belly, sitting there proudly with her hands on her thighs, and a triumphant grin spread across her face while Stan groaned beneath her.

"See?" she said smugly. "You're such a baby."

"Get off me!" Stan yelled. He was struggling, kicking his feet wildly as if that might somehow help him.

"Ask nicely," the girl said calmly. She had all the time in the world, and she'd let him suffer for as long as possible.

"No!"

"Then I'm not getting off you, you big baby," she replied, settling her weight even more comfortably on his stomach.

Ashby was laughing so hard he had to bend over, his laughter bubbling out of him like he couldn't control it even if he tried. My own smile grew wider as I watched. It was strange and funny to see Stan like this, not the loudest or wildest one for once. He was usually the one nobody could calm down, but this girl seemed to be doing something no one else ever managed.

"Someone help!" Stan groaned, trying again to push her off him, his face twisted with frustration.

"Ask nicely," she repeated, fixing him with an expectant glare.

"No, no, no, never!"

"What's going on out here?"

I turned my head toward the porch and saw Dad standing there, his eyes finding me first, then Ashby, and finally landing on Stan and the girl tangled up on the grass. He didn't even wait for an answer. His expression shifted into amusement, and he let out a low chuckle. "Ah, you're finally back," he said. "No one else has been able to stop that whirlwind all summer."

The girl glanced over her shoulder with a wide, proud grin. "Hi, Mr. Statler!"

Dad lifted his hand in a quick wave. "Be good, kids. Come inside if you want a snack." Then he turned around and went back into the house.

Stan huffed and puffed underneath her for a few more seconds, his legs still kicking, and his hands pressing uselessly against her arms. Then he stopped moving completely. His face scrunched up like he was chewing on something really bitter.

"…Please," he muttered. "Can you get off me, please?"

The girl raised a brow, clearly surprised, and even Ashby stopped laughing. Then she grinned, looking satisfied, as if she had just won something. "See? That wasn't so hard."

She pushed herself up and stood, brushing dirt off her knees, while Stan rolled onto his side and sighed dramatically, holding his stomach like he had survived a great battle.

I stared at him, fascinated. I had never seen Stan act like this. Ever. He was loud and stubborn, always doing whatever he wanted, and now he had just…listened.

The girl turned toward Ashby as he climbed down the playground. His face lit up, and so did the girl's, and as they met each other halfway, they hugged tightly.

"I'm so happy you're back from Australia!" he said excitedly. "I thought you weren't coming back, ever!"

I noticed two things: Ashby's eyes were brighter than they'd ever been, and my heart was beating hard, but in a painful way. I didn't like the way it felt. Not one bit. So I tried to ignore it.

"Mom wanted to visit family," the girl said as she

stepped away from him. She scrunched her nose. "I liked it, but I missed home and all of you guys."

"We didn't miss you," Stan muttered from where he still sat in the grass.

The girl rolled her eyes hard. "I sure hope I'm not going to be in your class in second grade."

I was fascinated by her. She talked like a grown-up, and she wasn't afraid of anything. She was confident and loud, but not obnoxiously like Stan. She was kind and funny, and Ashby liked her. And when Ashby liked someone, I had to like them too.

Stan groaned loudly. "I'll have my parents get me to switch. Actually, now that you're back, I'll ask them if we can move away."

As dramatic as he was being, I knew he couldn't dislike her that much. She was super cool. Cooler than any girl I had ever met. Maybe Stan was intimidated by her.

She didn't respond and turned to face me next. She looked at me differently than Stan had the first time he saw me. She wasn't confused or telling Ashby that I shouldn't be there. She looked curious, tilting her head and smiling.

"I'm Scottie," she told me, taking a few steps closer. "Are you new here?"

I felt them all looking at me now. My heart continued to beat loudly in my chest, but I wasn't scared. Just… worried. That maybe she'd change her mind about me the second I lifted my hands.

But Mom and Dad always told me to be brave in situations like these.

I quickly glanced at Ashby, then slowly lifted my hands to sign.

[I'm Milow.]

She watched my hands as I lowered them, and I braced myself for her honest reaction. But before she could say anything, Ashby stepped in. He took my hand in his and smiled proudly. "She lives here now."

Scottie's smile didn't fade. If anything, it grew warmer. "Cool," she said easily. "Nice to meet you, uh…"

"Milow. Her name is Milow. She fingerspelled it for you, but she also has different name signs for all of us. This is the sign for her name," he explained, signing an M, and then flicking two fingers away from his right eye. Mom taught us about this. That people who signed created unique signs as identifiers, instead of fingerspelling the names every time. My special name sign was my initial, and then the indication that my right eye had two colors.

Ashby's name sign was a combination of his initial and the sign for water, because he was a swimmer. And Stan's name sign was a little funnier, but it fit just the same: his initial, and the sign for clown. I came up with that one, and I was proud of it.

"And she's way cooler than you," Stan added, now standing a few feet away from us, but with still enough distance to get away from Scottie if he needed to.

I didn't mean to ignore Stan's words, because he had never really said anything so nice to me. He was never rude or mean to me, but I had never heard him say I was cool. But I couldn't stop staring at Scottie. Something about her made me curious, and while that strange feeling was still lingering in my chest, I really wanted to be her friend.

Stan just couldn't let it go. "You want to know why she's way cooler than you? Milow never chases me or pushes me to the ground, and she always lets me use her colored pencils. And she has a way cooler name," he said, breathing heavily as if what he had said upset him. "You have a boy's name. Girls aren't supposed to have boy names."

That confused me, because Wesley once said that my name wasn't really for girls, either. He said it was a…a…uniform…*no*, a uni-something name…*um*… I couldn't remember the word for it. But he said my name was rare, and it made me special.

Scottie's expression changed, and she looked angry now. She glared at Stan and huffed as she crossed her arms, still standing her ground. "I'm named after my dad, whose name was Scott, and he died just before I was born, so you're being very *insensitive*, Stanley."

That shut him up, and it made me stare at her even harder.

Her daddy was gone too.

She understood what it meant not to have a father.

Maybe that's why I was so fascinated by her. She was strong even after losing someone important.

"Stop it now, Stanley," Ashby muttered, sounding ashamed by his best friend's behavior. He was still holding my hand, and I squeezed it gently to get his attention.

When he looked at me, I smiled and lifted my hands to sign. [I like her.]

Ashby's eyes widened, and his expression turned happy again. "Yeah, I really like her, too." He looked at Scottie with an apologetic smile. "I'm sorry Stan is being so mean."

"It's okay." She looked at Stan and shrugged. "He's only mean to me because he really likes me."

Stan gasped louder than he had ever gasped, stemming his hands onto his hips. "I do *not* really like you!"

"Do too!"

"Nuh-uh!"

"Yuh-huh!"

I watched them bicker, and when they finally stopped, Scottie turned toward us with a grin. She reached out and touched Ashby's shoulder, shouting, "Tag, you're it!" before she ran away laughing.

I was frozen for a moment, still so very confused yet excited about this new girl who had suddenly appeared in our garden. It was on that hot summer day that I gained another friend, who had taught me to be fearless and strong.

———

Ashby

Tuesday, August 4th

I put the pencil down and leaned back a little, studying the drawing carefully to make sure I hadn't forgotten anything important. The sky was blue, the grass was green, and the playground stood right in the middle of the page, exactly how it looked in real life. I sat up straighter then, pleased with my artwork. This was another drawing Milow could hang on the wall in her bedroom.

I held it out to her with a grin.

"Here, Milow. For you."

She lifted her gaze from her own drawing and scooted up on the mattress so she could sit properly. She took the paper from my hands and looked at it closely, her eyes moving slowly over every line and color. She didn't want to miss a single detail.

Her eyes shone with happiness. That was my favorite way her eyes looked, especially when they shone like that for me alone.

"Do you like it?" I asked, impatiently waiting for her to tell me what she thought.

She nodded right away and carefully set the drawing down on the bed beside her. Her hands lifted. [It's amazing. You're an artist!]

Her words made my heart feel so full, like it would actually explode right there in my chest. My grin stretched even wider. "Thanks," I said, then added honestly, "but I'm a way better swimmer."

A loud groan came from the direction of my desk. "How many more drawings are you going to make for her?" Stan complained, slumped in the chair while pulling apart the Lego he'd been working on.

"As many as I can," I said without hesitation. "For the rest of my life." I didn't even think about it before saying it. It just felt true. Like a promise I had already made to myself and had no intention of ever breaking.

Stan scrunched up his nose and shook his head a little. "It's like you're in love with her or something."

I frowned and stared at him for a few seconds, then my eyes drifted back to Milow. She was watching me now, her eyes wide and curious. She was waiting to see what I would say next.

I knew other kids my age would've made gagging noises or denied that statement. They'd argue that it wasn't true, and that it was weird and silly to be in love with someone because love was for grown-ups. But I didn't feel like doing any of that because the truth was simple, even if the words felt too big to admit.

I was in love with her.

And even though I was only seven, I knew that was exactly what I felt for Milow.

PART 2

11

Milow

Friday, September 5th
16 years old

I wasn't as fearless or strong as my younger self would've liked me to be. I was anxious all the time, and some days, I couldn't figure out how not to seem weak. I was smart, though, which was at least something good, but it didn't cancel out the rest of it. I was still vulnerable, and I pretended I was fine just so no one would worry. I hated seeing that look on my family's and friends' faces when they thought something was wrong with me, so I made sure they never saw it. At first, it was easy. I was younger, and hiding things was simple. As I got older, it became harder to keep everything contained and carry it all without letting it show. Speaking about it felt impossible, because that would mean exposing even more of myself, and vulnerability only seemed to invite more problems.

God, I sounded unbearable even inside my own head. Of course, no one would want to sit there and watch me complain about my thoughts and feelings.

So I did what I always did. I pushed everything down and moved on with my day like nothing was wrong. Summer break was over, and school had started again this week, which meant schedules, expectations, and piles of work waiting to be done.

Not that the workload bothered me. I always asked for extra assignments anyway, because I finished what the teachers gave us during class or lunch. I liked keeping my brain busy. Reading the same kinds of books or doing Sudokus and crosswords every day wasn't enough anymore. It didn't compare to learning something new, to being challenged, and feeling like my mind was doing exactly what it was supposed to do.

It was Friday, and I had just gotten home from school. Tonight there was supposed to be a back-to-school party at Scottie's house. Of course, I wanted to go. I just hadn't asked Mom and Dad yet, and since I was only sixteen, I wasn't sure I even wanted to bring it up out of fear of their answer. However, I had a feeling they'd say yes. They wanted me to do things, to go out, to have fun. To experience new things. They wanted me to live.

I wanted that too, at least in theory. In reality, I often struggled to fit in, no matter how much I tried.

The reason was my silence.

Mom and Dad never pushed me to talk. They never told me to use my voice, never acted like it was something I could simply decide to do. I appreciated that more than they probably knew. But the truth was, if I could have spoken, I would have done so a long time ago. I wanted to. I just couldn't.

Ever since I was little, people had told me I had selective mutism. That I was one of those kids who had gone through a lot of trauma, who had shut down and stopped talking because of it. They said that one day I would choose to speak again, because I had once used my voice, and that meant it was still there.

And I knew I had spoken before, so something didn't add up.

"Hey, Milow."

I had been so lost in my thoughts that I hadn't even noticed anyone else was in the house. I turned my head and saw Evie sitting on the couch, her smile as soft and warm as it always was. Her brown eyes had a kindness that made everyone feel at ease. Ever since she and Wesley got together, she had spent every holiday and every birthday with us. Now that they both graduated from university earlier this year, she was here even more. She practically lived here, though they were planning to move into their own apartment. Dad was completely on board with that, saying they were old enough and had their near future figured out. Mom would keep them here forever if she could. I wouldn't have minded that either.

I smiled back at her, set my backpack down, and walked into the living room. [Hi, Evie. What are you doing?]

Like everyone close to me, Evie had learned to sign. I had never asked anyone to do it for me. They just did, out of love, out of patience, out of wanting to include me without making a big deal out of it.

"Oh, I'm just looking through some of Iris's old cookbooks. I want to make something for dinner tonight because she won't be home from work until later." She glanced down at the thick book resting in her lap, lips pursed in thought. "I'm just not sure what yet..."

I sat down beside her, tucking my legs under me as I

leaned in to look at the open page. I pointed at the picture of eggplant parmigiana, then waited until she looked at me before signing again. [This one looks delicious.]

"Hm, yeah…but Wesley isn't so keen on eggplants."

I pressed my lips together and glanced back down at the cookbook, scanning the page once more before lifting my hands. [You can make half of it like a normal lasagna, and use slices of eggplant for the other. It will practically be the same.]

"You're right." She nodded, already convinced. "I'll do that."

Satisfied, I pushed myself up from the couch. [I have to put my things away. Can I help you cook after?]

"I'd love that," she said, smiling up at me.

[Great. Where's Wesley, by the way?]

"He's in bed. He had a pretty intense practice this morning. He's just resting for a bit." Then she tilted her head. "What about Ashby? Didn't you drive home with him?"

I usually did. Almost always. But today had been different. After school, I went to the library. I needed a few books, and even though Ashby would've waited without complaining, I didn't want to keep him waiting. I'd assumed he'd be home before me anyway.

I shrugged lightly. [No. I haven't seen him since lunch.]

Evie nodded and turned back to the cookbook. I headed for the stairs and slung my backpack over one shoulder.

Upstairs, my room greeted me just the way I'd left it this morning. The bed was perfectly made, and the room was orderly, with every single thing sitting neatly in its place. I closed the door behind me and set my backpack on the chair before unzipping it. Books came out first, and

I stacked them neatly on the desk. Then I pulled out my notebook and pencil case.

After making a mental to-do list for the weekend and getting excited about all the extra work I took home today, I went back downstairs and found Evie in the kitchen. She was pulling ingredients from the fridge and setting them out on the counter. I washed my hands and took the knife she handed me, starting on the vegetables while she worked on the sauce.

At some point, the front door opened and closed again, and Ashby's voice echoed through the hallway.

"Milow!"

"She's here," Evie called back.

A second later, Ashby appeared in the kitchen doorway. He was wearing his hat backward as usual, with his messy hair peeking out from underneath, and one of his vintage T-shirts. His eyes found me immediately, and relief flickered there before being replaced by worry.

"I was looking all over school for you," he said, stepping fully into the kitchen. "And you didn't text me back."

I froze for half a second, then remembered… [I left my phone at home.]

His brows pulled together. "All day?"

I nodded.

He let out a breath and ran a hand over his face. "Jesus, Milow. I thought something happened. You weren't at your locker. You weren't in the parking lot. I checked the library and the study rooms. Stan said he hadn't seen you after school, either."

Guilt settled heavily in my chest. I hadn't meant to make him worry so much. [I went to the library. I needed books. I didn't mean to—]

"I know," he said quickly. "I know. I just… I was worried."

Evie glanced between us. She always had that look in her eyes, like she knew something we didn't. "Why don't you sit for a second, Ash?"

He huffed but didn't sit. Instead, he stepped closer to me, lowering his voice. "Next time, just come find me and let me know. Okay?"

I nodded again, my gaze lifting to meet his dark-brown eyes. Ashby had changed a lot over the years. He was tall, well over six feet, with broad shoulders and strong arms from years of training. His swim team demanded it from their best swimmer, and he took that responsibility seriously. His body had grown, becoming something entirely different from the boy he used to be. Not that I minded. He looked healthy and handsome.

But his eyes had never changed. They were still kind, still full of loyalty and an easy, unmistakable warmth that always made me feel safe and loved.

He relaxed then, his shoulders dropping as his gaze stayed on me. He eyed me carefully, then his hand moved, squeezing mine once before letting go again. The small gesture sent a familiar jolt through me. It wasn't unusual for us to hold each other's hands. We had been doing it since we were little. It was comforting, but lately his touch made me nervous.

"I'm gonna shower," he told us.

I nodded as a small smile tugged at my lips. I watched him turn and head for the stairs, already reaching back to take his cap off his head as he went. I listened to his footsteps until they disappeared upstairs, only realizing how closely I'd been watching him.

Evie didn't say anything right away. She just hummed to herself, pretending to focus very hard on chopping vegetables, though the corners of her mouth kept lifting like she was holding back something she found very amusing.

"You know," she said casually, not looking at me, "most boys don't run all over school looking for someone unless they really like them."

I felt my face flush instantly and dropped my eyes to the counter. She knew Ashby always worried about me. It didn't matter in what context. Whenever I wasn't close to him, he always made sure I was okay. Even when we were in class, he sent me short texts, and I always responded with a thumbs-up.

"And most people," she continued, finally glancing at me with a knowing smile, "don't look at someone the way you two just did unless there's more going on than either of you is ready to admit to."

I shot her an embarrassed look, and she laughed quietly with a shake of her head. "I think it's very sweet."

[He's just extra worried every time a new school year starts. Because of the changes and all.]

"I know, I know." Evie smiled softly, reaching out her hand to squeeze my arm. "And I'm glad you two have each other as best friends." She turned back to the counter and continued cleaning up. "If I hadn't had Wesley during high school and college, I don't think I would've made it through."

They had been best friends once too. Until one day, Wesley just openly admitted his love for her in front of his whole hockey team. And the whole town. Because he did it on the ice after they won the state championship.

It was the sweetest thing I ever witnessed, but it didn't come as a surprise. I knew they were meant to be together. I knew from the day I saw that one interaction at the pool many years ago.

12

Milow

"*...and Coach said I'll have to push harder if I want to* have a chance against those guys from Dunst High."

I turned my head as Ashby and Wesley walked into the dining room. Ashby's hair was damp from the shower, and he had brushed it back, which was a rare sight. This look left his face completely open and unobstructed. I realized I wasn't used to seeing him like that, without his hair falling into his forehead the way it normally did, but even so, or maybe because of it, he looked really handsome.

Wesley walked beside him. His hair had lightened the way it always did in the summer, turning from light blond to nearly white from the sun because of all the time he spent outside. Sometimes I thought the sun did the same thing to his eyes. As pale as they already were, they always seemed a few shades lighter in the summer months. Especially when he got a tan from working out outside, they looked striking.

"You're already pushing hard," Wesley said, his tone

firm as he looked at Ashby. "I just talked to Dad about it a few days ago. You're already doing a lot, and we're worried your coach is making you work too hard for your own good."

Wesley didn't look pleased at all, and as I watched Ashby's shoulders tense slightly at his words, I knew I agreed with him. Ashby was at swim practice three times a week, sometimes more when competitions were coming up, and on the weekends, he often had meets that took up most of the day. On top of that, he had just started his senior year of high school, and even though he wasn't struggling and had always been a good student, the workload wasn't going to get any lighter.

With the constant pressure from his coach layered on top of everything else, I worried that one day it would all become too much, even for someone as strong and determined as Ashby.

It had gotten to be too much for Wesley back when he was in high school, and there had been a time when he almost quit hockey altogether. Back then, the pressure had been constant, from school, training, expectations, and the simple fact that there never seemed to be enough hours in the day.

Luckily, Mom and Dad had stepped in before it broke him, rearranging his schedule so that there was enough free time to breathe and rest, and to feel like a normal teenager once in a while. Because of that, he hadn't burned out. He had graduated, made the U Sports team at the University of British Columbia, and now he played for one of the best teams in all of Canada, the Vancouver Redwinds, as well as for the national team.

The boys were talented athletes with bright and

promising futures ahead of them. And then there was me. I didn't have anything that impressive figured out yet, no clear path or plan laid out in front of me. But I still had time to work it out.

"It'll be fine," Ashby said, frowning as he let out a heavy sigh. Then a grin tugged at his lips. "I don't have time to worry about that right now. I've got a party to attend tonight."

His eyes flicked to mine, and I smiled back immediately. Just looking at him made my heart flutter uncontrollably.

"And Milow is coming with me."

My eyes widened, and I quickly lifted my hands. [I haven't asked Mom and Dad yet.]

"That won't be necessary," Wesley said easily. He walked over to where I was sitting at the table and squeezed my shoulder in a brief but reassuring gesture, before sliding his arms around Evie, who had just walked in carrying two plates.

"Hot, Wes, the plates are hot," she warned.

He pressed a quick kiss to her cheek, then took the plates from her and set them down on the table.

I frowned slightly and looked up at him. [Why won't it be necessary?]

"Because Mom and Dad won't be home until later," Wesley explained. "Dad texted earlier and said he's picking up Mom from work so they can go on a date. Which means I'm in charge tonight, and I say you absolutely can go to that party."

I bit the inside of my cheek, looking over at Ashby, who was still grinning at me like this was already settled.

"Great."

I furrowed my brows. [I'm scared.]

Ashby's expression softened immediately. His grin faded while Wesley laughed under his breath. "Scared? To go to a high school party?"

I shrugged and looked back at him. [It'll be my first official party. I don't know what people do at parties.]

"They dance and have fun," he said with an easy smile. "And some people get blackout drunk. But since we're a non-alcohol-consuming family—"

"And we're underage," Ashby cut in quickly.

"—you'll just have to dance."

I scrunched my nose and dropped my gaze to my hands, flexing my fingers against my lap. Evie carried in two more plates and set them down on the table. Once everyone was seated, she glanced around with curiosity. "Whose party is it, anyway?"

"Scottie's," Ashby replied. "So, yeah, it'll probably be a wild one. But it'll be fun. She only invited people she actually likes, not every student at Bowen High."

"That does sound fun," Evie said, nudging my side with her elbow. "You should go."

I lifted my gaze and looked at all three of them sitting at the round table, all watching me with the same expectant expression, as if this decision mattered more than I realized.

I set down the fork I had just picked up and signed, [What if I get bored?]

"You won't," Ashby said quickly. "I'll be there, and I'll entertain you. And if I'm not entertaining enough, you can just watch Stan make a fool out of himself."

A smile tugged at my lips. I did like watching Stanley do stupid things and then deal with the consequences afterward. He was still a whirlwind, loud and always pushing things too far.

"I'd pay to watch that boy embarrass himself," Wesley said, stabbing into the lasagna with his fork. "Remember your tenth birthday, Ash? When he dared himself to run around naked at the public pool. God, what a clown."

Evie laughed softly, while Ashby let out a heavy sigh, unable to defend his best friend. "Yeah…not his brightest moment."

"There are never bright moments with that one," Wesley said, then he turned his attention back to me. "So here's the deal. You go to the party, and if for any reason you feel uncomfortable and want to come home, you text me and I'll come and get you. Deal?"

I studied him for a moment, trying to picture what a party at Scottie's would actually be like. It wasn't that I had never been to parties before. There had been Ashby's birthday parties, and Wesley's too. But Mom and Dad were always nearby then, and I could always disappear upstairs if things got too loud. I had been to Scottie's birthdays too, but this was different. This was her first real house party without her mom around. There'd be older kids I didn't hang out with at school. And apparently alcohol.

"I won't leave your side," Ashby said calmly. "I'll hang out with you all night."

That was too nice of him, and it was too much. I didn't want him to give up his night just to be sure I was okay. I shook my head and signed, [You don't have to do that. But I'll come.]

His grin came back instantly. "Perfect."

After dinner, I lingered in the dining room, pretending to listen to Wesley and Ashby talk even though my mind wasn't focused on it at all. The party sat heavily on my mind now that I was going. I had agreed to it. I had no idea what I was supposed to wear, and that uncertainty made me nervous all over again. It was a minor thing, but choosing an outfit to go anywhere had always put pressure on me.

Maybe it was because I appreciated every single item I had in my closet. Before being adopted, I remembered only ever wearing an oversized T-shirt, a pair of underwear, and socks with holes in them.

I glanced toward the kitchen, where Evie finished putting the plates in the dishwasher. She was always so calm and looked like she belonged wherever she was. I envied that about her. She probably never worried about her clothes. She didn't have to. She looked beautiful no matter what she wore. After a moment of sitting there and arguing with myself, I finally walked over to her.

She looked up when she noticed me hovering. "What's up?"

[Can you help me pick something to wear for the party?]

Her face immediately softened into a warm smile. "Of course I can," she said without hesitation, like there was never any doubt. "I'd love to."

Relief washed over me, glad I didn't have to do it alone.

Once she was finished cleaning up, we headed upstairs. I opened my bedroom door and stepped inside, flicking on the light. Evie stepped in and glanced around with a small smile. "Okay," she said, clapping her hands once softly. "Let's see what we're working with."

I walked over to my closet and slid the doors open, suddenly too aware and overwhelmed with how many clothes I owned. Yet, none of them felt like the right choice for the party. I looked back at her, a little unsure, and signed, [I don't want to look weird. Or like I'm trying too hard.]

She came over and looked at the clothes, running her fingers through the fabrics. She had a look of understanding in her eyes. "You won't," she said easily. "We'll find something that'll make you comfortable while still looking cute."

Thirty minutes later, I stood in the middle of my room, staring at my reflection while Evie watched me with a wide, approving grin. "I think you look super cute," she said, pleased with herself.

I looked at the jean skirt and the white top again, taking in how unfamiliar it felt to have so much skin showing. I had no issues wearing my bikini at the pool, but this was different. I bit my lower lip, shifting my weight from one foot to the other.

"You don't like it," Evie said gently, her smile fading as she crossed one arm over her stomach and rested her cheek in her hand.

I shook my head. [I like it. It's just...I feel naked.]

"Naked?" She tilted her head and looked me over again. Her eyes drifted from my outfit to my closet, then back to me. "Okay. That's easy to fix. You can layer."

She walked over and pulled out a light-green cardigan, holding it up in front of me. "This will look really pretty."

I studied it in the mirror, then nodded and slipped it on. I buttoned the top button and let the rest hang open so the white top beneath was still visible. I felt more like myself almost instantly.

"Better?" she asked.

I tilted my head to take another close look at myself, then signed, [Yes. This is perfect.]

"Good," she said with a satisfied smile. She crouched and grabbed a pair of white-and-brown Adidas sneakers. "And these. Trust me."

I put them on, laced them, and stood up just as a knock sounded at the door.

"Milow?" Ashby's voice came through the wood. "You ready?"

Evie shot me a knowing look. "Come in."

The door opened, and Ashby stepped inside. He stopped short the second he saw me. His eyes moved over me slowly. He looked at me the way he always did. With a kind of gentleness that always made my heart beat a little faster. Then he smiled.

"You look really pretty," he said, almost surprised by his own words.

My chest squeezed in that familiar way again, and I felt heat creep up my neck. I signed a small thank-you.

Evie cleared her throat. "Will Wesley drive you to the party?"

Ashby didn't look away from me as he answered her. "Yeah…he will."

"Good." Evie smiled again, then gently squeezed my hand. "Have fun, okay? And if you feel like leaving, text Wes."

I tore my gaze away from Ashby and looked at her, nodding once.

Evie left, and I stayed where I was, standing in front of the mirror with my hands loosely clasped together. Ashby was only a few feet away. He was always welcome in my room, always had been. When we were little, he had the habit of sneaking into my bed. As we grew older, he stopped doing it. I missed it, but I knew we couldn't keep sleeping in one bed with each other. We were in high school, and not little kids anymore.

Ashby didn't speak right away. He shifted his weight, one sneaker scuffing against the carpet. His hands were still shoved into his pockets. I watched his reflection instead of looking at him directly.

"Hey," he said finally.

I turned toward him then. He took a step closer, then another, stopping just in front of me. It always was.

"I was actually really worried earlier," he admitted, his brows drawing together. "When I couldn't find you at school."

A small smile tugged at his mouth, but it faded quickly.

My heart squeezed as I listened. I knew that when he had come home earlier and found me safe in the kitchen, the relief he'd felt hadn't stayed with him for long. With Ashby, it never really did. His worry always went deeper than simple explanations or missed messages. He didn't just wonder where I had been. He worried about why. If someone had stopped me. If someone had meant harm. He always carried that fear with him, even on days when there was no reason for it at all.

I needed to let him know that nothing had happened. [I just went to the library right after class, and I thought you had probably left already, so I went home.]

His shoulders relaxed, but only a little. "That makes sense." He let out a breath, rubbing the back of his neck. "I just kept thinking maybe something happened. I know that's stupid."

I quickly shook my head. [It's not stupid.]

He looked at me for a long moment, with his eyes searching my face. Then he stepped closer and opened his arms, giving me time to pull away if I wanted to.

But I didn't. I never did when he wanted to hug me.

I moved into him, my arms settling around his waist as his wrapped around my shoulders. His hugs always made me feel like nothing bad could ever reach me. His chin rested on top of my head, and I breathed in his scent, which always sent me back to the most comforting moments of our past.

"I'm glad you're okay," he murmured. "I don't like not knowing where you are."

I pressed my cheek against his chest, my fingers curling into the fabric of his shirt. I hated it when he worried.

After a while, he pulled back and smiled at me, taking in my outfit before saying, "You really do look amazing. I mean it."

My cheeks flushed, and I dropped my gaze to avoid his.

He laughed quietly and reached up to gently pinch my cheek with the backs of his fingers, "You ready?"

I nodded, feeling nervous and excited all at once. But I knew he would stay close to me all evening and make the night bearable.

13

Milow

"*Text me when you want me to pick you up, okay, Milow?*"

I looked at Wesley through the open car window and nodded, smiling as I gave him a quick thumbs-up.

Then he shifted his attention to Ashby, his expression turning serious. "You look out for her."

"I will. I won't leave her side." Ashby said it with certainty. He had already promised me that earlier, and he didn't need to repeat it. I knew he meant it.

"Good." Wesley nodded once. "Then…have fun, kids."

[Thank you.] I waved as he drove off, watching the car disappear down the street. When I turned to Ashby, I waited for him to lead the way toward the wide-open front door of Scottie's house, where music and voices drifted out into the warm night air.

He stepped closer to me, taking my hand in his as I looked up.

"Once we go in there…" he started, his brows pulling

together like whatever he was about to say weighed on him. "I really need you to just…enjoy it."

I tilted my head, waiting for him to continue.

"I mean," he went on, "I want you to have fun. I know this isn't your ideal Friday night, but I think you might like it. And if you don't…" He shrugged lightly. "We go home."

This time, I frowned and shook my head, gently pulling my hand free so I could sign. [If I want to go home, you don't have to come with me.]

"I know, I know." He exhaled and smiled at me. "But honestly…I only said yes to this party because I thought you'd want to go. For Scottie."

That changed things for me. A smile tugged at my lips. [You didn't have to.]

"Yeah," he said, shrugging again. "Still. If you want to leave, we leave. Okay?"

I studied his face for a moment, then nodded slowly. [Okay.]

"Good. Let's go inside."

The noise hit me full force the moment we stepped inside.

Music thumped through the house, vibrating the floor and going straight into my body. Voices overlapped, and there was laughter and shouting everywhere. The air smelled like cheap perfume and sweat. Almost like the girls' changing room at school. It wasn't my favorite smell, and I tried to ignore it. People crowded the entryway, standing in loose clusters with cups in their hands and bodies swaying even when they weren't dancing.

I stopped when a guy stumbled into my path, and Ashby immediately put himself between us. He shot the guy a glare, and without needing another warning, the guy lifted his hands in defense and left.

Ashby looked at me. "You okay?"

I nodded.

We continued walking, and he slowed his pace, angling his body slightly toward me to create space. I reached out on instinct and grabbed a fistful of his shirt at his back, my fingers curling into the fabric. He glanced down at me to make sure I was okay, and I gave him a tight smile to ease his worry.

"Let's go to the kitchen," he said, leaning closer so I could hear him. He gestured ahead, toward the packed hallway.

I had never seen Scottie's house this full, but it was big enough to hold all these people. Ashby gently cleared the path with his shoulders, murmuring quick apologies when someone bumped into him. I stayed close, almost pressed into his back, and my hand was still gripping his shirt.

People glanced at us as we passed. Some smiled, some looked curious, their eyes lingering on me before flicking back to Ashby. At first, I thought maybe they were staring because I was a year younger. Most of these kids were seniors. Some I didn't recognize at all, but they looked even older. I hadn't seen anyone from my year yet, but I doubted Scottie had invited them. I was the only junior she hung out with.

I kept my gaze down, focusing on the familiar feel of his clothes under my fingers and the way he moved through a crowd with confidence. The living room opened up to our left, and I saw someone dancing on a coffee table. Someone else spilled a drink and laughed about it, and a group of girls cheered on a guy who drank a clear liquor straight from the bottle. I felt like I was walking through a movie scene.

Ashby glanced back to check on me once more. I smiled tightly, even though my heart was beating so fast that it hurt. I was still so nervous, but I tried my best not to show it.

The hallway narrowed, and the vibe shifted. It was still loud, but more with voices than music. The closer we got to the kitchen, the more I smelled food.

Then we reached the doorway. The kitchen was crowded too, but it was less chaotic. People leaned against counters, sat on the edges, and talked in tighter groups. Near the center of it all, Scottie stood facing Stan, both of them looking tense. Their voices were raised enough that even over every other sound, I could tell they were arguing. Well…their expressions gave it away first.

Ashby slowed to a stop the moment we stepped into the kitchen, and I felt the tension in his body immediately. His shoulders lifted, then dropped with a heavy sigh. I stayed behind him, close enough that my shoulder brushed his back as I peeked past him to whatever was unfolding in the center of the room.

"And what the fuck do you want me to do about it?" Stan said loudly, his voice sharp as he threw his arms up into the air. "I wasn't the one who sent out all those messages about the party."

Scottie looked furious. Her jaw was tight, and her brown eyes flashed with anger as she faced him head-on. "I sent them to my contacts, Stan. People I personally know. That message wasn't supposed to be forwarded to anyone else."

"I just sent it to two of my friends I train with."

"And that's where you messed up."

"Right. So it's my fault all these people you didn't invite showed up."

Scottie looked like she was ready to walk away, but her hands curled into fists at her sides, and instead of leaving, she whipped back around and stared him down. "Yes, Stanley. It is your fault. Because your two friends then invited their whole fucking college group."

"Oh, man…" Ashby muttered under his breath.

I looked up at him, my lips pressed tightly together as my fingers tugged at the fabric of his shirt. He turned his head and sighed once more, then leaned in enough so I could hear him.

"Don't worry," he said quietly. "I'll handle it."

Ashby guided me forward, leading me toward our friends. The second Stan noticed us, his expression shifted. The tension melted right off his face and was replaced with a wide, familiar grin.

"Ace, my girl!"

He barreled past Scottie and wrapped his arms around my waist, lifting me off the ground the way he always did. Stan had started calling me Ace during my first year of high school because I kept getting A's. The nickname never bothered me, and it had grown on me, actually.

Stan had gotten huge over the years. He wasn't much taller than Ashby, but he was just as broad and packed with muscle. He was super strong, which he needed to be as an MMA fighter.

I smiled, unable to stop myself. No matter how chaotic he was, no matter how rough things between us had been when we were younger, we'd grown close. All four of us had. Scottie and Stan just…clashed sometimes. One day, they were inseparable, holding hands in front of the whole school. And the next, they were at each other's throats like this. But they were friends. Or something more.

"Put her down," Ashby said, his voice tight with worry again.

Stan laughed, setting me back on my feet. I adjusted my skirt, smoothing it down, then I waved at Stan. Soon after, my attention went straight to Scottie.

She leaned against the counter with arms crossed over her chest, and her expression was still hard. Her gaze was fixed somewhere past us. I pressed my lips together and stepped closer to her, gently placing my hand on her arm and giving it a gentle squeeze.

She didn't look at me right away.

I waited, giving her a moment to let her breathe. When her eyes finally lifted to meet mine, the edge in her expression softened, and she smiled gently.

"I'm sorry you had to see that," she said. Then her smile widened just a little. "You came."

I nodded. [You asked me to.]

"Yeah," she said quietly. "Thank you."

"What's going on?" Ashby asked, stepping closer. His hand closed around Stan's arm to keep him there.

Scottie sighed and shook her head, her gaze dropping to the floor. "Nothing."

"Yeah," Stan muttered. His voice was low and edged with guilt. "Now it's nothing."

Ashby and I both looked between them. The tension was thick and so familiar. I shifted my weight and then glanced up at Ashby, waiting for him to do what he always did—step in, calm things down, and make them like each other again.

He looked at Stan again and asked, "Who did you invite?"

Stan scrubbed a hand over the back of his neck. "Two guys from the club. That's it. I didn't think they'd forward the message to anyone else."

Scottie let out a humorless laugh. "You never think."

Stan flinched at that. For once, he didn't fire back. His expression shifted. The defensiveness drained away and was replaced by pain. He hated fighting with her just as much as anyone would hate fighting with someone they were close to.

"I'm sorry," he said. His voice carried a weight that sat heavy in the room. He stepped closer and reached for her hand. She could've pulled away if she wanted to, but she didn't. "I fucked up. I wasn't trying to ruin your night."

Scottie hesitated, then her fingers curled around his.

"You always do this," she said, but there was no real anger left in her voice. But she sounded exhausted instead.

"I know," Stan replied softly. "And I hate that I do."

He tugged her closer, and when she didn't resist, he pulled her into his arms. Scottie let out a breath and leaned into him, her forehead pressing against his chest as her arms slid around his back. He leaned down and buried his face in her dark-blond hair, breathing her in deeply.

I watched them and smiled. This was how they always found their way back to each other. There was a long history between them. One that would take way too long to tell. But I was hopeful that, as they got older, the thing growing between them would become clearer.

Ashby's shoulders finally eased beside me, and he

turned toward me with a smile. "Do you want something to drink?"

I nodded and let my gaze wander around the kitchen. Bottles crowded the counters and the table. There were cups everywhere. I scrunched my nose and looked back at Ashby. He was scanning the room too, his expression tightening. "What were you planning, Scott? Giving everyone alcohol poisoning?"

Scottie turned her head toward him, her arms still wrapped around Stan as she sighed. "Mom only bought maybe a third of that," she said. "Other people brought the rest."

Scottie was seventeen, but her mom bought the alcohol for her. I knew it was because she trusted her. I knew Scottie wouldn't drink a lot, but you couldn't have a house party without alcohol, right?

"I put Pepsi in the fridge for you, Milow," Scottie added, looking at me.

That was thoughtful of her. [Thank you.]

"Of course." She smiled softly and finally loosened her hold on Stan, who looked more than satisfied that they made up. "There's finger food over on the table, but if you want something else, just check the fridge."

"Are you hungry?" Ashby asked me, and I shrugged.

[No. I would like something to drink, though.]

He nodded. "I'll get you something."

He went to the fridge, and Stan followed him like a little puppy, talking about whatever was on his mind again. When they came back, he pressed a cold can of Pepsi into my hand.

[Thank you.]

He smiled, the corner of his mouth lifting. "I won't

be far," he told me, then he went to stand next to Stan and a group of guys I recognized. They were all seniors, and they often sat with us at lunch.

I turned toward Scottie and nudged her arm as I popped the tab. She sighed heavily and leaned into me, resting her head on my shoulder for a moment.

"I'm sorry you always have to see us fight," she said quietly.

I took a sip, then shook my head as I set the can down behind me. [It doesn't bother me. I don't like seeing you hurt.]

Her jaw tightened. She looked away from me, her eyes drifting across the kitchen until they landed on Stan. He was laughing now, gesturing wildly as he talked, completely unaware of the way she was looking at him. Or maybe he was aware and didn't know what to do with it either.

"That's the thing," she whispered. "He hurts me without even trying. And somehow, he's also the only one who makes me feel so…" Her hand lifted and pressed against her chest. "Good. And seen."

I kept my hands at my sides.

"I have all these intense feelings for him. Good and bad ones," she said, the words rushing out like she was afraid they'd get stuck if she slowed down. "I don't even want to pretend I don't feel this way. And I hate it, because he's the same person who can make me furious in five seconds flat." Her eyes stayed on him. "How can one person do both?"

My chest ached for her. Those were complex feelings, and I wished I could help her figure them out. But I struggled with the simplest feelings myself. Still, I tried to give the best advice I could.

[I think…you know he matters to you more than others,] I signed when she looked at me. [He's always been around, and you two have always had a special connection.]

She swallowed hard. "That's what scares me."

[I know,] I replied. [Having someone this close gives them the power to hurt you. But it also means what you feel is real. And I don't think that should be ignored.]

Scottie blinked. "You always make things sound so simple."

[I don't think it's simple,] I signed. [I think you're just brave enough to feel it instead of running from it.]

She let out a shaky breath. "God. You're just too wise for your own good."

I shrugged, feeling a little embarrassed. I reached for my drink again. I didn't think I was wise. I just felt things deeply, loved without restraint, and retreated into my mind when my emotions grew too loud. Thinking always felt safer than feeling when everything threatened to spill over.

Across the room, Ashby's eyes met mine. He was half turned toward Stan, but his attention was fully on me. I smiled to let him know I was okay, and his shoulders eased, just a fraction, before he turned back to the conversation.

Scottie followed my gaze and smiled softly. "He really looks out for you."

[He always has.]

Her eyes drifted back to Stan once more, softer now. "I wish loving someone didn't feel like standing in the middle of a storm."

It wasn't the first time she used the word love when talking about Stan. It wasn't surprising to me. Not when it came to the two of them. They had tried to push each other away since childhood, but something stronger always pulled them back.

I waited for Scottie to look at me again before I signed. [I think the right people are worth standing in the storm for.]

Scottie nodded slowly. Across the kitchen, Stan laughed loudly and from the heart, and out of the corner of my eye, I saw Scottie grin.

"He's such an idiot."

I agreed. But he was her idiot.

14

Ashby

I wanted to go home.

Not because anything was wrong or because Milow wasn't doing okay, but because I was exhausted after a long school day and an even longer swim practice. My shoulders still ached, my head felt full, and all I could think about was how much nicer it would be to spend a Friday night at home with her instead. Sitting on the couch. Watching some random movie we'd both half ignore. Or watching her solve what felt like her millionth crossword or Sudoku, completely focused, with her tongue pressed lightly to her cheek the way it always did when she concentrated.

Still, Milow looked happy.

She smiled often, stood close to Scottie, and followed conversations easily, even chiming in with her hands now and then. No one other than us four here understood sign language, but Scottie never missed a beat, always translating Milow's words out loud like it was the most natural thing in the world. I loved her for that. I loved anyone who made things easier for Milow without making a big deal out of it.

Milow had come out of her shell as she grew older. Slowly, and in her own way. She still struggled to fit in sometimes, and I didn't think that was a bad thing. She didn't blend into the background. She didn't disappear into crowds. She was different, and to me, that difference felt fragile and precious. I carried this quiet fear that one day she'd change in a way I couldn't protect anymore. That she'd wake up and decide she didn't need me hovering around her all the time.

I'd had nightmares about it.

About her suddenly finding her voice and using it to tell me to back off. To stop worrying. In one dream, she'd looked right at me and called me an asshole for never leaving her side. I'd woken up sweating, and with my heart racing, shaken by the words even though they weren't real. And as bad as the dream was, there had been this awful part of me that clung to the sound of her voice in it. Because I had never heard her speak. No one had. And I hated that whatever had happened before she was adopted had hurt her so badly that she'd learned to keep that part of herself locked away.

"Ash…Ashby, dude, where'd you go?"

Stan's voice cut through my thoughts, sharp enough to pull me back to reality. I blinked, my vision clearing as I realized I'd been staring into the void.

My eyes went straight to Milow.

She stood beside Scottie, smiling softly as she listened to a girl talk. Milow nodded along, her posture relaxed and present, like she belonged right there.

"Hm?" I snapped my gaze to Stan.

He was grinning at me with that knowing, slightly annoying grin he always wore when he thought he'd figured something out—which was rare. He followed my line of sight back to Milow and then looked at me again.

"Dude," he said, lowering his voice just enough that it wouldn't carry across the kitchen. "One day you'll just have to admit your feelings and—"

"Stop." I shot him a sharp look and turned away before he could finish the sentence, reaching for my Pepsi on the counter. I took a long sip.

"I know, I know," he said easily, completely unfazed. "It's hard hearing the truth." He leaned his hip against the counter, arms crossed. "But you're suffering here, buddy."

"Suffering?" I raised a brow at him, lowering the can. "That's a bit dramatic."

"Yeah." He nodded, looking all serious now. "You are. You've been madly in love with her since we were kids. Everyone sees it. I think it's time."

I shook my head slowly, already feeling that familiar knot tightening in my chest. My love for Milow wasn't something I could just say out loud. Not now. Maybe not ever. I didn't know how she felt, and her feelings mattered more than anything. We were best friends. We had grown up together, shared every moment, no matter how small or big. We were each other's safe space. And that was everything to me. *She* was everything to me.

Admitting what I really felt would change things. It would put something fragile at risk. And I wasn't willing to do that.

I reached out and squeezed his shoulder. "Thanks," I said quietly, "but I think you should focus on your own love story."

His grin came back instantly, wide and confident. "Oh, I'm really focused."

Before I had the chance to roll my eyes, Scottie appeared beside us, clapping her hands once to get our attention. "Okay," she said, smiling up at us. "We're going outside. Garden time."

Stan perked up immediately. "Beer pong?"

"Obviously," she shot back. "But, please, don't embarrass me."

"I make no promises," he said, already moving.

Scottie rolled her eyes and then looked at Milow, her smile softening. "You coming?"

Milow nodded, stepping closer to me. I felt her shoulder brush my arm, and without looking down, I adjusted my stance so I was just a little closer to her. There were small moments like these that only we noticed. No one else saw the way we looked at each other, with all the trust we had, and no one noticed that every single touch—purposeful or not—sent a shiver down my spine.

"Let's go," Scottie said, following Stan to the back door.

We headed outside, and the noise of the house faded slightly. There were fewer people out here, but still more than I had expected. We stood near the table where four girls were finishing a game of beer pong. Before I could say anything, Stan stepped forward and tugged Scottie in beside him, already claiming his spot.

"Ash, Milow, come on," he said, jerking his chin toward the other side of the table, clearly expecting us to join in.

I turned my head and looked at Milow, leaving the choice up to her. She hesitated, her gaze moving between the table, the cups, and the people standing around it. I doubted she even knew what the game was, and for a brief second, I forgot myself and only then remembered there was alcohol in every single cup.

"We'll pass," I said instead.

I felt Milow relax instantly beside me, her shoulders easing the tiniest bit. The back of my right hand brushed against her arm, the soft fabric of her cardigan touching my skin. I wanted to take her hand. I knew it would calm her even more, and it was dark enough out here that no one would notice. The thought of those small, secret touches made my head feel light.

"Fine," Stan said, already distracted. He scanned the group and pointed toward two of our friends standing nearby. "Jasper, Bennett. You're up."

Both were in our grade. Jasper was on the swim team with me. Unlike some others at school, he and Bennett actually called Stan out when he went too far. They didn't look thrilled about playing against him, but they stepped forward anyway and started refilling the red cups.

"It's unfair," Jasper said, shaking his head.

Stan raised a brow, tossing the ping-pong ball into the air and catching it again. "What's unfair?"

Jasper nodded toward Scottie. "She's a pro at this game."

Scottie grinned unapologetically, lifting one shoulder in a small shrug. "Don't worry, boys," she said lightly. "I'll go easy on you."

"Thank fuck," Bennett muttered under his breath.

I couldn't stop a chuckle from escaping. When it came to Scottie, most boys at school kept their distance. But not because they were scared of her. They were scared of getting rejected. I knew it bothered her, and she wished more people would see her as just a friend rather than someone they might get to date. Though Scottie only had eyes for Stan, and most guys knew that.

The game started again, laughter and groans mixing with the thud of the ball hitting plastic. I stayed where I was, watching absentmindedly. My attention kept drifting back to Milow, who stood slightly behind me. She was close enough that I could feel her body's warmth. She shifted her weight. The movement was small, but her hand brushed mine again.

This time it lingered, and it wasn't accidental. I didn't move right away. I didn't want to spoil the moment. Then, slowly, I turned my hand so my fingers were open instead of curled, and I let it rest there like an invitation I pretended not to notice. A second passed, then another.

And, finally, her fingers slid into mine.

It was suddenly quiet between us, even with the noise around us. She stood a little behind my shoulder, close enough that no one could see our hands. We just held on, both of us aware of how fragile this moment was.

Her hand was just a little cold, and it fit perfectly in mine. My thumb brushed against the side of her finger, and she answered by tightening her grip just a little.

I swallowed and kept my eyes on the game, pretending to care whether Stan made the shot or not. My heart was beating too fast for that. Every nerve in my body felt attuned to that single point where our hands met. No one noticed. Stan was too busy talking trash. Scottie was laughing, already lining up her next throw. Jasper was complaining loudly. And everything carried on like normal.

But for me, everything felt different.

Milow leaned in a fraction closer, her shoulder brushing my arm now, and I had to tell myself that this was nothing, even if it was everything. I squeezed her hand once gently, and she squeezed back.

I didn't know what this meant or what she thought about it. If it was just a simple touch she needed to feel to steady herself, or if she felt the same as I did. But what I did know was that for the first time all night, I stopped wanting to go home.

"Hi, Ashby."

Milow's hand slipped out of mine immediately. The loss of her touch felt like a sharp knife going straight through my heart. The hairs along the back of my neck stood up, and that awful mix of being caught and being irritated settled deep inside of me.

I turned my head and found Hailie standing far too close. Aspen hovered right behind her. Both of them were in Milow's grade. I knew they shared classes. I also knew exactly how obnoxious they were.

"Um, hey."

"Cool party, huh? I totally needed to come," Hailie said, smiling too widely. Her two front teeth were too big for her face. "Aspen heard from Leah, who heard from Molly that there was a party tonight, so we just had to show up."

I raised a brow without meaning to. Leah and Molly were in my grade. Scottie actually liked them. I was sure they'd been invited. Hailie and Aspen, though? Definitely not Scottie's friends.

"We've totally missed parties," Hailie went on. "I was in Italy with my family all summer, and Aspen was in

Florida, so we didn't see anyone from school. It was sooo boring."

I didn't care. Not even a little. Still, I wasn't a jerk. I didn't want to be rude. I pulled my mouth into a tight smile and nodded once. "Cool."

"Totally cool," Aspen echoed, her voice high-pitched and practiced.

They both stared up at me with those expectant looks. Their blond hair was straight, and it looked—and smelled—burned. Their makeup was layered on thick. They used way more than any seventeen-year-old needed. But that wasn't my business.

I shifted my weight, angling my body just enough to check on Milow. I needed to see her. To know she was still right there. She was watching the beer pong table, her face calm, focused elsewhere. But I knew better. She was listening in on this one-sided conversation.

I wanted to reach back for her hand. To slip my fingers into hers again and disappear into that quiet, hidden space we'd created just moments before. I wanted that calm back, but I didn't dare.

It was too risky.

"So, Ashby…" Hailie said, tilting her head and pursing her glossy pink lips. "Aspen and I were thinking."

"We were *totally* thinking," Aspen added quickly.

"We were thinking that maybe the four of us could go on a double date?" Hailie said, her tone light, as if this were the most natural idea in the world.

I furrowed my brows. Four of us, who? They definitely didn't mean Milow…

"Us two, you, and Stan," Aspen clarified, her eyes lighting up when she said Stan's name.

Oh.

"Uh, I don't really—"

"Go on dates, ugh, we know," Hailie interrupted, rolling her eyes. Then she grabbed my forearm with both hands and gave it a playful tug that felt wrong. And too aggressive. "But we think you need to take time off sometimes and actually have fun. You're always at swim practice."

How she even knew that, I had no idea. Sure, people talked. I was good at what I did. But it still annoyed me that she spoke as if she knew me.

"And since you and Stan hang out all the time anyway," Aspen continued, "and Hailie and I are always together, we figured it'd be easy. Just all of us hanging out."

I looked at Aspen. Then back at Hailie. My jaw tightened.

I hated this. I hated it so much that it made my head feel hot. I wanted to tell them to fuck off. Plain and simple. The words were right there on my tongue, and I was just about to let them loose when Scottie stepped in front of me.

Hailie finally let go of my arm.

"Why are you here?" Scottie asked. Her voice was flat.

Hailie sighed dramatically and crossed her arms over her far too exposed chest. Not that I was looking. It was just impossible not to notice. Her boobs were pushed up to her chin in an unnatural way.

"We got invited."

"By whom?"

Hailie didn't have a straight answer to that, so she stayed quiet, her mouth opening and closing like she might invent one if given enough time.

"We're here now anyway. You can't kick us out,"

Aspen said, confidence spilling out of her as if she'd never been told no before, which was probably the case.

I didn't see Scottie's face, but I could hear it in her voice. She was amused but had already had enough of this conversation. "Right. Actually? I can. This is my house. Besides, you're juniors. This party is for seniors."

Hailie's frown deepened. "Then what is the mute doing here?"

Something in me snapped immediately.

I stepped around Scottie without thinking, putting myself fully in front of Milow, and blocking their line of sight. My body knew what to do before my brain caught up. I'd protect Milow. Always, and with no hesitation.

"All right," I said, trying to keep my voice low. "You weren't invited. You should leave."

"But that's not fair," Hailie shot back, pointing past me like Milow was an object she could argue over. "If she's here, we can be here too. We're enjoying the party more than she is anyway. No one even understands her."

Milow's fingers brushed the back of my shirt, and my body tensed so much I was ready to explode. But I kept it together for Milow's sake.

Scottie stepped forward again, this time fully beside me. "You're done," she said. There was no humor in her voice now. Just pure authority and a hint of anger. "Leave my house. I'm not asking."

Aspen scoffed. "Wow. Okay. Power trip much?"

"Yes," Scottie said calmly. "My house. My rules. Out."

They stood there for a second longer, clearly hoping someone would back them up. But no one did. People had started to watch it all go down, and I needed this to be over before things got worse.

Hailie huffed and turned on her heel. "Whatever. This party sucks anyway."

"Yeah," Aspen muttered, following her. "So lame."

They disappeared back through the house, flicking a few cups off the tables on their way out.

I sucked in a deep breath and shook my head, turning back to Milow just as Stan showed up at my side. His brows were drawn together. "What just happened? They looked like someone murdered their egos."

"They were being rude," I said flatly.

"As usual," Scottie murmured, then added, "And, apparently, they have the hots for you two."

"Us?" Stan repeated.

I gave a short nod, then shook my head again because I hated even thinking about ever letting those two girls close.

Stan blinked once, then his face twisted as if he'd just put something awful in his mouth. "Ew. Them? Never. The only two girls I'd ever go out with are Scottie and Milow."

I looked at Milow then. Her cheeks flushed just a little, a soft pink that reached her ears. It was subtle, but I saw it. I always did. Always noticed the smallest things about her. I smiled at her and shoved my hands deep into my pockets, forcing myself to keep them there instead of reaching for her like every instinct told me to. I leaned closer anyway. "You okay?"

She nodded right away and lifted one hand. [Witches.]

A laugh slipped out of me before I could stop it. "Yeah. They are."

And she really was okay. That was the thing. She always was. Shit like that didn't cling to her the way it clung to me. I carried those moments around, stored them deep inside of me, and let them linger. When people talked badly about Milow, I held on to it because there would always be opportunities to hold it against them if they ever tried to switch up on her. I was resentful, but she wasn't. She never held on to it. She let it pass, like it wasn't worth the space in her head.

It was fascinating seeing how she always chose calm over bitterness, and that quiet kindness of hers was exactly what made me so proud of her.

15

Milow

It had bothered me. A lot, actually. The way Hailie and Aspen talked to Ashby. The way they talked about me without a single ounce of shame in their voices. I had learned early not to give them the attention they were desperate for. That was what they wanted most. A reaction. A reason to continue being mean. But it seemed that even with my silence, they got more annoyed.

I'd always had trouble with them, from the very beginning. On my first day of school, they decided it was their job to explain me to everyone else. They told every single kid in our grade that I was mute. They told them I was different and that I didn't talk because I thought everyone else was stupid.

None of that was true. I never even dared to think things like that. I was just a scared seven-year-old, trying as hard as I could to listen to the teacher, understand the rules, and be good and obedient, like my father had taught me to be. I was brave every single day I walked into that classroom, even though I sat alone in the very front. Even though I could hear the whispering and giggling behind me, and all the comments that were never meant to be kind.

I remembered one day clearly. I turned around in the middle of class after Hailie called me an unwanted, parentless orphan. The words hurt, and I wanted to tell her two things. First, that "parentless" and "orphan" meant the same thing, and second, that she was being cruel.

But I couldn't say a word. All I could do was stare at her…and flip her off.

She told on me, of course, and I had to listen to my teacher explain why flipping someone off wasn't okay.

There had been more moments like that over the years, but I learned how to survive them without making things worse. I never gave Hailie and Aspen what they wanted, and I focused on school and my friends. I stayed silent, because there wasn't anything I could do. Even when they laughed, even when they talked about me like I wasn't right there, I learned how to ignore it. Or at least how to pretend I did.

I picked at the loose skin around my thumb, my gaze locked on my hands while the party carried on around me. Usually, I only picked at my skin when I was anxious, but sometimes it happened out of boredom. At some point, we'd moved into the living room. People filled the space, but I'd stopped listening a while ago. My focus shifted to staying awake because my eyelids kept drooping, no matter how hard I fought it.

My body slowly sank deeper into the couch. Ashby must have noticed. He leaned closer, his shoulder brushing mine.

"Tired?" he asked quietly.

My gaze flicked up to his, and I gave a small nod.

"Do you want to go home?" There was a hint of hope in his voice. He'd only come for me. I knew that. But I also knew he'd been having fun—at least before Hailie and Aspen showed up and ruined the mood.

I shrugged and glanced around the room before looking back at him. [Do you?]

He shrugged too. "Yeah. I think I do."

Relief settled in my chest. I nodded again. [Okay.]

His mouth curved into a smile, like he'd already made the decision before I did. He reached into his pocket and pulled out his phone. "I'll text Wesley," he said.

He typed quickly, his thumb moving fast across the screen. I watched him with a smile on my lips. Ashby was always ready to get me out of places I didn't want to be. It made me feel protected, but sometimes, it also saddened me. Because what would happen when we got older? As adults, he couldn't be by my side the way he'd been all this time. He'd move on. He'd go to college, most likely become a big athlete, and find someone new. It was selfish of me to think that he'd stay by my side forever, but I desperately wanted him to.

"All right," he said a moment later, slipping the phone away. "He's on his way."

My shoulders finally loosened. I leaned back into the couch, the tiredness catching up with me now that I knew I didn't have to stay much longer. Ashby remained right there beside me, his knee brushing mine, and I told myself not to think too hard about that simple touch.

"I'm really sad you're leaving already," Scottie said moments later as she wrapped her arms around me and hugged me tight, "but I'm really glad you came." She pulled back just enough to look at me. "Did you at least have fun?"

I nodded, and when she let go, I smiled and signed, [Lots of fun. Thank you for inviting me.]

"Are you kidding?" she said immediately. "Next time, you'll be the only one I invite." She scrunched her nose, glanced around the room, then lifted her hands again. [I'm sorry those girls were being so mean to you.]

[It's okay. I'm used to it.]

Her brows pulled together. "Yeah, but you shouldn't be. Next time they act like that, you come and tell me—"

"Or me," Stan added from her side. "I seriously can't stand those girls. It's bad enough that every word they say is filled with hate, but they also reek of rotten eggs, which really doesn't help their case."

I pressed my lips together and looked up at him, trying not to smile at his words. As much as I disliked Hailie and Aspen, I refused to be cruel the way they were. Sure, I'd flipped them off more than once over the years, and yes, in my head, they were still witches, but that was as far as I ever went.

"Thanks for that, Stanley," Scottie said, patting his arm before turning back to me with a smile. "I'll see you on Monday."

I nodded. [See you at school.]

"Bye, Ashby," she added, pulling him into a quick hug before he and Stan fell into their usual handshake routine.

Stan turned to me next, winked, and pulled me into a hug that lasted a little too long, like it always did. "You're way smarter and way prettier than those girls," he said firmly. "And you always smell nice. Don't forget that."

When I stepped back and looked up at him, his blue eyes were serious. There was something else there too. Anger, maybe. He'd always hated seeing anyone go after me, which, when we first met, I had thought he'd never be nice to me. Thankfully, Stan turned out to like me, which made me happy.

[Thank you, Stan.]

"You're very welcome, Milow," he said with a grin. Scottie rolled her eyes next to him.

"If he were even half as charming with me as he is with you…" she muttered.

"Hey, I am charming with you," Stan argued. "You're just always mad at me."

"I'm not always mad at you," she shot back. "And when I am, it's because you make me mad."

They kept bickering, the same way they always did, while Ashby gently guided me out of the house and toward the street, where Wesley's car was already parked and waiting.

As we got closer, I noticed Evie sitting inside with Wesley. She smiled as soon as she saw us and lifted her hand to wave. I waved back before Ashby opened the door for me, letting me slide in first, then climbing in beside me.

"Hey, you," Evie said warmly, turning in her seat to look at me. "How was it? Did you have fun?"

[Yes, it was fun,] I signed, my smile a little restrained. [I don't think parties are really for me, though.]

She nodded, as if she understood that completely. "That's okay. At least you tried it once." She reached back and gently rubbed my knee, then glanced at Ashby for a brief moment before looking at me again. "How do you feel about ice cream?"

"Ice cream?" Ashby repeated, eyebrows knitting together. "Right now?"

"Yeah," Evie said easily. "I'm craving it." Then she smiled at me. "What do you say?"

I was exhausted, and my head felt foggy from the tiredness ready to overcome my body, but there was no world in which I would ever turn down ice cream. [I'm up for ice cream.]

"Perfect," Evie said, grinning as she turned forward again. "Let's go to Sutter's."

Wesley gave a nod and reached out his right hand, placing it on Evie's thigh. She placed hers on his, and, immediately, it reminded me of Mom and Dad. Holding hands had always meant something to me. It was strange. I had no one to hold hands with—not like Mom and Dad, or Evie and Wesley. But I used to hold Ashby's hand a lot before falling asleep next to him when we were younger. We didn't do that anymore. But when he held my hand back at the party, in secrecy and hidden from everyone around us, it made me wish I could hold his hand again more often.

I let my mind drift, looking out of the window as we drove to Sutter's. Sutter's was the only gas station in Bowen, and the only place in town that somehow had better soft-serve than any fast-food place. We'd been going there since we were little. Some of my favorite memories were the hot summer afternoons when Wesley took Ashby and me there, just for ice cream or a cold can of pop, the three of us sitting outside on the wooden porch when we had nowhere else to be.

"By the way," Wesley said, pulling me out of my thoughts. "Mom and Dad are still on their date. They went to the city, and they'll stay the night."

I smiled at that. I always missed them when they were gone, but it made me happy knowing they were still so in love and still choosing to spend time alone together. Now that we were older, and Wesley was home to look after us, they went on dates more often. I loved that for them.

"That's nice," Ashby said quietly beside me.

I turned my head toward him at the same time he looked at me. Our eyes met, and for a second, neither of us looked away. We both smiled, and my heart, as it always did, picked up its pace and throbbed hard in my chest.

My gaze drifted down from his brown eyes to his hand resting on his thigh. His fingers flexed, like he was thinking about it too. My own hand curled in my lap.

We were thinking the same thing, but neither of us moved. We were too shy and too aware of the moment that we just kept smiling, pretending not to notice that what we felt for each other had already grown into something bigger than we were ready to understand.

At Sutter's, we went inside and headed straight for the soft-serve machine. The shop was empty except for Sutter himself, who shuffled out from behind the counter to refill the stack of paper cups beneath the dispenser. His long white beard moved as he spoke. "You kids doing okay?"

"Doing great," Wesley answered easily. "You?"

"Ah, you know…" Sutter grunted as he straightened and ran a hand through his beard. "Same old, same old."

"I heard a rumor you're closing up," Wesley said, and the old man immediately frowned.

"That's all it is, boy. A rumor."

"Good," Evie chimed in with a grin when she started filling her cup. "Because you have the best ice cream in all of B.C."

Ashby handed me a cup, and I took it, thanking him by leaning into his side. "What will you get? Vanilla?" he asked.

I pursed my lips and studied the four soft-serve flavors. I always chose vanilla. It was my favorite, and Sutter's vanilla actually tasted like vanilla, unlike the bland kind from other places. For a brief moment, I considered something else, my gaze lingering on the hazelnut option, but I decided against it and nodded.

Once everyone had their ice cream and Wesley paid, we said goodbye to Sutter and stepped outside to sit on the wide wooden porch steps. I started eating right away, but my attention kept drifting back to Ashby because tonight, instead of his usual chocolate, he had chosen hazelnut.

When he caught me staring, he smirked and leaned closer. "You wanna try?"

I met his eyes, realizing he had only picked that flavor because I had hesitated earlier. He had noticed something so small, and it meant more to me than I could explain.

I nodded quickly, and when he held the plastic spoon out to me, I leaned in to take a bite. He watched me closely as the ice cream melted on my tongue. "Do you like it?"

I nodded again. It was really good. In all the years we'd come here, I had only ever gotten vanilla. Sometimes chocolate. Never hazelnut or strawberry. I didn't like strawberries. Wesley and Evie loved it.

[It's delicious.]

"Do you want to switch?"

I thought about it for a few seconds. [Okay.]

"Baby, you want to switch too?" Wesley asked Evie, his grin teasing.

She laughed softly. They had clearly been watching our little exchange. Then she nodded and handed her strawberry soft-serve to Wesley, who had also chosen strawberry.

"You suck," Ashby muttered, though a smile tugged at his lips.

Heat crept into my cheeks, and I dropped my gaze to my new ice cream, suddenly very focused on not looking at him. Because if I had, my whole face would've turned bright red.

16

Ashby

The moment we got back home, Milow signed goodnight and headed upstairs. I didn't follow her right away. I didn't want to crowd her or risk annoying her. I knew she would never get tired of me, but I wanted to give her space.

She was exhausted. It was late, and I didn't want to keep her up any longer after a party I knew had drained her more than she let on. I followed Wesley into the kitchen instead. He grabbed a glass of water, and I leaned back against the counter, one elbow resting behind me.

"What's bothering you?" Wes asked.

I furrowed my brows. He always knew when something was off. It annoyed me sometimes, because there were moments I didn't want to talk about things. Even though, in the end, I was always glad I did.

I took a breath and gave a small shrug. "A few things, really."

Wesley stood across from me, leaning against the island, his glass in hand. "Shoot."

I chose just one thing. I was tired too, and I didn't want to drag this out. I also didn't want to keep him up when Evie was already in bed, probably waiting for him.

"There were these girls at the party," I said. "They were being mean to Milow."

Wesley's brows lifted slightly as he waited for me to continue, his jaw tightening as he tried to rein in the anger I knew was already there. When it came to Milow, we were both overprotective.

There had been too many moments over the years where we had to step in, making sure other kids didn't hurt her—physically or emotionally. But since Wes was out of school, he couldn't always be there to jump in.

I was there. But even I wasn't with her all the time. I was a grade above her, and I only saw her during breaks, lunch, and after school.

"I think they've bothered her before," I said. "She brushed it off tonight. Just ignored them like they weren't even there."

"That's not a bad thing, is it?" Wesley said, though he sounded like he was still thinking it through.

"I know. I just…" I rubbed the back of my neck. "She's good at pretending things don't get to her. And I know it affected her."

Wesley took another sip of his water, studying me closely. "If something actually hurt her and got under her skin, she'd tell us."

I frowned. "You don't know that."

"I do," he said calmly. "Milow doesn't complain just to complain. She never has. When she brings something up, it's because she wants it solved. She doesn't waste energy on things she can handle on her own."

"That doesn't mean it doesn't still suck," I muttered.

"No, it doesn't," he agreed. "But there's a difference between something being annoying and something actually damaging. And if it crossed into that second category, she wouldn't keep it to herself forever."

I stayed quiet, staring at the floor.

"And you're there," Wesley continued. "Every day. You see her at school more than anyone else. You notice when she's off. If those girls really became a problem, you'd pick up on it."

"I try," I said. "But I'm not with her all the time. I'm not in her classes, but those girls are."

"Still," he said. "You're around. You walk her to class. You eat lunch with her. You notice the small stuff. And if someone messes with her when you are there, you don't let it slide. That counts for something."

I sighed. "I just hate that I can't fix it. That people still think it's okay to be assholes to her. Or anyone, for that matter."

"Yeah," Wesley said. "I know. I hate that too. But you can't control everyone. What you can do is exactly what you're already doing."

I looked at him. "Which is?"

"Being there," he said. "Making sure she's not alone. Making sure she feels safe. And trusting her enough to believe she'll let you know when she needs help."

I shifted my weight. "I just don't want to miss something."

"You won't," he assured me without hesitation. "And if you ever do, we'll deal with it then. Together."

I nodded slowly.

"And Ash," Wesley added, his voice softer now. "You're

not failing her just because you can't shield her from every shitty person she meets. You're doing fine. And so is she. That girl is stronger than we know."

I didn't doubt that.

I let his words sink in, grateful for his advice like I always was. I could always count on him for advice and perspective when I needed it. "Okay. Thanks, Wes."

He nodded once and set his glass down on the counter, then stepped closer and pulled me into a hug. He patted my back before letting go, giving me an encouraging smile. "Anytime, kid. Now go to sleep. You can barely stay upright."

I huffed out a laugh and ran a hand through my hair. "Yeah…night, Wes."

Heading upstairs, I took the steps carefully, moving as quietly as I could until I reached the third floor, where Milow's room and mine were. The narrow hallway was dark, and I stopped in front of her door and stared at it for a moment.

It was closed, and no light showed beneath it.

She was probably already in bed. Still, I reached for the handle.

I opened the door slowly, just enough to peek inside.

Her room was dim, lit only by the faint glow of the moonlight. Milow was curled on her side beneath her blankets, with her hair spread across the pillow. She was already fast asleep.

I stood there for a second longer than necessary, watching her, and trying to prove to myself that she was okay. When I had somewhat convinced myself of it, I closed the door as carefully as I could, not to make a sound.

I woke up late the next morning. I hadn't been this

tired in a long time. School had only started again a few weeks ago, and before that, during summer break, I'd been able to sleep as much as I wanted. My body clearly hadn't adjusted yet.

I stayed in bed for a while, staring at the ceiling until I felt awake enough to move. When I finally checked my phone, it was already close to ten thirty. Everyone else in the house was probably up. Even so, I didn't rush. I took a quick shower, pulled on sweatpants and a clean white T-shirt, and then headed downstairs.

Before going down, I stopped by Milow's room and peeked inside. She wasn't there.

Downstairs, I found her sitting at the round dining room table with Mom and Dad, eating breakfast. Wesley and Evie weren't there, so I assumed they had gone out for the day. I smiled when I saw Milow and took the empty chair beside her. "Morning. How was your date?" I asked, looking at Mom and Dad as they ate.

"Hey, champ," Dad said, leaving the answer to Mom.

"Oh, it was wonderful," Mom said. "We went to Vancouver and had dinner at this really cute French restaurant. I tried escargot for the first time."

I scrunched my nose and glanced at Milow, who made the same face. I grinned and looked back at Mom while grabbing a slice of sourdough bread. "And? Did you like it?"

"Oh, yes," Mom said, smiling at Dad. "Who would've thought snails could be so good?"

Out of the corner of my eye, I saw Milow swirl her spoon around in her cereal, suddenly a lot less interested in eating while Mom talked about snails. I chuckled and decided to change the subject. "What about the hotel? How was it?"

"Expensive, but nice," Mom said, shooting Dad a quick look. "But we had a great night."

"I'm glad," I said as I spread butter and then honey onto the bread.

When Mom and Dad drifted into another conversation, I turned to Milow. "What are you up to today?"

She shrugged and set her spoon down to sign. [I have some schoolwork to do.]

"Me too," I lied. I needed an excuse to spend time with her. "Want to do it together?"

Her expression changed right away, her eyes lighting up. [Okay.]

"Perfect."

About an hour later, I sat on my bed with a random textbook open, waiting for Milow to join me. She came in holding four books against her chest, her pencil case tucked on top. She smiled when she saw me and turned toward my desk like she planned to work there, but I stopped her and patted the space next to me on the bed.

"Come here."

She paused and looked at me, clearly weighing whether she wanted to be more comfortable or closer. I tried to keep my face neutral, but my heart still jumped when she chose the bed and walked over. She sat down, leaving a careful gap between us.

She set her books down neatly, opened the first two she wanted to start with, then took out a pencil and immediately focused. There was no hesitation. When Milow studied, she did so with no excuses. I kept my science book open, but I wasn't reading it. I kept watching her instead, as if I had the damn right to.

After a minute, I noticed the faint color creeping into

her cheeks. She was sitting there, writing, but she was blushing. Did she notice me looking at her? Probably. Milow was always aware of her surroundings, and she noticed the smallest things.

She shifted, then finally glanced up at me. Her eyes moved to my open book, then back to my face.

[Do you need help with something?]

I blinked and quickly glanced down at my book, pretending I had a clue about what was written in it, then I looked back at her.

"Uh. Maybe," I said. "I haven't really started."

She nodded like that made sense and went back to her work, the redness still on her cheeks. I stayed where I was, pretending to read, fully aware of her beside me and trying not to think too hard about why her presence continued to affect me so much.

About forty-five minutes later, I was bored. I sat leaning back against the headboard of my bed, tossing a baseball up into the air and catching it again. Milow was still studying, her focus sharper than anyone I'd ever seen. She hadn't looked up once. It was impressive, and even though I wasn't doing much, I liked watching her work.

In the time she'd been in my room, she'd finished several pages of math problems, read about twenty pages of a book I'd only ever seen the movie version of. When she got stuck on a few questions in another worksheet, she pulled out a Sudoku puzzle and worked through it first to clear her head. It was like it helped her think. Somehow, it did. Watching her switch between things so easily was fascinating, and honestly a little intimidating. What sixteen-year-old had that kind of focus? That kind of drive to get things done so efficiently and so calmly?

Not me. And most definitely not the boy who just walked into my room unannounced.

"What are you doing?" Stan asked, staring at us like he couldn't believe his eyes. "It's Saturday, and you guys are studying? I can't believe this." He slapped a hand to his forehead. "I thought I raised you better."

I grinned and looked at Milow, waiting for her reaction. She never let Stan get away with mocking her for long. She scrunched her nose and set her pencil down before signing, [School is important, Stanley.]

"Not if you want to be a professional athlete like Ash or me."

[I don't want to become a professional athlete.] Milow's hands moved fast, her expression amused.

"No...but you could still change your mind." He pulled out the chair and dropped into it, grabbing the first thing off my desk, which happened to be my water bottle. "You could try dancing. Or soccer, like Scottie."

Scottie was great at soccer, but she wasn't planning on doing it forever. She wanted to be a doctor. What kind of doctor, I didn't know. But she was ambitious, and I could see her reaching her goals.

[I'm not good at sports.]

"You can always learn," Stan said with a shrug. Then he switched topics, because I knew talking about the future made him uncomfortable. "I was thinking we could hang out today. Once you're not busy, I mean."

"Milow's not done studying," I said, glancing at her.

[Almost done,] she assured me.

"She just can't resist me," Stan teased.

Milow shook her head at that, her lips pulling into a smirk, clearly unimpressed. She went back to her work without another word, and Stan started talking about something that happened at the party.

Once Milow finished, she stacked her books and closed her pencil case, and we all headed downstairs. We made ourselves a quick snack, nothing special, whatever we could find, and then took it outside. We spent the rest of the afternoon in the garden, sitting in the sun and staying there as long as we could, knowing the warm days were already starting to run out.

17

Milow

Monday, September 8th

On Monday morning, before my first class, I waited for Ashby at my locker. Every Monday, before most people were even awake, he went to swim practice. Usually, he trained at the Dunst Aquatic Center, about a fifteen-minute drive from Bowen. But since our high school had an indoor pool, even if it was fairly small, he used it whenever he could. And every Monday morning, his coach even drove over from Dunst just to be there while Ashby trained.

His coach, Ruben, had been with him since he first started swimming, back when he was only four years old. Ruben had promised Ashby that he would stick by his side until Ashby won his first Olympic medal. That was a huge promise to make, but if anyone could win an Olympic medal, it would be Ashby.

While I waited for him to walk over to the main building, I organized my books in the order I would need them for the day. Students stood around me in small groups or rushed past in the hallway, most of them clearly not as excited for classes to start as I was. The halls always made me anxious, especially when none of my friends were nearby. I kept my head down, half inside my locker, and tried to ignore everything around me until someone familiar showed up.

Juniors and seniors shared the same side of the building, and since I was now a junior, I had been moved to a new locker. Not everyone was lucky enough to end up closer to their classrooms, but I had a feeling Mom and Dad had something to do with it. They had probably emailed the school, asking for my locker to be closer to Ashby, Scottie, and Stan.

I was glad about it, but at the same time, I hated being treated differently. I was still perfectly capable of walking a few extra steps to get to class. And I would have seen my friends during the big break and lunch anyway.

This morning, Scottie was the first one to reach me. She leaned against the locker next to mine and smiled, but her eyes gave her away. She looked exhausted. "Hey, girly. How are you?"

I smiled back and closed my locker. [Good, thanks. You?]

She lifted one shoulder in a small shrug. "It's Monday morning," she said, as if that explained everything.

It wasn't that Scottie hated school. She just wasn't a morning person. And when something was bothering her, it usually showed in her mood, even if she tried hard to hide it. She never liked dragging other people down with her, and she always forced a smile, even when she clearly didn't feel like it. Sometimes I wondered if things were weighing on her that nobody else knew. Not even me. Or Stan.

[Something on your mind?] I asked. I was always ready to listen if she needed to talk.

"Yeah," she admitted, letting out a quiet breath. "A few things, actually. But that's something for another time. I don't want to dump it on you first thing in the morning."

[You never bug me,] I signed, giving her a reassuring smile.

Before she could respond, Stan appeared at the end of the row of lockers, already grinning like he was about to say something stupid. Scottie spotted him instantly.

"Oh, great," she muttered. Then she pushed off the locker and straightened up. "I'll see you later, okay?"

She gave me a squeeze on the arm and took off down the hallway before Stan could reach us, leaving me standing there just as he came to a stop in front of my locker.

He watched her walk away with that same look of longing he always had when it came to her. Then he let out a breath and crossed his arms over his chest. They had fought again. That much was obvious. Lately, it felt like that was all they did. Either they were arguing, avoiding each other, or barely speaking at all. And then, every once in a while, they were inseparable again, like nothing had ever been wrong. It made me sad every time I noticed it. I hated seeing them like this. I wished I knew how to fix it, or at least make it easier for both of them.

When Stan noticed the look on my face, his expression shifted fast. The heaviness disappeared, replaced with something more casual. "Good morning," he said. "Hope you're having a better morning than I am."

I pressed my lips together, already preparing to let him know that things with Scottie would work themselves out. That they always did. That whatever this was, it wouldn't last forever. But before I could sign anything, he spoke again, changing the subject.

"Is Ashby not here yet?"

I shook my head. [He's probably still at the pool.]

"Yeah." He paused, then pulled his backpack off his shoulder and dug through it until he found a single sheet of paper covered in scribbled math problems. He held it out to me. "Hey…can you look this over and check for mistakes? I really don't want to have to redo the whole thing."

I took the paper without hesitation. I liked helping my friends, and I loved math, so any free chance to look at problems like this, I took without thinking twice. The page was filled with algebra. Basic stuff. Easy for me. But I knew Stan hated math, and the fact that he had even attempted this was already a big deal for him.

"I didn't even Google anything or use my calculator," he added quickly. "I did it all with my big brain."

I glanced up at him and smiled before looking back down at the paper. He really must have put all his effort into it, because as I worked through each problem, I realized there wasn't a single mistake. Not one. I handed the paper back to him and nodded, then signed, [No mistakes. Good job.]

His eyes widened as he stared at the paper, then at me. "For real? Don't mess with me, Milow."

I grinned. [I'm not messing with you. You did great.]

He let out a heavy, relieved sigh and pressed the paper to his chest. "Thank fuck. I literally sat for three whole hours working on this."

Three hours was a long time to spend on ten algebra problems, but I was still impressed. The fact that he could even sit still for that long said a lot. He slid the paper back into his backpack, and when he looked at me again, he smiled.

"You know," he said, "I would give anything to have a brain like yours. But I just…like other things better."

[And that's okay,] I assured him.

"Yeah…I guess so." His smile faded as his gaze shifted past me, and that familiar protective look settled in his eyes. I didn't want to turn around. I was scared of what he was seeing. But then I heard Ashby's voice, and my head snapped toward him.

He was walking toward us, and Aspen was right behind him. Ashby didn't look happy about it, but he wasn't pushing her away either. I felt that tight feeling in my chest again, the one I always tried so hard to ignore. It wasn't jealousy. Not exactly. It felt more like betrayal.

I turned back to my locker and opened it again, forcing myself to focus on something other than the sight of them walking together.

My body tensed as they came closer. When they stopped next to us, I peeked up from behind the curtain of hair that had fallen over the side of my face, only long enough to catch a quick look at Ashby. He was already watching me. His hair was still damp, and he looked tired, like he always did after practice. I looked away again, pretending to search for a specific book in my locker.

"What's up?" Stan asked.

I was sure the question was meant for Ashby, not Aspen, but she answered anyway. "Hi, Stan. Ashby and I were just at the pool, swimming some laps. It's sooo nice getting a little workout in before school. Totally keeps me energized for the day."

My fingers tightened around the books tucked against

my chest, and my other hand curled into a fist inside the locker. The feeling that rose in me was unfamiliar and sharp. It felt like anger, and I hated it. I wasn't an angry person. I simply didn't like Aspen. And I really didn't like the way she talked as if she and Ashby were friends. They weren't.

"Um, cool," Stan replied, clearly uninterested.

"Milow," Ashby said my name softly. When I didn't react—which I hated, because I didn't want any of them, especially Aspen, to think she had gotten to me—he stepped around Stan and leaned against the locker beside mine. He tilted his head down so he could see my face better. "Hey."

My heart did that stupid flutter again, and my eyes lifted to his without thinking. The whites of them were a little red, probably from the chlorine. The crowd in the hallway faded out the way it always did when I looked at him. He smiled at me, giving me his full attention, making it clear he didn't care that Aspen was still standing there.

I bit the inside of my cheek as a smile pulled at my lips. I lifted my hand in a small wave.

"Will you be at the pool again tomorrow morning, Ashby?" Aspen asked.

I tucked a strand of hair behind my ear and closed my locker, watching as Ashby finally looked away from me and toward her. "No." That was all he said. No explanation. No follow-up. No alternate plan. I was pretty sure he hadn't even known she'd be there this morning, and that he'd just dealt with it because he wanted to practice.

Aspen pouted, but only for a second.

I was ready for her to leave, but then Hailie walked up. "As, here you are!"

"Oh, hi, Hails."

They hugged. Then Hailie turned and flashed a bright smile at Ashby and Stan, very clearly ignoring me. "Hi, boys."

Stan's face twisted in annoyance, unable to hide how he felt about them. Ashby stayed quiet, already done with the conversation. Hailie looked back at Aspen. "Where were you, As?"

"Swimming with Ashby. I told you I'd be here early this morning, remember?"

"Oh, yeah, totally. I must've forgotten."

"Whoa, wait a second," Stan said, amusement creeping into his voice. "You call her 'As'?"

Hailie tilted her head, eyes narrowing. "Yeah. Why?"

"As in 'ass'?"

"Yeah. Why?"

She still didn't get it. Ashby and I did. I glanced at him, pressing my lips together to stop myself from smiling. One corner of his mouth lifted, just slightly, his eyes flicking to mine with quiet amusement.

"You don't see an issue with that?" Stan asked Aspen.

"No. Why?"

While Stan tried not to laugh, Ashby shifted enough to reach for my hand. His finger brushed mine first, then curled gently around two of my fingers. Stan stood directly in front of us, blocking the view, hiding our touch from everyone else in the hallway.

I kept my eyes on Ashby and focused on that small, secret touch. I wanted to hold on to it. I wanted it to last.

"If one of my friends had a nickname like that for me, I'd be pissed," Stan added.

"Well, I don't mind," Aspen said, sounding irritated now. "Anyway…Ashby?"

I pulled my hand back, my heart racing. I was too scared that someone might have seen it, even if the touch had lasted only a second. Ashby's brows pulled together when he looked at her, clearly annoyed.

"See you around?" she said.

"Um, sure."

When they finally left, Ashby let out a heavy sigh. "God, they're obnoxious."

"Tell me about it. She literally calls her friend 'ass.'"

I hugged my books closer to my chest and waited for one of them to move. Classes were about to start, and I didn't want to be the last one walking into the room again. Ashby clearly didn't want to keep talking about them. He shook it off and looked at me instead, his expression softening. "I'll walk you to class."

"Me too. I'll walk you to class too," Stan added, then muttered under his breath, "Because my girl walks herself to class."

I pressed my lips together and reached out to touch his arm to get his attention, tucking my books under my arm to sign. [Do you want me to talk to her?]

He looked tired. "No. But thank you," he said quietly. "I'll handle it myself."

I glanced at Ashby then, giving him a quick look that said everything I was thinking. I'd ask Scottie later what was going on anyway. I hated seeing them like this, and I hoped that, maybe, after school, they could talk it through. Whatever it was. Ashby gave me a quick nod, reassuring me that he'd check in on Stan.

When we reached my classroom, I turned toward them and smiled. [See you later.]

"Yeah. See you later," Ashby said, smiling back at me.

The moment stretched, and I could feel the same pull I knew he felt too. The urge to reach out and to touch. But we didn't. We just stood there a second too long, looking at each other, until I finally turned and walked into the classroom. I could still feel his eyes on me until I took my seat.

I sat down near the window like always, set my books on the desk, and opened my pencil case, ready for another morning of learning.

18

Ashby

I was alone by the pool when Aspen showed up, wearing a bright-pink bikini that didn't really cover what it was supposed to. I had just finished warming up, stretching my arms and legs, and I was about to get into the water when she walked in.

I was usually the only one swimming this early in the morning. Normally, my coach, Ruben, came with me, but this morning he'd texted to say he had to stay home because his daughter was sick. So I came by myself. Training alone didn't bother me. I was used to it. Still, with Ruben there, things were easier. He pushed me when my motivation dipped, corrected my form, and sometimes filmed me swimming laps so I could watch myself afterward and fix what needed fixing next time.

My first instinct when I saw Aspen was to ignore her. Maybe she'd decided to start swimming too. This wasn't my private pool. Any student could use it, and sometimes I wasn't alone. Jasper came here too, and other, younger kids came to swim occasionally. Some were from the swim club I was part of. They never bothered me. They came to swim and then left. Unlike Aspen, as I quickly realized.

"Hi, Ashby," she said, smiling brightly.

She was wearing makeup, which struck me as odd if she actually planned on getting into the water.

"Hey," I replied. I'd been raised to be polite and kind. I never wanted to give anyone a reason to think otherwise. Still, when it came to Aspen or her friend, I would've preferred to say nothing at all.

"So nice swimming this early, right?" she went on. "I'm totally an early bird. Sometimes I'm up so early I don't even know what to do before school. Then I remembered you saying you come here every Monday."

I hadn't told her that. Not directly. Not ever. She must've overheard a conversation I'd had with someone else. I was sure of it. She and Hailie had a habit of listening in, then talking about me like we were friends. We weren't. We had never been, and I had no interest in changing that. Especially not when they were the same two people who had spent years saying cruel things to and about Milow. From the moment school started, I'd known they were part of the reason she kept her head down and always tried to stay unnoticed. Milow did everything she could to take up as little space as possible, and their behavior was tied to it.

I didn't respond. I gave her a tight, polite smile and walked along the edge of the pool toward the starting block in lane two. I hated swimming on the outer lanes, and since the pool was empty, I could choose whichever one I wanted.

I pulled on my cap and adjusted my goggles over it,

trying to shift my focus back where it belonged. When I swam, everything else usually fell away, and it was just my body, my breathing, and the water. That was it. Swimming was the one thing I knew I was really good at—the one thing I wanted to do professionally.

I'd been working toward this since I was four years old. When I was little, I didn't even know professional swimming was a thing. But the older I got, the more people told me I was good, and the more records I broke, the more serious it all became. I wanted more. I was on the right path, and I wasn't about to let anything—or anyone—pull me off it.

As I tried to pull my focus back to myself, Aspen suddenly stepped up beside me. She was still smiling, standing far too close. Personal space seemed to be a foreign concept to her. I had to fight the urge to groan. Instead, I glanced at her with a raised brow. "Can I help you?"

She giggled, like I'd said something funny. "No, I think I've got it. I'm a good swimmer too, you know. I swim all the time in summer, and I was thinking about joining the Dunst Swim Team."

"Cool," I said flatly.

"Totally cool." She exaggeratedly bit her bottom lip, then let her gaze drift over me in a way that made my body tense.

I was wearing my usual jammer. Actual training gear, like any serious swimmer would wear, unlike Aspen. Her bikini felt out of place here, especially if she honestly thought about joining a competitive team. I almost told her she'd need proper gear if she were serious. That she'd need a kneeskin suit, like every other girl on the DST wore. But I stopped myself. I didn't want to encourage her.

Her eyes lingered on my crotch, and it made me uncomfortable. The jammer was tight, the way it was meant to be, but I wasn't used to being looked at like that. Usually, people were focused on their own training. They were respectful and didn't stare at others wearing skin-tight stuff. But Aspen wasn't respectful. She kept staring. I cleared my throat and turned toward the starting block, stepping up onto it and shaking out my arms and legs.

Without saying anything else, I pulled my goggles over my eyes and took a deep breath, filling my lungs with all the air I needed. Aspen was still standing there, close enough to be distracting, but I forced myself to ignore her. I'd come here for a reason. I wanted to focus on myself, just like I'd planned.

After fifty laps, I pushed myself out of the water and peeled off my cap and goggles. I only ever did fifty here in the school pool, mostly because I didn't have more time. In actual practice at the aquatic center, I usually did close to 200, sometimes more. Fifty was fine for a Monday morning.

Aspen was still there. Sitting on the bench along the side, watching me like I'd given her permission. I forced myself not to dwell on it. I'd just finished a solid practice, and all I wanted was to shower, then find Milow. I missed her. I hated coming to school without her, but I didn't want to make her get up earlier than she had to just so I could swim before class. I knew that on mornings she didn't drive with me, Mom or Dad took her instead, depending on who left for work first.

As I walked over to where I'd left my towel, Aspen stood up and moved too close again. "I was thinking..." she said.

She hadn't been in the water once. She'd just sat there

the entire time, watching me. I wanted to tell her how much that bothered me, but I didn't.

"About the double date," she continued. "Hailie and I really want to try that new restaurant in town. You know, the Italian one?"

I frowned. Stan and I had never agreed to a double date. I was sure we'd made that clear at Scottie's party. I hated how entitled she sounded, like she could decide things for us. I dried off and wrapped the towel around my hips, partly to keep warm and partly to make sure she wouldn't stare at my crotch. Before I could answer, she kept going.

"We were thinking Friday might be good. Do you have time? Can you ask Stan? Maybe you could give me your number so I can start a group chat with all four of us."

I didn't want that. Not now. Not ever. The patience I'd been holding onto finally snapped. "I'm sorry, Aspen, but I'm not interested. And neither is Stan. He's dating Scottie."

"Dating?" She laughed. "They're not dating. They fight all the time."

She talked about my friends like she knew them the way I did. My jaw tightened as I shook my head. "We're not interested," I said again.

"Oh, well…maybe you'll change your mind if, you know, if you see this."

It was a moment. A single second in which she lost all her self-respect and decided to flash me. She pulled the bikini top that barely covered her tits to the sides, her green eyes not showing an ounce of shame. I wasn't looking at her tits. I was staring into her eyes, shocked by what she had just done.

"Do you like them?" she asked, tilting her head to the side, trying her hardest to flirt with me. "Every guy at school does."

And that was the fucking problem. I knew she'd slept with a lot of guys at this school already. I wasn't slut-shaming her. It was just facts. And her pulling this stunt proved, once again, how low she'd go to get someone's attention. The worst part was that once she got the attention she so desperately craved, she'd move on to the next guy. I was never going to be one to check off her list. Neither was Stan. We had principles. We weren't up for a quick fuck just for the hell of it, and we surrounded ourselves with two of the most good-hearted girls in this whole town. Stan and I wanted something real. Not girls who did shit like this to get someone's attention.

I wanted to shout at her. Lecture her about the fact that what she was doing could be categorized as sexual harassment. But no words came out. I turned around and headed straight for the showers, relieved that there were separate boys' and girls' changing rooms. Although after what she pulled, I bet she'd still intrude on my privacy and ignore simple rules. My mind was racing, and all I wanted was to get out of there. I took a shower, got dressed, pulled my backpack out of the locker, and headed out to the main building.

My mind was on Milow. I needed to see her. I needed her face in front of me to pull my thoughts away from everything. I couldn't tell her what happened. It would upset her, and that was the last thing I ever wanted for her. I found her quickly, standing by her locker with Stan, and relief hit me the second I saw her.

But it didn't last. Aspen was right behind me. She

wouldn't let up. She clung to me like a tick, stubborn and relentless, draining every ounce of patience I had left. No matter how hard I tried to shake her, she stayed there. Luckily, after Hailie showed up and Stan made fun of her nickname for Aspen, she finally backed off, and I got to walk Milow to her class. That alone made the morning feel manageable again.

The small, hidden moment we shared lingered in my mind. I found it fascinating how everything around us disappeared when our hands touched. I had noticed it back at Scottie's party, and then by her locker. That touch alone gave me enough to help me get through the morning. As she disappeared into the classroom, I already found myself counting the time to the next break.

During the first period, I tried to focus as much as I could. History had never really been my thing, but I knew that if I wanted to reach my goals and get into UBC— just like Wesley had—I couldn't rely on athletics alone. I needed solid grades too. Athletic success wasn't enough. Academics mattered just as much.

My focus broke when my phone buzzed. I usually ignored it during class, but whenever I got a text, my first thought was Milow. If she needed me, I wanted to know. I carefully slid my phone out of the front pocket of my hoodie and glanced down at the screen.

Aspen has added you to the group "DOUBLE DATE"

I frowned. Where the hell did she get my number?

My grip tightened around my phone. First, she showed up at the pool and watched me swim. Then she crossed a line I still couldn't fully wrap my head around. And now, after I had given her zero reason to think I was interested, she still wouldn't stop.

"Dude," Stan hissed from the desk to my right, near the back of the room.

I looked over at him. He was holding his phone low, the same message glowing on his screen. My jaw clenched. I had wanted today to be a normal day like it usually was. Instead, we were getting dragged into something we never agreed to and never wanted.

I typed a quick message to Stan, keeping my phone hidden from the teacher at the front of the room.

> **Me:** Exit the group.
> **Stan:** How'd she get our numbers? Did you give it
>   to them?
> **Me:** Fuck no.

I hesitated for a second, then decided to tell him what had happened earlier at the pool.

> **Me:** Aspen flashed me at the pool. She's still trying
>   to push this double date thing.

I heard Stan suck in a sharp breath before he quickly covered it with a cough.

> **Stan:** WTF?!
> **Stan:** You should report it.
> **Me:** Yeah...
> **Me:** Exit the group.

I did a second later, just as another message from him came through.

Stan: Honestly, what the actual fuck. She flashed you??

Me: Don't say anything to anyone. I'll talk to her older brother. He can handle it.

Stan: What a bitch. I'm sorry, man. That's not okay.

Me: Glad we're on the same page.

I glanced at him and gave a tight smile before sliding my phone back into my hoodie pocket. Stan just shook his head, still trying to process what Aspen had done. I thought about finding Lando, Aspen's brother. He was a senior too, and I only shared one class with him. But I wasn't sure I really wanted to tell him what happened. He might think I was lying. Aspen had a way of convincing people, and I was certain that he'd believe his sister over a guy accusing her of flashing her tits.

The thought of him taking her side made my stomach knot. I didn't want to start something bigger. It was already exhausting enough dealing with her at all.

By the time the teacher's voice pulled me back into the room, I'd decided to keep it to myself. At least for now. It felt safer that way. Even if it didn't feel right.

19

Milow

Scottie was waiting for me at my locker, and the second I reached her, I could tell her mood had dropped even more since this morning. Still, when she saw me, she smiled and slipped into that cheerful expression she always used. She did it without thinking. I never blamed her for it. I just wished that she didn't feel like she had to hide how she was really feeling around me.

"Hey. So, I was thinking," she said, a little too upbeat. "We could go to the mall after school. I need some new clothes, and we could stop by the bookstore and grab coffee. What do you think?"

I opened my locker and slid my books inside, then turned back to her and signed, [I'll have to ask Mom, but I'm pretty sure she'll say yes.]

"Perfect." She smiled, then tilted her head. "How was your morning?"

As we started walking toward the lunchroom, she automatically took my lunch from my hands so I could sign more easily. She was always like that. Always making small things easier for me without making a big deal of it.

[Good,] I signed. [I'm really liking the harder material. Junior year is going to be fun.]

She laughed softly. "You're literally the only person I know who enjoys school this much. I'm happy to inform you that senior year is even worse, so you can look forward to that."

[I've been looking forward to that since I was six,] I signed back, grinning. Although, once I was a senior, none of my friends would be at this school anymore. I looked at her more closely. [How are you?]

She shrugged, but her face tightened instead of relaxing. I'd asked her that question plenty of times before, and I already knew the answer I usually got wasn't the full truth. I asked anyway, even though I didn't expect much.

"I just want to go one day without feeling so annoyed."

[What's annoying you?]

We stopped in front of the large doors to the lunchroom. If this was about Stan, I knew she wouldn't want to talk about it once we were inside.

"Just…some stupid thing that shouldn't annoy me," she said, furrowing her brows before sighing.

[What happened?]

"He picked me up, and I thought we'd drive to school alone. But Ava was in the car with him."

I knew Ava. She was in some of Ashby's classes and had always been kind. She'd never given me a reason to dislike her. Ava was stunning. Not that Scottie wasn't. Still, Ava was tall, with beautiful brown curls and an effortless, movie-star kind of beauty that drew attention without trying. On top of that, she was genuinely nice. I could understand why seeing her in Stan's car had hurt.

"And I know I shouldn't be jealous," Scottie continued, her voice quieter now. "But she's perfect. Every guy at this school would give anything to date her."

Any guy?

Even Ashby?

The thought came uninvited, and I pushed it away just as quickly. It was pointless and inappropriate. There were rules. And even though Ashby and I had already crossed a line in small ways, I couldn't let my mind go there now.

[They're just friends,] I signed. [You know Stan has always had a crush on you.]

"Yeah," she said, her shoulders slumping, "but I keep giving him reasons not to anymore. I must be exhausting. It feels like I am."

[You're not exhausting, Scottie. And Stan isn't exactly perfect, either,] I signed. [He likes getting a reaction out of you. You know that. He just doesn't know how to show affection without being annoying.]

My words might have been harsh. I liked Stan, but it had always been like that. Even when they were kids, they'd teased and poked at each other constantly. Anyone who paid attention could tell it came from feelings neither of them wanted to admit out loud.

Scottie sighed and scrunched her nose. "Yeah. I know. Still…seeing them together like that hurt."

I understood. I reached out, squeezed her arm, and gave her an encouraging smile. [Trust me. Stanley only has eyes for you. He always has. And he always will.]

"Yeah…" She smiled, but it didn't quite reach her eyes.

"You're the best, Milow. You always know how to cheer me up."

That was what friends were for. I slipped my arm through hers and walked into the lunchroom with her, trying to ignore all the loud voices of the other students as I scanned the room for the boys. They were at our usual table, the one near the windows. As soon as we got closer, Ashby looked up. His face softened instantly, and he pushed a chair back for me without even thinking about it.

"Hey," he said quietly as I sat down beside him.

Scottie took the seat on my other side, directly across from Stan. He was already watching her, his posture stiff, like he wanted to say something but didn't trust himself to get it right. They still hadn't spoken. They just looked at each other. As tense as it was, I figured that silence was better than words they couldn't take back.

I turned toward Ashby and smiled. [Hi.]

"What did you bring for lunch?" he asked, leaning a little closer so he could see what I was unpacking.

I pulled out the turkey sandwich I'd made that morning and set it on the table, then opened my container with veggie sticks and sour cream dip. I glanced at him again.

[We can share this,] I signed, nudging the container closer to him.

His smile widened. He only brought a sandwich himself, and I knew that wouldn't keep him full until after school. "That's sweet. Thank you, Milow."

I smiled back and started eating, feeling that quiet comfort settle in my chest whenever I was surrounded by the people I trusted. Around us, the table slowly filled as

Jasper and Bennett joined, the conversation slowly picking up, and I just listened.

Once I finished my sandwich, I started snacking on the veggie sticks, my eyes drifting back to Ashby again and again without me really meaning to. He was fully pulled into the conversation now. They were talking about sports and then different video games, and just as Stan tossed another question into the mix, a girl stepped up to our table. I couldn't remember her name, but I knew she was a senior.

The table went quiet instantly. She didn't seem bothered by the attention at all. She smiled straight at Jasper.

"Hi, Jasper," she said.

He turned toward her, and the smile on his face made it obvious he was glad to see her. "Hey, Lacey. What's up?"

"I was just wondering if you want to go out with me tomorrow night," she said. "Maybe we could go watch a movie."

That caught all of us off guard. Lacey didn't hesitate, didn't seem nervous asking him out in front of everyone. There was confidence in her voice, and it sent a strange shiver through me. I wished I had that kind of confidence.

We all waited, watching Jasper closely.

"Yeah," he said after a second, smiling wider. "Sure. Sounds great."

"Cool," Lacey replied, her smile softening. "I'll text you."

"Yeah. Great."

"Okay. Bye, guys."

She walked away, and Jasper turned back toward us, clearly pleased with himself.

"Well, shit…" Bennett said. "How long has that been going on?"

Jasper shrugged. "We talked at Scottie's party and exchanged numbers."

"She's nice," Bennett said.

"Yeah," Jasper agreed. "She is."

At the end of the table, Stan let out a sharp huff, crushing a napkin in his fist. "Could be that easy."

Oh no.

I looked at Scottie just in time to see her expression shift.

"Shit," Ashby muttered beside me, already knowing where this was headed.

Scottie's shoulders tightened. She stood up fast, her hands hitting the table harder than necessary. Her eyes were sharp, and I was instantly glad I wasn't Stan. He'd only said four words, and they could've meant different things, but none of us doubted what he'd meant.

"And why on earth do you expect me to be the one to ask you out?" she said. She didn't wait for an answer. Before Stan could even open his mouth, she was already walking away.

"Man…" Jasper said, shaking his head.

"You really need to keep some thoughts inside your head," Bennett added.

"I swear to God…" Stan groaned, dropping his face into his hands. "She would've read my mind anyway."

I bit the inside of my cheek, wanting to tell him that things would be okay, but this wasn't my place. This was something the boys had to handle.

Ashby leaned forward and reached across the table, patting Stan's shoulder. "Go talk to her."

"What the hell am I supposed to say?" Stan shot back, looking at Ashby with wide, stressed eyes. "Everything I say gets me in trouble. I can't do anything right with her."

"Yeah, you can," Ashby said. "You just have to count to ten before you speak."

"Maybe twenty," Jasper added.

Bennett grimaced. "Thirty. But Ashby's right. You need to use your brain sometimes."

Stan shook his head and ran both hands through his pitch-black hair, clearly overwhelmed. He stayed quiet for once, and no one else filled the silence. I looked at Ashby and pressed my lips together. He gave me a tight, reassuring smile. He was worried too, but didn't want to make it worse. We all knew this wasn't over, but we also knew they'd find their way back to each other. It just wouldn't be easy.

After a moment, Stan stood up and grabbed his backpack. "Wish me luck," he said.

Before he could leave, I reached across the table and picked up the uneaten chocolate bar Scottie had left behind. I held it out to him.

"Stan," Ashby said, stopping him.

Stan looked at Ashby, then down at the chocolate bar. He sighed and took it. "Not sure this will help, but… thanks."

I shook my head slightly and lifted my hands so he'd look at me. He did, with his expression tired and unsure.

[Don't try to be funny,] I signed slowly, making sure he followed every word. [Just be honest. Tell her how you feel, even if it comes out messy.]

He swallowed and nodded once.

[And listen to her,] I added. [Don't interrupt even if it hurts. She needs to feel heard.]

Stan let out a quiet breath and gave me a genuine smile. "You're way too smart for all of us," he said.

"What did she sign?" Bennett asked. "I want to know."

"Not now," Jasper muttered.

I looked at Stan again. [I know. Now go.]

He nodded, adjusted his backpack, and finally walked off after her, the chocolate bar clutched tightly in his hand. Chocolate usually made me happy, so I didn't see a reason why it wouldn't help.

"They're like an old married couple," Bennett said, sounding more amused than concerned.

"Yeah," Jasper agreed. "They'll figure it out."

I knew they would. They just needed time, and maybe a really long and honest talk.

Ashby pushed his chair back and stood up, slinging his backpack over one shoulder. "Come on," he said, looking at me. "I'll walk you to class."

I gathered my things and stood too, giving the boys a quick wave before following Ashby out into the hallway. The lunchroom noise faded behind us as we walked side by side. We were close but not touching, but the urge was too intense to ignore. The halls were starting to crowd again, with students moving in every direction, and lockers slamming.

"I kind of wish I didn't have class right now," Ashby said after a moment. He glanced at me, then looked forward again. "We could go to the library instead. Sit there for a bit. I don't really feel like paying attention."

I smiled, already knowing what he was doing. He was

avoiding responsibility and avoiding everything that wasn't me. It was sweet, in a way, but I couldn't let him lose his focus.

I lifted my hands. [You can't skip.]

He groaned quietly. "I know. But the library's quiet. And we could hang out."

I scrunched my nose. [We can hang out after school. And you care about your grades. Don't pretend you don't.]

He huffed. "You're right. Sometimes, though, it's okay to skip a class."

[It's not, but nice try.] I smiled and kept walking, matching his pace. [You'd be mad at yourself if you skipped. And your coach would kill you if it affected your eligibility.]

"That's a good point," he admitted. "A terrifying one."

We stopped outside my classroom. Ashby shifted his weight, clearly not wanting to leave yet.

"I'll see you after," he said.

[Maybe. Scottie wants to go clothes shopping.]

"Oh."

I smiled tightly. [I haven't asked Mom yet.]

"She'll probably say it's fine." He didn't look happy, but he wasn't going to stop me from hanging out with Scottie. "Okay, then…I'll see you tonight."

I nodded, and he hesitated. "Okay. I'll go."

[Okay.]

I felt his eyes on me as I went to my desk, and when I was seated, I looked over to where he still stood just outside the door. He waved before he left, and all of a sudden, I wished I had said yes to skipping class.

20

Milow

Scottie and Stan had talked things out. Scottie talked about it the entire time we were shopping. It didn't bother me. I listened, glad they actually seemed to have reached some understanding this time. When I asked her if they had finally decided to go on a date, she said no. Instead, they agreed to stay friends for now and give it a few weeks without fighting before even thinking about dating.

It sounded reasonable. Probably smarter than jumping into something while everything was still messy.

When I got home, Mom and Evie were in the kitchen, cooking dinner together. Dad was still at work, and Wesley was at practice. I went straight to my room and unpacked my backpack, laying out my books in the order I wanted to work on them later. After that, I took out the two books I had bought at the bookstore. I'd had just enough money for two paperbacks. Two books I'd been wanting to read for a while, and I was already trying to figure out when I could start one of them.

I read the blurb on the back of the first book, then the second, going back and forth as I tried to decide which to read first.

"You're back."

I snapped my head toward the door and saw Ashby standing there with a smile on his face. I smiled back and nodded, lifting the two books to show him before setting them down on the bed. [I got new books.]

"Yeah? Can I see?"

I nodded and stepped aside, letting him walk over and pick one up. "A psychological thriller?" he asked, glancing back at me. "You like those?"

I shrugged. [I haven't really read one before, but this one's supposed to be really twisty, so I thought I'd try it.]

"Sounds good," he said, then picked up the second book. It was the same genre. "Can I read this one? It actually sounds pretty interesting. We could read together."

The idea of reading books together excited me. It reminded me of the days we looked at children's books when we were little, so I nodded quickly. [Okay.]

"Perfect." He grinned and sat down on the edge of the bed, the book resting in his lap as he leaned back on his elbows.

I turned to my desk and finished putting my things away, stacking my schoolbooks and sliding my notebooks into place. When I glanced over, he was still watching me, looking extremely comfortable in my room. I smiled, enjoying his presence. It seemed that lately we'd been hanging out more often again, and I liked that.

Mom called us for dinner from downstairs a while later, and Ashby sighed as he stood up. "Wanna read together after dinner?"

[I have to do my homework first.]

"That's fine. I'll start the book already so I can get a head start."

I'd finish the other book faster than he would. That was for sure.

[Okay.]

———

Friday, September 12th

Every Friday, I had a free period before lunch. I always spent it in the library. No one bothered me there. Even with other students around, they were the kind who actually worked instead of sitting around making noise. I was in the middle of a math problem when my phone buzzed inside my backpack. I pulled it out and saw a message from Ashby. He was supposed to be focused on class, but that clearly didn't matter to him. He also knew I had a free period.

Ashby: Are you in the library?

I pressed my lips together and typed a quick reply.

Me: Yes.
Ashby: Perfect.

I was about to warn him not to come—because he definitely had somewhere else to be—but I didn't get the chance. Seconds later, he was walking toward my table with a smug grin. I put my phone down and frowned. [You should be in class.]

He dropped into the chair next to me. "I should," he said quietly. "But I'd rather hang out with you."

I studied him for a moment, taking in the tired look in his eyes. [I'm working on math problems.]

"I can see that." He leaned back in his chair. "Keep going. I'll watch."

I didn't mind him watching while I worked, but I wished he'd take school a little more seriously. [Are you missing something important?]

"No, I—"

"Quiet, please," Mrs. Chancey, the librarian, hissed from her desk near the entrance.

We both looked at her, then at each other.

Talking wasn't an option for him anymore, but there was a simple solution to that. Ashby lifted his hands and signed instead. [I'm not missing anything important. Just boring geography.]

I pursed my lips. [What did you tell your teacher?]

He shrugged. [Nothing. I just excused myself.]

Of course he did. And of course, his teacher let him go. Being the star athlete came with its perks. I knew it wouldn't last forever, though. One day, someone would stop letting him skip class. Until then, he'd probably miss fifty more. [Mom and Dad won't like that.]

[Mom and Dad won't know.] He raised a brow, then sighed. [Practice was intense last night. I didn't sleep well. I'm tired. My body hurts. I don't want to use my brain right now.]

I watched him for a moment longer. I understood. I didn't want him slipping into something he couldn't easily climb out of. For now, he had things under control. He was allowed to feel worn down, especially after a long swim practice.

I smiled softly. [Okay. I still need to finish these.]

[That's fine.] He smiled back. [I'll watch.]

I went back to my worksheet and forced myself to focus, my pencil moving across the page as I worked through the next problem. I was aware of Ashby sitting beside me the entire time, but he wasn't distracting. He made me feel safer and more relaxed. After a few minutes, he shifted his chair closer.

His hand moved toward my left, where I was holding the pencil, and he hesitated for a moment before he took it, his fingers wrapping loosely around my hand. His gaze dropped and settled on my thumb, and I felt a familiar twinge of embarrassment when I realized how raw the skin looked. I hadn't even noticed that I'd been picking at it today.

Ashby's expression changed subtly, his jaw tightening as he turned my hand to look more closely. He didn't comment on it or pull his hand away. Instead, he brushed his thumb gently over mine, as if he was trying to stop the habit with a simple touch.

I swallowed and glanced up at him. [Sorry,] I signed with my other hand.

He shook his head immediately and tightened his grip, his expression firm but kind. "You don't have to apologize."

I pulled my hand out of his and stared down at my thumb, feeling a familiar wave of frustration as I took in how red and irritated the skin looked. I hated that it was so obvious again, hated that I hadn't even realized I'd been doing it until he noticed.

As much as I wished I could stop, and as much as it hurt when the picking got really bad, I honestly didn't know how. Dad once told me it was just a habit, something I could break if I focused hard enough and really tried, but I had tried. I'd tried more times than I could count. I'd been doing this since I was five, ever since fear started settling into my body in ways I didn't know how to explain. Picking had always been a way to ground myself when everything else felt too loud, and in the end, I started doing it subconsciously.

When I looked back at Ashby, his expression had shifted, worry written plainly across his face. He wanted to help, I could tell, but he didn't know what to do, and neither did I. I didn't expect him to fix this for me. It was mine to deal with. I told myself I'd grow out of it eventually. That once school wasn't a constant source of pressure and anxiety, maybe my hands would finally rest.

[I really want to finish this,] I signed, reaching for my pencil again and turning back to the worksheet.

"Okay," he said quietly, staying right where he was.

I worked through the last few problems with him beside me in the quiet library, and even though the anxiety never fully left, it didn't feel as heavy when he was there.

21

Ashby

At lunch, I couldn't stop thinking about ways to help her with the skin picking. I knew she'd been doing it for as long as I could remember, but the older she got, the worse it seemed to become. Sometimes it got so bad that she bled, which was why she so often had a bandage wrapped around her thumb. She never talked about how much it bothered or hurt her, never made it a big deal, but I knew it did. It had to. No one could keep tearing at their own skin, leaving it raw and irritated, without it affecting them. I made a quiet mental note to look it up later, to see if there was anything that could actually help. Maybe there were techniques she hadn't tried yet. Maybe a doctor could do something more than tell her to stop.

I was pulled out of my thoughts when Bennett said Milow's name. I looked up just in time to see him slide a small container of strawberries across the table toward her. "You want one?" he asked casually, and I immediately frowned.

"She doesn't like strawberries."

Milow shifted in her chair and gave Bennett an apologetic smile.

"Who doesn't like strawberries?" Bennett said with a laugh. "Come on, they're probably the last ones you'll eat this year."

She shook her head, and I repeated myself, more firmly this time. "She doesn't like them."

Bennett's brows pulled together as he looked at me, then back at Milow. "Shit, sorry."

[It's okay,] Milow signed, her smile tight. She didn't want to make it awkward.

"She said it's okay," I translated.

Bennett nodded and smiled at her again. "What fruit do you like, then?"

I didn't know why my mood had shifted so sharply, but I didn't like this conversation. Even though Bennett was my friend, even though he'd always been nice to her, I didn't want him getting closer to her. I didn't want him learning her preferences or trying to make her laugh.

Milow studied him for a moment before signing, [I like blueberries and oranges.]

Bennett glanced at me, waiting. I sighed and translated. "Blueberries and oranges."

He grinned. "So if I take you out for dinner, will you share a blueberry shake with me?"

Stan let out a low whistle from across the table. "Did you just openly ask out my girl?"

His girl? If anyone had a claim like that, it was me. He'd better stick to calling her Ace. And since when was Bennett interested in Milow like that? How did he imagine taking her out when he couldn't even understand her without someone else speaking for her?

Milow's cheeks flushed bright red, and the tight feeling in my chest only got worse. I'd never thought of myself as the jealous type, but whatever this was, it flipped something I didn't know I had in me.

"I'm just messing with you," Bennett said quickly, a smirk still tugging at his mouth, and when he noticed the way my expression hardened, he rushed to correct himself. "I mean, I'm not messing with you. I was trying to be funny. Not that I wouldn't date you. You're beautiful—"

"I think that's enough," I cut in, my voice sharper than I intended.

The table went quiet for a moment. Bennett blinked as he realized he'd pushed too far, and leaned back in his chair with his hands raised, backing off without wanting to make it worse. "Okay. Yeah. Sorry," he muttered.

Milow kept her eyes on her lunch, with her shoulders hunched. I noticed the small movement of her hand in her lap. I dropped my gaze and watched as her fingers found her left thumb. She started picking at it without even realizing she was. Her focus drifted inward.

I tensed. Carefully, without drawing anyone's attention, I slid my hand under the table and reached for hers. My fingers closed gently around her hand, stopping the motion before she could break the skin again. She startled, then relaxed when she realized what I was doing.

She looked up at me, her expression soft but embarrassed. She hadn't meant for anyone to notice, but I knew she hadn't even noticed herself. I gave her hand a gentle squeeze to remind her that she wasn't alone and didn't have to deal with it by herself. She let her hand stay in mine, and after a moment, she took a slow breath before using her right hand to finish her lunch.

I needed to get my emotions under control. Snapping at my friends wasn't like me, and I didn't want any of them to start thinking I was turning into someone unpleasant or unpredictable. Even more than that, I didn't want to risk pushing Milow in any way. The last thing I ever wanted was to make her feel cornered, especially by me. Right now, she seemed okay with my hand holding hers, and I stayed aware of that, ready to pull back the second she needed space. What she didn't know was that feeling her hand in mine helped me stay calm when everything inside me felt like a storm brewing.

———

That same night, I got out of bed and sneaked across the hall to Milow's room. I couldn't sleep, and I knew she'd still be awake, reading. I knocked and slowly opened the door just a crack to look inside. "Milow?"

She turned her head, sitting up in bed as she lowered the book to her lap. Without needing to ask for permission, I stepped inside and closed the door quietly behind me before crossing the room. Only her bedside lamp was on, but it was enough to light up her face. She moved on the bed, making space for me like she always did. I gladly accepted the invitation. I lay down next to her, careful not to crowd her, then turned onto my side so I could look at her. She met my gaze and hesitated, but only for a moment. Then she set the book on the nightstand and lay down, facing me.

I didn't talk. There didn't feel like a need to. We just lay there under one blanket, and with our heads on the same pillow. Her breathing was even, which automatically made me breathe slowly too. I watched her eyes soften, admiring the colors in them as I so often did. And she watched me right back. I reached out, unable to fight the urge not to, and rested my hand on hers. She didn't pull back. Instead, her fingers slid into mine. After a while, my eyes drifted to her hand. Even in the low light, I could see the redness on her thumb. Slowly, so I wouldn't startle her, I brushed my thumb over hers carefully.

Her eyes dropped to our hands, then lifted back to my face. I recognized the look immediately. She was about to apologize again, and that familiar flicker of embarrassment showed in her eyes. I hated it. She felt guilty over something she had never had any control over. It had to hurt her, and she looked so lost every time she tried and failed to stop picking at her skin. She had done it for as long as I could remember. Since we were kids. And it made me angry that no doctor had ever helped her or even taken it seriously enough to try. I knew it had to be tied to her anxiety, but even then, I didn't fully understand where it all started or what had caused it in the first place.

"You don't even notice when you do it," I said quietly. I wasn't accusing her. "It happens when you're anxious, right?"

She swallowed, her fingers twitching as she nodded.

I tightened my hold just a little, still moving my thumb over hers. "If you ever feel like that again," I said quietly, "I want you to hold my hand instead. You can squeeze it if you need to. As hard as you want." I hesitated for half a second, then added to make it sound simpler, "Think of my hand as a fidget toy. Just something to keep your hands busy when your thoughts get too loud."

Her eyes widened, surprised by my offer. I couldn't be around her when we were in school, and my idea would be useless then, but whenever I was close to her, I wanted her to remember this.

She nodded, and a smile tugged at the corners of her mouth. Then her gaze dropped to our hands, and she tested my proposal, giving my hand a gentle squeeze. She looked pleased when she looked into my eyes again, and with a smile, I added, "I don't want you to hurt yourself. I want to help however I can."

She nodded slowly, then shifted closer to me, closing the gap between us. Her eyes drifted shut, and I stayed still, watching her face soften again. My gaze lingered on her lips longer than it should have, and I hated the strange feeling that followed. We had been close for so long. We were never supposed to be more than friends, but I had never really called her my foster sister, either. Not because I didn't accept her as family, but because I had always known that we were meant to be something different.

Against everything my head was telling me not to do, I shifted onto my elbow, not letting go of her hand. Her eyes flew open again, and I moved slowly, giving her enough time to pull away if she wanted to. But she didn't. She lay on her back and looked straight at me. Her lips were parted, and she just watched me, her attention fully on every single one of my moves.

I lifted our joined hands and placed them gently beside her head, getting us both into a more comfortable position. Her eyes were wide, and she looked nervous, but she didn't push me away. Her fingers stayed intertwined with mine, and that alone made my head spin. I leaned down slowly, giving her one last chance to stop me. When she didn't, I pressed a soft kiss to her cheek. It was brief and careful, and I didn't linger longer than I should have. My heart was racing so hard that I was sure she could hear it in the quiet. I could've sworn I heard hers beating in her chest.

When I pulled back and met her gaze again, there was no panic in her eyes. She still looked nervous, but not scared. I realized I was nervous too, standing right on the edge of something I didn't know how to name, and unsure if I had just crossed another line.

"Was that okay?" I asked in a whisper.

She nodded, her eyes dropping to my lips. My chest squeezed my lungs, making it hard to breathe.

"Don't," I said, shaking my head. "Don't look at my lips like that, Milow."

She looked back up at me, confusion flickering across her face. Her brows drew together, trying to understand what I meant. Her hand slipped out of mine and came to rest on my chest instead. Her fingers curled into the fabric of my shirt, and she tugged me a little closer. She was really testing me here, even if she didn't mean to. I didn't move at first. I was stuck in my own head, trying to figure out what the right thing to do was supposed to be. The problem was that I honestly didn't know anymore. Keeping my distance felt like the responsible choice, the one I was supposed to make, but leaning closer felt better in a way I couldn't just push aside and ignore.

I had always thought of myself as confident, especially when it came to girls, but none of that confidence mattered here. It didn't help me at all. I had kissed two girls before, and neither of those moments had meant anything to me. Both times were during forgettable games of spin the bottle with girls from school. I didn't think about those kisses afterward and didn't really care to remember. Kissing random girls was never something I wanted to keep doing, and after that, I never felt any real urge to kiss anyone again.

Not until now.

I knew she had never been kissed. That knowledge made my stomach twist with fear of doing something wrong. So instead of kissing her lips and risking ruining everything, I leaned down slowly and pressed my mouth to her jaw. It was another careful kiss, but this time, it lingered. She sucked in a breath, and her hand moved from my chest to the nape of my neck. I followed the line of her jaw, moving lower. I moved slowly, still giving her time to pull away if she wanted to. But she didn't and instead tilted her head more to the side to expose her neck. I pulled back and held my breath, fighting another urge to leave this bed immediately. My mind wouldn't listen. This was all my heart's doing.

She was melting against me, and it was the sweetest thing I had ever felt. The air in the room started to feel thicker, and the heat under the blanket grew, making me want to kick it off us. But I knew the blanket was giving her some comfort. I wanted to stay like this forever, and a need to taste more of her took over. I wanted to explore this newfound territory with a devotion that bordered on worship.

I pulled back enough to see her face, to make sure she was still okay with this. Her lashes fluttered against her cheeks, and her lips were still parted. The sight was my undoing. "You're so damn beautiful," I muttered, unable to hold the words back.

I lowered my head, bypassing her lips and pressing a series of soft, open-mouthed kisses along the side of her throat. I started just below her ear, feeling her pulse beat against my lips. It was a frantic but steady rhythm that mirrored my own, and I lingered there with my tongue darting out to taste her skin. She rewarded me with a tug at my hair.

My hand slid from her waist to the small of her back, pressing her even closer as my kisses trailed lower. I could have spent the rest of the night like that, just kissing her neck and learning what she liked. But I had to stop eventually, scared I'd push this to a point she wasn't ready for.

I finally stopped, lifting my head to rest my forehead against hers for a moment. Then, I looked down at her. Her eyes were still closed, and the serene expression on her face made me feel more at ease. Unable to resist the pull that still tugged at me, I leaned in and pressed a final, lingering kiss to her cheek, close to the corner of her mouth.

"Come here," I whispered, shifting so I could wrap her up completely. I rolled us until she was tucked into my side, pulling her into my arms until her head settled under my chin. I stroked her hair, her back, any part of her I could reach, and let myself settle until my heartbeat was steadier.

I didn't say another word, and she fisted my shirt with one hand. She didn't let go, and I kept stroking her back, listening as her breathing got deeper and more even. When her grip on my shirt loosened, I knew she had fallen asleep. My arm was starting to go numb pinned under her, but I didn't move. I didn't want to wake her up. I waited a few minutes to make sure she was fully out, then carefully reached my free arm toward the nightstand. My fingers found the lamp switch and clicked it off, plunging the room into darkness. I settled back against the pillow, tucking her head under my chin again, and let myself close my eyes with the certainty that she'd stay in my arms all night long.

22

Milow

The second I opened my eyes, my heart started beating as fast as it had the night before. I could still feel his lips on my neck, my skin tingling where he had pressed his mouth. I had never felt anything like that, never thought that he could make me feel even more than when he simply held my hand in secret. Maybe it was because I wouldn't allow myself to think further. I wasn't sure what was happening between us, but I didn't want to question it. I was scared it would end quicker than it began, and if I could feel his lips on me like that again, I didn't want to risk it by addressing it.

When he kissed my neck last night, a thick knot built in my throat. My body tried to find a way to let him know how good he made me feel, and I knew in moments like that, most girls would've made a noise. I've seen it in movies and read it in books. When something felt good, you automatically made soft sounds because you were feeling incredible. But as much as I wanted to allow my throat to make a sound to show Ashby how nice his kisses felt, nothing came out. Instead, I had to keep moving my hands through his hair, tugging at it to tell him I didn't want him to stop.

There was something wrong with my throat. I've always known that if I were truly capable of making even the tiniest sound, I would have a long time ago. But no matter how hard I tried or put my mind to it, no sound ever came out. Sometimes I wondered if it was because I had stopped talking at four years old. Maybe I had been silent for so long that my vocal cords just rusted and stopped working. Whatever the case, I could have Mom ask my doctor soon, since she had made an appointment to get me checked overall and have my vaccines updated.

I was still in bed with Ashby lying next to me. He was asleep on his side, facing me, with his right hand tucked under his cheek and his other hand resting between us on the mattress. His lips were slightly parted, but he was breathing slowly through his nose. I didn't want to wake him, knowing he enjoyed sleeping in on the weekends when he didn't have a swim meet. So I watched him, taking in every inch of his face. There were faint freckles splattered across his nose and cheeks, ones that had always been there. When he was little, the freckles were more prominent, but they had faded as he grew. I could still see every single one. I had memorized them. I felt the urge to lift my hand and trace them, but I kept my hands to myself, not wanting to risk waking him.

Sometime during the night, we had stopped cuddling. His arms had been around me tightly, and our legs were tangled as we fell asleep. His warmth had given me comfort, and while I wasn't lying in his arms anymore, he was still next to me. He hadn't left, which had to mean something.

Careful not to disturb him, I slid my legs out from

under the covers and sat on the edge of the bed. I looked back at him one last time, making sure he was still asleep, before tiptoeing out of the room.

As soon as I walked down the stairs, I could hear music drifting up from downstairs. An upbeat eighties song was playing, and I knew Mom and Dad were making breakfast. It wasn't unusual for them to be up early to prepare breakfast for the whole family, and when they did, they often turned up the radio. I crept down the next stairs, passing Wesley's closed bedroom door, and when I got to the kitchen, I saw exactly what I was expecting.

Mom was at the stove, flipping pancakes in one pan while another cooked scrambled eggs. She was wearing her apron over her pajamas, and she was swaying her hips to the rhythm, singing along to the chorus of Depeche Mode's "Just Can't Get Enough." Dad was standing by the island, chopping fruit with rhythmic precision, but he wasn't just standing there. Every few seconds, he'd do a little shuffle step, spinning around to show off to Mom before going back to the cutting. They were both laughing, lost in their own world, completely unaware I was standing there watching them.

I didn't want to move and interrupt this moment. I loved watching them because it proved every time that they were still so very much in love with each other. I had learned about how they met a while back, when they told the story at Christmas once. They both went to school together at Bowen High, just like all of us kids, and though there was attraction on both sides, Mom let Dad really work for it. I was glad Dad never stopped showing interest, because if he had, they would've never married and adopted me. I owed this life to his persistence.

I was ripped from my thoughts when Wesley appeared next to me, an amused frown pulling between his brows. "They're such teenagers," he said, grinning down at me.

I looked up at him and smiled, giving a small shrug because I would rather have parents like this than ones who fought all the time.

"My babies!" Mom called out when she finally noticed us. She came over to us with a big smile on her face, reaching for each of our hands. "Dance with me. You know this song, right? It was your Dad's favorite song in high school."

She moved to the music, and Wesley and I had no choice but to follow. If there was one place I felt comfortable enough to dance, it was in this house and with my family. I scrunched my nose when Dad wrapped his arms around me from behind, grabbing my hands and flaring them in the air to the music, while Mom spun around, really feeling the rhythm.

"I'm glad all of this will forever stay hidden from the world," Wesley said, clearly joking.

"What, are you ashamed of us, son?" Dad asked, spinning me around before letting go of my arms to grab Wesley into a dancing position. "Iris, darling, take a video of us. We'll play this on his birthday in front of all his friends."

My grin widened as I watched Mom grab her phone to film the two. Wesley rolled his eyes, letting Dad lead, and as annoyed as he looked, I knew he was having just as much fun.

"Wonderful, boys. Do a little spin, Wes," Mom encouraged.

I wanted to laugh. It's what every normal person

would've done in moments of joy and happiness. But, as always, no sound came out. I didn't want to make this moment bad by ruining everyone's mood, so I forced myself to push those thoughts aside and just let the happiness show on my face.

"Aw, Wes, you're a princess."

I turned my head to see Ashby standing in the doorway with a grin on his lips. He looked tired, with his hair sticking up in every direction. He looked at me for a second longer, his eyes softening when they met mine. I smiled at him, unable to stop myself, then turned away because I felt my cheeks flush.

"Morning, guys," he said as he stepped into the kitchen, his voice still rough with sleep.

"Morning, champ," Dad replied, finally letting Wesley break free from his dramatic dancing.

Mom clapped her hands once, then turned down the music. "All right. Let's eat before this turns into a party."

We all sat down, passing around plates while Mom brought all the food to the table. As everyone started eating, I looked around the table.

[Where's Evie?]

Wesley swallowed his bite and shook his head. "She's not feeling so good this morning."

[What's wrong?]

"She has a migraine," he told me, looking pained as he said it.

"Oh, Wes, you didn't tell us that. We've been blasting music down here all morning," Mom said with a worried expression.

"It's fine, Mom. It wasn't that loud."

Evie suffered migraines, and it could take hours and often days until she'd feel better. I couldn't imagine just how painful migraines were. I had only ever had headaches before, but I knew that pain was nothing compared to what Evie felt.

We continued eating, and I tried not to make it too obvious that I was thinking about Ashby and what we had done last night.

———

After we all helped clean up the kitchen, I went upstairs to work on some homework. I tried to stay focused, but my eyes kept drifting to my bed, to the place where Ashby and I had slept the night before. Every time I looked at it, my mind filled in the memory on its own. Him leaning over me. His mouth on my neck. The way my body had reacted without me telling it to. My toes curled every time the feeling came back, and I had to force myself to look back down at my notebook and keep working.

I couldn't stop wondering if Ashby was thinking about it too. If he replayed it the way I did and thought it had been a mistake. Or if he wanted it to happen again, the way I secretly hoped it would. The thoughts crowded my head and, for the first time, made it genuinely hard to get through my work. I frowned and leaned back in my chair, my hands lifting toward my face without me really noticing, and I started picking at my thumb again. This time it wasn't because I was anxious. I was nervous, but more than that, I was restless, and even though I knew exactly what I was doing, I couldn't make myself stop.

I pinched at the loose skin on the inside of my left thumb and pulled until a small piece came away. Then

I did it again, lower down where the skin was already red, where there was another thin flap I kept worrying at until a sharp sting finally made me freeze. A tiny drop of blood surfaced, and I clicked my tongue quietly, annoyed with myself for letting it go that far. I should have stopped sooner. I always should have. But sometimes I couldn't stop until it hurt, like the pain was the only thing strong enough to break the cycle. Only momentarily.

I pushed my chair back and got up from my desk, then walked out of my bedroom and into the bathroom. I opened the cupboard and started digging through my things, looking for a bandage. The pack I found was empty, but I knew I had another one somewhere. I always did. I went through bandages too often not to.

"What are you looking for?"

I turned my head and saw Ashby standing in the doorway, his swim cap and goggles looped together in one hand.

[A bandage,] I signed, then held up the empty box so he could see.

"I think I have some."

He turned around and headed back to his room, and I followed him down the hall but stopped at the doorway instead of going all the way in. He set his cap and goggles on the bed, then bent over his backpack and dug through it before pulling out two loose bandages. "Here," he said, handing them to me.

[Thank you,] I signed, smiling at him.

He didn't look away. His gaze stayed on me, trying to figure out what I needed the bandage for. He probably already knew, or at least suspected it, and that made me instinctively curl my hand inward, trying to hide my thumb. The movement sent another sharp sting through it, and that was enough to convince me I shouldn't wait any longer to cover it up.

I turned and went back into the bathroom, rinsed the small wound, and carefully wrapped one of the bandages around it. As I did, I could feel that familiar presence again, knowing I was being watched even without turning around.

"What happened?" Ashby asked from behind me, worry clear in his voice.

I turned to face him and gave a tight smile. [Nothing.]

"You picked your skin again," he said. He wasn't accusing me, just stating it as fact. His eyes flicked down to my thumb for a brief moment before coming back to my face.

[Yes, but it was nothing. I just got distracted for a moment,] I signed.

He kept studying me with that quiet concern in his eyes that made it obvious he was trying to read more into it. He wanted to know whether it was because I felt anxious. I could see it in his expression. He was looking out for me like he always did.

[I'm fine. I promise,] I added.

He held my gaze for another second, then gave a short nod. "Okay."

[Are you going to practice?] I asked next, glancing at the swim cap and goggles he was holding again.

"Uh, yeah. I wasn't planning on it at first, but Ruben texted and said the pool's closed to non-club members today. Since it's usually packed on weekends, I figured I'd take advantage of it."

[That's nice.]

"You want to come?" he asked. "You could swim too, or you could just hang out in the café and watch."

I used to go with him more often when we were

younger, back when Mom or Dad took him to the aquatic center for practice. While he swam, we'd sit in the café on the upper floor, the one with the floor-to-ceiling windows that overlooked the entire pool. They had a vending machine with the best hot chocolate there, and just thinking about it made the decision easy.

[Okay,] I signed without hesitation.

His expression shifted into a smirk. "Perfect. I need to finish packing, and then we can go. Are you ready?" he asked, his eyes briefly scanning what I was wearing.

I glanced down at my loungewear and decided it was comfortable enough for sitting around and watching, so I nodded.

"Great. Give me fifteen minutes." He turned and disappeared back into his room, and I went to grab my new book so I could bring it with me.

On the drive to the Dunst Aquatic Center, which was only a few minutes from our house, I kept my eyes fixed on the road ahead. Even though we had been close our entire lives, sitting alone with him in the car suddenly felt different. The radio was on, but it wasn't loud enough to drown out the nervous thoughts crowding my head.

I wanted to start a conversation just to kill this silence, but he was driving, and he couldn't watch me sign while keeping his eyes on the road.

So instead, like that made more sense, I turned my head and looked at him.

Ashby was focused, his hands tight on the wheel and his attention fully on the drive. I could already tell he had shifted into practice mode. Swimming did that to him. He cared about it deeply. That sport went beyond routine or obligation, and I had always admired him for that.

Not many people had something they felt that strongly about.

I liked to think I was passionate about school, but it wasn't the same. School was practical and necessary, and, truthfully, the only thing I was good at. It would eventually help me get somewhere, once I figured out what I actually wanted to do with my future. Swimming was different for him. It was something he chose, something he poured himself into, and watching that focus settle over him every time made me feel proud of him.

The corner of his mouth lifted, but his eyes stayed on the road. "What?" he asked. "Do I have something on my face?"

Handsomeness. That's what he had on his face.

I pressed my lips together and lowered my gaze to my hands resting in my lap as warmth crept into my cheeks. Ashby chuckled softly and reached over, brushing his fingers against mine before letting his hand settle there. He didn't need to say anything. He was relaxed, and that ease carried over to me.

When we arrived at the aquatic center, we went inside and found Ruben already waiting near the entrance. He pulled Ashby into a quick hug, then turned to me with an easy smile. "Hey, kiddo. You here to swim too?"

I smiled back and shook my head.

"She's just watching," Ashby said, shifting the strap of his sports bag higher on his shoulder.

"Good, good." Ruben nodded toward the stairs leading down to the changing rooms. "Jasper's here too."

"Great, thanks." Ashby looked back at me and smiled. "Go ahead. I'll come up later so we can eat something."

I nodded. [Have a good practice.]

"Thanks."

I waved before heading up the stairs toward the café. The upper level was empty, and while it was usually staffed, the people who worked there weren't around. There was no reason for them to be when only club members were allowed in today. Along the back wall, vending machines lined up, offering hot drinks, snacks, and sandwiches. I bought myself a hot chocolate and sat at a table by the window.

The pool area below was empty. The water was smooth and undisturbed, and the entire center was quiet, with only the faint radio music playing from the speakers. I pulled my book from my tote bag and set it on the table, then leaned forward to look down at the pool deck. Ruben appeared first, slipping his stopwatch around his neck and tucking his clipboard under his arm. A moment later, Ashby came out with Jasper beside him. Jasper's dirty-blond hair was already hidden under his cap. Ashby turned around, scanning the upper level until he spotted me. He waved before pulling his own cap into place.

I waved back. Jasper followed Ashby's gaze and looked up at me too, lifting his hand with a friendly smile. Then he pointed at Ashby and grinned, keeping his eyes on me as he mouthed, "He's going down."

I scrunched my nose and watched them bump shoulders and laugh as they walked toward the pool. That was another thing I admired about Ashby. He built friendships that were destined to last forever, and I felt immense gratitude not only for watching those friendships grow, but also for Ashby allowing me to see them as my friends too.

23

Ashby

I wasn't pleased with my performance. Practice itself had gone well, and Jasper and I had raced each other three times just to push ourselves. Normally, and without trying to sound arrogant, I would have won all three races. This time, I only won one, and even that was by a millisecond. It didn't actually mean anything. I was still swimming well, and Jasper was a strong swimmer too. We had joined DST at the same time when we were kids, and we had never treated each other like rivals. If anything, we had always done the opposite. We pushed each other. We cheered for each other, even when we raced in lanes right next to one another.

There was no reason to be frustrated with someone else for being faster. Swimming was individual. You swam for yourself, and that should have been the only focus. Still, I couldn't stop thinking about how unfocused I had felt in the water. Blaming it on school felt lazy, especially since Jasper was a senior too and had the same academic pressure I had. He didn't seem as weighed down by it. That probably made it easier for him to clear his head once he hit the pool.

Jasper held out his hand, looking down at me from the edge. I was still gripping the block, not quite ready to climb out after our last laps.

"You all right, dude?" he asked.

"Yeah," I said, taking his hand and letting him pull me out. "I've just got some things on my mind."

"I'm here if you ever want to talk," he said, running a hand through his damp hair.

I appreciated that. I knew I would take him up on it one day, but not right now. "Thanks, Jasper."

"Anytime."

"Boys."

Ruben stood up from the bleachers after finishing his notes and walked over to us, scratching the side of his buzzed head. "I'm happy with today's performance. If there's one thing I want you both to work on, it's not neglecting your kicks. Your arms are strong, your strokes look good, but it seems like you forget about your feet sometimes. Did you notice that too, or am I just nitpicking?"

Jasper shrugged. "I didn't notice, but I'll keep it in mind."

"Same," I said.

"Good." He glanced back down at his clipboard, then continued, "There's a swim meet here in two weeks with teams from all over the province. I haven't signed you up yet, but I can if you want in." He looked up at us again. "It's friendly. Nothing high pressure."

"Sounds good," I said, nodding. "I'm in."

"Yeah, me too," Jasper added.

"Great." Ruben smiled and pulled us both into quick hugs. "Enjoy your weekend. Take it easy. The door locks automatically when you leave," he said, then headed out.

I looked up to where Milow was sitting and saw her completely focused on the book in her hands. She had only started reading it a short while ago, yet I could already tell how many pages she had gotten through. She was a fast reader. I'd always known that. Still, it never failed to amaze me how quickly she moved through a story. I felt a small rush of excitement at the thought of asking her about it later, of hearing her explain what it was about once she finished.

"How is she doing in school?" Jasper asked. He was looking up at her too.

Part of me wanted to say she was doing more than fine, that she was thriving, but we both knew how people could be to her. "She's doing well," I said instead, rubbing my towel over my hair. "Very focused."

"I saw her on the first day back," he said, a grin pulling at his mouth. "She came into Mr. Kallio's class right after the lunch bell and handed him a note asking him for extra worksheets to work on. I like math, but the kind of stuff she does is seriously hard."

I chuckled. "She's a genius with numbers." And with a lot of other things too.

As if she felt us talking about her, she glanced down. I smiled up at her, and my heart kicked harder than it had during practice.

"She's a genius with a kind heart," Jasper said, still looking at her. "People like her usually end up doing great things."

"Yeah…" My smile softened as I pictured Milow in

the future, doing something meaningful and big. "She will too."

I lifted my hands before Milow looked away.

[I'm going to take a shower and then I'll come up,] I signed.

She nodded and signed a quick okay before returning her attention to her book. I glanced at Jasper as I started toward the showers. "You want to come up there and eat with us after?"

"Yeah, sure," he said easily.

After showering and getting dressed, Jasper and I headed upstairs together. We dropped our duffel bags by the door and walked over to the table where Milow was sitting.

"Hey, Milow. What are you reading?" Jasper asked as he took the seat across from her.

She lifted the book and showed him the cover, then set it aside on the table.

"A psychological thriller. Is it any good?" he asked.

She nodded and gave him a thumbs-up before turning to me with a smile. [You guys looked good down there.]

"Thanks," I said, keeping my voice light even though I felt anything but calm inside. "It felt good." I hesitated for only a second before asking, "What sandwich do you want?"

She pressed her lips together as she looked toward the vending machines lined up against the wall, then signed, [Cheese, please.]

I nodded and turned to Jasper. "You?"

"I'll come see what they've got," he said, getting up again.

We walked over together, picked out our sandwiches, paid, and grabbed drinks before heading back to the table. I set Milow's sandwich in front of her.

[Thank you.]

"Of course." I slid a bottle of iced tea toward her as well. "I grabbed this for you too."

She smiled again, and we settled into eating. Jasper talked about the upcoming swim meet, going over possible teams that could show up, and I chimed in when I felt like it. When his phone buzzed, and he pulled it out to read a message, my attention drifted back to Milow.

She smiled at me, her sandwich nearly finished. Without thinking, I shifted my leg until my knee brushed against hers. I just needed the contact. She didn't pull away. Instead, she pressed her leg gently against mine, holding it there. It was a small gesture, a moment no one else would notice. It told me that what had happened between us last night hadn't been a mistake, and that it could happen again. I hoped it would.

"You guys want to hang out at the diner tonight?" Jasper asked, breaking the moment as he looked up from his phone.

I turned to him. "Who's going to be there?"

"Lacey and some of her friends. Bennett too," he said. "You can bring Stan and Scottie if you want."

"Yeah, I'm in."

He looked at Milow with a friendly smile. "You coming too?"

She nodded.

"Awesome. It'll be fun."

———

"Milow!" Stan came straight toward us the second we stepped into the diner, his arms already wide open. "My sweetest girl. I missed your face."

Milow tried to hide her grin, but she didn't succeed when Stan pulled her into his arms and hugged her tight against his chest. If this had been any other guy, I would've stepped in without hesitation. But Stan was just Stan. He'd always treated her like a sister, and I knew there was nothing behind it.

Though when the hug dragged on longer than necessary, I reached out and patted his shoulder. "Let her breathe, buddy."

"Three more seconds," he muttered, squeezing her once more before finally letting go. "I had the worst day. This just made. everything better."

Milow had that effect on people, though Stan also tended to exaggerate. I chuckled. "What happened?"

"I had to help my mom clean out the garage," he said, shaking his head. "I knew she liked garden gnomes, but there were literally over a thousand of those little fuckers down there."

"Literally?" I asked, smirking.

"Li-ter-al-ly."

"Right." I gave his shoulder another squeeze. "But you survived."

"Barely."

Milow smiled up at him and lifted her hands. [I like your hair like this, Stan.]

I hadn't paid close enough attention to notice it before. "Did you cut it?"

Stan grinned and wiggled his brows. "Sure did. Well, Ava's mom did."

I stared at him for a moment, unsure if he fully understood whose mom he had let cut his hair. I knew Scottie hadn't enjoyed sitting in the backseat of Stan's car while Ava rode in the front. "Where? Does she have a salon?"

"Yeah," he said proudly. "In her basement."

Milow looked up at me, her lips pressed together. She was thinking the same thing I was.

"That's…nice, man," I said carefully.

"Yup." He turned back to Milow, grinning again. "You like it?"

She nodded. [You look like a young James Dean.]

"Well, shit," he said, clearly pleased. "At least you think it looks good. Scottie just frowned at me." He jerked his head toward the back of the diner. "Come on. Everyone's been waiting."

He walked ahead of us toward the booths. Two were already filled with people we knew from school. Jasper sat next to Lacey and lifted a hand when he saw us. Two girls whose names I didn't bother remembering sat across from them. In the booth behind theirs, Scottie sat by the window, looking bored. Bennett sat next to her, talking, though she looked like she wasn't listening at all. He might as well have been talking to a wall. As we reached the table, I let Milow slide in first before taking the seat beside her. Stan pulled over a chair and dropped into it at the end of the table, his attention immediately drawn to Scottie.

"Hey," I said, exhaling as I let my body relax.

"Hey, man," Bennett replied. He turned away when Scottie started signing to Milow, and I took that as a sign to give them some space. I glanced at Stan and noticed he was watching the girls closely.

"Stan," I said quietly, giving him a telling look.

He sighed and looked away as he leaned back in his chair. I was still unable to make sense of the two of them. When we were younger, I had honestly believed their constant fighting would stop the moment they admitted they liked each other. I thought naming it would fix everything. Apparently, that was much harder for them than anyone could've expected. All I wanted was for them to get along. To stop clashing over every little thing and maybe sit down for an honest conversation without it turning into another argument. Even though they had already done that just a few days ago and agreed to try being friends, it clearly wasn't working the way they had hoped.

It didn't help that Stan seemed mostly oblivious to the fact that he sometimes got a little too close to people Scottie didn't like seeing him with. Of course, he was allowed to hang out with whoever he wanted, and I knew he never crossed any lines. Still, there were moments when he should've paid more attention to what Scottie needed instead of shutting her out whenever things became overwhelming for him. I knew he liked her just as much as she liked him, but if they kept going like this, the tension between them would only turn more toxic.

24

Milow

Scottie and I went to the bathroom after we finished our burgers and fries, and when we came back, she stopped at the counter to order dessert for both of us. She picked apple pie without hesitation, and because it looked too good to pass up, I went with the chocolate cake.

[It's too much for me alone,] I signed once the waitress set the two plates down in front of us.

"That's fine," Scottie said easily. "You can share with Ash. He likes chocolate too, right?"

I nodded. I'd always shared food with him without thinking twice. Still, the idea of it now made me feel strangely uncomfortable. No one knew about how close we'd been lately, and no one would've suspected anything either, but just thinking about sitting there with the cake between us made me feel exposed.

We both reached for our plates and turned around, only to nearly bump straight into Hailie and Aspen. I frowned without meaning to. It was an automatic reaction whenever they were near, and I never quite knew how to hide it in time.

"Oh, look," Hailie said, her voice louder than necessary, "the bitch and the mute."

Aspen laughed like Hailie had just said something genuinely clever, her amusement coming too easily.

I let the words slide past me because I was used to their cruelty by now, but my attention immediately shifted to Scottie. She hated the two of them. Actually, she disliked more than a few people, and everyone knew that once you crossed her, she didn't let it go quietly. She made sure you remembered it every time you met her.

Hailie and Aspen clearly thought they were untouchable. They said whatever they wanted without stopping to consider how ugly their words were or who they might hurt. I kept glancing at Scottie, hoping I could somehow keep her calm, but I already knew it was too late.

A slow, dangerous smile spread across her lips, and she tilted her head slightly as she looked straight at Hailie. "What did you say?"

Hailie looked startled for just a moment before her expression shifted into a smug and pleased smirk. She thought Scottie had taken the bait, and she was ready to start a fight.

This won't end well.

"I said it's the bitch and the mute," Hailie repeated, crossing her arms over her chest and staring at Scottie without a hint of shame.

"Oh, okay," Scottie said with a laugh. "For a second there, I thought I didn't hear you correctly."

"No, no. You did. And if I'm honest, you're totally in my way."

"Oh, am I?" Scottie clicked her tongue and waved her free hand. "Gosh, I'm so sorry. I didn't mean to bother you."

I stared at her, unsure if she was being serious or just putting on a show. It was hard to tell, and even though I knew my best friend inside and out, she was now hard to read. But before I could question whether she had just lost it completely, her expression shifted. Her eyes narrowed, and her jaw tightened.

It happened fast. The apple pie flew through the air and landed squarely on Hailie's face. I slapped my hand over my mouth in shock, but there was something new that stirred in me—a dangerous sort of satisfaction. I felt a rush of something I hadn't allowed myself to ever before. It was a small, guilty thrill at seeing her get a taste of what she'd dished out for so long. After all the years of their bullying, maybe it was okay to feel this. *Schadenfreude*. I had read it in a book once, and I thought it was the right word for how I felt.

Gasps and "oh shits" erupted through the diner as Stan and Ashby rushed toward us. I quickly set my plate on the counter and grabbed Scottie's hand, intending to pull her away from the two girls who seemed determined to make other people's lives miserable. But she planted her feet firmly, refusing to back down.

"You want to repeat that for me?" she said, her voice sharp. "Your words might sound sweeter now that you've got apple pie all over yourself."

"Milow, come here," Ashby said quietly next to me, sliding his hand into mine.

My body relaxed immediately, letting him guide me aside while Stan stepped in front of Scottie, putting himself between her and Hailie. He gently took the plate from her hands and set it on the counter. "Let's go," he said to her. He wasn't angry at her at all, which showed that even when she did something extreme, he would protect her. I had to admit, throwing pie at a bully felt completely justified. It had been years of torture without any consequences for them.

"No, I want her to apologize first," Scottie said, trying to step around Stan.

"They won't mean it anyway, Scottie. Come on, let's go," he said, holding her steady, his hands sliding around her waist.

"You slut!" Hailie screeched, finally making sense of what had happened. "You'll pay for this! I'll tell my dad. He won't let you walk away if he finds out!"

Scottie laughed, throwing her head back in delight before she dared her to follow through. "Tell him," she encouraged, still trying to get out of Stan's hold.

"Baby," Stan said, keeping his voice calm as he slipped his hands around her waist again, "they're not worth it."

"Step aside, asshole!" Hailie shrieked. "I'll kick this mentally ill slut's ass."

Those words made Stan go rigid, and everyone in the diner understood it was a mistake to call Scottie that. Now she had fully unleashed the beast in him.

I squeezed Ashby's hand tightly, bracing myself for what came next. He stayed calm next to me, but I could feel the tension. We all knew Stan wouldn't actually hurt anyone, but the way he turned to Hailie, his eyes locking on hers with a deathly glare, made my stomach turn.

"Listen here, you trashy, attention-seeking goblin—"

"Damn," Ashby muttered with a chuckle beside me.

"If you ever, and I mean *ever*, mess with my girls again, I will personally drag you to your house and tell your daddy exactly what you've put all of us through over the years. No one likes you, you're a brat, and your mouth is open way too much for nothing smart ever to come out. Now, apologize to Scottie and Milow."

He didn't give them an ultimatum. He didn't need to. He meant every word, and the scariest part was that his voice stayed calm.

"You too," he added, shooting a sharp glare at Aspen. "I know what you did back at the pool, so don't think you'll get a pass here."

Ashby tensed beside me, and I looked up at him, catching the pained expression crossing his face. What had she done at the pool? Did I even want to know?

"Apologize. Now."

Hailie wiped her face, shaking her head as her eyes watered. "I can't believe she did this."

"I said, now!"

Aspen muttered a barely audible "I'm sorry," without looking at us.

Hailie still resisted, but when she finally looked at Stan and saw the seriousness in his eyes, she mumbled an apology. It sounded forced, completely lacking sincerity, but at least she said the words.

"Good. Now stay the fuck away from my girls. Both of you." Stan released Scottie and guided her away, then called back to Marjorie, the waitress. "Sorry about all this, Mar. Those two will clean up."

Ashby led me outside, keeping his hand in mine. When we reached his car, I watched Stan cup Scottie's face with both his hands. She had adrenaline written all over her face, and her eyes were glimmering with tears she refused to shed.

"I'm okay," she muttered, sniffling.

Stan nodded, studying her carefully before pulling her into a tight hug.

I looked at Ashby, who was still holding my hand. His eyes were filled with concern, and I couldn't help but smile to reassure him. I let go of his hand and signed, [I'm okay too.]

"Good. I'm sorry they always bother you like that."

[It's fine. I'm used to it.]

His jaw tightened. He hated that statement, but I couldn't lie. It was the truth. I was used to the bullying, and I learned to live with their cruelty.

"But you shouldn't be."

I gave a little shrug. It was all I knew, and nothing would change, anyway.

He sighed then, not pleased with any of what happened. "I think it's best if we just go home," he suggested, glancing over at Scottie and Stan, who were still wrapped up in each other's arms.

"I don't want to go home," Scottie murmured, her voice quiet but firm.

Stan looked down at her for a moment, then back at Ashby. "Mind if we hang out at your place for a while? We could watch a movie. Get their minds on something else."

I liked that idea.

"Yeah, sure," Ashby said with a nod. "Let's go."

We all got into Ashby's car. Scottie and Stan settled in the back, while I took the front seat, still feeling my heart race from the chaos at the diner. I was glad the boys had been there, and that the situation hadn't escalated into something worse.

Even so, a knot of worry twisted in my stomach. Thoughts of going back to school on Monday crept in, scared that Hailie and Aspen would come after us for revenge, and I felt that familiar urge rise again. My fingers drifted to my thumb, and I started picking at the skin around the bandage still wrapped around it. The anxious habit took over before I could stop myself.

At home, we found Wes and Evie on the living room couch. Wesley was sitting upright, and Evie was lying beside him with her head on a pillow in his lap. Wesley looked up when we walked in, and he caught the tension right away.

"Hey, what's wrong?"

"Two girls were bullying Scottie and Milow," Stan said. The anger was still written all over his face.

Wesley sighed. "The same two?" He looked from Scottie to me. "Are you girls okay?"

I smiled at him and nodded. Scottie answered for both of us. "Yeah. Thanks. Stan handled it."

Wes gave a tight nod, then said, "You guys wanna stay down here? We were just about to head to bed." His hand moved gently through Evie's hair. She looked asleep.

"Yeah, I think we'll hang out here," Ashby said. "Where are Mom and Dad?"

"Mom's sleeping. Dad's at the fire station." Wesley carefully stood up, lifting Evie bridal-style without any effort.

Now that I could see her face clearly, it was obvious she still wasn't feeling well. The TV was on mute, which meant Wesley was making sure not to worsen her pain.

I looked at her, worried, and signed, [How is she feeling?]

"Better than this morning," he said quietly. "She just took her migraine meds. They're knocking her out." His voice stayed low. "Try not to be too loud, okay?"

"We won't," Ashby assured. "Night."

"Good night." Wesley carried Evie upstairs, and I watched until they were out of sight.

"Poor Evie," Scottie said with a sigh. "Migraines suck."

I nodded. I had watched Evie suffer migraines for years, and I wouldn't wish that kind of pain on anyone. Not even my bullies.

Scottie and Stan were already getting comfortable on one of the couches. Ashby stood there for a moment, scratching the back of his head, thinking something through. "I think I'm gonna change into something more comfortable first."

I wanted the same thing, so I signed, [Me too.]

Without waiting for a response, we headed upstairs toward our rooms. When we reached the last step, Ashby caught my hand and pulled me toward him. His eyes searched my face, and my heart started pounding hard against my ribs.

"Are you sure you're okay?" he asked. His voice was low and filled with worry.

He was standing too close for me to sign comfortably, but I didn't want to anyway. I wanted to stand here with him and look into his eyes for as long as we could.

"I'll look out for you on Monday," he added. "I know you're worried about that."

He read me too well. There was no point in pretending otherwise, so I nodded.

He kept his eyes on my face a moment longer. I watched him swallow hard before he leaned in and pressed a kiss to my cheek. I closed my eyes, holding on to the feeling, and without thinking, I leaned into him. My hands came up to his stomach, resting there to steady myself.

He pulled back slightly so he could look at me again. I met his eyes, and that was a mistake. Heat rushed into my cheeks, and the urge to lean in closer and kiss him hit me hard. I didn't know if I should, or if I would be any good at it. He had only ever kissed my cheek or my neck. Maybe he knew that anything more would cross a line.

Or maybe he didn't want to kiss me at all. Maybe I was reading this wrong. Maybe he didn't feel what I felt. The thought ripped me out of the moment, and my body stiffened as I took a step back. [I'm going to change now.]

"Yeah." He cleared his throat and ran a hand through his hair. "Me too."

Neither of us waited. We disappeared into our rooms, and I took my time changing into my pajamas. I didn't want to run into him in the hallway again. I didn't want to risk making this awkward.

25

Ashby

Scottie and Stan seemed to have reached a quiet agreement not to fight tonight. It had to be the way Hailie talked about Scottie that got under Stan's skin. It was enough for him to stand by her side and protect her instead of letting her handle it alone. What happened at the diner made it clear how much he cared about her. There was no denying that, even when things were messy between them, he still stayed.

I knew Scottie didn't take that lightly. She always tried to fix things between them. Even when she pulled back or felt worn down, she never pushed him too far away.

I turned on the first movie I found and set the remote on the armrest. Scottie and Stan were curled up together on the other couch. I sat about a foot away from Milow, who had tucked herself under a blanket. I wanted to pull her closer and hold her the way Stan was holding Scottie, because I knew it would calm her and maybe calm me too, but I'd already made things tense upstairs when I kissed her cheek, and I didn't know how she had taken it. At first, she leaned into me and held my gaze like she wanted more, and then she pulled away so fast it felt like she needed distance immediately. Maybe I needed to slow down. Maybe I needed to back off and give her room, instead of pushing for the closeness I clearly relied on more than she did. I told myself that space didn't mean rejection, even if it felt that way. I glanced over at her anyway, to make sure she was okay, and to see if she still looked comfortable sitting there beside me.

My phone buzzed on the coffee table, and I leaned forward to grab it. "It's Jasper," I said, already answering and bringing the phone to my ear. "Hey."

"Hey, buddy. Are you guys all right?" he asked.

"Yeah, we're good. What's up?"

"I just wanted to check in and let you know Marjorie kicked the two girls out. They're banned from the diner."

I pressed my lips together, satisfaction settling in. "Seriously? That's good news."

"Yeah. Figured you'd want to know. How's Scottie?"

I looked over at her, curled into Stan's side. "She's fine."

"And Milow?"

"Yeah. Milow's fine too," I said, my eyes drifting back to her. "Thanks for checking in."

"Sure. Have a good night."

"You too. Bye, Jasper."

I ended the call and let the phone rest in my lap. "Hailie and Aspen are banned from the diner."

"Good," Stan said, letting out a short laugh. "About time they faced some consequences."

Saturday, September 27th

Two weeks later, I sat on a bench in the changing room, feeling more nervous than I ever had in my life. Nervous didn't even cover it. My chest was tight, my stomach twisted, and my whole body shook like it was about to shut down. The music blasting through my noise-canceling headphones didn't help at all, and I knew drinking that Red Bull minutes earlier had been a mistake. My hands wouldn't stop shaking. I didn't feel ready to swim, even though it was just a friendly meet, and none of this was supposed to matter. Still, my heart raced like I was about to step into something irreversible, and I had this over-whelming sense that if I took one wrong breath, I would break down crying right there in front of everyone.

I tried to understand what was happening to me, why this fear felt so sudden and so extreme, and why my brain kept telling me I wasn't good enough for anything at all. It wasn't new, not really. I had felt the same thing three days earlier at school, right before that stupid physics test I knew I was going to fail. I hadn't paid enough attention in class. I hadn't studied the way I should have. I knew that. I also knew it could have been avoided if I had just focused and put in the effort. But instead of fixing it, my thoughts spi-raled, jumping straight to worst-case scenarios—messing up the entire school year, letting everyone down, proving I didn't belong on the swim team either.

The more I thought about it, the worse it got, until it felt like everything I cared about was slipping out of reach at once. School. Swimming. My future. It all blurred together into this heavy pressure inside of me, like I was already failing before I even got the chance to try.

A hand landed on my shoulder, and when I looked up, Wesley stood there. Everyone had come to watch me swim today, and even with all that support, I didn't want to step out there. One look at his face was enough. I sighed, and that was when I couldn't hold it in any longer. I pulled my headphones off and dropped my face into my hands as my eyes burned. I couldn't stop the tears.

"Oh, buddy…" Wesley sat down beside me and wrapped his arms around me, rubbing my back gently. "Jasper told me to come back here. Said you looked unfocused."

That explained why he was here with me instead of out on the bleachers with the rest of our family.

I didn't speak. I just let him hold me while I tried and failed to get control of my self. I had never felt this exposed before. Nothing had ever pushed me to this point. Or maybe it had, and I'd just ignored it. Maybe I had always been good at burying the bad thoughts and pretending they didn't exist. But whatever I used to do wasn't working anymore.

"What's on your mind, Ash?" he asked, his voice calm. "Talk to me."

I wanted to talk. I wanted to tell him everything that was piling up in my head, but I didn't know if saying it out loud would actually fix anything. I let him hold me a little longer, trying to control my breathing, before I turned my head to look at him.

"It all feels too heavy," I whispered, wiping my eyes with the back of my hand. "I don't know how to do all of this at the same time."

Wes kept one hand on my back. "I wish I could tell you it gets easier," he said honestly. "But I won't lie to you."

That didn't scare me. If anything, it made me want to listen to him. He had lived this already. I'd watched him juggle school and ice hockey for years, watched the exhaustion, the frustration, the nights he came home silent and angry at himself. I saw him break down more than once, and yet, it had worked out for him in the end. But none of it had been smooth.

"But," he continued, tightening his arm around me, "you get stronger. You learn how to carry that weight without it crushing you."

I shook my head. "I feel like I'm failing at everything. I can't focus, then I panic, and then I mess up even more. It's like I'm already behind before I even start."

"You're not failing," Wes said immediately. His voice was firm now, but not harsh. He was speaking with certainty. "You're overwhelmed. There's a difference."

"It doesn't feel like one."

"I know," he said. "It didn't for me either. I thought if I struggled, it meant I wasn't good enough. That if I had to work this hard, then maybe I didn't deserve it." He paused, making sure I was listening to every word he said. "That was bullshit then, and it's bullshit now."

I let out a shaky breath. "What if I go out there and screw this up?"

"Then you screw it up," he said. "And the world keeps turning. One swim doesn't erase who you are or how hard you've worked."

I swallowed, lowering my head. "It feels like it does."

"That's the pressure talking," he replied. "Ash, you

love the water. You started so young, and even then, you were so passionate about it. That won't just disappear."

I knew he was right. "I still love it."

"Good. Then pour your heart into it the way you always have. You don't have to be flawless today," he continued. "You just have to swim your race."

My heart still ached, but his words slowly eased the pain.

"And about school," he added, giving a little shrug. "We'll figure that out together. We can find tutors. Change your training schedule so you have more time to study. Whatever you need. You don't have to go through this alone, even if your brain keeps telling you that you should."

I pressed my forehead against his shoulder, taking in a deep breath that finally helped me calm down.

"You're allowed to struggle," Wes said quietly, cupping the back of my head with his hand. "It doesn't make you weak."

I nodded again, managing a smile as I hugged him. We stayed like that for a moment until the noise in my head slowly disappeared. It wasn't gone fully, but it dulled enough·for me to think again.

Wes shifted and held me at arm's length, looking at me with a serious expression. "No matter what happens out there, we're all on the bleachers cheering you on. Every single one of us."

I sniffed. "Thanks, Wes."

"We'll be loud, too," he added with a raised brow. "Embarrassingly loud. Mom already warned me she's going to scream your name."

My face twisted, and I decided not to fight that because

I couldn't get Mom not to do something she already set her mind to. "Great."

He grinned and got up, then offered me his hand. I took it and let him pull me up.

"And, Ash."

"Yeah?"

"You don't have to be fearless. Being scared or nervous is part of life. Just don't let the fear make the decisions for you."

I appreciated his words, and as much as they meant to me, I was starting to get amused. "All right, dude. Stop talking before you turn into some wise old man."

He grinned and gently patted my cheek. "Eh, too late. Comes with being the older brother. And having this hair." He pointed at his head of bright-blond, almost white hair. Then his expression turned serious again. "You've got this. No matter what the time says, I'm proud of you."

"Thank you."

"Anytime," he said. "Now go do your thing. We'll be right there."

He gave me one last firm pat on the shoulder before heading back toward the door. I watched him leave, then put my headphones back on and used the time I still had left to warm up.

After a few minutes, I shook out my arms and legs, then picked up my phone from the bench. There was a message from Milow that she had sent just a minute ago. I opened and read it, a smile immediately spreading on my face.

Milow: Good luck, Ash. I'm so proud of you! <3

I stared at the message longer than I probably should have. And while Wesley's pep talk did enough to make me feel better, her message somehow gave me the last push I needed to get out there and do my best.

I typed a quick reply.

Me: Thank you, Milow. <3

I locked my phone and slid it into my locker with the rest of my things. After taking another deep breath, I pulled on my cap and goggles, grabbed my towel, and stepped out onto the deck to join Jasper and the rest of my team.

"Are you feeling okay?" Jasper asked.

"Yeah. Thanks, man."

He gave me an encouraging smile before shifting his focus again, and I turned my head toward the bleachers. They were packed today, and it took me a moment to spot my family. I finally found them sitting near the middle, all of them already looking at me with proud smiles on their faces.

I lifted my hand and waved, and they all waved back. I expected Mom to call out my name like Wes had warned me about, but instead she held up a colorful sign that read **GO ASH GO** in big bubble letters. I recognized it immediately. It was the same sign they had made for me at my very first swim meet when I was seven. The fact that Mom had kept it all these years sent a wave of emotions through me, but I forced myself to hold it together.

I decided then that no matter how I placed today, having them there cheering me on was what mattered most.

26

Ashby

Thursday, October 2nd

"How did what I said get me detention?" Stan asked. His expression was serious as we walked down the hallway toward Milow's locker.

"You told Ms. Sartre you have something called Brain Lag Syndrome and that if she didn't give you a B, you were legally required to sue her for malpractice."

Stan scoffed. "It's a legitimate thing, dude. Look it up."

I laughed and shook my head. "I won't look up something that doesn't exist."

"Okay, maybe the Brain Lag Syndrome isn't real, but if a teacher fails to teach you, that's negligence. I'm failing her class because she hasn't found the right way to teach my brain."

"Ever thought that maybe you actually just need to study for once? Ms. Sartre is a great teacher." And he knew that. But Stan was lazy when it came to things he didn't care about, which wouldn't help him graduate next year.

"I just asked for a different learning style."

"You asked her if she could explain algebra using cartoons," I said, laughing again.

"Uh, yeah! Visual learning," he shot back. "Very real."

"You also asked if sleeping during class counted as participation."

"I was just annoyed at that point," he muttered. "All I was trying to say was that a C-minus was basically a crime against my future, and by the Geneva Conventions, she's obligated to fix it."

"Stan," I said, stopping for a second because this was getting ridiculous. "The Geneva Conventions apply to war crimes."

"Exactly." He stared at me with wide eyes and raised brows, as if his point made any sense.

I shook my head and patted his shoulder. "You're a basket case."

We continued walking, and Stan wouldn't let up. "I was just trying to compromise."

"It got you detention."

"That's a temporary setback," he said with a shrug, adjusting his backpack. "She can silence me, but she can't silence the truth."

"The truth being you're an idiot."

We stopped at Milow's locker, and Stan leaned in closer, lowering his voice like he was sharing classified information. "For the record," he said, "I think detention is proof I was onto something."

"Of course," I replied.

He grinned, proud of himself. "Revolutionaries are never appreciated in their time."

"Right." I pressed my lips together and leaned back

against the locker. Then I laughed with a shake of my head, unable to keep a straight face. "I still think you should start taking school more seriously."

"I *am* taking it seriously," he shot back. "I just sometimes am not in the mood for school."

That, unfortunately, made sense. I often wasn't in the mood either. The difference was that I knew I didn't have the luxury to ignore it. No matter how heavy everything felt, I couldn't afford to mess this up. I had goals I wanted to reach in the future.

We waited there, both of us glancing down the hallway every few seconds for Milow. She should've been here by now.

Instead of her walking up to us, Lando did.

He walked toward us fast, with his shoulders tense and his jaw locked. His face was tight with anger, and before I could even register what was happening, he was in front of me. His hand grabbed the collar of my sweater and slammed me back against the lockers.

The metal hit my spine hard.

"You sick fuck," he hissed, his face inches from mine. His eyes were wild. "You always go around messing with girls?"

"What the fuck are you talking about?" I tried to pry his hands off me, but his grip was solid. If there was anyone I didn't want to fight, it was Lando. He trained MMA like Stan, and he was stronger than he looked. And right now, he wasn't thinking, which was the kind of mindset he usually had in a fight.

"Jesus, Lando, get off him!" Stan yelled, trying to push him off me.

"Step back," Lando growled, never taking his eyes off

me. "Think you can mess with my sister and get away with it?"

"I don't know what you're talking about," I said, my jaw tight. Panic crawled up my chest.

"Don't play dumb, Statler," he snapped. "You harassed her."

"Whoa," Stan said, his voice louder now, and trying again to pull him off me. "Slow the hell down. I think you've got the wrong guy."

Lando yanked my collar again and shoved me back into the lockers. Pain shot through my shoulders. My muscles were already sore from practice, and this made it worse. I lifted my hands to protect myself. I wasn't going to fight back. I didn't want this to escalate. I also wasn't convinced I'd win if it did.

"You fucking harassed my little sister," he repeated, like saying it again would make it true.

I swallowed hard. "I swear to you, Lando, I never even talked to her," I forced out. His fists pressed too close to my throat. If anything, I'd done the opposite. I'd avoided Aspen at all costs, and I was nice to her, even when she didn't deserve it.

"Don't act all innocent now," he snarled. "I'm gonna fucking kill you."

Stan snapped at Lando's threat. "Oh, you wanna fight? Fight me, bitch."

He finally got a solid grip on Lando and shoved him hard. Lando stumbled back and slammed into the lockers across the hall with a loud crash.

"Stan," I warned. My chest rose and fell fast. "Let it be."

"No," Stan said, stepping forward. "If he wants to fight, he can fight me. Not that he has a chance."

A crowd had formed around us, watching it all go down with curiosity, waiting for someone to cross a line.

Lando straightened slowly, his breathing heavy. He looked between us, trying to decide whether it was worth it. Then he pointed past Stan, straight at me. "He touched my sister inappropriately."

I shook my head immediately. "I didn't."

Stan let out a dry laugh. "Who'd ever want to touch her?"

That earned him a deadly glare. But Lando didn't move toward him. He knew better than to rile up Stan. He was a menace when he fought.

"What's going on?" Jasper broke through the crowd. Bennett was right behind him. Jasper's eyes moved from Stan to Lando, then landed on me. "You good?"

"Yeah," I said. "I'm fine."

Jasper turned back to Lando, unimpressed. "So what's this about? Why are you losing your mind?"

Lando repeated his accusation, and I finally snapped, unable to hear him blatantly lie any longer. "She flashed me. Out of nowhere. I was swimming, and she showed up and flashed me."

"Liar," Lando spat.

"Shit," Jasper said suddenly. "She did it to you too?"

Everyone froze, and the students around us gasped.

Jasper looked straight at Lando. "About a week ago. She came to the pool and flashed me. Same thing."

Stan whistled low. "Damn," he said, eyes wide and dancing with amusement. "Your sister's kind of out of control, eh?"

Lando looked like he might blow up again, but his expression shifted. The tension in his face didn't disappear fully, but doubt crept in and settled in his eyes. We weren't laughing. We weren't scrambling to defend ourselves. We weren't acting guilty. We had no reason to lie, and he finally saw that.

"Let it go, man," Jasper said calmly. "You should probably talk to your sister about this."

"She does have a habit of lying," Stan added immediately. He had no damn filter. He shrugged, as if commenting on the weather. "She's a crazy witch, if we're being honest. Just saying."

I shot him a look, hoping he wouldn't go further and turn Lando's initial anger on himself. Luckily, Lando had other worries now. He dragged a hand through his hair. He was clearly fighting the instinct to keep defending her. If we had actually harassed her, his reaction would've made sense. But we hadn't done shit.

Stan crossed his arms over his chest, satisfied. "You owe my friend an apology."

Lando muttered something under his breath.

Stan leaned forward, cupping his hand behind his ear. "Sorry, what was that? We didn't quite catch it."

Lando clenched his jaw, then said it louder. "I said I'm sorry."

"There it is," Stan said, nodding like a proud coach. He reached out and patted Lando's shoulder, completely unbothered. "Growth. Accountability. Love to see it. See you at practice, buddy."

Lando didn't respond. He just turned and walked away, disappearing down the hallway with stiff shoulders.

I finally let out the breath I'd been holding and shook my head slowly. "Jesus."

Stan grinned. "You're welcome."

"What happened?" Scottie appeared once the crowd around us thinned out. Instead of answering her myself, I let Stan explain everything while my attention shifted past her to Milow, who had come up behind her.

She looked worried. As soon as she reached me, she lifted her hands while her eyes searched my face. [Are you okay?]

"I'm okay," I told her, forcing a tight smile.

[I heard shouting.]

"I know." I sighed and reached out, rubbing her arm gently to ease her worry. "It's fine. Really."

She wanted to believe me, and though her shoulders relaxed, her expression stayed tense. She didn't push me for further explanation, but I knew she wasn't happy with the answer I gave.

I couldn't tell her the truth, though. I didn't want her to know what Aspen had done. I didn't want her getting upset, or worse—wondering if I'd somehow provoked it. It was irrational. She knew me. She knew I wasn't that kind of guy. Still, the thought of her hurting over something so stupid made my stomach twist.

I smiled at her again, then turned to her locker and spun the combination. It wasn't a secret. I'd asked her for it on her first day of high school, and since getting this new locker for junior year, she hadn't chosen a new one. I glanced back at her once the door opened. "Hungry?"

She nodded and slid her books inside, then grabbed the container with her lunch.

"Good. Me too."

"She did what?!" Scottie's voice cut through our quiet moment, and we all turned as she stared at Jasper, then snapped her gaze to me. "Seriously?"

My stomach dropped, and Milow stiffened beside me. *Shit…*

"She flashed you?" Scottie's eyes went wide. "What a bitch."

"It's fine, Scottie—" Jasper said, but she cut him off immediately.

"It's not fine. That's sexual harassment. You've reported her, right?"

My hands curled into fists at my sides. I hated that Milow was hearing this. She was looking at me, trying to piece together what was going on, but I didn't dare meet her eyes. I knew they'd be full of hurt.

"Lando's taking care of it," Stan said casually.

Scottie shot him a death stare. "Taking care of it? Are you even hearing yourself? She flashed her tits at them, and you don't think that's worth reporting?"

She was right. We were brushing it off. If a guy had done that to Scottie or Milow, I'd be dragging him straight to the principal's office without a second thought. I lifted a hand and rubbed the back of my neck, then looked at Jasper. When he met my eyes, I saw the same realization there. He nodded slowly.

"God, sometimes I really wonder if you guys even have brains," Scottie muttered, shaking her head. Then she looked straight at me. "I expected more from you."

Milow lifted her chin. I glanced at her from the corner of my eye and saw how serious she looked.

[Me too.]

That hit harder than anything else.

"You're right," I said, turning fully toward her. "Jasper and I will go report it to the principal. We should've done it right away."

Milow still wasn't looking at me. Her jaw was tight, and her lips pressed together. That was exactly what I'd been trying to avoid. I didn't want to make things worse, but I couldn't ignore this either. It would only upset her more.

"Milow," I said quietly.

She hugged the food container to her chest and turned her head to the side.

"Milow." I was trying to find the right words.

"He probably didn't even look, Milow," Stan said, trying to help.

Scottie rolled her eyes. "That's not why she's upset."

I frowned and looked between Scottie and Milow. Milow finally looked at me, a bright fire burning in her eyes, and she shifted the container under one arm and signed, [I'm mad because you didn't react right away. She and Hailie get away with things like that without real consequences, and I'm sick of it.]

She wasn't mad at me. I finally understood that. She was angry because there were no real boundaries or fairness when it came to those two girls, and she hated that Aspen wasn't being held accountable. Especially when we should have spoken up much sooner. I slipped an arm around her shoulders and gave her a gentle squeeze. "Milow's right," I said, looking at Jasper. "We should've reported it immediately."

He nodded. "Yeah. Let's go now."

I nodded back, then turned to Milow. "I'll come right after. Go eat."

She looked up at me again, her eyes less fiery now. [Okay.]

I wanted to hold her longer. Pull her close and kiss her. But this wasn't the place or the moment.

"All right, ladies," Stan said, slinging an arm around Milow and Scottie, pulling them into his sides. "Let's eat."

I watched them walk away. Milow glanced back at me once before turning the corner, and then I looked at Jasper.

"All right," I said. "Come on."

27

Milow

Friday, October 10th

Today was the last day before Thanksgiving break, and while I was excited to spend more time at home with my family again, I was even more excited about finally going to the doctor's appointment Mom had set up for me. School was nice today, and all the teachers seemed to be glad to get a week off. For once, no homework was assigned, so everyone could actually enjoy the week-long break. I knew I'd still end up doing a few worksheets on my own, though. I liked keeping my brain active, even when I didn't have to.

I was putting my books into my locker after my last period when Ashby came to stand next to me. He leaned against the locker beside mine in that casual way of his. He smiled, and my cheeks immediately flushed. As much as I loved him, there were moments I resented how effortlessly good he looked.

"Are Mom and Dad picking you up?" he asked, loosely crossing his arms over his chest.

I nodded, closing my locker before turning toward him. [Yes. They'll be here in five minutes.]

"I'll walk you out." He pushed himself off the locker and nodded down the hallway.

I fell into step beside him as we started walking. [Are you coming to the doctor too?] I asked, keeping my body angled toward him while we moved.

"No," he said. "I'm going to Dunst. Ruben's free to come down, so Jasper and I are getting an extra training session in since he won't be around next week."

He'd had practice just yesterday. And on Wednesday. And Monday too. He stayed so focused all the time, and even though he'd gotten better at managing his schedule, I still worried he might be pushing himself too hard again.

[Take it easy, okay?]

He grinned and gently nudged my shoulder with his. "Don't worry about me, Milow. I'm fine."

He'd said that before. And not long after, he'd broken down before that friendly swim meet a couple of weekends ago. Wesley had told me about it later. I'd wanted to help, but I never brought it up. Whatever Wesley had said to him must have helped, and if Ashby had already moved past it, I didn't want to drag him back there again.

We headed outside toward the parking lot and stopped by the benches. He sat down, leaning back and sliding his hands into his hoodie's pocket. When he looked up at me, he wore that lazy smile that always made my knees go weak.

"Sit," he said, nodding to the space beside him.

I bit the inside of my cheek and studied the spot next to him before sitting down, wondering why something so small felt like such a big deal when we had sat next to each other plenty of times before. I blamed it on how close we had gotten lately, and on this new thing that was slowly but steadily growing between us.

I couldn't get too close to him in public without worrying that someone might figure out he had kissed me that night. Okay, there hadn't been an actual kiss yet, but I was scared that wanting to kiss him was written all over my face.

"You're tense," he said, cutting through my thoughts.

I snapped my head toward him and pressed my lips together before giving a small shrug.

"Are you scared to go to the doctor?"

I shook my head and dropped my gaze to my hands resting in my lap. The urge to pick at my skin came instantly, but I stopped myself and tugged my sweatshirt's sleeves over my hands instead. I didn't want him to notice and worry.

"Then what is it?" he asked.

He looked calm. His body was loose against the bench, like nothing in the world weighed on him the way it did on me. Students walked past us on their way to the parking lot. A group of boys stood only a few feet away, messing around and shoving each other. I wondered if any of them noticed how close we were sitting or how stiff my posture was, and whether they noticed that his knee was pressed against mine.

I dared to look at him again. [It's nothing. I guess I'm just tired.]

He raised a thick brow. An amused spark flashed in his eyes. "Tired? You? I don't buy that. You're never tired after school. You're literally the only person I know who goes home and immediately starts doing more schoolwork."

I was proud of that. I'd always been. I never lost focus in school. Still, I hated how easily he saw through me. He knew I was lying. And even though he didn't demand the truth, I couldn't keep the thoughts from spilling out anyway.

[Aren't you scared others will notice?]

My eyes flicked back to his. He tilted his head slightly. "Notice what?"

[Us.]

His brows pulled together, then his eyes widened a little when he understood what I meant. But he still didn't look worried. "Why would I be?" he asked.

[Because we can't—] I dropped my hands, then threw them into the air as frustration slipped through before I could stop it. [What if people figure out what we did?]

I was serious. My chest squeezed, and my thoughts were spinning, but he didn't match my intensity. Instead, the corners of his mouth lifted in a smug grin. "I kind of like the idea of getting caught," he said easily. "It's not like anyone could make us stop feeling what we feel for each other."

That made my heart slam so hard against my ribs that I felt it rise into my throat. He had just admitted his feelings. And he'd spoken mine out loud too. I wanted to stay in that moment and keep talking about this, but I couldn't. It felt too exposing right here in public.

He went quiet for a second, then leaned forward, resting his elbows on his knees. His voice dropped as he spoke. "I get it," he said. "I know this is fragile. But no matter what happens, or who says something, I'm staying by your side. My feelings won't change."

And that, somehow, scared me just as much as it comforted me.

[I don't know if I'm ready to let this be public information.]

That got a chuckle out of him, and it instantly made me frown.

[What?]

"Public information?" he said, clearly amused. "You want to hold a press conference about it while we're at it?"

I scrunched my nose and dropped my gaze back to my hands, feeling stupid for how serious I made it sound.

"I'm kidding," he said, leaning in a bit closer. Just when he opened his mouth again, a car slowed down behind us.

I turned my head to see Mom and Dad inside, and I pushed up from the bench right away.

"Milow."

I paused for a second and looked back at him, then kept walking toward the car.

"We'll talk about this tonight, okay?" he said as he followed me.

I gave him a short nod as we stopped beside the car. He offered a tight smile and opened the door for me. "See you later."

I waved and slid into the seat, pulling the door shut behind me.

"Hey, sweetheart," Dad said, reaching back to give my thigh a quick squeeze. "How was school?"

[Good, thanks.] I smiled at him, then waved at Mom before she turned toward the window and rolled it down.

Ashby leaned in, resting his forearms on the open frame. "Hey. I'm headed to Dunst."

"Training?" Mom asked. "Today?"

"Yeah. Just a quick session since Ruben's not around next week. I'll be home before dinner."

"Okay." Mom reached out and touched his arm.

"Take it easy, champ," Dad added.

"I will. Bye."

He tapped the door as he stepped back. The car started rolling, and I kept my eyes on him until he disappeared from view.

As much as I wanted this to be simple, like any other couple walking out of school together, touching without thinking about others judging, I wasn't even sure that's what this was. I didn't know if we were moving toward something serious or if I had read too much into all the stolen looks and quiet moments. Maybe I had filled in the blanks because I wanted them filled.

I pressed my lips together and stared at my hands in my lap, trying to calm the thoughts spinning through my head. I wanted clarity, but I didn't know how to reach it without being vulnerable. I would have to open up to him and be honest about what I felt, which, generally, wouldn't be an issue. But it meant risking rejection, and I had never thought I handled that well.

There was a new wallpaper in the waiting room at the doctor's office. It had a jungle theme, with trees and leaves layered over each other, and while it was probably meant to calm patients, it made me anxious to find every animal hidden behind the bushes before I got called in. The longer I looked, the louder my thoughts became. My head buzzed again. No matter how hard I tried, I could only ever truly slow my mind down when I went to sleep.

I had wondered if I had ADHD before, but I knew I didn't. Stan definitely had it. I secretly diagnosed him with it many years ago. I pursed my lips and kept staring at the wall while Mom and Dad flipped through a magazine together. They spoke in low voices, snickering softly as they pointed at something on the page. My eyes snapped to them for a moment, and I smiled at the sight. They always looked so happy, which, in return, made me happy.

My foot bounced against the tile.

This was supposed to be a normal appointment—a general checkup, nothing more. Yet the longer I sat there, the stranger the feeling in my chest became. As if some part of me already knew something was off, even if I couldn't explain it—or knew that nothing was wrong.

When the nurse called my name, I pushed the feeling down and stood. We followed her down the hallway, where she made me go through the usual routine. Scale. Blood pressure. Height. All normal. I'd grown a few inches and now stood at five-three. It was a stupid thing to be proud of, but I was anyway. She took a small blood sample from my finger, then smiled and told us to wait in the exam room.

I perched on the edge of the table while Mom and Dad sat in the chairs near the wall. Dad leaned back with his arms crossed, and they both looked calm.

The doctor finally came in with a clipboard and an easy smile. He greeted my parents first, then nodded at me. "Good to see you, Milow."

I waved and watched him sit down at his desk. He looked at his computer screen for a moment, humming quietly to himself.

"I have your stats here, and everything looks good," he said at last, then paused. "But…"

My stomach dropped.

But what? But something's wrong. But there's a problem. My thoughts jumped too fast, spiraling before he even continued. *You have diabetes. You have cancer. You're dying!*

He glanced back at the screen, his eyes narrowing slightly. "You do have low iron levels."

Gosh, he could've set that up differently.

I stared at him, unsure how to react.

"Do you eat meat, Milow?" he asked.

I nodded.

"Not a vegetarian?"

I shook my head.

"All right. That's easy to fix," he said. "Iron-rich foods can help raise your iron levels. Red meat. Spinach. Broccoli. All the good stuff."

I smiled tightly and nodded again. Mom and Dad always cooked balanced meals, and I ate everything they cooked for us.

After checking a few more things on the screen, his gaze lingered on me. It shifted to my throat, and there was a question in his eyes. *You're still not talking.* But he didn't say it. He just watched me a moment longer before turning to my parents.

"Have you already discussed the surgery?" he asked.

I frowned.

The surgery?

I looked at Mom. Then Dad. Neither of them spoke. Their calm expressions cracked, panic flashing across their faces so fast it made my stomach twist.

Confusion rushed in hard. My hands lifted without me thinking, moving automatically as I searched for answers. Maybe he had mixed me up with another patient. Maybe he meant someone else.

[What surgery?]

Mom's posture stiffened, and Dad cleared his throat. They weren't looking at me.

"I think maybe this isn't—" Dad started, but the doctor cut him off gently.

"I'm sorry," he said. "I assumed this had already been discussed. She's going to be eighteen soon."

Only in two years.

My hands hovered in my lap, frozen mid-thought, as one question drowned out all the others.

What surgery were they talking about?

What was wrong with me?

And why were Mom and Dad not looking at me?

28

Ashby

"Tell me again why you're here?" Jasper asked, glancing at Stan, who was grinning from ear to ear.

"I'm here to dive. Duh." Stan pointed dramatically toward the diving tower, his face dead serious now. "You guys swim your little laps, and I get to have fun jumping from the ten-meter platform."

I chuckled. Stan had sprinted over to my car just before Jasper and I got in and practically begged to come with us to the aquatic center. He hadn't brought swim shorts or a towel, but luckily for him, I always kept a second pair of jammers in my locker. That was what he was wearing now.

"At least you'll look professional jumping," I said, pursing my lips in amusement.

He grinned again and reached down, cupping his crotch with one hand. "They're pretty damn tight, but I guess I won't be losing them when I hit the water."

"Definitely not," Jasper added with a laugh, shaking his head.

"Boys!" Ruben called from the other side of the pool. "Let's get this session started. Warm up with ten laps. Nice and easy."

I dropped my towel on the bench and slapped Stan on the back. "Go play, kiddo."

He smirked. "Thanks, Dad."

He jogged off toward the diving pool, and I rolled my eyes as Jasper laughed again.

"He'll be like this at fifty."

"Oh, I know. I'm prepared for that."

After our warm-up laps, Ruben wasted no time and sent us straight into a race. Once that was over, he had us move out of the water for a round of strength exercises. My shoulders were already burning when we started lifting.

"How often are you going to the gym?" he asked.

"Twice a week," Jasper replied without hesitation. And it showed. His arms and shoulders had filled out, and even his legs looked noticeably stronger than they had a few months ago.

"Good," Ruben said, then shifted his attention to me. "Ashby?"

I flinched. I hadn't set foot in the gym in weeks. Mostly because I hadn't had the time. And when I did, I usually didn't have the energy or the motivation. "I haven't been in a while," I admitted carefully.

Ruben hummed, studying me while I lowered the dumbbells to my sides. My shoulders screamed in protest as the muscles worked hard.

"You feeling strong enough with just swim practice?" he asked next, his eyes staying locked on mine as if he already knew the answer.

"Yes, I do," I said honestly. "But I plan on getting more workouts in." It sounded like a promise, not just to him, but to myself. I knew skipping strength training could set me back, especially with the goals I had. I didn't want to risk that.

"You can come work out with me," Jasper chimed in. "I go to the gym every Tuesday and Thursday before school. Even Stan shows up sometimes."

"Sounds good," I replied, giving him a tight smile. "Thanks."

"Of course, buddy."

Before we could say anything else, a loud, pained cry echoed through the entire aquatic center. We all turned toward the diving pool just in time to see Stan hauling himself out of the water. His face was bright red, twisted in pain, and when he stood upright, his chest was the same alarming shade.

I grimaced. "You okay, Stan?" I called over.

"No," he choked, one hand clutching his chest, the other firmly guarding his crotch. "I think I broke my balls."

Jasper laughed and shook his head, clearly unwilling to feel even a shred of sympathy. I could've warned Stan not to jump from that height without knowing any actual diving techniques. But even if I had, he would've done it anyway.

"My balls," Stan groaned again, drawing out a dramatic breath. "I need to go to the hospital."

"You'll be fine, son," Ruben called back, not sounding nearly as amused as the rest of us. He'd known Stan since he was little. He was well aware of his reckless tendencies, and he'd stopped feeling sorry for him a long time ago.

"My balls are aching, Ruben!" Stan cried, still cupping

himself. Then he tugged the jammers away from his body and glanced down. "Holy shit…they're turning blue. Come look," he urged, turning toward us.

"No, thank you," Jasper said immediately, already turning back to lift his dumbbells.

Ruben turned away, clearly done with Stan and his theatrics.

I chuckled. "Maybe stop jumping from up there. You'll break your neck next time."

"Hey, I'm a great diver," Stan shot back defensively. "I should've picked that as my sport instead of MMA."

"No, Stan," I said dryly. "You're doing just fine in MMA."

"But I'm a good diver."

I didn't respond.

"Ash, dude," he called. "Tell them I'm a good diver."

"Don't encourage him," Jasper warned without looking over.

"I won't," I replied, smirking as Stan groaned in frustration.

———

On our drive back to Bowen, Stan wouldn't stop whining about his balls. And while any other person would've gotten annoyed by his whining, I started to feel bad for him. He was in real pain, and being a guy with balls myself, I knew how hurtful that could be.

I looked at him through the rearview mirror, grimacing when I saw the pain lingering in his eyes. "Sure you don't want to go to the hospital?"

"And tell the doctors my balls hurt? Thanks, but I don't want to embarrass myself like that," Stan huffed.

"You might get your balls checked out by a hot nurse," Jasper added. He wasn't taking this as seriously as I was, and it showed through his amusement.

To be fair, it was funny. But then again, the pain Stan was feeling wasn't.

Stan's expression changed, and I prepared for a clever response. "When you put it that way…get me to the fucking hospital so I can get my balls checked out by a hot nurse."

Jasper and I laughed.

"Jokes aside," I said, focusing on the road again. "Hospital. Yes or no?"

He thought about it for a good thirty seconds, then shook his head. "No. I'll just put a pack of frozen peas on it, and the swelling will go down."

We were quiet after the mention of his swollen balls until Jasper broke the silence. "How are things with Scottie?"

A loud sigh ripped out of Stan. "Fine? Bad? I don't know. I texted her this morning, but she ignored it."

"What did you text her?" I asked.

"If she wants to come over tonight, so we can Netflix and chill."

He said it so nonchalantly, I flinched. "Dude…"

Jasper sighed. "Stan."

"What?"

"Come on. You can't possibly be the only guy who doesn't know what that stands for," I said, half surprised at how unaware he was. We had grown up together. We were best friends. But sometimes it felt like he missed things that were so obvious to me. Maybe it was his fuck-everyone's-opinions-other-than-mine mindset, but he couldn't possibly be that oblivious to something so obvious.

"To watch Netflix and chill. It's literally in the saying," he explained, but he was painfully wrong.

"No, Stan," I said, laughing because I couldn't believe I had to lecture him on simple teenage slang. Granted, he didn't use his phone often. Didn't have all those social media apps everyone else was addicted to. But he must've heard that phrase somewhere.

"You asked her to hook up," Jasper told him, turning his head to look back at him.

I glanced into the rearview mirror again, watching his reaction. He was frowning, genuinely baffled.

"No, I didn't. I asked her to come over to watch a movie and relax. Okay, maybe I hoped to cuddle with her or whatever, but definitely not hook up."

"That's what it means," Jasper went on. "It used to mean actually watching a movie and hanging out, but it turned into this euphemism for having sex."

"Yup," I said.

"No way…"

"Maybe that explains why she ignored the text," I suggested with a shrug. "Try taking it back."

"Shit, shit, shit, shit." I heard him fumble for his phone in his backpack, then he spoke again, probably recording a voice message. "Scottie? Ignore my last message. I didn't know that Netflix and chill means sex. I don't want sex with you—"

I glanced at Jasper, who was looking at me with the same amused expression.

"I mean, shit, I do want to have sex with you someday because you're, like, so hot and my best friend. But I want it if you want it too. But not tonight. Tonight I want to hang out with you and actually watch a movie or two, and you can talk during them and tell me all the silly little facts you know. And then we can order pizza, and I'll even let you order the one with anchovies and olives. I'm sorry, Scottie. I didn't know. Motherfucker…"

"I hope that last bit you didn't record," I said, peeking at him again.

"No." He frowned, sighing heavily. "Goddammit. Who takes something simple and innocent and twists it into something that can be misinterpreted?"

Jasper laughed. "To be fair…you're the first one to turn innocent things sexual. Even if you don't mean to."

"Right," Stan muttered.

We stayed quiet until I pulled over in front of Jasper's house. He leaned forward to grab his backpack from the floor, then turned toward me. "Thanks for the ride. Happy Thanksgiving."

"Yeah. Happy Thanksgiving," I said. "See you after the break."

"Bye, Jasper," Stan added.

Jasper shut the door behind him and headed up the walkway. Stan climbed into the front seat, and I waited until he buckled his seatbelt before pulling back onto the road.

"She texted back," he said.

"Yeah?" I glanced at him. "What'd she say?"

He looked down at his phone, then groaned. "Ah, damn…"

"What?"

"She said, 'I would've said yes to Netflix and chill, but you took it back.'"

I lifted a brow, then pressed my lips together. "Well…"

"I could've had sex tonight," he blurted, then waved it

off. "Shit. Never mind. Hold on." His thumbs moved fast. "Now she texted again. 'JK. I'd love movies and a pizza.'"

Scottie was obviously messing with him, but I was relieved neither of them seemed eager to push things into something messy. Or messier than they already were. "That's good," I said, a small smile pulling at my mouth.

"Yeah. I guess it is."

"Don't fuck it up."

He let out a dry laugh. "Yeah. Like that's not my strong suit."

"You're not that bad," I said. "You just need to use your brain a little more sometimes."

"Heard that before."

"So try listening. People don't tell you that for fun. We mean it."

He sighed, then nodded, resting his head against the headrest. "I know. And I do appreciate it."

"Good." I turned onto his street and slowed in front of his house. "If Scottie comes over tonight and you actually want to impress her, maybe stop by the store first."

"And get her what?"

"Her favorite chocolate," I said. "A book she might like. Something that shows you've been thinking about her."

He studied me with those deep blue eyes for a second, then nodded. "Yeah. I might."

I pulled to the curb. He grabbed his backpack, opened the door, then paused. "Hey," he said. "Thanks. For all of it."

"Anytime," I replied. "And put those frozen peas on your balls."

He chuckled and shut the door, then jogged up the

driveway as I drove off. My parents' car was already in the driveway when I pulled up to the house, and I parked beside it, cutting the engine before getting out. I was ready to unwind and let my body relax. My thoughts kept drifting back to Milow, hoping her doctor's appointment had gone well. I'd missed her all afternoon, and I caught myself hoping she'd want to watch a movie with me tonight.

But when I entered the house, excited to see her again, my stomach dropped at the sight of her.

29

Ashby

"What happened?" I asked, my heart thudding hard against my ribs. "Why is she crying?"

My eyes moved between Mom and Dad, then landed on Wesley. I held his gaze longer than the others, silently begging him to explain whatever they were keeping from me. His ice-blue eyes were red and swollen. He looked like he'd been crying too.

"What happened?" I asked again. I couldn't bring myself to look at Milow again. She was staring down at her hands, with her shoulders drawn in. She wasn't looking up at me either. Panic crawled up my spine. I hated this. Hated that everyone seemed to know something I didn't, and that they wouldn't just tell me.

"What the fuck happened?" I demanded, my voice rising despite myself.

"Come sit down, champ," Dad said gently, patting the space beside him.

But I ignored him.

I didn't want to sit next to Dad. I wanted to be next to Milow. So I crossed the room and sat down beside her instead, immediately taking both her hands in mine. I leaned closer, my brows knitting together. "Milow, are you okay?"

She didn't look up.

A sick, hollow feeling settled deep in my gut. Something was wrong. Something bad had happened, and my first irrational thought was that I'd done something. I knew I hadn't. I would never hurt her. Not her. Not anyone. Ever. Still, the questions kept coming. Why wouldn't she look at me? Why was she crying? Why was nobody telling me what the fuck was going on?

"Ash," Mom said softly, her voice breaking as she sniffed back tears. "There is something we want to tell you."

"What?" The word came out sharper than I meant it to. I didn't care anymore. I needed answers, and I needed them now. I tightened my grip on Milow's hands. I knew she wouldn't sign. Not in the state she was in. And I needed her touch to keep me calm. But on the inside, I was breaking apart.

Mom took a breath and looked at Dad. "Gus…"

He nodded and rubbed his hands together, staring down at the floor as if the right words were written there. When he finally looked up, his lips were pressed tight.

"Son," he said quietly, "I need you to be strong, okay?"

My chest tightened again. "Did someone die?" My head snapped toward Wesley. "Where's Evie?"

"Evie's okay," Wesley said quickly. "She's with her parents this weekend."

I looked back at Dad with my brows raised and my heart racing.

"Nobody died," Dad said. "Nobody's hurt. This is about Milow."

I felt my heart break for her, without knowing what it was. I'd been bracing for it without realizing.

"What about Milow?" I squeezed her hands harder, and she squeezed back. I still couldn't look at her. If I did, I knew I'd fall apart. I just needed to feel her there. To know she was with me, and that whatever they were about to say could be fixed. For her, I'd fix anything, no matter how difficult it would be.

I stopped asking questions then. Because the more I questioned everything, the worse my thoughts became. So, I waited.

"Your mother and I have been keeping something from you," Dad said slowly. He cleared his throat. "From all of you kids. Not because we thought we could hide it forever, but because we were waiting for the right time."

"Go on," I said, my jaw locking. My patience was gone.

Dad's eyes flicked to Milow. His face tightened, and his jaw clenched. His eyes filled with tears, but he fought them. He'd already cried today. All of them had.

"You see," he said carefully, "Milow...she's mute."

I frowned. "Yeah. No shit."

The words came out harsher than I ever spoke. This conversation was dragging something ugly out of me. It was turning me into someone I didn't want to be or had ever been.

"She chooses not to speak," I added.

Dad shook his head slowly. "That's not—" He stopped, glanced at Milow, then back at me. "She can't speak."

I stared at him. "What do you mean she can't speak?"

Nothing felt real. This had to be a nightmare. Some warped dream. Maybe I'd hit my head swimming. Maybe I was unconscious. But then Milow squeezed my hands again, and I knew I was wide awake.

"Milow doesn't have vocal cords."

The words didn't make sense. Everyone had vocal cords.

I just stared at him, my brows drawn together, unable to form another question. Were they messing with me? Was this a sick joke?

"You see, champ," Dad continued, his voice heavy as he let his head drop again. His hands rubbed together. When he looked up, he looked at Milow first. "Milow, how much can I tell him?"

"Everything!" I snapped. "Tell me everything!"

Milow looked at Dad and nodded slowly, giving him permission.

Mom reached out and rubbed Dad's back. He inhaled deeply, calming himself.

"When Milow was little," he said, "before we adopted her…she lived alone with her father. Her father was a doctor. A surgeon."

I couldn't look away from him. His face hardened, anger cutting deep lines into his expression. Whatever came next burned inside him. I had never seen him like this, and it scared me shitless.

Milow's fingers curled in my hands. She started picking at her thumb. I caught it immediately and threaded my fingers through hers, stopping her from hurting herself.

"When Milow was four years old—" Dad stopped.

My heart slammed against my chest.

"When she was four," he said, voice breaking, "her father removed her—"

A low, broken sound tore from his throat. He swallowed hard, forcing the words out before the tears fell.

"He removed her vocal cords. By surgery."

Dad was crying now. His jaw trembled, his hands curling into tight fists before he finally dropped his face into them. Mom stayed strong for him, holding herself together when he couldn't. Wesley, who had been sitting in the armchair, got up and moved closer. He sat beside Dad and wrapped an arm around his shoulders, pulling him in without a word.

I was too overwhelmed to even form a clear thought. Anger was there, but it tangled with disbelief. After what he'd just told me, it felt impossible that this was real life. It was like I was inside someone else's nightmare. I must've been asleep. There was no other explanation.

Why would a father do that? Why would anyone want to remove their daughter's vocal cords? What was the purpose? What could be gained from it? The questions piled up, one after another, each worse than the last. There was no logic to it. No explanation that could make sense. Just cruelty. Just something horrific done to a child who should have been protected.

I had never learned about Milow's past, and now… this. Her father was a sick bastard.

My chest hurt, and my head buzzed.

Finally, I looked at Milow. I needed to see her eyes.

"Milow," I said quietly.

I wasn't sure why I needed her to look at me. But even though I knew I wasn't the reason she was this upset, that bad feeling wouldn't leave. Guilt pressed down inside of me. I hated that I hadn't been there for her when her father did that to her, even if I would've only been a kid myself. I hated that I hadn't known the truth. That Mom and Dad had kept it from us. From me. From Wesley. And from Milow too. But why?

My head snapped toward my parents. "Did Milow not know? I mean…if she can't speak—"

I stopped myself.

I hated that I couldn't ask Milow directly. And the thought made my stomach twist. If she couldn't speak, why would she believe she might one day? But the second that question formed, I felt disgusted with myself. It wasn't fair. I had no right to accuse her of pretending or lying. This wasn't about me.

This was her story.

And I was getting upset over something I had no fucking right to make into a big deal.

"I'm sorry," I added quickly, shaking my head as I pulled my hands away from hers and ran them through my hair. "I just… I don't understand."

"It's okay, Ash," Wesley said. He moved again, this time coming to sit beside Milow. He reached around her back, squeezed my shoulder, and rested his other hand over Milow's. He was being the protective big brother he always had.

"No, it's not okay." I frowned, shaking my head again. "Has she been forced to believe that she would someday start speaking again if she wanted to?"

Mom looked at me first, then her gaze shifted to Milow.

Guilt sat heavy in her eyes, and I hated it because it told me everything. That was exactly what had happened. Still, I knew it couldn't have been easy for them either.

"We didn't want to overwhelm her," Mom said softly.

"She was little. She…" She stopped, her gaze returning to Milow with a smile that hurt more than it helped. "We wanted the best for her. At first, we hoped that maybe… maybe there was a way. That she could speak again someday."

I couldn't blame them.

Mom was right. None of this could have been easy. Finding out what Milow's biological father had done. Taking her in, trying to protect her, and figuring out how much truth a child could handle. None of this was their fault. If anything, they saved her. They gave her a real family. They gave all of us a home filled with love and safety.

We were all grateful for that.

I swallowed the shock and drew in a slow breath, forcing myself to stay calm. "Where is her father now?" I asked. "In jail? A psychiatric hospital?"

Milow stiffened beside me.

I turned to her immediately and took her other hand. "I'm so sorry," I said quietly.

She finally looked at me.

The pain in her eyes was deeper than anything I had ever seen. She looked broken in a raw and devastating way.

"Her father…" Mom started.

I looked back at her, bracing myself and hoping for something that would satisfy me.

"He died," Mom said. "Shortly before Milow came to live with us."

Thank fuck.

That bastard wasn't alive anymore.

Milow pulled her hand from mine and stood up. Fresh tears streamed down her cheeks, her body visibly shaking. She didn't want to sit here anymore. I could feel it.

[I'd like to be alone,] she signed.

"Are you sure, sweetheart?" Dad asked. He'd finally managed to calm himself, though his voice was still rough.

Milow nodded.

"What about dinner?" Mom asked, forcing a smile.

[I'm not very hungry right now.]

With that, she turned and headed upstairs.

I stayed where I was, frozen in place.

I didn't know how I was supposed to keep living like normal after what I now knew. All I knew was that I needed to stay strong. For Milow. And for myself.

———

I only ate because I was hungry after this afternoon's swim practice. Even then, I barely managed it. I ate just enough to keep myself upright, because I knew if I forced more down, I'd get sick. My stomach was already twisted. I couldn't stand the thought of Milow sitting alone in her room. She had asked for space, and I wanted to respect that. Still, every part of me wanted to hold her. To make sure she wasn't alone with this.

After dinner, Mom set a plate of food aside for Milow. She and Dad talked in low voices, their words muffled but heavy with the pain they had been carrying for years. Wesley and I headed upstairs to his room, and the second the door closed behind us, I broke.

I didn't just cry. I fell apart.

The sobs tore out of me uncontrollably. I'd held everything in for too long, and once it started, I couldn't stop. Wesley wrapped his arms around me and rubbed my back. I cried harder than I ever had in my life. I couldn't remember a time I'd cried like this. Not since before Mom and Dad adopted us. Not since before I ever felt safe.

"She's strong," Wesley murmured into the side of my neck. "She's getting through this. And we'll be there for her. Just like we always have been."

I nodded against his shoulder, not trusting myself to speak. I wasn't ready to let go yet. We stood there in the middle of his room for a long time before I finally pulled back. I wiped my face with the backs of my hands.

"I just can't imagine what she had to go through living with that monster," I said hoarsely. "What if he—" I stopped myself. I couldn't finish the thought. But the question that had been circling my mind wouldn't leave. "Why would someone do something so gruesome to a child?"

Wesley ran a hand through his bright-blond hair, then nodded toward the bed. We sat down side by side.

"He had a reason," he said quietly. "A sick and twisted one."

He knew more. I could hear it in his voice. And even though part of me wanted to stay ignorant, I needed to know.

My jaw tightened. "What did he do to her?"

Wesley leaned forward, resting his elbows on his knees, and rubbing his hands together. He had the same mannerisms as Dad. Always had. I'd joked about it before, that Wesley had to be his biological son. They were too alike.

I braced myself when Wesley started talking again.

"Milow was six when she found her father dead in his bed," Wesley said. "She'd been waiting for him to wake up. He never came downstairs. So she went to his room and found him there. Dad said he had a heart attack."

My jaw was locked, and I stayed silent. I needed to hear it all. Every single detail.

"That night," Wes continued, "Milow stepped outside the house for the first time in her life. Her father never let her out. Never took her anywhere. He never planned to. It's not clear if she understood that he was dead, but she went outside anyway, looking for help. She was wearing only her pajamas, and her father's boots and gloves. There was a lot of snow that night. She didn't know where she was going, but she walked until she reached the fire station. That's where Dad found her."

I stared at him. "What do you mean, Dad found her?"

Wesley held my gaze. "Milow's old house and the fire station are on the main road here in Bowen. Her house was at one end, and the fire station was on the other. She walked that entire stretch by herself in the dark. Dad was working that night. He took her in and called the police and child services."

It didn't sound real. It sounded like a nightmare someone made up to scare people. And then, realization hit me hard. Milow was only six years old when she found her father dead. She walked outside for the first time in her life. Alone. In the snow. Unable to speak and looking for help.

I couldn't make up my mind accept it. I kept going over it again and again, but it never settled.

It had to be a miracle. Or pure luck. Either way, she had made it to safety.

But what hurt the most was knowing how close she had been the whole time, and no one ever knew. While she was trapped in that house with that monster, we were only a few streets away, living our lives, safe and unaware of the cruelty that was going on in that house.

"How did she—" My voice cracked. "How did Dad figure out what was wrong?"

"He didn't, really. The police later did. Dad asked her questions, but she stayed silent," Wes said. "Apparently, after her father removed her vocal cords, he never taught her how to sign. Maybe one or two signs. But not enough to actually communicate."

Rage surged through me in violent waves. I wanted to punch the wall and scream at the top of my lungs. But I stayed still.

Then I realized he still hadn't answered my question.

"Why did he remove her vocal cords?"

Wesley let out a heavy sigh. He'd been avoiding this part.

"Her father abused her, Ashby," he said. "And because no one knew she existed—and because he didn't want anyone to find out what he was doing in that house—he silenced her."

That was it.

My stomach twisted violently, and before I could react, I doubled over and threw up right there on Wesley's bedroom floor.

"Shit," he murmured, immediately rubbing my back. "It's okay, champ."

But nothing was okay.

Milow had lived through hell.

Her voice was taken from her.

And with it, the innocence no child should ever lose got ripped away before she even had the chance to understand what was happening to her.

And her father? He got the easy way out.

"You feeling better?" Wesley asked as he handed me a glass of water.

He'd made me lie down on his bed after I threw up, even though I'd tried to argue and help him clean the floor myself. He hadn't let me. He'd told me to stay put. That's the way he always got when he knew I needed someone else to take control for a minute.

I hadn't expected my body to react like that. I'd never thrown up from shock or emotion before. But hearing what Milow had been through had caused this violent and uncontrollable reaction. My body hadn't been able to process it, and so it rejected that information.

"Yeah. Thanks," I said. I took a few sips of the water, forcing myself to keep it down, then set the glass on the bedside table. I leaned back against the pillows with a quiet sigh, staring at the wall while more tears rolled down my cheeks. "She's kept all of that to herself this whole time. She never told me."

I didn't think I was owed the truth. I knew this was her story and her pain. But it still hurt. I wished I had known sooner. I wished I could have been there for her. Maybe if I'd known, I could have held her tighter.

"And she's still here," Wesley said gently, his pale eyes watching me closely. "She's living. She's strong. Milow went through something no child should ever have to survive, and still, she's brave and has the kindest heart. It's not normal to have gone through something so heavy and end up a good person."

I looked at him as his expression softened further. He reached out and pressed his hand flat against my chest, right over my heart. "Just like you," he said quietly. "You've been through a lot of cruelty too. And you turned out to be an incredible person."

I didn't want to think about my life before Mom and Dad adopted me. I rarely did anymore. It stayed buried because the life I had now was safe and full of people who loved me. Thinking about the past always felt like opening a door I'd worked hard to keep closed.

I lowered my gaze and placed my hand over his, squeezing it gently.

We sat in silence for a moment. Then another question pushed its way into my mind. "What about her mother?" I asked quietly. "Was she not around when all of that happened?"

Wesley pressed his lips together and shrugged. "Mom and Dad asked the police about Milow's mother. They tried to find her. But there was nothing. No records, no contact information. She probably left not long after Milow was born."

That didn't make any part of the story easier. If anything, it made it worse. More anger settled inside me. I tried not to let it take over, because the more I let myself feel the bitterness and anger, the more my stomach threatened to revolt again.

"Okay," I said quietly, lifting my eyes back to Wesley. "Thank you for telling me, Wes."

"Yeah," he replied with a smile. He dropped his hand and patted my thigh before standing up. He crossed the room and opened the window, letting the cold air push out the sour smell still clinging to the floor. "You want to watch a movie? Just something dumb. Take your mind off it for a bit."

I shook my head. "I think I'm just going to go to bed."

"All right." He watched me carefully as I sat up and swung my legs over the side of the bed. "You need anything, you come get me."

"Thanks." I glanced at the floor and pressed my lips together. "And…sorry about the puking."

He waved it off without hesitation. "Don't worry about it."

I gave him a tight smile and left his room, heading upstairs. I needed to brush my teeth and get that foul taste out of my mouth.

30

Milow

I'd fallen asleep not long after coming up to my room. My mind had been exhausted from everything I'd learned today, and my body had followed. I hadn't fought it. The few hours of sleep I got had been deep, and when I woke up, I wasn't tired anymore. The clock told me it was past midnight. Sleep wouldn't come easily anymore. Not with how much my mind buzzed.

I lay on my back and stared up at the dark ceiling. After a few minutes, I reached for the book I'd been reading. I turned on the lamp and tried to focus, hoping the story would pull me in enough to let me forget about reality, or at least pull me back into sleep. I wanted my eyes to get heavy again, and I wanted my thoughts to quiet down.

But it didn't work.

The words on the page didn't make sense in my mind, and I read the same sentence over and over without absorbing any of it. My mind kept drifting and dragging me back to everything I didn't want to think about, and I couldn't escape. No matter how hard I tried, I couldn't shut it out.

Today, I learned the truth. Not the version I'd been fed as a child. Not the lie crafted by the man who was supposed to protect me and instead became my abuser. Deep down, I had always known I couldn't use my voice ever again. That knowledge had lived somewhere, buried deep, and was pushing its way out at the most convenient time. The nightmares I'd had over the years hadn't been dreams. They'd been on my mind, trying to tell me what my conscious self wasn't ready to face. But I'd been a child. I'd been naïve enough to believe in the story I'd been given. I'd believed that something magical had taken my voice away because I'd been good and obedient.

Now I knew the truth.

And the strangest part was that it didn't hurt the way I'd expected it to. Losing my voice itself wasn't the deepest pain. I'd already lived with that reality. I'd adapted to it, and I'd survived without it all these years.

What broke me was knowing why.

My own father had taken it from me to silence me. He had done it so I couldn't call for help and couldn't scream to get an outsider's attention when he abused me.

I squeezed my eyes shut, trying to suppress the memories of when I was just a child, but they still surged forward anyway.

All the nights in his bedroom.

The weight of his body over mine.

The way my body had frozen while my mind begged for an escape I knew I didn't have.

I tried to breathe, but my lungs wouldn't fill properly, and only when he let me go was I able to breathe.

I sat up abruptly and pulled my knees to my chest, wrapping my arms around my legs and resting my chin against them. I focused on my breathing.

I let the quiet voice inside my head speak. To remind myself where I was and that I was safe in this house. I wasn't trapped like I once had been, and I had parents who loved me. Parents who had chosen me and protected me in every way they knew how.

I wasn't angry with them for not telling me the truth sooner. I understood why they hadn't. They'd wanted to shield me from it and to give me a childhood that wasn't defined by what had been done to me. And honestly, I didn't think knowing earlier would have changed any-thing. I hadn't been ready then.

Maybe I was only just ready now.

I turned my head toward the door. My heart was pulling me toward Ashby on the other side of the hall. He was probably asleep, and I didn't want to wake him just so he could see me like this. I was restless, anxious, and barely holding myself together. But maybe he was already deep under, and maybe I could slip into his room the way I had so many times before. I would be quiet and careful, and I'd crawl into his bed without waking him at all.

Just the thought of being next to him calmed me, and the urge to go was now too strong to ignore.

I pushed myself off the bed and padded to the door, opening it slowly so it wouldn't creak. It was dark out in the hallway, and I crossed it on bare feet with cautious steps. My heart skipped a beat as I reached his door, and I paused there with my hand hovering over the handle. Then, I finally pushed the door open.

Just like I had expected, Ashby was asleep. He was lying on his back, with his head turned toward the door, and the sight of him made something deep inside me tingle funnily. I had felt that before, but I had always told myself not to let that exact feeling grow stronger. Now…I didn't feel like suppressing it, despite the line it would cross.

I stepped inside and closed the door behind me, moving closer until I stood beside his bed. For a moment, I just watched him. His face was soft, but his thick brows were gently drawn together, as if he was thinking about something he didn't like. Maybe he was having a bad dream. I reached out before I could stop myself, my fingers brushing his hand where it rested on the mattress.

I caressed his palm, feeling just how warm his hand was compared to mine. His fingers twitched, but he wasn't waking up. My eyes moved to the empty spot next to him. I wanted to lie down right there and press my body against his. I wanted to hear him breathe, and I wanted to put my head on his chest and listen to his heartbeat.

His fingers suddenly curled around mine, and I looked at his face again, my eyes wide.

Ashby stirred and turned onto his side, his eyes opening slowly. Confusion flashed across his face, then relief came over him as he saw me.

"Milow?" he whispered. He tightened his grip on my hand and pushed himself up to sit. "Are you okay?"

I shook my head. I couldn't lie to him.

His expression fell. Even in the dark, I could see the tears gather in his eyes. He didn't say anything else. He just reached for me and pulled me onto the bed with him. He shifted back until he was leaning against the headboard, then wrapped his arms around me and drew me close. I settled against his chest and closed my eyes. His heartbeat was fast under my ear, and his body was tense, holding in too much.

It was quiet for a moment, but then his breathing changed. It caught in his throat, and his chest hitched beneath me.

"I'm so sorry," he whispered, his voice breaking. "I'm so fucking sorry you went through that."

His arms tightened in a desperate attempt to hold me even tighter. I wasn't sure that was even possible, but this was okay for now. He was here with me, and his presence alone made me feel safe and protected.

His face pressed into my hair as his shoulders started to shake. He was crying, and at first, there were quiet sobs. But then they became louder, and everything he had been holding back was crashing down at once.

I quickly turned my head to look up at him. Tears were streaming down his face, and his breathing became an uncontrollable mess. I had never seen him like this. Not once had he cried in front of me.

I lifted my hand to brush his cheek, and I wiped at the tears that kept spilling over. My thumb traced his skin, trying to get him to calm down the same way he always calmed me down.

His eyes squeezed shut at my touch, and more sobs escaped him. It broke my heart into a million pieces, and the pain only got worse when I realized that he finally knew what had happened to me. He was hurting because of me.

Tears rolled down my face before I knew it, and I cried with him.

When he reopened his eyes and saw me crying in silence, something in him snapped completely. His expression turned angry, but that anger wasn't directed at me. It never was. He shifted, and his strong hands moved with urgency as he lifted me and settled me fully into his lap. He wrapped his arms around me tightly, with one hand cradling the back of my head, and pressing my face into his neck while the other locked around my back.

"I'm here," he said again in a broken voice. "Whatever you need. Whenever you need me, I'm right here. Always, Milow."

I didn't need him to promise it. He had been proving it for years, long before tonight, and long before the truth came out and shattered everything. He had always shown up, mostly in quiet ways. But he did show up.

I looked at him through wet lashes and smiled softly, then I placed my hand flat against his chest, right over his heart, and curled my fingers into his shirt.

He exhaled slowly, and it seemed that my touch helped him breathe again. His arms tightened around me once more, reminding me of their protection. One hand slid up my back, moving in slow strokes, and his chin rested against the top of my head.

In the quiet, my body relaxed against his. Exhaustion was finally taking over. At some point, his head tilted to the side, resting fully against mine, but his arms stayed wrapped around me, holding me close as we both drifted off in that position.

Ashby

It was early in the morning when I woke up. My body was stiff and sore, but once I remembered last night, I didn't care. I was still sitting upright with my back against the headboard, and with Milow curled up in my arms just like she had been hours ago. I wouldn't have wanted it any other way.

I moved carefully, stretching my legs a little before pulling the blanket higher to cover her properly. Then I looked down at her and ran a hand gently through her hair. She was still asleep, and I stayed like that, just holding her and admiring her beauty.

Unable to stop myself, I leaned down and pressed a soft kiss to her forehead, careful not to wake her. She shifted slightly against me, her fingers tightening in my shirt, and for a second, I thought she would stay asleep. But then her brow creased, and slowly, her eyes opened.

She looked at me with an unfocused gaze at first. When she realized where she was, her shoulders eased. I felt the tension leave her body as she settled back against my chest.

"Hey," I whispered. "I didn't mean to wake you."

She closed her eyes again, her lips parting as she took a deep breath.

I smiled and rubbed her back, letting her decide if she wanted to fall back asleep or stay awake with me. Selfishly, I wanted her to look at me again. Her eyes always brought a sense of safety.

I couldn't take my eyes off her. My gaze moved over her face, taking in her rosy cheeks, the tip of her nose, then her lips. Too many thoughts crowded my head at once. Some were gentle, and others felt wrong to have, given everything I now knew.

Her lips were beautiful. So soft and expressive. And they would never be used for what lips were meant for. She would never speak. The finality of it hit me all over again. But…she would still smile. She would still pout in that adorable way that always made my heart melt. But her voice? Her voice was gone forever. I would never get to hear it, and the heaviness of that fact hurt so deeply.

Anger rose inside of me, aimed at a man who no longer existed but had left damage everywhere. I didn't even realize I was holding her tighter until she startled.

Her eyes flew open. The moment she saw my face, she shifted, pushing herself upright to straddle my lap so she could look at me properly. Her hands came up, her eyes searching mine with concern.

[What is it? Why are you angry?]

My throat tightened. I struggled to keep myself together. "I don't want to use my voice," I said quietly. "Not if you can't. Not when yours was taken from you."

Her eyes widened, and she shook her head quickly, her hands moving with urgency. [But I don't want you to do that.]

"It just doesn't feel right, Milow. It isn't fair," I said, fighting to keep the emotions inside. Tears were already burning behind my eyes. My heart was racing and slam-ming against my ribs like it wanted out. I could feel myself slipping the harder I tried not to explode.

Her expression softened into sadness, and her gaze

dropped to my chest. My hands were still gripping her hips tightly. I needed to make sure she would stay right there.

Her breath shook when she inhaled. Then she looked back up at me, and her eyes held so much at once. Hurt, patience, understanding. But most of all, exhaustion. She was tired of explaining. Tired of reassuring everyone else. And that made me feel guilty. I was the one making her feel that way.

[A lot isn't fair in life, but I'm not mad.]

"But you should be," I said, my voice cracking. "You should be so damn angry, Milow."

My hands started to shake, and my body followed. The same uncontrollable tremor from the night before worked its way through me.

She shook her head again and placed both hands flat against my chest. She leaned forward until her forehead rested against mine, and I closed my eyes, focusing on her presence and on the pressure of her hands. Slowly, because of her, my breathing eased.

When she felt it change, she leaned back just enough to look at me. Her hands slid up to my neck, then one moved to cup my cheek. Her thumb brushed gently over my skin, and she held my gaze for a moment before pulling her hands back to sign.

[I don't want you to be mad. And I don't want you to stop talking just because I can't.]

I watched her as she paused. Her brows furrowed for a moment, then a small, almost shy smile touched her lips.

[I don't ever want you to stop talking, because your voice is the most beautiful thing I get to hear every day.]

I blinked. Her words weren't sinking in at first. But then they did, all at once, and every emotion I had tried so hard to keep inside me pushed out completely. I broke down, but this time, for a different reason than before.

She had the purest heart. Her kindness hadn't been destroyed, even after everything she'd been through. She had been silenced, and still, she chose gentleness. She saw beauty in darkness, and that was what undid me.

My fingers tightened at her hips as she lifted her hand again, wiping the tears from my face. I struggled to keep my breathing under control, refusing to let it turn into another spiral. I hadn't cried like this in years, but it seemed that since yesterday, I couldn't stop.

"Milow," I whispered, pulling her closer to me. I had so many things I wanted to say to her, but no amount of words seemed to be enough to tell her just how much I admired and adored her.

I still wanted to show her somehow, but the only way I thought of could scare her off. I didn't want to risk pushing her away, but I was just too selfish not to lean in closer and kiss her.

She stayed right there, close enough that I could feel her breath against my mouth. Her hands rested on my shoulders now, steadying herself while I tried to do the same for both of us. I swallowed hard as I leaned in closer, unable to stop myself. The pull felt inevitable, and I was careful not to move too fast. I was worried that one wrong move would shatter this moment.

"The world doesn't deserve you," I whispered. Tears kept rolling down my face. "I don't deserve you."

She shook her head and lifted her hands to sign, [But you do,] before she rested her hands on either side of my neck again. Her touch was so soft, it sent shivers through my whole body.

"No, I don't. But I'm so grateful that you let me be here with you, and that you trust me enough to stay by your side."

Her brows drew together as her eyes dropped to my mouth. The tip of her tongue came out, licking her lips before her eyes met mine again. That should've been my sign, but I was frozen. I couldn't believe that this girl had a heart of gold, and she was letting me have it.

She leaned in first, her lips parting slightly. My jaw clenched, and my fingers flexed on her hips before I moved them to her back. I rested one hand on her lower back, the other between her shoulder blades. I wanted to ask her if she was sure. If she truly wanted to kiss me, because we were both in vulnerable states, and I didn't want her to regret it. But there was no room for questions.

I pulled her even closer until my lips brushed hers, and with a small tilt of my head, I kissed her gently. It was a ghost of a touch at first, and I was terrified that she'd push me away. But she didn't, and she kissed me back just as softly, while her fingers dug deep into my shoulders.

My heart had never beat this hard, and my chest started to hurt from the throbbing. But if that's what kissing her would feel like for the rest of my life, I would deal with the pain.

I tilted my head a little more and parted my lips again, moving them against hers in a slow, careful kiss. Her lips moved with the same rhythm, and her body pressed more into me. She wasn't pushing me away, and with her fingers moving into my hair at the back of my head, she showed me she didn't want this to end.

I didn't want to stop either. I wasn't sure I could, not with how good this felt.

My right hand stayed at the small of her back, while I moved the other to her side, squeezing her waist gently. Her body shuddered, and her lips parted again in an attempt to deepen the kiss. I was going at her pace here, not wanting to force her into something she didn't want to do.

But this was all her doing.

Her fingers tangled in my hair, and she pressed her body into mine again as her hips slowly moved on top of me. She was still straddling my lap, and it seemed like she couldn't get any closer.

Carefully, I moved my tongue to brush along her bottom lip, and when she reacted with another tug of my hair, I slowly slid inside her mouth, my tongue softly brushing against hers.

Her body stiffened, but only for a split second. Because next, she was the one dipping her tongue deeper into my mouth and tilting her head more to the side. I couldn't help but smile. Milow had always been so shy, and I knew she'd never been kissed. But she was opening up to me, wanting this as much as I did.

I moved both my hands to her hips, pressing her harder against me as I curled my tongue around her in a slow and passionate kiss. Her fingers were still tangled in my hair, and I decided in that moment that her hands in my hair were my favorite thing ever.

The sun was rising outside, brightening up the room as the morning rolled in. But no matter what the world was doing, I only cared about Milow.

31

Milow

I had never felt every inch of my body tingle the way it did in that moment. I felt so many emotions at once, and as intense as they were, they were all positive. If I had to put how I felt into words, I wasn't sure I could. As many books as I read, and as smart as everybody told me I was, I had no words for this. All I knew was that I was in love, and no amount of words could ever explain what that felt like.

Ashby was a great kisser. Not that I had anyone to compare him to, but the way he made it feel had to mean something. He was so gentle and careful, and never once did it feel like I was being forced. He let me take the lead, and let me decide what came next, and I realized that maybe that wasn't such a good idea.

Because if it were up to me, we would kiss forever without ever stopping. Though, thinking about it more, that probably would've started to hurt our lips after a while.

After what felt like an eternity, I was the one who pulled back. I looked into his eyes, needing to make sure that what we had just done was okay. His lids were still lowered, and his gaze held that same soft and comforting admiration he always looked at me with.

His thumbs brushed slowly over my hips, and our breathing had settled into an easy rhythm that proved just how calm we made each other. My hands were still tangled in his hair, and I didn't want to move them. I could tell he liked it when I tugged at it. He made those low sounds deep in his throat when I did, and I had done it a few times during the kiss, to hear them again.

A slow smile spread across his mouth, and he leaned in once more, pressing one last gentle kiss to my lips. When he pulled back, I let my hands slide down to his shoulders, and he reached up to cup my face with both hands.

He studied me closely, his expression still so soft and sweet. Then he spoke, and the words he said made a big firework explode in my heart.

"I love you, Milow. I've always loved you."

I froze and just stared at him as my heart beat so hard in my chest that I could feel it in my throat. I didn't move, waiting for him to say more.

"I know this won't be easy," he continued quietly. "People will judge because of the way we were brought up. They'll probably look at us funny. And if you don't want this to be public, that's okay. We can keep it to ourselves. I don't care about that." His thumbs brushed along my cheekbones. "I just want to be with you. However you want that to look."

My mouth fell open as the words sank in. Had I heard correctly? Did he really say all that?

I pulled my hands to my chest, trying to find the right words before I signed, [You want to be my boyfriend?]

Ashby's eyes widened slightly. "Ah, shit…" He lifted a hand and ran it through his hair with a shake of his head. "I didn't mean to just…no, I don't—crap, I mean, yes. Yes, I want to be your boyfriend. I want it so goddamn bad, Milow."

His words rushed out, sounding messy and unfiltered, and then he stopped short. He searched my face as worry crept in. "I'm sorry," he said quickly. "I shouldn't have pushed that on you. I just—" He swallowed. "If that was too much, I need to know. I don't want to scare you or make you feel uncomfortable."

My throat tightened at the look in his eyes. He was scared of losing me. Of losing what we were and had. I reached for his wrist, stopping his hand where it hovered uselessly between us. He tensed at my touch, watching me closely.

[I want you to be my boyfriend, too.]

His breath left him in a shaky exhale. "You…you do?"

I nodded, my eyes burning now. [I love you too.]

For a second, he didn't move at all. Then a wave of emotions washed over his face. He laughed softly and pulled me into him by wrapping his arms tightly around my body.

"Okay," he whispered against my hair. "Okay. Thank fuck."

I scrunched my nose and smiled at his choice of words.

His hands slid up my back, and he leaned back to rest his forehead against mine.

"I promise," he said quietly, "I'll do this right."

I had no doubts about that. He had done it right all these years, even when we weren't boyfriend and girlfriend.

Ashby fell asleep again, and I carefully got out of bed and went downstairs when I heard sounds coming from the kitchen. Mom was already up. I joined her and helped prepare breakfast while the others were still sleeping.

I worked on the pancake batter without really paying attention. My thoughts kept drifting back to everything that had happened the night before. Mom and Dad had finally told me the truth about my past. Ashby told me he loved me, then he became my boyfriend. That part made my heart skip a beat, and I couldn't stop the smile that formed on my face.

"Milow?" Mom said softly as she stepped closer and placed a gentle hand on my back. "Would you like to share how you're feeling? Do you think it might help?"

I looked at her, unsure. I didn't feel ready to bring my past back up so soon. But a part of me worried that if I kept pushing it away, it would come back later and make it harder to deal with it. That was how bad things worked, didn't they? You ignored them for as long as you could, and then one day they caught up to you when you least expected it.

I gave her a tight smile and shrugged, then set the whisk down to sign. [I'm not ready yet, but I will come to you when I am.]

"Okay," she said, smiling gently as she rubbed my back. "How about we make a nice afternoon out of today? We could go to the mall. Maybe even get a haircut. I really need one," she added, flipping her long brown hair over her shoulder.

[That sounds nice.]

"Good. I think the boys can survive an afternoon without us," she teased.

I grinned and nodded in agreement. Even so, I knew I would miss them, like I always did. And I would miss Ashby the most.

———

On the way to the mall, I got a text from Ashby that made my heart thud incredibly hard. He was officially my boyfriend, and getting his texts now had a whole different meaning.

Ashby: Enjoy your day at the mall. Miss you already. I love you, Milow. <3

I smiled at the text, unable to be nonchalant about it, and just as I was about to text back, another one appeared. And another. He was spamming now.

Ashby: Forever, by the way.
Ashby: I love you now, and I'll love you forever.
Ashby: That sounds so cheesy.
Ashby: But it's true, and I just wanted you to know.

I covered my mouth with one hand, my nose scrunching at how adorable he was being.

Me: I'll love you forever too.
Ashby: And I've always loved you.
Me: I've always loved you too.
Ashby: Glad we're on the same page.

I kept smiling at his texts and watched the bubble come up one last time.

Ashby: I love you. Always. <3
Me: I love you. Forever. <3

By the time we reached the mall, the knot in my chest had loosened a little. But I still had our conversation present at the back of my mind. The last time I'd been at the mall with Mom was a long time ago, and the idea of spending an entire afternoon alone with her there excited me. But before we shopped, we headed straight to the salon. Mom had called before we left the house to check if they had any availability on such short notice.

Luckily, they did. Mom booked a haircut for herself, and I made a decision I'd never made before. I was going to get my nails done. I didn't want to cut my hair because I liked it long, and after Ashby's texts earlier, I felt unusually happy. So much so that I wanted to try something new.

Before Mom sat down for her appointment, she helped me explain to the nail technician which color I wanted.

[I really like this one,] I signed before pointing to a light, almost pastel green.

"That's very pretty," Mom said with a smile. She told the technician, then looked back at me. "I'll be right over there."

I nodded and smiled. [Okay.]

The technician guided me to a chair across from her, positioned so I could see Mom in the mirror. Mom gave me a small wave, and I watched her for a moment longer than necessary. I remembered the first time I'd seen her, before she and Dad adopted me. I had thought she looked like a princess back then. She still did. She hadn't aged much at all. For forty, she looked more like thirty. Dad too. He was only two years older and still looking young, even with his silly mustache.

The woman carefully took my hands and began the manicure. I watched every step. I had never done this before. I'd never even considered painting my nails. I'd never thought my fingers deserved that kind of care. The skin around my nails was torn and uneven. Some nails were shorter than others, and the red, irritated skin on my left thumb made me think my hands would never look nice.

My skin picking had always made me uncomfortable and insecure. Still, I hoped that having polish on my nails might help me stop. It was worth trying. And if it didn't work, then I would have to find another way.

The process was easier than I expected. The technician didn't seem bothered by how my hands looked. She even reassured me that the creams and oils she used wouldn't burn the open skin. I smiled at her, grateful that she didn't draw attention to something I already struggled with.

When she finished, I held my hands out in front of me and slowly turned them, taking in how they looked now.

"All done," the woman said, smiling when she saw my reaction. "That's a really pretty color on you."

My smile widened. [Thank you.] I wasn't sure if she understood, but the way she nodded and dipped her head told me she did.

I stood up and turned just as Mom got out of her chair. Her hair was shorter now, ending around her chest in loose waves. She'd gotten wispy bangs that somehow made her look even younger. I didn't know how that was possible, but she looked beautiful.

"Oh, sweetheart, let me see," she said, walking over with a bright smile. I placed my hands in hers, and she examined them closely, brushing her thumbs gently over my nails. "Looks amazing, Milow. Do you like it?"

I nodded quickly, then signed, [You're beautiful. The bangs really suit you.]

Mom grinned and carefully touched her hair. "I hope Dad's going to like it. He was never a fan of bangs."

[He'll love it. He'd love you even if you were bald.]

She laughed and took my hand in hers. "You're right. He's so easy to please," she joked.

Once Mom paid, we left the hair and nail salon and went into the first clothing store we saw. I browsed through the racks absentmindedly, occasionally spotting a cute sweater, but nothing that felt worth trying on. Mom, on the other hand, already had four items draped over her arm. She smiled at me. "Nothing catching your attention?"

I pursed my lips and gave a small shrug. [No. But I like what you've picked out so far.]

"I desperately need new sweaters. I'm getting sick of my old ones," she explained.

I studied her for a moment. [Can I have them?]

"My old sweaters?"

I nodded.

"Of course, sweetheart. But you should get some new clothes too. I really want to spoil us both today," she said with a smile.

[Okay.] I was sure I'd find something I liked in another store.

We continued through the store when a woman who looked familiar waved at Mom. "Iris, hi! Taking your daughter shopping?"

Mom smiled at her, and as the woman approached us, I saw Hailie and Aspen step up behind her.

Great. It was the weekend, and I still had to see them.

"Hello, Darla. Oh, yes. It's a much-needed outing," Mom said. Her voice was kind, but only people who knew her well would notice the annoyed undertone.

"Tell me about it," Darla replied.

Now that I looked at her more closely, with Hailie standing right beside her, it was clear she was her mother.

"Milow, gosh, you've grown so much, sweetie," Darla said, smiling far too brightly at me. "How are things at school? I've never had you over at the house. Maybe you and the girls can have a sleepover sometime."

I wanted to grimace. Darla clearly didn't know that her daughter and her daughter's best friend hated me. She probably also didn't know I was mute, and that spending time with them wouldn't even work since they didn't understand me. I didn't respond. I just gave a tight smile and tried not to look at Hailie and Aspen.

They were staring at me. I could feel it.

"She's not really our friend," Hailie said to her mother, her voice filled with disgust. "She's friends with that mentally ill girl."

"Hailie!" Darla scolded, turning to her daughter. "That's not a nice thing to say."

"But it's true," Aspen added. "We told you about her, didn't we, Darla? The girl who keeps starting fights with us."

I wanted to scream, but since I couldn't, I just stared

them down. They were talking about Scottie, and I hated the way they described her.

"Oh, don't be dramatic, girls," Darla said dismissively.

"Who are you talking about?" Mom asked. I was sure she already knew, but she wanted confirmation.

"Scottie Kepner," Aspen replied, her voice still dripping with disgust as she looked at Mom. "I wouldn't let my daughter hang out with a girl like that. She's such a bad influence. Maybe Milow shouldn't either."

Was she serious? How could they speak so disrespectfully about someone they didn't even know? Scottie was my best friend. She was kind and loyal. They were just angry because Scottie was one of the few people who always stood up to them.

I'd had enough. I turned to Mom and waited for her to look at me. [They're nothing but rude to Scottie and me at school.]

Mom didn't hesitate for even a second. She reached for my hand, and I slipped mine into hers as she faced Darla. "It was nice seeing you again, Darla. Enjoy your shopping."

There was no room for Darla to respond. Mom guided me toward the changing rooms. She was angry, which was something I rarely saw, and I hated that they had caused it. When we stopped near the changing rooms, Mom turned to me with worry written all over her face. "How long has this been going on?"

I shrugged. [It never really stopped.]

She knew what that meant. She knew about first grade, about the time I got in trouble for flipping them off. That had been the only time a teacher talked to Mom and Dad about Hailie and Aspen. I'd never really told them about everything else they put us through.

[But it's fine. Ashby and Stan are there to protect us.]

Mom wasn't satisfied with that. "If they're ever rude to you or Scottie again, please tell Dad and me, okay?"

I nodded.

She sighed, still upset, and reached out to gently caress my cheek. "I'm proud of you, Milow. For who you are. You have the purest heart."

Without meaning to, I felt proud of myself too. But maybe having such a pure heart wasn't always a good thing. I knew I forgave too easily.

I smiled and leaned into her, giving her a small hug before looking up at her again. [Go try them on,] I signed, pointing at the clothes on her arm.

And for the rest of the afternoon, we strolled through the mall, enjoying our time with each other.

32

Ashby

Dad, Wes, and I spent the afternoon in the basement, play-ing video games and eating whatever snacks we could dig out of the pantry. It wasn't something we did often. Wes and I played maybe once every other week, and only when there was truly nothing else going on.

Between school and practice, I rarely had the time, but today it felt good to shut my brain off for a while. Gaming was a distraction I hadn't realized I needed this badly.

After a few rounds of racing cars, we switched to another game, and since it was single-player, Dad and I ended up watching Wes completely demolish every monster that came his way. I was stretched out on one end of the big couch, watching the screen absentmindedly, and somewhat lost in my own thoughts when I heard a noise upstairs.

My heart jumped instantly. I sat up, suddenly unable to relax at all at the thought of seeing Milow again. "They're back," I said, already pushing myself to my feet.

Wes paused the game, and Dad turned his head toward

the stairs. I did too, just as footsteps started coming down. Mom appeared first, and all three of us had the same reaction when we saw her.

"Whoa..."

My jaw dropped.

Wes let out a low whistle. "You look beautiful, Mom," he said, while I was still trying to find actual words.

"Why, thank you, Wesley," Mom replied with a grin, tossing her hair over one shoulder.

"Very beautiful," I finally managed, smiling at her.

"Sweet mercy..." Dad's expression was priceless. He slapped a hand over his eyes, rubbed his face, then looked at Mom again with his mouth hanging wide open. "You're truly the only woman who can pull that off."

He meant the bangs. I'd heard him complain about bangs more times than I could count—which, to be fair, never really mattered. He didn't get a say in what anyone did with their hair. But that's exactly what made this so funny.

"You like it?" Mom asked, stepping closer to him.

"Do I ever!" Dad wrapped his arms around her waist and pulled her in, his eyes still fixed on her face and hair. "You look absolutely beautiful, Iris."

I pursed my lips and glanced at Wesley, who chuckled and shook his head.

Then Milow appeared on the last step, and my attention snapped to her immediately. She hadn't cut her hair, but something about her looked different. Softer, maybe. I couldn't quite place it.

"Hey, Milow. How was shopping?" Wes asked.

She pulled her gaze away from me to look at Wesley with a smile. [It was fun. Mom and I got some new clothes.]

I barely registered what she signed. Something else had caught my eye.

"You have nail polish on."

The comment made everyone look at me, but I kept my focus on her. Milow blushed and tucked her hands against her stomach.

I smiled. I knew how big this was for her. Realizing I might've embarrassed her, I walked over and stood in front of her.

"Can I see?" I asked gently.

She hesitated, then slowly lifted her hands. I slipped my hands beneath hers, lightly brushing my thumbs over the backs of her fingers. Wesley stepped closer to look too.

"It's pretty," I said after a moment. "I really like the color."

She smiled and pulled her hands back, glancing down at them before signing. [I like it too. But I already started picking at the polish.]

"That's okay," I said quickly. "It probably takes some time to get used to it."

She nodded, still staring at her hands. That's when an idea clicked.

"Hey…maybe nail polish could actually help with the skin picking."

Milow frowned slightly.

"What do you mean?" Wesley asked, gently taking one of her hands to look closer.

"I mean…instead of picking at your skin, you could pick at the polish," I explained. "That way it doesn't hurt, and you still have an outlet for when you get anxious."

It might've sounded stupid. I wasn't sure. But it made sense to me.

Milow looked at me thoughtfully, her lips pressed together.

"Actually, that's a really good idea," Mom said, stepping in beside us. "People do that all the time. It's kind of like those fidget rings. You peel the polish instead."

So it wasn't stupid after all. I smiled at Milow. "What do you think?"

She shrugged and glanced at her hand in Wesley's, then slipped it free to sign. [I could try. But then it won't always look pretty.]

"That doesn't matter," I told her. "You're wearing it for you. And you can always reapply it."

"Champ's right," Wes added. "Evie peels her polish all the time. I can ask her to bring some over tomorrow night if you want."

Milow's smile grew brighter. She nodded and clasped her hands to her chest.

God. She was adorable.

"I see you boys lived on junk food today," Mom said, amused. "Do you still have room for dinner?"

"I could eat," Wes said.

Dad and I nodded. "Same."

"Okay. I'm not cooking tonight. I'll be doing enough of that tomorrow. How about Chinese?" she suggested.

We all agreed. Before heading upstairs, she told us to clean up the basement.

While Dad and Wes went back to the couch, I turned to Milow and smiled. [Meet me in your room?]

She pressed her lips together and nodded. [Okay.]

I squeezed her hand lightly and watched her head upstairs before turning back to help clean up.

A few minutes later, I stood in Milow's bedroom

doorway and watched her by the bed as she pulled her new clothes out of the bags.

She turned when she heard me, and a bright smile immediately spread on her lips. My heart skipped, like it always did when I looked at her.

"Hey." I stepped into the room and closed the door halfway behind me, giving us some privacy.

She bit the inside of her cheek and lifted her hand in a small wave. Her eyes stayed on mine and widened with curiosity as I stopped right in front of her. I didn't try to stop myself. I didn't want to. I slid both hands around her waist and pulled her toward me before I leaned in and kissed her.

She melted right into me, with her hands coming up to my shoulders, where she held on tightly. I tilted my head and deepened the kiss. I took my time. I wanted the moment to last.

Her fingers brushed my hair at the nape of my neck. The touch sent a sharp rush through me. I moved my hands to her lower back, and I wanted to go lower. The urge was heavy, but I kept my hands where they were and pressed her closer instead, lining her body with mine.

I traced my tongue along her lips slowly, and she parted them for me before I slipped my tongue into her mouth, where it met hers. I didn't want to overwhelm her, and after one more deep kiss, I pulled back and pressed my lips to her cheek before looking at her again.

"I missed you today," I told her quietly.

She smiled, and I knew she had felt the same without needing to sign it. Instead, she wrapped her arms around my neck and hugged me.

I breathed her in and closed my eyes, tightening my

arms around her waist. I stood with her like that for a moment, pressing soft kisses to her neck, before finally pulling away.

"Wanna do a little haul?" I asked, interested in what she bought.

She nodded quickly and turned to her bed, showing me each of the six items she got. All of them were pretty, and they'd suit her perfectly.

[I like this one best,] she signed, lifting the navy-blue-and-red striped long-sleeve shirt.

"That one's my favorite, too," I told her with a grin, taking the shirt from her. "Kinda reminds me of one of my sweaters."

Her cheeks reddened as she clasped her hands together, a shy smile appearing on her lips. [It reminded me of you, so I bought it.]

"You're adorable," I said under my breath, chuckling softly. "When we go back to school in a week, we should both wear it."

Her eyes widened. [Really?]

"Yeah, why not?" I smiled and placed the sweater back on the bed. "We could match."

[I'd like that,] she signed, her eyes still wide.

"Good." I grinned and sat down on the bed. "What else did you do at the mall?"

Her face immediately fell, and my heart stopped. Something must've happened.

"What?" I furrowed my brows and watched her stare down at her hands. "Did something happen, Milow?"

She gave a little shrug.

"Milow..." I reached for her hands. "Everything's fine between you and Mom, right?"

It was a stupid question. Of course nothing had happened between them. Milow and Mom were tight, and it even felt wrong asking her that.

She frowned, and when she didn't respond, I said, "Sorry, that was stupid. But something happened."

Her gaze met mine, and I saw that mix of anxiety and worry flash through her eyes. Pulling her hands out of mine, she signed, [We ran into Hailie and Aspen in one of the stores. Hailie's mother stopped to talk to Mom.]

Ah…shit.

"Did they say something to upset you?"

She nodded. [They said mean things about Scottie.]

"In front of Mom?" But that shouldn't have been surprising.

[They called her mentally ill and said that Mom shouldn't let me be her friend.]

"Witches," I muttered, pulling Milow between my legs. I rested my hands on the backs of her thighs and brushed my thumbs along them. "You know that none of their opinions matter, right? What did Stan say about them again? That their mouths are open too much for nothing smart ever to come out."

A slow smile tugged at her lips, and I continued. "We both know Scottie is the most amazing friend, and she's nothing but loyal to you. And vice-versa. Hailie and Aspen are just sad and lonely, and it's clear that their friendship isn't even as strong as the friendship you have with Scottie."

Milow gave a small nod, her smile more genuine now.

[I told Mom that they've been nothing but mean to us.]

"Good. And next time they decide to be mean again, you tell us."

She nodded again, resting her hands on my shoulders as she looked down at me.

I smiled, giving her thighs a gentle squeeze. "I love you, and I'm proud of you, Milow. Don't ever forget that."

She shook her head and blushed harder, then she leaned down to hug me. I held her for a while, rubbing her back and silently reassuring her that I would always be there for her.

33

Ashby

Friday, October 17th

Thanksgiving break was almost over, and we had all des-perately needed the days off. But even then, Milow kept pulling out her math books, solving problems for fun like it was nothing. I often sat and watched, taking her in and admiring her like I always did.

This Friday afternoon, Mom and I sat at the computer and finally sent out my university applications. She had promised we'd get them done during the break so I could focus on school and practice afterward. I applied to fifteen universities. Still, there was only one I truly wanted to get into—the University of British Columbia.

That was the goal. Wesley had graduated from UBC. He was already a well-known athlete across the country because of it. He played for Canada's national hockey team and held a regular spot on the Vancouver Redwinds. He had made his dreams real, and I was proud of him. At the same time, watching how hard he'd had to fight to get there scared me.

I knew it wouldn't be easy for me either, no matter how good a swimmer I was. Success would cost time, pain, and sacrifice. But I was ready for that. I was willing to give everything it took.

What mattered most was that I wouldn't be doing it alone. My family was behind me. Supporting me. That was what I was most thankful for.

"Hey, champ." Wesley came up the stairs just as I stepped out of the bathroom. "Did you send out those applications?"

I'd needed a shower after today. For some reason, I'd been sweating more than usual. Important things like applying to uni made me nervous.

I ran a hand through my damp hair and nodded. "Yeah. Mom and I worked on it all day."

"Good." He smiled. "I know you'll get into UBC."

"I hope so." I let out a breath and gave him a tight smile. "What's up?"

"Uh, I wanted to talk to you about something."

"Sounds serious."

"It is, but it's nothing bad," he said, nodding toward my bedroom door. "Let's sit down for a second."

I followed him into my room and sat on the bed with him, leaning back on my hands to get comfortable. "Shoot."

Wesley cleared his throat and leaned forward, resting his elbows on his knees with his head tilted down. When he looked at me again, he said, "I told Evie about what happened to Milow. I thought you should know."

I watched him closely, giving myself time to feel the weight of his words and what that meant. After a moment, I nodded. "Okay."

"I asked Milow first, of course. She was okay with it, and she stayed with us while I told Evie."

"Okay," I said again, giving a short nod. "And how did Evie take it?"

He let out a quiet, amused laugh. "Not well. She cried."

That didn't surprise me. Evie was one of the most empathetic people I knew, and she'd been part of this family forever. She saw Milow as her little sister, and that news couldn't have been easy for her to swallow, just like it hadn't been easy for us.

"And now they're painting each other's nails," Wes added with a chuckle. "They kicked me out of my own room."

I laughed and sat up, giving his back a gentle pat. "You can hang out with me, buddy."

"Thanks. Do you wanna go back downstairs and play some more video games? We won't have that kind of time after the weekend."

I hated how true that was. Still, any chance to hang out with Wesley was one I never turned down. And I wanted Milow to have time with other people too, not just me. I didn't want to crowd her or make her feel like she only had one place to be.

I nodded and stood up from the bed, giving Wesley another quick pat on the shoulder. "Yeah. Let's."

———

I woke up the next morning with a stiff neck. After dinner with the whole family the night before, Wesley and I had gone back downstairs and gotten sucked into another round of video games. At some point, I must've fallen asleep down there.

Wesley wasn't around when I opened my eyes. I wasn't upset about it. He'd probably gone back to his bed to spend the rest of the night with Evie.

The TV was off, and as I pushed myself up to sit, I noticed my phone was lighting up on the coffee table. Someone was calling. When I reached for it, I saw Stan's name on the screen.

I frowned and checked the time—quarter to seven.

Why the hell was he up this early on a Saturday?

I slid my thumb across the screen and held the phone to my ear. "Stan? Are you okay?"

"Am I okay?" His voice was rough and raspy, like he had just woken up himself. "Hell yeah, I'm okay. I'm always okay."

"Right," I muttered, rubbing my eyes with my free hand. "Why are you calling? It's early."

"I know." I heard something crunch in the background, and from the way he was breathing, I could tell he was walking. "I'm on my way to the gym with Jasper."

I waited, giving him a second to explain himself. When he didn't, I asked again, "And you're calling me this early because…"

"Because I wanted to hear your voice, sweetheart," he said in a high-pitched singsong tone. Then his voice dropped back to normal. "And to ask if you wanna come, you goose."

I chuckled. "Shit, Stan. Why didn't you tell me yesterday? I would've been ready."

"I forgot. I was with Scottie and she—" He stopped short, then continued, "Are you coming or not? I'm almost at your house. I'll wait if you are."

"Yeah." I was already on my feet. "I'll be right outside."

"Great. Bring me a banana, an apple, and two protein bars. The peanut butter and caramel ones. Love you."

He hung up before I could argue. I sighed, not because I was annoyed, but because no matter how demanding and chaotic he was, I knew I'd never stop loving him as my best friend.

I quietly went upstairs to grab my gym bag. I didn't bother changing. I'd shower after the workout anyway. I slipped on a sweater, pulled a cap over my messy hair, and stepped back into the hallway. I stopped in front of Milow's bedroom door. It was cracked open, and I could see her lying in bed.

I needed to see her before I left, so I pushed the door open and stepped inside. With quiet steps, I went to sit on the edge of her bed. I leaned in and pressed a soft kiss to her cheek, careful not to wake her, but she stirred anyway, and I almost cursed under my breath.

"Hey," I whispered.

She frowned and sat up quickly, worry flashing across her face. [What's wrong?]

"Nothing," I said softly, rubbing her arm before cupping her cheek. "I'm going to the gym with Stan and Jasper."

Her brows pulled together as she glanced at the window, where the sun still hadn't come up. When she looked back at me, she signed, [Can I come?]

"To the gym?" I asked, surprised.

She nodded and bit the inside of her cheek. [I can bring a book.]

I grinned. God, she was so fucking adorable. "Yeah. I don't mind."

Her lips curved into a smile. She leaned in, kissed my cheek, then rested her head on my shoulder. [Thank you.]

I laughed softly and kissed the top of her head, wrapping an arm around her. We stayed like that for a moment before I whispered, "We should go now. Stan's already waiting outside."

She got out of bed right away and pulled on a hoodie that used to belong to Wesley. It was way too big on her, but she loved it. It had his hockey team's logo on it and his number. She pulled the hood up, grabbed a book, then turned to me with a smile. [Ready.]

I took her hand and laced our fingers together, lifting it to kiss the back of her hand before leading her downstairs. I packed the snacks Stanley had asked for, plus a few extra for Milow and me.

When we stepped outside, Stan was already standing at the end of the driveway, his gym bag slung over his shoulder. I let go of Milow's hand. As soon as he saw us, he broke into a grin and opened his arms.

"No way," he said. "Ace is coming to the gym with us?"

Even though their friendship was innocent, I felt a sharp flicker of jealousy. It was his nickname for her that caused it. And somehow, as her boyfriend, I didn't even have one for her.

I needed to fix that.

Milow smiled and waved as we walked over. When we were close enough, Stan wrapped his arms around her waist and lifted her.

"Being up this early is much more bearable when I get to see your face," he told her, squeezing her tight before setting her back down. "You gonna work out with us?" he asked, grinning.

She shook her head and held up her book. [I'm going to read.]

Stan's grin widened. "Of course you are. You know what, though? You make reading look sexy anywhere."

I pressed my lips together and watched Milow for a second, then looked at Stan and gave a short nod. "Morning."

"Morning." His grin stayed in place as he threw an arm around Milow's shoulders and started walking. "I'm focusing on cardio right now, but we can do legs and arms too. Did you bring the snacks?"

"Yeah."

"Good. After that, we're going to the diner for breakfast."

"Works for me," I said, glancing at Milow.

She looked pleased. [Will Scottie come too?]

Stan's expression tightened right away. "Uh, no. I don't think so. She got really angry with me again last night."

Milow's eyes filled with concern. [What happened?]

He dropped his arm from her shoulders and let out a heavy sigh, shrugging. "I honestly have no idea. I went to her place, hung out, and watched a movie. Right before we were about to fall asleep, she got up and trashed her room. It was like her personality flipped. She started calling me names and—" His voice broke. He cleared his throat, forcing himself to keep going. "I tried to calm her down, but she started scratching and hitting me. Scarlett was home, and she came up and pulled her off me."

Milow stopped walking, and so did we. She looked up at Stan and rested her hand on his arm before signing, [I'm sorry, Stanley.]

He sighed again and rubbed the back of his head. "I swear, I didn't say anything this time. I kept counting to ten before I spoke. Even when I just asked if she was hungry or wanted to watch a different movie."

I watched him closely. I believed him. I didn't think he

had said anything that Scottie could have taken the wrong way. But I also didn't believe she'd explode like that for no reason. Something was wrong.

"Have you talked to Scarlett about it?" I asked. "I mean, has she noticed the change in Scottie, too?"

"I don't know," he said. "I haven't asked. But she looked exhausted."

I shoved my hands into my pockets, trying to piece it together. Scottie wouldn't lash out like that without a reason. She loved Stan, and a year ago, their friendship had been solid. It always had been.

[I'll text Scottie later,] Milow signed, her gaze gentler now. [There has to be an explanation. We'll figure it out.]

Stan nodded. Before we started walking again, I squeezed his shoulder. "It'll be okay."

"Yeah," he said quietly. "I hope so."

———

When we arrived at the gym, Jasper was already there. Bennett had come too. After a quick greeting, I walked Milow to the corner where two large couches sat near a vending machine. As she went to sit, I placed a hand on her hip and stopped her, smiling down at her.

"If you need anything, let me know. Okay?"

She smiled back and nodded, tucking her book under her arm. [Okay. Enjoy your workout.]

"I probably won't," I said, grinning. I wanted to kiss her. Or at least pull her into a hug. But I could feel the guys watching, so I held back. "I love you, sweet girl."

Sweet girl.

Yeah. That felt right.

She reacted instantly. Her eyes widened, her cheeks

flushed, and her hands curled into my shirt as she ducked her head.

I chuckled, unable to hide how much I loved that reaction. The softness, the way she felt everything so openly. *Sweet girl* fit her perfectly.

"I'll be right over there," I said quietly, giving her hip a gentle squeeze before turning back toward the guys.

As I walked away, I glanced back once more. She was already settled on the couch, book in hand, and watching me with that shy smile.

And for the next two hours, I couldn't focus on my workout. Not with her sitting there, reading her book.

34

Milow

I tried to read, but I couldn't focus. Every time my eyes moved over the page, I felt Ashby looking at me. It didn't make me uncomfortable, but it made my cheeks burn. And it got worse every time our eyes met.

The others noticed. I could tell because they kept glancing between us. Jasper most of all. He had that knowing look on his face, like he'd figured us out a long time ago. But he didn't say anything.

When they finished their workout, Ashby came over to me with a smile on his handsome face. I closed my book and looked up at him, sure my face was bright red by now.

"Hey. We're going to take a shower, then head to the diner. Are you hungry?"

I nodded. I'd only had half a banana and one bite of Stan's protein bar. I still didn't understand how they ate those things. The taste alone felt like punishment. But apparently, it helped with their muscles or something.

[I'll wait here,] I signed, smiling up at him. [You looked good doing the shoulder workouts.]

My hands moved before I could stop them.

Ashby grinned. His shirt was off, and it was hard not to look. He needed strong shoulders for swimming, but everything else about him was perfect too.

"Yeah?" he said. "So you watched me?"

He already knew the answer. And he'd watched me too, even though sitting and reading wasn't exactly as impressive or sexy as him working out.

[Maybe.]

His grin widened. He glanced toward the others, already heading for the locker rooms.

When they disappeared around the corner, he turned back and leaned down, bracing his hands on either side of me on the couch. Then he kissed me.

I kissed him back right away. I'd missed his lips. I smiled into the kiss and lifted my hand to the side of his neck. He stayed close after pulling back, his eyes looking into mine.

"I love you," he whispered, rubbing his nose gently against mine.

I smiled and rested my forehead against his, closing my eyes for a second before looking at him again. [I love you too.]

"Forever?" he asked quietly.

I nodded. [And always.]

He smiled and pressed another kiss to my lips, then he stood upright and stretched his arms. "I'll be right back."

[Okay.] I watched him head to the locker rooms, and because I couldn't seem to focus on the book in this gym anyway, I decided to text Scottie and see how she was doing. I pulled out my phone and sent her a text.

Me: Hi. How are you, Scottie?

It only took her a few seconds to read my message. I waited for her reply.

Scottie: Hi. Good. I think.

I hesitated. I didn't have to tell her that I already knew about what happened between her and Stan last night. She probably suspected it, but I knew she wouldn't be mad about it.

Me: I'm here to listen if you want to talk about it. <3
Scottie: I know. You're the best. <3

I bit my lip, thumbs hovering over the screen for a while before I typed again.

Me: We're going to the diner for breakfast in a bit. Do you want to come?

I paused, then added another message.

Me: Stan will be there too. He's worried. I think he'd really like you to come.

Her reply took longer this time. I imagined her staring at her screen and thinking. Whatever had happened last night between them hadn't come from cruelty. I knew that. I'd felt a shift in her mood lately. She was more distant and fragile, but only in certain moments, and there was never really an obvious trigger.

Scottie: Okay. I'll come.

Relief settled in my chest. I replied right away.

Me: Do you want us to pick you up? Bennett's
     driving. His mom's minivan has room for all of us.
Scottie: No. I'll meet you there.
Me: Okay. See you then :)
Scottie: See you later :)

At the diner, Scottie wasn't there yet. She said she'd walk, so it would've taken her a little longer to get here. While she was on her way, we all squeezed into one booth. I was sitting between Ashby and Stan, and Bennett and Jasper were sitting opposite us.

We had already ordered our food, and while Bennett and Stan argued about some new video game, I looked out the window, hoping to see Scottie walk up to the diner soon.

Ashby's hand rested on my thigh, and I snapped my eyes to him, finding him already watching me. I smiled and placed my hand on his, and he turned his palm up to slide his fingers through mine.

"Do you want to hang out with me this afternoon?" he asked quietly.

It was such an innocent and sweet question that it made my heart skip a beat, and my cheeks turned red once again. Ashby had been my best friend since we were little, and I found it admirable and sweet that he still asked me to hang out, instead of just assuming that I would.

Of course, I would hang out with him even without him asking, but little things like that proved that he cared about what I thought and wanted.

I nodded slowly, tilting my head to the side and pressing my cheek against his shoulder in an attempt to stop my shyness. I had no reason to be shy with him. He knew me better than anyone else. And still, he managed to get me to blush and grin like an idiot.

His lips curled into a smirk as he squeezed my hand gently.

Needing to avoid his gaze before my face turned into a tomato, I looked out the window, only to see Scottie walking right toward the diner. I smiled, sitting up straighter.

Ashby followed my gaze, smiling when he saw her. "Did you text her?"

I nodded and turned my head when the bell above the door sounded, and seconds later, Scottie stood at the end of our table. I waved and smiled, and the others said hi to her. All but Stan. He just stared up at her while Scottie played with her fingers, avoiding his gaze. I was scared they would start to argue, and for a moment, it really seemed that way. But then Stan got up and pulled Scottie into a tight hug. He rubbed her back, and she clung to his sweater.

Relief washed over me, and Ashby's tension eased too.

"I'm sorry," I heard Scottie murmur into Stan's chest.

"You don't have to apologize," he assured her with a sigh. He pulled back and looked down at her with a smile. "I'm glad you came."

Scottie smiled back, and as they turned to sit down, Jasper got up from his spot and came to sit next to me, where Stan had been sitting before. He wanted them to sit together, and so Stan slid in next to Bennett, then Scottie followed.

I slid my hand out of Ashby's and waited for Scottie to look at me. [I ordered orange juice and chocolate chip pancakes for you. Oh, and a bowl of fruit we can share.]

She smiled at me and lifted her hands. [Thank you, Milow. You're the best.]

Our food came a moment later, and we all ate while holding casual conversations. I nodded or shook my head at questions thrown my way, and when we were all done, I tapped Jasper's shoulder to get his attention.

"Yeah?" he asked, smiling at me. "What's up, Milow?"

[I need to go to the bathroom.] I pressed my lips together, unsure if I should've told Ashby first, because I knew Jasper didn't know ASL.

But instead of frowning or looking at the others for help, Jasper asked, "Sign that again."

I blinked and lifted my hands. [I need to go to the bathroom.]

"Bathroom!" he exclaimed. "That's the sign for bathroom, right?"

My eyes widened, and I quickly nodded.

"Shit, dude…are you learning ASL?" Stan asked.

"Not really." Jasper smiled and got up, clearly having understood what I signed. "I read this book at my dad's office at the clinic. You know, he's an ENT and has that kind of stuff lying around. It's pretty interesting. I might actually start learning it."

"You should," Scottie told him. "It's pretty cool knowing how to sign. It's been like our secret language all these years."

I nodded again, thinking it was really cool of him to consider it. I knew he wasn't doing it for me directly, but I appreciated every single person in my close circle who put in the time and effort to learn to speak my language.

And while there had been many who understood me, there were still a couple of people I wished would've made things easier for me. My teachers, for example. I could never respond when I knew an answer, but my teachers already knew I knew a lot, and so they didn't even try to quiz me at random. I didn't want to linger on that. I was doing great in school, even though I wasn't being understood.

"Yeah, I'll look into it more," Jasper assured her, then smiled at me again. "You're the coolest, Milow."

"And the smartest," Stan added, lifting a finger to emphasize his words.

"And she's super beautiful too," Scottie said with a grin.

My face turned bright red for the millionth time today. They were being silly.

"Milow's just the best," Ashby said at last, standing up before Jasper had a chance to sit back down. He smiled down at me and placed a hand on my lower back. "Come on."

"Are you taking her to the bathroom?" Stan asked, looking amused. "You know, she's a big girl."

"I have to go too," Ashby explained with a roll of his eyes.

I bit the inside of my cheek, my body already tense. I really had to pee. Ashby led me to the back of the diner and through the swing door. I stopped in front of the women's bathroom and looked up at him.

"I'll wait here," he said, smiling gently.

I nodded. [Okay.]

After giving my hand a quick squeeze, I turned and disappeared. When I came back out, Ashby was waiting for me. He was leaning against the wall, his hands tucked into the pockets of his pants. He smiled and reached out with one hand.

"Come here."

I'd go anywhere he wanted me to. At this point, he could handcuff me to him, and I'd follow him without hesitation.

I stepped forward, sliding my hand into his while keeping my eyes on him. His smile stayed in place, and when I was close enough, he slipped his other hand around my waist and pulled me against him. My body pressed into his, and I rested both hands on his chest as one of his hands came up to cup my cheek.

He didn't say a word. He just looked at me, then leaned in and kissed me. I melted into him right away. Every time we kissed like this, hidden away from everyone, there was this fire inside me. It felt exciting to be sneaky like this, and even though I wished we didn't have to hide, I didn't want that feeling to disappear either.

Ashby's tongue traced the seam of my lower lip, and I parted my mouth for him to tangle with mine in that claiming way that always made my knees weak.

When my lungs started to give out, I pulled back and rested the side of my face against his chest, wrapping my arms around his waist. He put his arms around me and rubbed my back as we stood there in the narrow hallway.

"You always make me feel calm," he whispered, drawing in a slow breath. "I can't explain it. All I need is for you to be in my line of sight, and my heart slows down."

I closed my eyes, then squeezed him tighter to show him how much his words meant to me. Any guy could have said something like that to make a girl feel special, but I knew without a doubt that Ashby meant every word.

I tilted my head to look up at him again, smiling before pressing a soft kiss to his jaw.

"I love you so fucking much, Milow. I always have."

My expression didn't change. My smile stayed in place as I admired this boy I had somehow been lucky enough to call mine.

[I love you too.]

"Good. I don't think I could keep going if you didn't."

I scrunched my nose and reached up to cup both sides of his head before letting my hands fall again. [You'd be just fine.]

"No, I wouldn't. I don't think I'd be the same if you hadn't come into my life." His expression shifted, and the change made my stomach tighten.

He looked away, clicking his tongue in frustration as he rubbed the back of his head. "Shit, never mind," he said with a nervous chuckle. His eyes met mine again as he tried to smile. "Let's go back."

I wanted to ask what had caused the sudden shift, but he was already leading me toward the door. I had always known Ashby was adopted too—just like Wesley and me—but I knew nothing about his life before that. He never talked about it. Neither did Wesley. Mom and Dad had always looked forward, never wanting to drag our pasts along.

But just like mine had come to light, I had a feeling his would too. Maybe unexpectedly, maybe when he was finally ready to talk about it himself. I didn't want to push. I just wanted him to know I was here.

I wrapped both hands around his arm to stop him, and he turned to look at me.

[I'm here to listen. Always.]

His smile was small, but his eyes were full of gratitude. "I know," he said quietly, cupping my cheek and brushing his thumb along it. "Thank you."

I smiled wider, leaning into his touch before poking his side to get him moving again.

We went back to the table, and as soon as we sat down, Bennett said something that made pain and anger surface inside of me.

"Don't you think it's been long enough now? I mean…the not-talking thing. How do you think you'll make it through life?"

My body went rigid, and Ashby tensed beside me.

"Dude…what the fuck?" Stan said, elbowing Bennett in the chest.

"What? I'm just wondering." Bennett looked at me again, his brows raised. "You can't expect everyone to learn to sign just because you don't feel like talking."

"That's enough," Ashby warned. His voice was hard as he glared at him.

"Am I wrong?" Bennett shot back with a shrug. "My cousin did this too. He stopped talking for like a year. It's selfish, if you ask me. If you have a voice, why make every-one else work so hard to understand you?"

"I said enough!" Ashby stood, his gaze locked on Bennett. "I don't know why you think it's okay to talk to her like that, but you need to apologize. Now."

"Apologize for what? I was simply expressing my opinion."

"Yeah, well, it's a shit and ignorant opinion," Scottie said, standing up as well. "After all these years, I'd think you'd know better."

I didn't want them to fight, but I didn't know how to stop it. Ashby looked furious, like he was about to snap. I had never seen him like this, and it worried me. I reached up and touched his arm, trying to pull his attention back to me.

When he looked down, I signed, [It's okay. Please sit down.]

His brows knit together. "No, Milow. It's not okay. He's being a dick."

"A huge dick," Stan added. "Just apologize, dude."

Bennett crossed his arms and leaned back, staying silent.

"Ben, come on," Jasper said, looking at him expectantly. "Apologize."

But Bennett didn't. He just shrugged. "I think she should accept my opinion."

"Your opinion is an attack," Scottie snapped. "You're being fucking rude."

"Right."

"You are." Scottie glared at him. "How do you not see how insensitive you're being?"

[Please stop,] I signed, trying to cut through the argument. I looked up at Ashby, pleading. [Please.]

His jaw clenched as he shook his head, then he looked back at Bennett. His expression went flat. For a second, I thought he was going to say more, but instead, he reached for my hand.

"Come on, Milow."

I stood. Stan and Jasper followed, but Bennett stayed where he was.

"If you decide to apologize, you know where to find us," Ashby muttered, his grip tightening around my hand. He looked at Bennett one last time. "And don't ever assume shit about Milow again."

My head and heart were spinning by then. Everyone went quiet, and there was no space for more. Ashby led me out of the diner, our friends following, and without a single word between us, we walked down the street toward home.

35

Ashby

As much as I wanted to be alone with Milow, I was okay with the others coming home with us. Once we got inside, we said hi to Mom, who was on the couch reading, and then we headed downstairs to the basement. There was more space down there, and we could all hang out without feeling crowded.

Everyone took a seat on the couches while I paced the floor, rubbing the back of my neck. I was so fucking angry. Bennett had no right to say shit like that. He demanded that Milow start talking, just because he was too ignorant to put in even the smallest amount of effort to accept her for who she was.

"Ash," Stan said, resting his elbows on his knees as he looked up at me. "Come on, dude. Don't let him get to you like that."

"He was being an asshole," I muttered.

"He was. We all agree with you on that," Stan stated. "But you told him exactly what you thought. Now it's on him if he wants to apologize. We're all on your side."

I sighed and ran a hand through my hair before finally sitting down next to Milow on the couch. I looked at her, and like always, she wore that soft smile that told me she wasn't even half as angry as I was. I knew I'd have to learn to live with that, with how easily she forgave, even when people hurt her.

"You okay?" I asked quietly.

She nodded, wrapping her hands around my arm and leaning into my side.

"Please don't let what Bennett said affect you, Milow," Scottie said. She was still visibly upset, and I knew she wouldn't let this go anytime soon. If anything, she'd be even more protective now. She wouldn't let anyone talk to Milow like that again.

"And don't ever feel pressured to talk," Jasper added, smiling at her gently. "It's your choice alone."

Milow stiffened. She straightened up and dropped her gaze to her hands, fidgeting with her fingers. I watched her closely, noticing the shift in her posture and the worry settling over her face.

I wanted to ask if she wanted to be alone. If she needed space. But when she looked up at me, I saw something else in her eyes. It looked like desperation.

She was asking for help.

"What is it?" I asked softly.

Her gaze fell back to her hands. I didn't rush her. None of us did. We sat there in silence, giving her all the time she needed. Then, finally, she looked back at me and signed, [Can you tell them?]

I frowned, trying to understand what she meant. But then it hit me, and my chest tightened so hard it hurt.

She wanted me to tell them about her past. About why she would never speak.

"Are you sure?" I asked, my voice low. I hated that this was coming up because of Bennett. I hated that she had felt forced to share something so personal.

[I'm sure,] she signed, her smile tight.

I took a deep breath and nodded, taking her hand in mine.

"Okay."

I cleared my throat and gave her hand a small squeeze. As I searched for the right words, I looked at Milow, taking her in. She was so damn strong. She hadn't deserved any of it. None of what had been said and done to her. None of it had managed to break her, no matter how much it had tried. She stayed strong, and she grew from the pain I knew she still carried deep inside.

And somehow, she always put everyone else first. She never let her trauma spill onto others. Never made it their burden.

"Last Friday," I started, still looking at her, "Milow had a doctor's appointment."

The room went tense instantly. When I glanced at Scottie, terror flashed across her face. She was already thinking the worst. What I was about to tell them wasn't easier to hear—but it wasn't what Scottie was thinking.

"She's okay," I said quickly.

Relief washed over their faces all at once.

"But—"

"Ah, dude. Don't 'but' us," Stan complained, dragging both hands through his black hair.

I pressed my lips together and looked back at Milow, checking in with her. Making sure she still wanted me to go on. She nodded and smiled softly, her fingers brushing against mine in a calming motion.

It almost made me laugh. I was about to talk about the worst parts of her past, and she was the one soothing me. She was so incredibly special.

I took another breath and turned toward the three of them on the other couch. "But Milow found out something that day. Something that…isn't easy to swallow."

I knew that firsthand. I'd fallen apart when I found out. I hadn't been able to stop myself from breaking, and again, she'd been the one holding me together.

"Whatever it is," Scottie said, her voice tight with worry as she tried to stay steady, "we're here for you, Milow."

Milow signed a quick thank-you, then she looked back at me, ready for me to continue.

With a tight smile, I looked at the others again. The right way to tell them still wouldn't come to me. How could it? There was no easy way for something like this. No way to soften what had happened to her. Still, I tried. I chose my words carefully, making sure not to dump everything on them at once. I needed to ease them into it.

"You see…" I started, my body tense. "Milow didn't choose not to speak."

I saw the questions forming in their eyes, but no one interrupted me. They waited.

"She doesn't speak because…well. Because she can't."

Scottie's brows pulled together, her gaze snapping to Milow, and back to me. "What do you mean?"

I sucked in a ragged breath and tightened my fingers around Milow's hand. She leaned into me a little more, almost like she wanted to disappear into my side.

But she didn't want to stop me. She was just steadying herself.

"Milow can't speak," I said, forcing the words out, "because she doesn't have vocal cords."

Jasper sat up straighter, his blond head tilting slightly. "I'm so sorry, Milow. And you've never known?"

Milow shook her head.

"So you were born without them?" Scottie asked, her voice already shaking.

"She was," I said. "She, uh…"

It got harder then. My lungs suddenly started to ache. I lifted my hand and rubbed the back of my head, buying myself a second. My other hand stayed locked with Milow's, and she gave me a small, encouraging nod. She didn't want me to stop.

"Before Milow was adopted," I continued, "she lived in a house here in Bowen with her father. Her father…" I swallowed. "He wasn't a good man."

Scottie's eyes filled with tears immediately. Out of everyone here, she had probably already imagined the worst. And I hated knowing that some of what she was thinking wasn't wrong.

I cleared my throat before I went on. "He was a surgeon. And when Milow was little, he…shit. He—" I paused, my voice breaking despite my effort. "He removed her vocal cords."

Their reactions hit all at once. They gasped, and shock washed over their faces.

"What the hell?" Stan said, his face twisted with horror and confusion. "What…the fuck…"

A sob slipped from Scottie as she shook her head,

disbelief written all over her face. "That's so fucked up. Why would he—oh my god, Milow. I'm so sorry."

"I'm going to kill that motherfucker," Stan growled, his hands clenching into fists.

"That, uh…that won't be necessary," I said quietly.

"Is he dead? Good. I mean—shit. I'm sorry, Milow. But that wasn't your father. That was a monster."

I agreed with him, even if I didn't say it out loud. I looked at Milow, unsure if she wanted me to go on. For a second, she didn't look sure either.

"No more?" I asked under my breath.

She slowly shook her head.

"Okay." I pressed a gentle kiss to her forehead. "No more."

More sobs came from the other couch. When we turned, Scottie was sitting there, tears streaking her face, and looking overwhelmed and helpless.

Milow, being who she was, stood up and went straight to her. Scottie got up and wrapped her arms tightly around her best friend, crying into her shoulder.

"I'm so sorry, Milow. You didn't deserve that."

Stan got up next and joined them, putting his arms around both girls, his own eyes glassy. "I'm so proud of you, Ace. You're one of a kind."

I smiled at the sight. After exchanging a look with Jasper, we both stood and stepped into the hug too.

"We're here for you," Scottie mumbled into the group. "You're strong and beautiful and the best friend I could've ever asked for."

"Yeah," Stan added, resting his chin on Scottie's head. "And you're so freaking smart. You always help me with my math stuff. You're heaven-sent. A literal angel."

I couldn't stop the smirk. Even now, Stan found a way to lighten the moment. Not to take away from the truth, but to keep us all from drowning in it.

I patted his back, then squeezed his shoulder and Jasper's. "She's grateful to have you guys. Couldn't ask for better friends."

"We're grateful to have her too," Jasper said quietly, smiling.

As the hug slowly loosened, Milow looked up at all of us, tears still in her eyes. She'd cried too. But she was trying to stay strong for us.

[I love you guys. I couldn't have asked for better friends.]

"We love you too," Scottie said with a shaky voice.

"And hey," Stan added, wiping at his face, "we speak a language not many people do. I might be stupid and can't solve simple math problems, but I know sign language. All because of you."

Milow smiled and leaned into his side. I had always loved their bond, even if they had a rough start when they were little. Back then, Milow needed time to trust him fully, but over time, she learned that Stan was just a big goof who loved with all his heart and fiercely protected the people he loved.

"I'm definitely going to learn ASL," Jasper told us with a proud smile. "I saw there are videos online to learn."

"I can teach you," Scottie suggested.

"Sure, thanks."

I smiled at Milow, watching her admire our friends with wide eyes. And when she looked at me, I winked. She immediately blushed, her gaze staying on mine before a shy, secret smile bloomed on her lips just for me.

36

Milow

Monday, October 20th

On Monday morning, I woke up earlier than usual to go to the pool with Ashby. He had asked me the night before, and I said yes. But I told him that I didn't just want to sit around and watch him swim his laps, and he promised to spend some time with me in the water too.

So there I was, with my arms and legs wrapped around him, and my back pressed against the wall of the pool. Ashby had his hands under my thighs, holding me up. I smiled at him, admiring the way he looked with his damp face and wet hair. He'd taken off his cap and goggles after finishing his laps, and there were still faint marks left on his skin.

I lifted my hands and cupped his face, brushing my thumbs along the redness beneath his eyes.

"That'll go away," he told me, his smile soft.

I nodded, then wrapped my arms around his neck and pulled him close, pressing my body against his in a tight hug.

His hands slid along the underside of my thighs, then moved higher until he was cupping my butt. A shiver ran through me, and without meaning to, I pressed my hips forward. His body went rigid, but his hands didn't move.

"I want to be good, Milow," he murmured into my shoulder before pressing a kiss there. "Please don't make this hard for me."

I knew exactly what he meant. I wasn't clueless about these kinds of things. But I was still pretty innocent, and I wouldn't even know what to do. Kissing already felt like a lot for me to handle, mostly because he made it feel so good. But this, the way his body reacted to mine, was new.

He kept kissing my skin gently, trailing his lips up the side of my neck. His mouth moved slowly, and I felt his tongue brush my skin before every kiss he placed. My eyes stayed closed as I melted into him. I hoped no one else would come to the pool. Ashby had told me he was usually alone and that only one or two other students came by sometimes. But that was rare. Ruben also hadn't come today, because Ashby told him not to.

I wanted to wake up early every Monday morning if it meant I could have an extra hour alone with him like this.

His lips moved to my jaw, and his hands gave my ass a gentle squeeze, sending another jolt through me. I slid my hands into his hair, tangling my fingers in it.

When I tugged a little harder, he let out a breath and pulled back, his hands moving to rest on my hips. "Shit."

I leaned back to look at him, frowning. Had I done something wrong? Had I upset him?

I didn't need to sign anything for him to understand what I was thinking. My expression said it all.

"Everything's okay," he said, a crooked smile on his lips. "It's just…you can't move your body like that. And you can't tug at my hair. That drives me crazy."

I pressed my lips together, feeling my cheeks heat up. But I felt like teasing him too. [I can't do that ever?]

He let out a soft, nervous chuckle. "No. You can do all of that whenever you want. I just…" He hesitated, rubbing the back of his neck. "I need you to understand that everything you do makes me feel things a thousand times stronger. And I'm worried that when things get…more intense, you won't be ready."

Oh. So he thought I couldn't handle more than making out. Maybe he was right. Or maybe he was trying to protect me.

[We'll take it slow,] I signed, keeping my eyes on his.

His shoulders relaxed as he nodded. "Yeah. We'll take it slow."

He leaned in again, but before his lips touched mine, his gaze flicked upward, and his eyes widened. "Shit," he muttered.

My whole body went rigid. I was scared to look, but I still turned my head. Jasper stood there in nothing but his jammers, staring at us, frozen just like we were.

"Oh, uh…" He let out a chuckle and scratched the side of his head. "Hey."

I pressed my lips together. The initial spike of panic faded into relief, though the awkwardness lingered.

"Hey," Ashby said. Despite the surprise, he didn't push me away. His arms stayed around me tightly.

Jasper kept looking between us, probably running through a thousand questions in his head. "So…you're dating?" His tone wasn't judgmental. Just curious.

"We're together," Ashby said with a hint of pride in his voice.

"Cool." Jasper smiled genuinely. "I'm happy for you."

"Thanks, dude."

That was it. Jasper didn't ask any more questions. He accepted it and moved on without a single weird look.

"I didn't mean to interrupt," he added. "I found out I have a free period, so I thought I'd come for a swim."

"Oh, sure. No worries," Ashby replied, glancing at the large clock on the wall. "We need to head out anyway. Still gotta shower and all."

Jasper nodded and headed toward the benches to put his towel down.

I looked at Ashby. He smiled at me and pressed a soft kiss to my lips. "Come on. We don't want to be late."

Once we were out of the pool, I wrapped my towel around myself and watched Jasper pull on his cap, tucking his blond curls underneath. When he noticed me watching, he grinned.

"I already learned something in ASL. Watch this."

He lifted his hands and signed, [Hi, my name is Jasper and I love to swim.]

His fingerspelling was a little shaky, but I understood him perfectly. I smiled widely, that familiar warmth spreading through my chest. [That was great!]

"Good job, dude," Ashby said.

"Thanks. I watched some videos last night. I also FaceTimed Scottie so she could teach me more. It's actually really fun."

That made me happier than anything. I never assumed anyone would learn to sign for me. Still, seeing someone care enough to try to learn my language meant everything.

"All right, I'll see you at lunch," he said with a wave.

I waved back, then followed Ashby to the changing rooms, where we showered and got dressed separately. I'd kept my hair in a bun so it wouldn't get wet. I didn't have time to dry it before class. I brushed it quickly in front of the mirror, packed my bag, and headed into the hall to wait for him.

When he appeared, the first thing I noticed was his sweater. It was the same one I was wearing—navy blue with red stripes.

I smiled and tugged at my own sleeves. He'd kept his word from two Saturdays ago, when I came home from shopping with Mom and showed him what I'd bought.

"We're matching," he said with a smirk. "We look great."

[We should match more often.]

"We definitely should." He cupped the back of my head and kissed my forehead, then took the bag with my towel and bikini. "I'll walk you to your locker."

[Okay.]

I wanted to hold his hand on the way back to the main building, but I kept my arms at my sides. His arm brushed against mine now and then, and that was all I'd get until we were alone again. It was enough for now.

When we reached my locker, he opened it as if it were his own and placed the bag inside. Then, because he knew my schedule, he grabbed the two books I'd stacked neatly on the bottom shelf and tucked them under his arm before leaning against the locker next to mine.

He studied me for a moment, his face gentle and soft. "Did you like it at the pool?"

I nodded quickly. [I want to come every Monday morning.]

"Yeah? I wouldn't mind." His smile shifted into a smirk, then faded as his expression turned serious. "But you might become too big a distraction, and I really can't afford that with all the swim meets coming up."

My eyes widened. [I don't want to distract you.]

He chuckled and reached out, tucking a loose strand of hair behind my ear. "I'm just messing with you, sweet girl. I want you around as much as possible. Living in the same house and going to the same school really isn't enough."

I scrunched my nose and gently bumped my fist against his chest. [You're silly.]

"Silly, huh?" His grin returned. "I don't care what you call me, as long as you still call me your boyfriend."

For a second, I was scared someone around us might have heard him. But the students in the hallway were too busy to pay us any attention.

My face burned bright red. God, he deserved an award for how easily he could make me blush.

[I will forever call you my boyfriend.]

"Boyfriend?" Stan suddenly appeared beside us, slinging an arm around my shoulders. "Whose boyfriend are we talking about?"

I glanced at Ashby. For a moment, we both hesitated. Jasper already knew. Stan was our best friend too. Telling him wouldn't hurt, and he'd probably figure it out soon anyway.

"Uh…" Ashby scratched the back of his head and looked at me again.

I gave a small shrug. [He can know.]

"I can know what? Just spit it out," Stan whined, looking back and forth between us.

I smiled at Ashby and nodded, waiting for him to say it.

"We were talking about Milow's boyfriend."

Stan frowned. "Why are you talking about yourself in the third person?"

It took Ashby and me a second to realize what he meant. He already knew.

"Don't look so shocked. Did you really think I wouldn't figure it out?"

"I figured you would eventually," Ashby said with a chuckle. "I just didn't think you already had. We've only been together a few days."

Stan's frown deepened. "Really? I thought that had been going on for at least four months."

My eyes widened. Had we really made it that obvious? We had always been close. Ashby had never shied away from showing affection. Still, I didn't think we'd ever done anything that made it look like we were dating.

Ashby laughed. "Okay, well…you got it right, dude."

Stan grinned down at me, but his expression quickly twisted. "This means I'll be third-wheeling from now on."

I pursed my lips and nudged his side with my elbow. [You have Scottie.]

"Not really. We're still not a couple," he said with a heavy, theatrical sigh.

"That's because you've yet to ask me out on an actual date." Scottie stepped up beside Ashby, her arms crossed over her chest.

Stan immediately tensed next to me, and I braced myself for another argument. But instead, Scottie stayed calm. She glanced between us, then broke into a grin. "You're matching."

I nodded quickly and smiled back at her.

"Of course they're matching. They're boyfriend and girlfriend," Stan said, like it was the most obvious thing in the world.

"What?" Scottie's eyes widened as she stared at me, trying to piece it together. "Are you serious? Since when?"

[About a week,] I signed. My heart started beating faster just thinking about the night we made it official.

"Oh my god. Guys!" She wrapped an arm around Ashby's side before pulling me into a tight hug. "I knew it. I knew since we were kids that this would happen. I've just been patiently waiting for this day."

I hugged her back and looked up at Ashby, who was smiling down at us. He looked pleased. Now our closest friends knew we were together, and I didn't really care about anyone else at school. The people I was afraid to tell were our family, but that was for another time.

"I want a hug too," Stan said, his eyes fixed on Scottie.

I pulled back and gave them some space, watching Scottie turn to Stan with a playful expression. "You'll get your hug when we're on a date."

"Oh, come on," Stan cried. "That's so not fair."

"Actually, pretty damn fair if you ask me," Ashby said.

"We barely even have time for a date," Stan argued. "I go to the gym one night, and the other night you're at soccer practice. We barely have time to go out."

"If you truly wanted to go out with me, and eventually call me your girlfriend, you'd make time," Scottie said calmly. "Besides, we hang out on weekends all the time. Could've made one of those times a date."

"She's right about that too," Ashby added, clearly trying to rile him up. And it was working.

Stan groaned and ran his hands over his face. "I'm honestly trying my best here," he said, looking back at Scottie. "Okay. Saturday. Since we'll probably hang out anyway. Do you want to go on a date then?"

"No."

Ashby laughed, and I grinned. I didn't want the bell to ring because this was incredibly entertaining. While we watched them, Ashby reached for my hand and gently curled his fingers around mine. It felt secretive enough but not hidden. I smiled up at him, then turned my attention back to Scottie and Stan.

"Why not?" Stan asked, looking confused and annoyed at the same time.

"Because I have a soccer game on Saturday," Scottie said. "And I actually wanted you guys to come."

"Sure, we'll come," Ashby said easily, and I nodded along.

I loved going to her games.

"Um, hello?" Stan said. "I'm trying to get this girl to go on a date with me. You're not helping."

Scottie's grin widened. She let it drag out for another second before finally freeing him from the torture. "You may take me on a date after my game."

Stan's eyes went wide. He threw his fists into the air, celebrating as if he'd just won another MMA fight. "Let's fucking go! You hear that, dude? I'm going on a date with the hottest girl on this planet!"

Ashby laughed. "Congrats, buddy. Don't fuck it up."

"Oh, I won't," Stan said quickly, looking back at

Scottie with a grin that reached both his ears. "I swear, I'll make this the best date."

The bell finally rang, and with Scottie and Stan already heading down the hall, Ashby led me to my classroom. "I'll see you later," he told me.

[Okay. See you later.] I looked around before adding, [I love you.]

He smiled and lifted his own hands. [I love you too, sweet girl.]

With that, I turned and quickly went to sit at my desk before my knees gave in.

I went to the bathroom before the next period, but, unfortunately, Hailie and Aspen decided to do the same. I did my business, then went to wash my hands, hoping to get out without them saying a word.

I had no such luck. As I finished drying my hands and turned toward the door, Hailie shoved me hard, making me stumble sideways. My hip slammed against the edge of the sink. I managed to stay upright, but the pain that shot through me made it hard to keep my balance.

"Did you really think you could get away with what you did to us at the mall?" Hailie's eyes were filled with rage. I never fully understood how someone so young and beautiful could carry so much hate. She had makeup on again, but I've always thought it looked pretty on her. However, I was sure that underneath it all, she was just as beautiful. There was no time to think about it. She kept going, throwing words at me that were meant to hurt.

"And you really think wearing the same sweater as Ashby will make him like you more? Please. You're literally the weirdest girl at this school. And you keep disrespecting us by not speaking."

Aspen stood right behind her with her arms crossed over her chest. She looked at me with the same disgust, but there was something else in her eyes. Something that didn't match the way she held herself.

"And you're doing it again," Hailie squealed. "You know you'll have to talk eventually. You're nothing special."

I furrowed my brows and avoided her gaze. The way she looked at me with so much rage hurt more than the words themselves.

"Go on, attention whore. Apologize to us."

I didn't know what for. I had never done anything to hurt them. I had never said anything mean. Obviously.

I crossed one arm over my stomach and held the other close, trying to protect myself. Even if I used my hands, they wouldn't understand. It would only make them angrier.

"She won't," Aspen said with a sigh. "We're wasting time here."

But Hailie shook her head. "It's never a waste to teach others some manners."

She stepped closer and reached for me. I tried to pull away, but she pinched my skin through my sweater. Pain bloomed instantly, and she didn't let go. I could already feel my skin bruising under her grip.

"Apologize," she said again, anger flashing in her eyes. "Go on, *mute.*"

I clicked my tongue and turned away until she finally released me. But the moment she did, she shoved me again—harder this time. I fell, unable to catch myself. I hit the floor on my butt, and the back of my head slammed into one of the stall doors. The pain was so harsh that my ears rang, and my vision blurred.

I forced my eyes open, terrified of passing out. I already got a taste of what she could do to me, and I didn't want to risk getting hurt more while I was unconscious. It was a sickening thought, but knowing Hailie, I knew she'd go that far. I scrambled to my feet and grabbed the door handle to steady myself. Seconds later, another sharp pain struck when Hailie slapped the side of my head with her palm.

"Are you stupid or something? Just apologize. It's one simple word."

My body was shaking now, and my lips trembled. I didn't want to cry. Not in front of them. But it was hard not to when I was being shoved and hurt like this.

[Please stop.]

"We don't speak your stupid language, bitch."

She swung again, her fist landing hard against my temple.

Tears streamed down my face now, and my chest felt so tight I could barely breathe.

[Please. Please.]

"Hailie, let's just go," Aspen pleaded, which somehow didn't surprise me. She had looked uncomfortable standing there, watching Hailie bully me. But she still hadn't stopped her.

"Tsk." Hailie's hands were clenched into fists at her sides, ready to swing again at any given moment.

I stared at her hands, terrified she would use them to hurt me again. But she didn't. She didn't move either. And I knew I couldn't stay there.

I wiped my cheeks with my fingers. Gathering all

the strength and courage I had left, I rushed past them and out of the bathroom. The pain was unbearable. My head throbbed as I walked, and I reached back to touch it, checking for blood. When my fingers came away clean, I let out a sharp breath. Then I forced myself back into class, desperate to forget that any of it had ever happened.

37

Ashby

Saturday, November 1st

It was a day before my eighteenth birthday, and while I should've been excited to celebrate the next day, I couldn't stop thinking about how quiet Milow had been over the past few days. I had asked her if something had happened, but she reassured me that she was just more tired than usual. Maybe she was studying too hard again, not giving her mind enough time to rest. I decided not to keep pushing, knowing that if something was wrong, she would've told me.

At least, that's what I hoped.

On the way to Scottie's soccer game in the afternoon, we stopped at a gas station to grab some snacks. Stan insisted. After letting him loose in the shop for about ten minutes, we walked back out with drinks and way too many snacks. Stan was happy about it. Milow was too. So I didn't argue.

Once we arrived at the soccer field, I parked in the lot beside it. We got out and headed toward the stands, taking a spot near the middle, so we had a perfect view of the field. Both teams were already warming up, and I scanned the field until I found Scottie.

She wore the number 17 on her back. That number had always been hers. She started playing when she was just six years old, and I still remember the day she told us about the new jerseys they got and how she chose her number.

She had been so excited about it that I asked her why she picked 17. She never told me. Not then, not ever. Growing up, with that question still stuck in my head, I eventually figured it out myself. She chose it because Stan's birthday was on the 17th of February.

Even when she was little—when Stan treated her like she was contagious—she still loved him.

"There's my girl!" Stan shouted, pointing toward Scottie on the field. "Woohoo, go baby!"

She turned her head toward the stands, spotted Stan, and grinned. She shook her head with an exaggerated eye roll, then lifted her hand and waved. We all waved back.

"Let her focus, dude," I said, reaching out to grab his hand and pull him down into his seat.

He sighed but stayed standing for another second, watching her. "She's just so beautiful in that jersey and with her hair pulled back like that," he said, finally sitting down beside Milow. "What's that hair style called? You know, when girls pull their hair back with gel and all."

Milow smiled at him. [A slicked-back ponytail.]

"Right, that. She looks so fucking hot with a slicked-back ponytail." He looked back toward the soccer field, with his jaw dropped as he watched Scottie. "Jesus Christ…just look at her. And that hair…"

I chuckled. [What, you got a hair fetish now?]

"I think I've always had a hair fetish. But only when it comes to her hair. I mean, fuck…look at it swaying back and forth. And that curl at the ends…so fucking perfect." He tsked, still staring at her. "She reminds me of a doll I used to have when I was a kid."

Milow grinned. [You had a doll?]

"He still has it," I told her.

Stan never took his eyes off Scottie, continuing to admire her from afar. "Thank fuck girls don't go bald like most men do. And I hope she never cuts it."

"She won't," I assured him, though, some girls liked to experiment with hair. "But maybe one day she decides to shave her head. You know, to try a new look."

That caught his attention, and he stared at me wide-eyed. "Fuck, I know I don't get to say what she can or can't do, but I would literally cry if she ever decides to shave her head."

[She'd look beautiful even without her long hair,] Milow signed, smiling at the idea of it.

"Yeah, for sure. But, shit…" He looked back at the field with a shake of his head. "I need her to keep it that way."

"She will, buddy." I leaned back and placed my hand on Milow's thigh, glancing at her as she ripped open a chocolate bar. She bit into it, and when she noticed I was watching her, she smiled and held the chocolate to my mouth.

I leaned in and took a bite, smiling at her as she bit into it again herself. I gave her thigh a squeeze, and when she finished the chocolate, she pocketed the wrapper and tugged at Stan's shirt to get his attention.

[How many goals do you guys think she'll score today?] she signed once we both looked at her.

"Oh, definitely two. Or more," I said. Scottie was a natural goal scorer. She played left wing, and even though her role was supposed to be assisting the strikers—which she did constantly—she still managed to score herself. Her crosses were always perfect, landing right in the penalty area where her teammates were waiting for the ball.

"She'll score a hat trick," Stan said confidently, like it was already a fact.

[I'll say a hat trick too,] Milow signed, smiling proudly.

The game started soon after, and we all focused. Scottie's team was on fire. It felt like every single player had been waiting for this game all summer. The break had been long, and I'd heard Scottie complain more than once about not having any matches. Now the season had finally started, and they'd be playing every weekend for the next ten or so weeks.

By halftime, the score was 2–1 for Bowen FC, and one of those goals belonged to Scottie. They'd earned a free kick after one of her teammates was fouled. The position was far from the goal, far enough that most players would've passed it off. But Scottie did what Scottie did best. She placed the ball, took three steps back, lifted her gaze to the goal, and sent the ball straight into the net.

The crowd erupted. Stan shot his fist into the air. "That's my girl!"

Scottie glanced up toward the stands and blew him a kiss. I grinned, watching Stan melt on the spot. "You truly can't fuck up that date, dude."

"Oh, I won't," he said, sitting back down. "I prepared everything. I sent my parents away so we'll have the house to ourselves. I bought all of Scottie's favorite foods. Mom even baked a cake. We're gonna have a picnic on the floor, with the TV playing one of those fake fireplaces. I thought of everything."

Milow smiled and squeezed his arm before signing, [She'll love it, Stan. You're amazing.]

Stan grinned from ear to ear. "I know. I can't wait to see her face light up when she sees it."

I reached behind Milow and patted Stan on the back. "Proud of you."

The match continued, and after two more goals scored by Scottie, the final score was 4–1.

"I told you she'd score a fucking hat trick," Stan said proudly. "God, she's such a talent. She should go pro."

I chuckled and leaned back, finally relaxing now that the game was over. I rested my hand on Milow's thigh. "She was incredible."

Milow nodded. [I'm so proud of her.]

We watched the two teams shake hands, and after a quick talk from their coach, Scottie headed over to us, where we had moved closer to the side of the pitch.

[You're the greatest, Scottie! Those goals were incredible.]

"Thank you, Milow." Scottie grinned and gave her a quick hug, then looked at all of us. "I didn't think we'd win, because that other team has always been super strong. But we did it."

"You sure did," Stan said, pulling her into a tight hug. "And you were the star, as always. You're amazing, baby."

Scottie smiled, then grimaced as she pushed against his chest. "I'm all sweaty and gross."

"Just how I like you."

"Ew, Stanley," she whined, playfully slapping his arm. "I'm going to take a shower. Will you wait?"

We nodded. Before heading toward the changing rooms, she rose onto her tiptoes and kissed Stanley's jaw.

"Today, my friends, I will finally be an official boyfriend," Stan said confidently once she was gone. "I just know it. Things are going well."

"I believe in you, buddy," I said, squeezing his shoulder. Then I pulled Milow closer to my side and smiled down at her. "What should we do tonight?"

She shrugged and wrapped her arms around my waist. She was leaving the choice up to me. And I already knew what I wanted. Before my birthday arrived, I wanted time alone with her. Just us. Hanging out in my room and watching movies.

Whatever we did, with her by my side, everything felt right.

"I didn't know what the fuck to do, Ash. She just stood up, and then she fainted and—" Stan's voice was frantic on the other end of the phone. It had only been three hours since we'd left the soccer field, and now he was calling to tell me he was at the hospital. Scottie had suddenly fainted.

I tried to calm him down, but he was rambling, probably pacing the floor without stopping.

"Did you call Scarlett?" I asked. I stood in the middle of my bedroom, my phone pressed to my ear. Milow sat cross-legged on the bed, watching me with wide, worried eyes. She looked helpless.

"Yeah. She's on her way. Shit, Ash…it happened so suddenly. We were eating the cake my mom made. She was happy, laughing, and then…then…" A sob tore out of him.

My chest tightened. "Do you want us to come to the hospital, Stan?" I asked. I needed to be close to him. And I knew Milow would want to be close to Scottie too.

"I don't know…the doctors and nurses haven't even come out yet. They haven't told me what's wrong with her." Another sob followed, deeper this time, and raw with fear. "Yes. Please come."

"Okay." I looked at Milow and nodded once. She was on her feet instantly. "We'll be there in fifteen."

"Okay. Thanks."

"Of course. Hang in there, buddy."

We hung up. I let out a slow breath. "Scottie's in the hospital. She fainted at Stan's house and didn't wake up."

Milow covered her mouth with both hands. Her eyes filled immediately.

"She'll be okay," I said, even as my own stomach twisted. I pulled her into my arms and held her close. I kissed the top of her head, murmuring soft reassurances. "Scottie's strong. Whatever caused it, she'll recover."

Milow's body trembled. When she pulled back, she looked up at me and signed. [What if something's wrong?]

"She's in good hands," I said. "They'll figure it out. They'll make her better."

But I knew what she meant. I'd noticed it too. Scottie had changed over the past few months. She had always been bright, loud, and energetic. Lately, there had been moments that didn't feel like her at all. Her mood changed at the flip of a switch, and she went from laughing to getting angry. And Stan had been the one who had to deal with it the most.

Milow wiped at her eyes and lowered her gaze to her hands.

"She'll be okay, sweet girl," I said again, reaching out to cup her cheek. "We can stop at that little gift shop at the hospital and get Scottie flowers and chocolates, hm?"

She looked up at me and nodded, smiling gently. [Okay.]

I smiled back and pressed a soft kiss to her lips, then one to her forehead. "Let's go."

Milow slipped her fingers into mine as we headed for the door, holding on a little tighter than usual. I squeezed her hand back, steadying us both.

Whatever waited for us at the hospital, we'd face it together.

38

Milow

Stanley was hunched over in a chair in the hallway, elbows resting on his knees, and his face buried in his hands. His body was trembling, and my heart squeezed at the sight. When we reached him, I gently placed a hand on his back, careful not to startle him.

"Hey, buddy," Ashby said quietly. He was holding a bouquet of colorful flowers and a box of chocolates in his arms, the ones we'd bought at the gift shop on the ground floor.

Stan looked up and let out a heavy sigh. "Hey. Thanks for coming," he said as he sat up straighter and wrapped an arm around my waist.

I let him pull me in, knowing he needed this now. I slipped my arms around his shoulders and leaned in to press a kiss to the top of his head.

"How is she doing?" Ashby asked next, setting the flowers and chocolates down on one of the empty chairs. "Have you seen her yet?"

Stan shook his head. "No. Scarlett's in there right now, talking to the doctor." His voice cracked. "I just want to know if she's okay. My heart keeps aching in my chest, and it hurts like hell."

I rubbed his back before sitting down beside him, waiting until he looked at me. [Scottie's strong. Whatever it is, she'll get through it. And we're all here for each other. Always.]

He tried to smile, but it didn't quite reach his eyes. "I know. I can't stand not knowing what's wrong. They could at least tell me if she's okay."

Ashby stood in front of us and reached out to squeeze Stan's shoulder. "I'm sure they'll come out any minute. Do you need anything? A drink? Something to eat?"

"No, thanks," Stan said quietly. "I'd probably just throw it back up if I tried to eat."

I pressed my lips together and reached for his hand, holding it gently between mine.

Stan squeezed my hand and took a deep breath as he leaned back against the chair. "It was horrible," he whispered. "I've never…seen anyone faint before. It was so fucking scary."

"I know," Ashby said as he sat down in the chair on Stan's other side, his body turned toward us. "I can't imagine how that must've felt. But you did great. You called the ambulance right away, and you let Scarlett know."

Stan stayed quiet for a moment, slowly shaking his head. "I don't even want to think about what would've happened if she'd been alone. Scarlett was working this afternoon. Scottie would've been home by herself if it weren't for the date."

I gently caressed his fingers, trying to steady him. His

grip tightened around my hand, like he was afraid to let go. I didn't pull away, wanting to give him all the support he needed, even though I was hurting inside too.

We sat in silence a while longer before the door across from us finally opened. All of us straightened at once. When Scarlett stepped out, Stanley was on his feet immediately, moving straight toward her.

"How is she? Can I see her?" He tried to look past Scarlett, but the doctor who had followed her out had already closed the door.

Scarlett smiled gently. Her face was so much like Scottie's. Or maybe it was the other way around. They looked so much alike, with the same dirty-blond hair and brown eyes.

Both of them were beautiful, inside and out.

"You can go in in just a minute, Stanley," she said softly, rubbing his arms. "The nurse is just finishing up a routine check. She's awake and doing okay. She's just a little dizzy."

I watched Stan's shoulders sag with relief as he dropped his face into his hands. When he looked up again, his voice was quiet. "Okay. Good. That's good."

Scarlett gave him a tight smile, then turned her attention to us. "Milow, Ashby…hey, you two."

I gave a small wave and stood to hug her.

"Hey, Scarlett," Ashby said as he came up behind me. "You look great."

"Oh, you're a charmer," Scarlett said with a soft laugh as she rubbed my back. When I stepped away, she hugged Ashby too. As she pulled back, she smiled and added, "Scottie told me you watched her soccer game today."

"We did," Ashby said proudly. "She was amazing. Scored a hat trick in true Scottie fashion."

Scarlett's smile widened. "I wish I could've been there. I asked my boss if I could get Saturday afternoons off so I can come watch her. At least for the home games." She let out a quiet sigh, exhaustion etched clearly across her face.

Scarlett had always been incredibly hardworking. It had only ever been her and Scottie since her father had died from a heart attack at only thirty-six years old. Scarlett worked as a restaurant manager at a high-end hotel in Vancouver, and even though the job was demanding and stressful, she pushed through. She made sure they had a good life, and she never let Scottie miss out on anything.

"Come on, let's sit," she told us, leading us back to the chairs.

We sat down again and waited in mostly silence until the nurse finally came out.

"You can go in now," she said with a gentle smile. "Just try to keep the volume down so she doesn't get overwhelmed."

"Okay, thank you," Scarlett said, already on her feet.

We followed her, Ashby picking up the flowers and chocolates from the chair. "Do you want to give this to her?" he asked, tipping the bouquet toward me.

I smiled and nodded, taking it from him.

When we entered the room, Stanley went straight to Scottie's bedside. She looked tired but happy, propped up against the pillows and smiling up at him.

"Hi," she said softly, reaching for his hand. "Why are you crying?"

My gaze flicked to Stan. I could only see the side of his face, but his cheek was flushed red, with tears sliding down.

That alone almost made me cry. I had never seen Stan like this. He was so worried about her that his usual humor had completely disappeared.

"I hate seeing you like this," he choked out, his shoulders shaking.

Scottie laughed quietly and squeezed his hand. "I'm okay," she promised. Then she looked past him and smiled at me. "Those are so pretty."

I smiled back and stepped closer, placing the flowers at the foot of her bed. [How are you feeling, Scottie?]

"Good. Just a bit dizzy, and my head hurts a little." Her smile faded slightly as she glanced at Ashby, who set the chocolates beside the flowers.

"Glad you're okay, Scott," he said, gently squeezing her foot over the covers.

"Thank you, Ash. But I'm truly fine," she said, looking around the room again. "I really don't understand why you're all acting like I'm dying."

"Because you randomly fainted, Scottie. I was scared shitless," Stan cried, rubbing at his eyes. "I was so fucking scared."

Scottie's eyes softened, but for a split second her expression went sharp, like she might snap back at him. She didn't. Instead, her face brightened again, and her voice turned light and amused. "I think I was just so overwhelmed by what my boyfriend did for me that I fainted."

Stan frowned hard. "It's not funny, Scottie."

"It's a little funny," she said, still holding his hand.

Even now, Scottie was trying to lighten the mood. She hated seeing people worry about her. And it worked on everyone except Stan.

"It's not funny. Not even a little."

Scarlett stepped in before he could spiral again. "You did everything right, Stanley. I'm glad you were there. She's okay. She's stable. And she told me what you did for her. The picnic? That was very sweet."

"He's the best boyfriend ever," Scottie added, using that word again, clear as day.

Everyone heard it except Stan.

He just kept frowning, and I scrunched my nose because it was honestly getting ridiculous. He had been trying to earn that title for years, and now that Scottie had handed it to him, he completely missed it.

I gently smacked his arm. [Are you even listening to her? She's called you her boyfriend twice now, and you haven't reacted at all.]

"Yeah, dude, you're fucking it up again," Ashby said, clearly enjoying this.

It took a second. Then Stan's eyes widened. "Shit…" He rubbed the back of his head with his free hand, the other still locked with Scottie's. "Wait. Are you serious? You actually want to be my girlfriend? You're not just messing with me because I'm crying at your hospital bed like a baby?"

Scottie grinned and shook her head. "I'm dead serious."

"Fuck… I mean—motherfucker—"

"Stanley," Scarlett warned, though she was smiling. "Language."

"Right. Sorry. Uh." He looked back at Scottie, gently cupping the side of her head. "Yes. I mean. Okay. Yes."

"Pull yourself together," Ashby said, laughing.

"Shhh," Stan snapped, shooting him a glare. "I'm trying. All of you watching is making this worse."

Scottie laughed softly, and I watched them with a smile and watery eyes. They were painfully sweet.

Stan cleared his throat, clearly bracing himself. "I should've asked you out a long time ago. Like, when we were ten or something."

"That would've been way too early," Scarlett said calmly.

"Right. Okay. Fifteen."

"Sixteen."

Stan groaned and looked at her like he was begging for mercy. "Come on, Scar. You're just messing with me now."

"Maybe a little," she said with a shrug.

Scottie looked delighted.

Stan turned back to her, serious again. "I should've asked you out a long time ago. I hated that I didn't. But I was always there. I always loved you the same."

"You've been in love with me since kindergarten," Scottie said proudly.

"No way—"

"You absolutely were," she said.

"Can confirm," Ashby added.

Stan sighed. "Fine. Since kindergarten. All I'm trying to say is…I love you. And I want to be with you."

Scottie's grin softened into a smile that I had always admired so much. "I love you too, Stan."

That was it for me. I clasped my hands to my chest, biting my cheeks, my emotions everywhere. This was always supposed to happen. Everyone knew it.

Stan leaned down to kiss her, then paused and glanced back at us. "Can you, like…give us some space?"

Ashby laughed and laced his fingers through mine. "Yeah. We're happy for you."

I nodded to agree with Ashby's words before letting him pull me toward the door.

Scarlett followed, but before she left, she turned back. "Take it easy, Stan. She still needs to rest."

"Don't worry," he said quickly. "Our first time won't be in a hospital bed."

I slapped a hand over my mouth, eyes wide.

"Oh, man," Ashby muttered, laughing.

"That's not what I meant," Scarlett said flatly, raising a brow before she closed the door.

When we were out in the hall, she shook her head with an amused smile. "I always wanted a son. But that one's exhausting."

She was joking, and I knew she was delighted to have Stan as her unofficial son-in-law. But I agreed with her. Stanley was chaos in human form. But underneath it all, he was loyal, protective, and deeply in love.

Scottie would always be safe with him.

39

Ashby

When the visiting hours were over, we went back into Scottie's room to say goodbye. As we were leaving with Stan and Scarlett afterward, she explained that Scottie had apparently suffered a circulatory collapse, which was why she had fainted so suddenly and without warning. I didn't know much about medical stuff, but something about a seventeen-year-old having a circulatory collapse didn't sit right with me.

Scarlett seemed to feel the same. I could see the concern on her face, the way her jaw tightened when she talked about it. Still, I didn't question it out loud. I didn't want to make anyone worry more than they already were. Scottie needed rest, and I trusted that Scarlett would make sure the doctors ran every test they needed to.

We got home late. Dad was the only one still awake, sitting on the couch with the TV on low. He looked over at us right away, his expression concerned. I had texted him earlier, letting him know where we were so he wouldn't worry about Milow and me.

"Hey. How is she?" he asked, sitting up straighter.

"She's okay," I said. "Apparently, she had a circulatory collapse."

Dad frowned. "At seventeen?"

"Yeah. That's what I said."

"Does she have any history of heart problems?" he asked.

I shook my head. "No. She's always been healthy."

Milow nodded beside me, her face tight with worry and confusion. [I feel like that's not what caused her to faint.]

Dad pressed his lips together, studying both of us for a moment. "I hope Scarlett makes sure those doctors check her thoroughly," he said. "I'm glad she's doing better, though."

I nodded, but the uneasy feeling stayed with me.

I looked at Milow then, rubbing her back gently. "She'll be okay," I assured her.

[I know. I just hate that she's all alone at the hospital tonight.]

"She'll be out in no time. I'm sure of it."

Milow leaned into me, still tense, and I held her a little tighter.

I told myself it was nothing, but deep down, that strange and uncomfortable feeling stayed.

———

"Come here, boy." My father's voice always made me want to run and make myself invisible. But in a one-bedroom apartment, of which he kept the door locked, I had nowhere to hide.

I walked toward him slowly, already knowing I had done something wrong even though I didn't know what it was, because with him, it was always something. Sometimes it felt like I was being punished for simply existing. But it wasn't my fault or my wish to be here with them.

The room smelled like beer and smoke that never really left, no matter how often the window was opened. He sat in his chair, a bottle of something strong-smelling on the table, and a cigarette burning between his fingers. The way his eyes were fixed on me made my stomach twist.

"You're too slow," he said, his voice low and irritated. "Everything you do is slow. You do it on purpose to piss me off."

I shook my head, but it was barely noticeable as I stared at the floor. Looking at him only made things worse. As I stopped in front of him, my hands were clenched so tight at my sides they hurt.

"Open your mouth."

I froze.

My heart started beating so fast it felt like it was going to burst out of my chest. I didn't want to do it, and I knew what he wanted before he even moved, but I also knew what would happen if I didn't listen.

Daddy's hands were big and strong, and they hurt the most when he balled them into fists.

"I said open your mouth," he repeated, already leaning forward.

My lips trembled as I obeyed. My jaw was stiff, and my breath shallow and uneven. I tasted smoke before he even touched me. His hand grabbed my chin, forcing my head up as his fingers dug into my skin.

"Look at you," he said. "Can't even stand still. You're useless."

Then he pressed the cigarette against my tongue.

The pain was instant and overwhelming. The burn lasted

longer than something so small should have. I squeezed my eyes shut as a broken scream tore out of me, but he didn't pull away. He held it there, twisting and pressing the cigarette on my tongue like it was an ashtray, and he kept going just long enough for my body to jerk and shake.

"Shut up," he barked. "You make everything worse."

He finally let go, shoving my head back so hard I stumbled and nearly fell. My mouth burned and throbbed, saliva spilling out because I couldn't swallow that awful thing. I pressed my hands to my face, choking on my own sobs.

"You're pathetic," he said, leaning back like he hadn't just burned my tongue again. "Crying over nothing. You're lucky I'm teaching you how to toughen up."

I looked at my mother then, because I always did. Because some part of me kept hoping that this time she would stand up and say something, or at least look at me. She was sitting on the couch with her legs crossed, and her eyes fixed on the TV. Her expression was flat and distant. And she didn't move.

"If you didn't act like this, he wouldn't get so angry," she said calmly. "You always push him."

My father laughed cruelly. "Hear that? Even she knows it's your fault. Everything is your fucking fault, boy."

My mouth hurt too much to speak. I tasted blood and smoke and something bitter. I wiped my face with my sleeve and tried to make myself small.

"Go sit in your corner," he said. "And don't make a sound. I don't want to hear you cry like a little girl."

I did what he told me, because I always did. I sat on the floor near the wall, with my knees pulled to my chest. My mouth was still burning, and my body shook even though I tried to stop it.

I stayed quiet and still, and I didn't dare to believe that this would ever stop.

———

I woke to a hand gently running through my hair. I smiled, keeping my eyes closed so I could enjoy her touch for a moment longer.

"Hmm." I slid my hand over her waist and pulled her closer, fitting her body tight against mine.

She melted into me, her leg slipping between mine as her fingers curled softly in my hair.

When I finally opened my eyes, hers were the first thing I saw, and my heart skipped without warning. If there was one thing I could choose to look at for the rest of my life, it would be her eyes. Their color still caught my attention every time, the blue in her right eye standing out clearly against the dark brown. It was as unique and perfect as Milow was.

"Morning," I murmured, pressing my hand flat against her lower back. "Have you been up long?"

She shook her head, then brushed her nose gently along my jaw before leaning in to kiss me. I kissed her back without hesitation, meeting her halfway and pulling her closer. It was a slow kiss, and it made everything around us feel far away and unimportant. It made me want to stay right here with her, wrapped in each other's arms, without getting up any time soon. I slid my other hand along her spine, feeling the curve of her back as she arched it, then moved it up to cup the back of her head to keep her right there. I deepened the kiss just a little, still moving my lips slowly against hers. I was taking my time because there was no rush.

When she pulled back, she pushed herself up to sit, and as she moved, I rolled onto my back. I looked up at her with one arm tucked behind my head and the other resting easily on her thigh, my thumb brushing over her skin without thinking about it. She looked calm and happy, her hair slightly messy from sleep, and her eyes soft as she looked down at me.

[Happy birthday, Ashby.]

I grinned, letting out a quiet sigh when it fully sank in. "Shit…I forgot."

She scrunched her nose and placed a hand on my stomach, her fingertips slowly tracing the creases of my abs. She did it unconsciously, but it made me grin wider.

"Thank you, sweet girl. I can't believe I'm eighteen. I'm getting so old," I said jokingly.

Milow rolled her eyes. [You're still young, and you have your whole life ahead of you.]

"You're right," I said, my grin turning into a slow smile. "And I can't wait to spend it all with you."

I gave it exactly one second before her cheeks burned bright red, and I smirked, lifting my left hand from her thigh to cup her cheek. "I should put making you blush on the list of things I'm great at."

Milow sucked in her cheeks to stop herself from smiling, but it failed. [Stop it,] she signed, before slapping my chest.

I chuckled and dropped my hand back to her thigh, gently brushing the skin beneath the hem of her pajama shorts.

I smiled. "I mean it. I'm glad I can spend my birthday with you."

Birthdays had always been my favorite. Not just mine, but everyone else's too. Growing older never scared me. Every birthday meant I'd survived another year and that I still had the people I loved close to me.

[I got you a present,] she signed, her cheeks staying pink as she glanced away for a second before looking back at me.

"Yeah?" I lifted my brows. "What is it?"

She reached over to the nightstand, picked up something, then handed it to me. I sat up, taking in the plaid wrapping paper before looking at her again. "Thank you, Milow."

[Open it,] she signed, her eyes bright with excitement.

"Okay, okay." I carefully unwrapped it, peeling the paper back and lifting out what was inside.

I grinned the second I saw it. A dark-brown trapper hat rested in my hands. The ear flaps and the front part were lined with lighter brown fur. I ran my fingers over it, already knowing I'd wear it every winter from now on. The weather was already turning colder, and I never left the house without a trapper hat in winter anyway. It had always been my thing.

Ever since Dad bought me my first blue one when I was little, it stuck. It became a habit and a comfort piece.

"I love it, Milow. It's perfect," I said, pulling it on with a grin. "How do I look?"

She smiled and clasped her hands together, pressing them to her chest before signing, [Very handsome.]

"Thank you," I said, chuckling. "I was actually thinking about getting a new one."

I leaned in and kissed her, one hand resting at the side of her head. When I pulled back, she lifted her hands again.

[There's something hidden on the inside.]

"Hidden?" I frowned and took the hat off, turning it over. The lining inside was dark blue, and I paused for a second. The hat's colors reminded me of her eyes. I didn't think she had picked it specifically because of that, but I liked to think she did subconsciously.

She pointed, and I leaned closer. Stitched neatly into the lining with white yarn were our initials, tucked inside a heart.

I smiled and looked back at her as she signed, [I embroidered it. If it's too much, I can take it out.]

"No," I said immediately, shaking my head as I traced the stitches with my thumb. "Don't. It's perfect. I want it exactly like this."

Her smile grew, and I pressed the hat to my chest before leaning into her to kiss her again. "I love you, Milow."

Always and forever.

40

Ashby

I spent my eighteenth birthday the way I always liked to spend it. Eating breakfast with my family, then hanging out together, talking and laughing while we ate cake. Stan was here too. I had called him earlier to check in. To see how he was doing and if he'd heard anything from Scottie. She was still undergoing additional checkups and tests, with Scarlett staying by her side. I didn't want him sitting alone with his thoughts all day, so I told him to come over and spend the day with us instead.

It took him a bit to loosen up. His usual humor was weighed down by worry, and I could tell he was forcing himself to act normal. But the moment Wesley suggested Mario Kart in the basement, Stan snapped right into it. He put on his game face immediately, talking shit about everyone else and declaring himself the self-proclaimed king of the game.

And honestly, he was. Mostly because he'd played it almost every day growing up.

We settled onto the couches, controllers in hand, and the game loading on the screen.

"I'm not good at this," Evie said, turning the controller over as if it might bite her.

Wesley leaned closer, pointing things out patiently. "It's easy, love. Press this one to go, and use this to steer."

Stan snorted, leaning back with his feet on the coffee table, ankles crossed. "She's gonna lose. And so are the rest of you."

Wesley shot him a look. "You be nice to my girl. You hear me?"

"Or what?" Stan shot back, raising his brows. "You gonna cry, big guy?"

"You better watch your mouth, buddy."

They kept going back and forth, and I just sat there watching, amused.

"You wanna fight, hockey boy?" Stan stood up suddenly, puffing his chest and dropping his controller onto the couch beside me. "Because that's another thing I'm better at than you."

"Oh no, please don't fight," Evie said, her tone dripping with sarcasm. She loved this and would find an excuse to see them mess around whenever she could. It was funny, really. Even though Stan trained in MMA, Wesley could throw a punch too. He'd been in enough ugly fights on the ice to prove it, which you wouldn't expect from how calm he usually was.

But on the ice, Wesley was different. It was the only place he allowed himself to throw punches when necessary.

He handed Evie the controller and rolled up his sleeves. "Thought you'd learned by now that you don't stand a chance, Whitt."

"Oh yeah?" Stan grinned, bringing his fists up like he was about to step into a real fight. "Show me what you got, Statler."

Seconds later, they were on the floor in front of the TV, wrestling like idiots. I laughed and cheered when Wesley managed to pin Stan down.

[He really never learns,] Milow signed, shaking her head, and suppressing a smile.

"Never," I agreed.

"You're so weak, Stanley," Evie teased, enjoying this more than anyone.

"Hey, I'm not weak," Stan argued, trying to shove Wesley off. "Get off me, puck face."

"Good one, dude," I said, laughing.

"Say I'm stronger than you," Wesley demanded.

"Never."

"Just give up," I told him, still entertained.

He struggled a while longer before giving up with a frustrated sound. "Fine. You're stronger than me. And more handsome, even with your white grandpa hair and demonic, icy eyes."

Wesley grinned and patted his cheek. "Good boy."

They got up, and Stan sulked his way over to Milow, dropping down beside her and wrapping his arms around her. "Everyone's always so mean to me, Ace," he said, pouting.

Milow patted his arm, her lips pressed together as her mouth turned down in sympathy.

"You'll survive," Wes told him with a grin. "Toughen up, buddy."

Around five that afternoon, Scarlett called Stan to tell him Scottie was allowed to go home. I thought it was strange. They still hadn't figured out what actually caused her to faint, yet they sent her home anyway, hoping it wouldn't happen again. That didn't sit right with me.

Stan left immediately to go to their house. We told him to give Scottie a tight hug from all of us, but not to overwhelm her. She needed rest more than anything, and having Stan there would be enough for now.

Milow was still visibly worried. She had already sent Scottie a text, letting her know she was there for her no matter what, anytime she needed it.

For dinner, Dad ordered pizza, like he always did when one of us had a birthday. I appreciated it. I didn't want anyone cooking a big meal or making a big deal out of it. Pizza was enough after the day they had already given me. We sat in the living room with music playing softly in the background, eating and talking without any rush.

That was all I needed. My family was around me, and the girl I'd loved since we were kids was right by my side.

41

Milow

Monday, November 3rd

Ashby didn't go to the pool this morning. Instead, we picked up Stanley at his house, then drove to Scottie's. Scarlett had decided to keep her home for another day or two, just to be sure she was actually feeling better before sending her back to school. It felt like the right call. The doctors had let her go too soon, at least in my opinion, and I hadn't liked it at all. But I trusted Scarlett because she always took care of her daughter the way she should.

When we walked inside, Scottie was curled up on the couch with a blanket pulled around her shoulders. She looked up when she heard us and smiled, and I went to her right away, even before Stan did. I had been worried nonstop, and seeing her like this made my chest squeeze all over again.

"Hey," Scottie whispered as I leaned in to hug her. "I'm okay." Her voice sounded light, as if she truly was all right.

I held her a second longer before sitting beside her. [I'm glad you're doing better.]

"Me too," she said with a soft smile. "They pumped me full of strong meds, and look at me now. Good as new."

"You still fainted," Stan said. He didn't look convinced. Not even a little.

"So? It's not like I died."

"You're still treating this like it's funny."

"It's not funny," she said. Her expression hardened for a brief second, then it softened, and she reached for him. "Come here. I want to kiss my boyfriend."

Stan hesitated before taking her hand. He sat beside her and leaned in to kiss her. When he pulled back, his tone stayed serious. "I don't think this was random. And it definitely wasn't a circulatory collapse. You're physically fit. You're healthy."

"It could happen to anyone, Stanley," she said calmly, keeping his hand in hers. "I'm fine. The tests will prove it."

I wanted to believe her. Still, something twisted deep in my stomach. It was a feeling I couldn't shake. Something was wrong, but I couldn't prove it.

"Just rest another day or two," Ashby said gently. "There's no rush. You'll be back on the field scoring hat tricks in no time."

Scottie looked at him with a tight and hopeful smile. "I can't wait."

Scarlett came back in with a steaming cup and set it on the coffee table. Then she looked at Scottie. "I'm cutting up fruit. And I put toast in the toaster. Are you hungry yet?"

"I am. Thanks, Mom."

Scarlett looked at the rest of us then. "Thank you for

coming by. You're the sweetest. But it's time to go. You'll be late for school."

I nodded and gently rubbed Scottie's arm before I stood, stepping closer to Ashby as his hand settled at my lower back.

Stan didn't move. He stayed glued to Scottie's side, still holding her hand. Then he grimaced and clutched his stomach with a groan. "I don't feel so good, Scar. Maybe I should stay here so you can take care of me, too."

Scarlett rolled her eyes, laughing softly. "Nice try. Come on. School's waiting."

"But my stomach hurts," he whined, standing up reluctantly.

"Then maybe stop stuffing your face with donuts before sunrise," Ashby said, grinning.

"That's not my fault," Stan shot back. "My mom buys them and then guilt-trips me into eating them before they go stale." He turned to Scarlett, pulling out his most piti-ful look. "Please, Scar? I'd really love some freshly cut-up fruit, too."

She shook her head. "You need to go. Chelsea won't be happy if you skip."

"Mom won't care," he said. "She'd rather see me taking care of my girl than zoning out in class."

I pressed my lips together. He wasn't wrong, but he still had to go. I tapped his arm to get his attention. [Scottie needs rest. We can come back after school.]

He frowned, then sighed. "Fine." He looked back at Scottie. "I'll come straight here after."

She smiled. "I'll be right here. Waiting."

"Good. I love you."

"I love you too, Stanley."

I loved them. Both of them. And I loved them together.

[Bye, Scottie. See you later,] I signed.

After one last round of goodbyes, we headed out and climbed into the car, where we had to listen to Stan whine throughout the drive about how he hated school and how he'd rather be at Scottie's side, guarding her from fainting again.

I couldn't argue with that. I'd rather be close to my best friend too in a time like this. And for reasons I couldn't explain, the heavy feeling in my chest only grew the closer we got to the school, like my gut was trying to warn me, telling me I shouldn't be there at all.

When the lunch bell rang, I went straight to my locker. I needed to put my books away, grab my lunch, and then wait for Ashby and Stan. I stood there for a few minutes, checking the hallway every so often, but they didn't show. After five minutes, I pulled out my phone to text Ashby.

Unlocking it, I saw he had already sent me a message.

Ashby: On our way. Teacher held us back.

I didn't want them to rush on my account, so I answered quickly.

Me: I'll head to the cafeteria. Meet me there.

I slipped my phone into the pocket of my hoodie, closed my locker, and started down the hallway. Only a few students were standing around the hallway, with the noise from before mostly gone. Then I turned the corner and saw Hailie and Aspen standing there. Bennett was with them, which caught me off guard. All three looked irritated, as if my presence alone had ruined their day.

I stopped. My throat tightened as I tried to decide what to do. I could turn around and text Ashby to meet me back at my locker. I could wait there. Or, I could stand my ground. The decision hadn't been simple, even though it should have been.

I wanted to leave. I always wanted to leave when I found myself alone with them. But my feet wouldn't move.

"God, just looking at her makes me want to vomit," Hailie said. "Do you own anything that doesn't make you look poor? Or is this really the best you can do?"

I frowned. That was it. That was the insult. I looked *poor*.

My clothes were clean. They fit, and there was nothing wrong with them.

"And she's still not talking," Aspen added, louder than necessary. She glanced at Bennett when she said it. She was meaner than usual, and she was clearly looking for his approval. "It's so weird."

"Yeah, and it's disrespectful," Hailie said, crossing her arms and shifting her weight to one hip. "Our beating clearly didn't help."

The word made my stomach drop. I felt the pain all over again. I looked down at my hands and started picking at the loose skin by my thumb, the habit soothing and useless at the same time.

"Beating?" Bennett asked quietly. "You hit her?"

He sounded concerned, but was he really? I didn't look at him to check. He hadn't been kind to me lately, and I didn't want his attention now. I just wanted Ashby. I wanted Stan. I wanted this hallway to stop feeling so small, and for my lungs to work normally.

Hailie clicked her tongue. "We had to. She was being rude."

"How was she being rude?" Bennett asked. He sounded genuinely concerned now, and I couldn't help it. I needed to see his face.

I lifted my gaze to him. He was frowning, his attention fully on me this time.

"I mean," he continued, "did she talk back to you or something?"

I bit the inside of my cheek, hugging my lunchbox to my stomach. He still thought I had selective mutism, that I would eventually start talking once I got over it.

He didn't know. None of them did. But I had a feeling that even if they knew the truth, they'd still treat me like this.

After what happened at the diner, I replayed Bennett's behavior over and over in my head. People's behavior didn't just change without a reason. Something in his life must've pushed him far enough to become someone he wasn't. The same must've been the case for Hailie and Aspen. That kind of anger must have had a source. It didn't come out of nowhere.

"No, she didn't say a damn word. Just kept her stupid mouth shut and—" Hailie stopped short, because there was nothing else to add. I hadn't done anything to them in the bathroom. Not a single thing. They had gone after me out of boredom.

My jaw locked. I needed to move. I needed my body to listen to me and get away from them.

"I hate her face," Hailie continued. "She thinks she's

something special by acting like a disabled person. But she's worthless. And she's a liar."

My brows pulled together. I usually didn't let her words get to me, but that one landed differently. Maybe because, for once, she had said something true. I was disabled. And for a split second, the thought crept in that maybe that really did make me worthless.

Aspen laughed and crossed her arms, copying Hailie's stance. "Or maybe she actually is disabled. Wouldn't surprise me. Maybe that's the reason why she hangs out with that other disabled girl."

"No," Hailie said. "The one you're thinking of is just severely mentally ill."

They both laughed. I saw Bennett grinning behind them, as if this was entertaining, like he hadn't been friends with us before.

I felt sick. How was he not stopping this? He had always been kind to me. At least he used to be. And I didn't understand why he was even standing with them. Didn't he have limits? Didn't he care and see how hurtful they were being?

Anger rose inside of me, and my whole body burned with overwhelming emotions. I hated the way they spoke about Scottie.

"I heard she fainted at her soccer game," Hailie said. "Such a loser. Maybe she should stop popping pills."

That was it.

I wanted to tell them exactly how I felt. I wanted to unload every thought in my head. But no amount of signing would make them understand, and they didn't deserve my explanations anyway. So I chose to do the one thing I knew they would understand without question.

I tucked my lunchbox under one arm and flipped them off.

With both hands.

Their laughter stopped instantly. Aspen recovered first, bursting out laughing again, but Hailie didn't. Her face twisted, eyes dark, clearly taking it for what it was.

An attack.

And without a second thought, she came straight at me.

I barely had time to react, but instinct kicked in, and I threw my arms up to shield my head, my lunchbox falling to the ground. My shield didn't help. Hailie's fingers tangled in my hair anyway, her fists closing tight as she yanked hard enough to make my vision blur.

"You bitch. How dare you?"

All I had done was flip her off. One small gesture. Something people did every day without thinking twice. And somehow that was worse to her than every word she had thrown at me for months, worse than every look, every shove, every whisper meant to make me smaller. It was enough to make her want to hurt me.

She kept pulling, jerking my head back and down, and I clawed at her hands, trying to get free. She didn't loosen her grip. She was stronger than I was, and she knew it. The pain shot through my scalp and down my neck, and no matter how hard I struggled, she wouldn't let go.

I stumbled sideways when she shoved my head down again, my body folding forward, and then it happened so fast I didn't even realize it at first. Her knee came up and slammed into my face, straight into my nose. The pain exploded through me. My hands flew to my face on instinct, and immediately they were wet.

"Hailie." Bennett's voice was filled with shock, or maybe I only imagined it, because he still wasn't pulling her off me. He didn't step in.

"You're a whore. A useless, disabled whore," she screamed, her grip on my hair never easing.

The pain in my scalp faded into the background, swallowed by the deep, pulsing ache in my face. Blood kept pouring out of my nose, soaking my hands, and running down my wrists. The fabric of my sweater stopped it from running down my arms, but there was so much that it dripped onto the floor.

"Hailie, come on. That's enough," Bennett said again. But he was still standing there.

My body started to shake as tears spilled over. My breathing came in short and uneven pulls. As if the bleeding wasn't enough, she started hitting the side of my head. Her punches weren't hard, not like the knee, but they landed again and again, each one adding to the pressure and the ringing until dizziness crept in.

The hallway tilted, and my legs felt weak and useless. If she hadn't been holding me upright by my hair, I would have collapsed. I wanted to scream. I wanted to make noise and draw attention to what was happening to me, but a voice deep inside of me told me I wasn't worth it as my body stayed silent. I was trapped like I always was. I had no voice to call for help. My father had made sure of that a long time ago.

I didn't think about him often anymore. I tried not to. But in that moment, with pain tearing through me and nowhere for it to go, I was pulled straight back into those memories, back to being small and powerless, and completely alone.

I couldn't even compare the pain. It had been so long. And I had been so young. But the helplessness felt the same.

Hailie must have burned through whatever strength she had left, because her grip in my hair finally loosened. She shoved me hard, and I stumbled straight into the lockers. One of the doors was open, and I recognized it was Hailie's because of all the pictures of her and Aspen stuck to the inside. I walked past her locker every day, and every single day she stood there and looked at me like I didn't belong.

"Let's just go, Hailie," Aspen pleaded, her voice tight. "Maybe we should call the nurse…"

"Shut up!" Hailie screamed. "I'm not done with this whore yet."

My head was spinning. I kept one hand clamped over my nose, trying to stop the blood, while the other searched blindly for balance. Before I could steady myself, she grabbed both my wrists. Her fingers dug in hard and twisted, wrenching my arms at an angle that sent pain shooting straight through me. That's when I saw her face again. The fury in her eyes was violent and unfiltered. She didn't look like a girl anymore. She looked older and meaner. Like the hatred had carved something ugly into her features and dragged it to the surface.

"Come help me," Hailie snapped, looking up at Aspen.

"I don't think I—"

"You're such a bitch, Aspen! If you're my friend, you'll help me." She twisted my wrists harder, and from the way my head was tilted, I felt the blood slide down the back of my throat.

It was thick and warm and made my stomach lurch. It made me gag.

"What are you going to do?" Aspen asked. She was closer now.

When she stepped into view, I saw the pure horror in her face. She was staring at me, at the blood on my hands, my hoodie, the floor. And still, she didn't help me. She didn't move toward me. She didn't tell Hailie to stop.

I wondered why. Was she scared Hailie would turn on her next? Did she think being loyal to someone this cruel was better than doing the right thing?

"We're going to break her fingers," Hailie said calmly. "She doesn't talk, so we'll make her."

The words didn't make sense at first. They floated somewhere above me. How did she expect me to start talking when I quite literally didn't have vocal cords? Breaking my hands wouldn't change that. It was pointless. It was cruel for the sake of being cruel. I knew she didn't know, but I didn't think she'd understand, anyway.

"Hailie…" Aspen whispered.

"Are you helping or not?" Hailie snapped. "God, you're the worst friend. And don't think I don't know you made out with Bennett when he asked me out."

Oh.

That explained a lot.

I struggled again as my vision tunneled.

"He asked me out first," Aspen cried.

"Just help me already," Hailie said. "Grab her wrists."

Aspen obeyed.

Her hands closed around my wrists, though not as tightly as Hailie's. It was enough to hold me still. Hailie crouched in front of me and forced my arms sideways until my fingers curled around the sharp edge of the open locker door. For a split second, I thought they were lifting me and helping me.

But I should've known that wasn't their intention.

Then, without a warning, Hailie slammed the door shut.

Metal crushed against my fingers, and pain exploded so violently it felt like my entire body folded inward. Before I could even process it, she did it again. And again. The locker rattled with the force, and each slam sent another wave of agony tearing through my hands, up my arms, and straight through my whole body.

My mouth opened, but no sound came out. Not even air. The pain was so deep and overwhelming that for a second, I swore my voice had come back.

But in reality, I stayed silent.

Aspen let go immediately and stumbled backward. Her voice shook as she spoke. "What did you make me do? Oh my god…Hailie, stop."

I ripped my hands back and pressed them to my chest, curling inward instinctively, and trying to protect what was left of me. My fingers throbbed and burned. The pain was endless and trapped inside my body, with nowhere to go.

"Hey! Get the fuck off her!"

Ashby.

The sound of his voice cut through everything, and I let go all at once. I stopped fighting. I stopped trying to protect myself. I could finally give in, because he was here now, and I didn't have to hold myself together anymore.

My body folded in on itself. The pain in my nose kept

growing, but the rest of my face and my hands started to go numb, like my body was shutting parts of me down to survive it.

"What the fuck did you do!" Ashby roared.

I couldn't look up. I couldn't move my hands. I stared at the dark pool spreading across the floor beneath me, and my thoughts spiraled in useless circles. Was all of that really mine? Had I lost that much blood? Had I hit her back without realizing it, making her bleed too?

"Milow."

Ashby was in front of me now, down on his knees. His hands were careful and warm as they cupped my face. "Fuck, Milow, are you okay? Look at me."

His voice was shaking with raw fear, and when I forced myself to meet his eyes, I saw tears burning there. He looked horrified, like he couldn't quite process what he was seeing. He was trying to make sense of something that shouldn't have happened. "Did she do this to you?" he asked, his jaw tight.

I nodded slowly. I didn't know what else to do. Blood kept pouring from my nose, soaking his hands, and dripping onto his jeans. He didn't even seem to notice. His eyes stayed locked on my face as he searched for something, his head shaking over and over. "I'm so sorry, Milow. God, I'm so fucking sorry."

I didn't understand why he was apologizing to me. He hadn't hurt me. This wasn't his fault.

My hands trembled as I lifted them to sign, even though they were throbbing. [I'm okay.]

His expression hardened immediately. "You're not okay," he said, his voice sharp now. "God, Milow, your hands…"

I frowned and looked down at them. The blood had already started to dry on my skin, and as I stared at them, I realized that's not what he was so worried about. My knuckles on my right hand were swollen.

"I'm taking you to the hospital. You've lost a lot of blood."

I shook my head without thinking. We didn't have time to go to the hospital.

[We have lunch. And we're going to see Scottie again after school.] I immediately regretted signing. The pain in my hands had overtaken everything else, drowning out even the agony in my nose.

"We're going to the hospital," he repeated, his tone leaving no room for discussion.

He sounded angry now, and panic flared inside me. Was he angry at me? Had I done something wrong? My thoughts scrambled, grasping for reasons and apologies that might make it better.

[I'm sorry. I'm sorry.]

"Can you stand up?" he asked, softer again. "I've got you."

I frowned and grabbed onto his arms, letting him pull me to my feet. The moment I stood, the room tilted violently. A hot rush shot through my head, and my stomach twisted. Blood filled my mouth, and it felt like my nose would never stop bleeding.

"Put this under your nose," Ashby said quietly, forcing himself to stay calm. He pressed a piece of fabric into my hand and guided it up. "Don't tilt your head back. Let it come out."

I looked at him, blinking fast as bright spots exploded across my vision. His face doubled, then blurred, and the world around us spun so badly I had to focus on the sound of his voice just to stay upright.

"You're a fucking coward!"

The shout made me flinch, and I turned my head too fast, sending another wave of dizziness crashing through me. I hadn't even noticed what was happening around us until then, but when my vision cleared, I saw Stan slamming Bennett back against the wall, his hands twisted in his sweater.

"You're a coward and a fucking joke!"

"Stan," Ashby snapped. "He's not worth it."

Stan didn't listen. He shoved Bennett harder, rage pouring out of him. "You're dead to me. After all these years, after everything, you let this happen to her?"

"Stan," Ashby said again, his voice strained. "I have to take Milow to the hospital."

No. No hospital.

I tugged weakly at Ashby's sleeve, my fingers protesting with every move as I shook my head and let the fabric fall so I could sign. [We have to eat lunch.]

"No," he shouted, the sound ringing in my ears. "You're going to the fucking hospital."

I froze. The anger in his voice knocked the air out of my lungs, and all I could do was stare at him.

Why was he mad? Why was I always wrong?

[I'm sorry.]

"Stop," he said, interrupting me as he dragged a bloody hand through his hair. He picked the fabric back up and held it to my nose himself, his touch careful but controlled. "Stop apologizing, Milow."

I nodded because that seemed like the only right thing I could do to stop him from being angry.

42

Ashby

"Hey, hey, hey!" Mr. Riveira shouted as he came running toward us, with Mr. Kallio and Principal Madigan right behind him. "What is going on here?"

I didn't look up. I kept one arm locked around Milow's back to keep her upright. My other hand covered hers, making sure she kept pressing the shirt from my backpack against her nose. My stomach churned violently. The amount of blood was unreal. There was too much of it. Way too much. It smeared across her hand and arms, soaked into the fabric of her sweater, and continued to drip onto the floor in dark splashes that made my head spin.

I forced myself to focus on her. On keeping her awake. Her body felt limp against mine, and her head tipped forward like she couldn't quite hold it up anymore. It had to be the blood loss making her this drowsy.

God. There was so much fucking blood.

"Stanley, get off him," Mr. Riveira ordered, grabbing onto Stan's arms. "Come on, buddy. Let's calm down."

"Calm down?" Stan snapped, twisting against his grip. Before Mr. Riveira could fully pull him away, Stan drove his fist straight into Bennett's face.

"All right. That's it!" Principal Madigan roared. "Enough!"

I barely registered it. My attention snapped back to Milow as her knees buckled in my hold. I tightened my arm around her immediately. "Hey," I said quietly, my voice shaking despite my effort to keep it steady. "Stay awake, okay? Stay with me, sweet girl."

"What happened here?" Mr. Kallio asked, stepping closer and carefully sliding an arm under Milow's other side to help support her. "How did it escalate like this?"

"I don't know," I muttered, my eyes never leaving her face. She looked so fucking pale, and the blood just kept coming. "But I do know this school has done absolutely nothing to protect its students from bullies."

Mr. Kallio let out a slow breath, sounding tired more than surprised. He didn't argue with me. "I'm calling an ambulance," he said. "We'll get her to the nurse's office so she can lie down."

"She shouldn't be lying down with a nosebleed," I snapped. "Jesus Christ, how fucking incompetent is this school?"

"Language, Ashby," he warned sharply.

Right. My language was the problem. Not the pool of blood on the floor. Not the fact that Milow was barely standing.

I pulled Milow closer to my side, subtly shifting so Mr.

Kallio's hold loosened. I didn't want anyone else handling her. I didn't want anyone else touching her. I should've been there sooner. That thought wouldn't let me go, and I needed to be the one holding her now.

"To my office. Now," Principal Madigan barked, gripping Stan and Bennett by the arms. "You too," he added, jerking his head toward Hailie and Aspen.

I didn't look at them. I couldn't. All I could see was Milow in my arms, and the terrifying truth that no matter how much I held her, I couldn't stop the pain.

"Dear heaven! What happened?" The nurse, Mrs. Bouchard, stared at us in open horror as I guided Milow down onto the bed.

I didn't answer. I hadn't seen it happen, and that alone made me want to put my fist through the nearest wall. But I didn't need to see it. Milow had confirmed it. I already knew who had done this. I knew it had been Hailie.

"She's lost a lot of blood," Mr. Kallio said. His voice stayed controlled, but I could hear what sat under it. No teacher could witness this and feel nothing.

"We'll get you cleaned up, darling," Mrs. Bouchard murmured, clicking her tongue. "Oh, you poor thing."

I kept my arm around Milow and slowly rubbed her back to comfort her. I had her right hand in mine, holding it in my lap. She looked gone. Her eyes were wide and empty, and her lips were parted from the pure shock. Her whole body trembled, and I cursed myself repeatedly for not being there to stop the horrendous attack from happening.

"I've got you, Milow," I said quietly. "I'm right here."

Her head turned with effort until her eyes found mine. She looked at me for a long second, then lifted her left hand. [Sleepy.]

Her fingers didn't move right. The motion was clumsy and delayed, but I understood anyway.

"I know," I said. "But you can't sleep. You have to stay awake, okay?"

Her hand dropped back to her side. When her gaze followed it down, I saw the skin around her eyes darkening already, bruises blooming fast and ugly. Whatever Hailie had done had been violent. It had split her open and left her bleeding without mercy.

"I'm here, Milow. I won't let you go," I whispered, but my own voice seemed far away. Nothing felt real, but I forced myself to stay strong and focus on her.

My vision burned. Tears stung behind my eyes, but I swallowed them down.

I couldn't fall apart. Not now. Not with her slipping right in front of me.

Mom and Dad arrived even before the ambulance sirens could be heard. They were out of breath when they entered the nurse's office, and after scanning the room, they came over to where we were sitting.

They crouched down, cooing to her with that frantic, trembling tenderness only parents could manage, and I didn't let go of her, not for a second, even as the flood of anger, helplessness, and exhaustion washed over me in waves that made my heart ache impossibly hard.

"My baby," Mom whispered, her voice breaking as she cupped Milow's now-clean face in her hands. Her nose was still bleeding, though not as much as before, and I held a cold compress against the bridge of her nose with gentle pressure. I was afraid to hurt her more. Afraid that any wrong move could tear her further apart.

Mom's eyes were glistening with tears that refused to

fall. She scanned every inch of Milow's face. The swelling, the bruises forming under her eyes, the pain she couldn't voice but that radiated in every line of her body. I caught Dad out of the corner of my eye, dragging a hand over his own face like he was trying to erase the horror he felt from his expression. They were both clearly broken, yet they tried desperately to stay strong for her. They wanted to be a shield even when their own hearts were cracking, because that's what parents were supposed to do.

"Who did this?" Mom asked, her voice barely above a whisper.

I tightened my jaw, forcing back the rage clawing at my throat. I swallowed it down because I didn't want to make the moment worse. The weight of everything pressed down too hard already. "The same girl who's been bullying her for years," I said, keeping my voice low and measured, but it was edged with all the fury I couldn't let spill outward.

Mom's face twisted. I recognized the shame immediately because it mirrored the same crushing shame I felt for not being able to protect Milow the way I knew I should have. The way I had promised her I would.

"I'm going to speak to that girl's parents," Dad said through clenched teeth. He couldn't keep his anger inside any longer. He reached out for Milow, brushing the hair from her face with the gentlest touch possible before leaning forward to kiss the top of her head. "I love you, sweetheart," he murmured, his voice shaky. The weight behind his words nearly broke me because I felt the helplessness, the love, and the rage all at once.

We were all at a loss for words. There were so many things I wanted to tell her, so many words I wanted to spill to soothe her. I wanted to promise her she was safe, to make her pain go away, and yet nothing I could say felt like it would be enough to make this moment any better.

She was suffering, and yet, the moment the pain on our faces registered, she pushed her own hurt aside and forced herself to stay calm so we would not fall apart. Even with what little strength she had left, she focused on soothing us instead of letting herself be the one who needed comfort.

While the three of us were drowning in fear and anger, Milow acted as if she was not the one who had been hurt. She kept herself composed despite the blood and the pain, ignoring the exhaustion shattering her body. Her expression was clouded with worry for us, and I felt a sharp sting in my heart because she had already carried enough. She had already fought more than anyone her age should have, and still she tried to take away our pain when it was supposed to be the other way around.

She lifted her hands, trying to sign something to us, but we couldn't understand her. Her fingers weren't moving properly, and they were all bruised and swollen.

I shook my head and lowered her left hand to my lap, needing her to rest it. Even the smallest movement could make the swelling worse and the pain sharper.

"You don't have to do anything right now, Milow," I said quietly, trying to keep my voice from shaking too much. "Let us take care of you, okay? Let us hold you this time."

Her eyes searched mine, as if she were trying to fully understand the idea that she could allow someone else to carry even a fraction of her pain. I realized that she had never once believed she was allowed to hurt. That somewhere along the way, she had learned to swallow her pain whole and carry it quietly, convincing herself that her purpose was to soothe and comfort. To hold everyone else together, even when she was breaking. Just the idea of being held in return, of letting herself be weak, felt so foreign to her that it barely existed at all.

Her selflessness was astonishing.

I kept holding her, forcing myself to steady my breathing until the paramedics finally arrived. Only after they had lifted her carefully onto the stretcher and secured her inside the ambulance with Mom at her side did I let go. I fell into Dad's arms, letting him hold me as I cried. My body trembled violently, and my stomach twisted so hard it made me sick. I stumbled away from Dad, and before I could stop it from happening, I threw up on the sidewalk.

All the tension and fear that gathered inside me for the last hour poured out of me uncontrollably, and it only stopped when there was nothing left inside.

43

Milow

They brought me into a small room where a doctor exam-ined my face, pressed carefully around my nose, and sent me for X-rays of my face and hands. He talked the entire time, explaining things to Mom, but I didn't really follow any of it. My head felt thick and slow, and my eyes kept slipping shut no matter how hard I tried to keep them open. I remembered Mom staying close, her hand never leaving my arm. Everything else blurred together until there were gaps I couldn't fill anymore.

When I opened my eyes again, I was lying in a bed. The room was dark and quiet, with only a dim, warm light glowing in the corner near the window. For a moment, I didn't know where I was or how long I had been asleep. I knew I was awake, but my body didn't feel like my own, and it felt like I was experiencing everything from afar. As I shifted my gaze, I noticed someone sitting beside the bed.

Ashby was there. He sat on a chair pulled close, hunched forward with his arms folded on the mattress and his head resting on them. He was asleep, looking completely worn down, with his shoulders tense even in rest. I watched him for a long moment, the sight of him making my stomach twist. I wanted to poke him. I wanted him to know I was awake. But my hands felt too heavy to lift. There was a splint on my left hand and a cast on my right. They were resting in my lap, and I stared at them when everything came back all at once in an overwhelming wave.

Hailie had done this to me. She had snapped in the middle of the school hallway and turned into this vicious person, and she had hurt me without anyone stopping her.

She had attacked me unprovoked. No…that wasn't the full truth. I had flipped her off. I had reacted to her words, but only because of what she said about Scottie. I couldn't stand hearing her mouth tear into someone I loved, but still…I had provoked her right back.

And maybe I shouldn't have.

Maybe if I had just looked away, if I had swallowed her cruelty like I always did and kept walking, my face wouldn't be aching, and my hands wouldn't be wrapped in thick white bandages. Maybe none of this would have happened if I had stayed small and invisible the way I was supposed to.

My body tensed as tears burned behind my eyes. I just sat there, staring at the back of Ashby's head and replaying everything over and over to try and make sense of it all.

No one exploded like that for no reason. No one got that violent without being pushed. That was what made sense. Which meant this had to be my fault, at least a little.

I stayed still, afraid that if I moved, the pain would only get worse. I wanted to reach out and touch him, to feel something familiar under my fingers, but my hands stayed where they were. They felt heavy and useless.

A soft knock pulled me out of my thoughts, and I looked toward the door as it slowly opened.

Wesley stepped inside, closing the door quietly behind him. He paused when he saw me awake, his expression shifting instantly. Relief flashed across his face before it tightened with anger and sadness. I wanted to believe that the anger wasn't directed at me, but after going through what happened in my head, I just couldn't shake the truth that I had still done something to provoke Hailie.

He crossed the room and stopped at the side of the bed opposite Ashby, and I watched his eyes drop immediately to my hands before slowly lifting to my face. His mouth tightened for a second before it softened into a smile, and then he reached out, resting one hand carefully on my arm. "Hey, Milow," he said quietly. "I'm really glad you're awake."

I bit the inside of my cheek and just looked up at him, my eyes wide. My body was still too tired to respond properly to anything. Not that I really could, anyway.

"How are you feeling?" he asked, lowering his voice even more. His thumb moved slowly along my arm, and his eyes never left my face.

I nodded. That was all I could manage. I wanted to lean into him, needing to feel his comfort. Wesley seemed to understand without me having to explain. He let out a quiet, shaky breath, then stepped closer and wrapped his arms around me carefully. I leaned into his chest without hesitation and closed my eyes, resting my head against him as his heartbeat thudded hard beneath my ear.

"You're so incredibly strong, Milow. I'm so sorry."

I wasn't sure what he was apologizing for. He hadn't done this to me. Nobody here had. If anything, it had been my fault. I should've known better.

He pressed a soft kiss to the top of my head and rubbed my back, and I let myself stay there for a little while longer, letting him hold me. I didn't have the energy to pull away anyway.

"Everyone's here," he told me quietly, his voice reassuring. "Mom and Dad, Evie…Stan, Scottie, and their parents too. They're downstairs in the cafeteria. We've all been waiting for you to wake up."

I turned my head slightly to look up at him, and he smiled at me, even though I could see how much it hurt him to do it. He was trying to cheer me up, without lessening the truth of it all. I let my gaze drift to Ashby, still slumped over the edge of the bed.

"Ash hasn't left your side," he added softly. "I tried to get him to come eat, but he refused. He didn't want you to wake up alone."

My throat tightened. I wanted so badly to reach out to him, to run my fingers through his hair because I knew he liked it when I did that. And I wanted him to stop worrying. Even asleep, he carried my pain like it was his own.

"Do you want me to wake him?" Wesley asked, his hand coming up to cup the back of my head.

I nodded and gave him a grateful look, then watched as he moved around the bed and stopped beside Ashby's chair. He rested a hand on Ashby's back and rubbed slow circles there, not wanting to startle him. "Ash," he said quietly. "Hey, buddy. Wake up."

Ashby shifted, mumbling something under his breath before he lifted his head from the mattress. It took a second for him to orient himself, but the moment his gaze landed on me, and he realized I was awake, he straightened fast. The chair scraped against the floor as he leaned forward, one hand coming to my forearm. "Milow…"

His voice broke when he said my name, and the look on his face made my heart ache. He looked exhausted, with dark circles under his eyes and his jaw clenched like he hadn't relaxed it once. The worry he'd been holding on to was so obvious on his face, and it hurt knowing that all of it was because of me.

44

Ashby

The nurse was checking on Milow while I stood with Wesley near the door, where he was trying for the third time to convince me to eat something.

"I'm not hungry," I muttered again, never taking my eyes off her.

She looked fragile in that hospital bed. Her face was bruised, and her hands were wrapped in a splint and cast. And still there was that familiar calmness in her, that quiet strength she always carried. It had always been like this with her. Even now, when she was allowed to be the one who hurt, she was still trying to hold herself together for everyone else.

"Come on, buddy," Wesley said gently. "She's not going anywhere. You need to eat something."

"I'm not hungry," I repeated, jaw tight. But my body betrayed me instantly with a loud growl rolling out of my stomach.

Wesley raised an eyebrow. "Right. And I'm Santa Claus."

I rolled my eyes but couldn't hide the amusement. "You got the hair right. Just need a beard and put on some weight."

Wesley grinned and patted my back. "There we go. Go on now. The cafeteria won't be open all night."

I turned to Milow. The idea of leaving her alone didn't sit right with me. "Can you…" I started, glancing at Wesley. "Can you just get me the food? Bring it up here?"

"Ash."

I sighed. "Fine. Will you stay with her, then?"

"Yeah, I can stay. I've already eaten," he told me.

"Okay." I sucked in a breath, tilting my head to get a better look at Milow around the nurse. "I'll be back soon, Milow. Wesley will stay with you."

She looked at me and nodded, her lips curling into a reassuring smile.

"I'll bring her dinner in just a minute," the nurse said, glancing at Wesley. "Will you help her eat? Otherwise, I can do it."

"I'll do it," I said, already stepping toward the bed.

"No, Ashby, I'll feed her," Wesley said calmly, his voice leaving no room for argument. "Go eat."

My jaw clenched, and I let out a heavy sigh. Leaving her side felt impossible when all I wanted was to stay and help. But I had to tell myself that she'd be fine. Wesley would take care of her, and maybe it was even better this way. I'd been by her side this entire time, and I didn't want her to get sick of me. Even when I knew that she probably wouldn't, crowding her right now wouldn't help anyone.

"Okay." I looked at Milow one last time before stepping back toward the door, and as Wesley turned his back
to me, I signed, [I love you so much.]

Milow's smile deepened, and the reassurance in her
expression was enough to carry me out of the room, but
not enough to calm the storm in my stomach.

I found everyone sitting around a couple of tables
in the cafeteria. Everyone was there, even Scarlett and
Chelsea.

"Hey, champ," Dad said, pulling up an empty chair
next to him. "I got you a sandwich and a muffin."

I sat down. "Thanks. She's awake."

"She is?" Mom straightened, a gentle smile pulling at
her lips. "Oh, good. How is she doing?"

"I don't know, Mom. How does anyone do after being
brutally assaulted?" The words left me before I could stop
them, and suddenly the table went quiet. I hated that I'd
snapped, hated that the anger still burned in my chest.

Dad rubbed my back. "We know, champ."

I clenched my teeth and stared down at the sandwich,
then lifted my gaze to everyone. "I'm sorry," I murmured
with a sigh. "Wesley's helping her with dinner. We should
give her a moment to eat."

Mom nodded, but I could see the impatience in her
eyes. I felt it too. I wanted to go back up there.

"You should eat too," Dad said again. "You haven't
eaten all day."

I didn't feel like it. My stomach had emptied hours
ago, and my throat still ached, but I picked up the sandwich anyway and took a bite.

Stan and Scottie sat across from me, their expressions
just as tired and worn as mine. Scottie, even though she'd

only just been in the hospital over the weekend herself, hadn't stayed home to rest. She'd chosen to be here, to be close to Milow instead of taking care of herself first. I could tell she was still weak, but she had put Milow above her own comfort.

Evie was sitting next to Stan's mom, Chelsea, at the end of the table, and she let out a sigh before picking up on a conversation they must've been having before I arrived. "I just hope there are real consequences this time. I'm glad you called the police," she told Dad.

He nodded slowly, running a hand over his face. He looked exhausted. "The suspension was the first step. The police will be looking more into it now that they admitted to doing it."

"They admitted it?" I asked, surprised.

"Yeah," Stan said, clearing his throat. "I was in the principal's office with them."

I remembered him punching Bennett in the face while Madigan, Kallio, and Riveira all stood there. "Did you get suspended too?"

Stan shrugged. "Just for a day. Hailie and Aspen got a month."

Good. It wasn't long enough, but at least it was something. I nodded. "And Bennett?"

"He got a week," Stan said.

Chelsea reached out and ran her hand through Stan's hair, smiling gently. "I'm proud of you all. For sticking together like that."

"So you're proud of me for punching a guy in the face?" Stan asked, a hint of amusement in his eyes.

"You punch guys in the face all the time," Scottie reminded him.

"Yeah, but…this time I wasn't legally allowed to."

Chelsea laughed softly. "I'm proud of you for protecting your friends and holding another guy accountable for not being man enough to help."

Stan grinned, leaning into his mother's touch and kissing her cheek. "Love you, Mommy."

The others laughed, and I found myself grinning too. Stan was a real mama's boy, and he wasn't ashamed to show it.

The pull to go back upstairs to Milow was unbearable, but I tried to hold myself in place. I told myself that things would get better for her, that the worst was over. She had already endured too much, and I wanted more than anything to make the pain stop and to give her the life she deserved. A normal life. A life where she could go to school without fear and be surrounded by people who loved her exactly as she was.

I knew I couldn't fix everything. I couldn't erase the past and the memories. But I could protect her better. And I would, because until now, I had failed her.

45

Milow

When the nurse came back with my dinner, she explained that my nose wasn't broken, but that I'd just taken a hard enough hit for it to bleed a lot. The swelling and bruising would fade over the next couple of weeks, she said, and the pain was already starting to ease because of the medication they had given me.

My right hand hurt the most. It was the one in the cast. She told me I'd fractured all four fingers, but that I would regain full use of them after keeping them immobilized for about a month. My left hand wasn't as bad. It was in a splint, but I could move my fingers a little without them hurting, and she assured me it would heal quickly if I held it still for a while.

After placing the food in front of me, she left the room. Wesley picked up the knife and fork and cut the chicken breast into small pieces. He smiled at me before spearing a bite and lifting it toward my mouth.

I let him feed me, and I appreciated his patience. I felt

tired and sore, and was grateful for the way he took care of me without making a big deal of it. He stayed quiet, and I could tell he was searching for the right thing to say, weighing every word before letting it out. I knew it wasn't easy for him. It wasn't easy for any of them to see me like this. Still, I felt proud to belong to a family that stayed and showed up in the worst moments. They loved hard and didn't walk away when things hurt.

As I took another bite of the chicken and rice, Wesley drew in a slow breath, finally ready to speak.

"I don't know why people are so cruel, or what drives them to want to hurt others," he started, watching me with those pale eyes of his. "But I do know that someone as strong as you, with a heart as gentle and honest as yours, is rare."

I kept my eyes on him, unable to look away, and unable to do anything but listen.

"You know…I've always known you were special. From the very first day you became part of our family, something shifted for the better. I was happy before Mom and Dad adopted you, I really was, but you…" He stopped and drew in a shaky breath, his eyes shining now. "You completed us. You filled in the space we didn't even know was empty. You were the missing piece, and I couldn't have wished for a kinder or braver baby sister."

My brows pulled together as tears burned behind my eyes. I wanted to lift my hands and touch his face, but I couldn't, so I just kept looking at him.

"And I know everyone else feels the same," he continued quietly. "You don't see it, because you're too busy worrying about everyone else, but we see you. We see how hard you try to make everyone around you comfortable. We see how much you give, and none of this happened because of who you are. It wasn't your fault."

His voice stayed firm, even as the tears started rolling down his cheeks.

"You matter, Milow. Your pain matters. And you don't have to be strong for us all the time. We've got you."

I swallowed hard as my throat started to burn. It was that familiar pressure building the way it always did when too many feelings bubbled up inside of me, and my body begged for a sound to escape. But like always, nothing came, and I was left forcing it all back down, trapping it inside my chest where it ached and lingered.

I looked at Wesley through the blur in my eyes, and at the way he was trying so hard to stay steady for me. I felt that same pull I had felt my whole life. Wesley was someone I watched and learned from without him ever realizing it. I had grown up measuring myself against his kindness and patience, and the way he was always right there without needing to be asked. If I knew how to be brave at all, it was because I had watched him do it first.

He wiped at his tears and rubbed his eyes with the back of his hand, letting out a slow breath as he pulled himself together.

"I love you, Milow, and I'm always here for you. No matter what, okay? Whenever you need me, for whatever you need me, I'm right here."

I smiled and gave a small nod, then leaned in just enough to rest my forehead against his. He cupped the back of my head and held me there for a moment before pressing a soft kiss to my temple and pulling back. Then he picked the fork up again.

"Let's finish this," he said, sniffing as he lifted a forkful of chicken and rice. "Before it gets cold."

He fed me the rest of the meal without rushing me. When the plate was finally empty, he stood, set it on the table near the window, then folded the movable tray away and slid it to the side of the bed. After that, he paused, looking around the room like he was checking that everything was in its place, and that I was safe. Then his eyes came back to mine. "Do you want me to call Mom and Dad?"

I nodded immediately, my eyes brightening despite the heavy feeling in my heart. I missed them so badly it hurt, even though I feared what it would be like to see their faces when they walked in. They were going to look worried, but they would see that I was okay.

"Okay," he said softly. "I'll shoot them a text."

I watched him type the message on his phone, and when he set it down again, he pulled the chair closer and sat back beside me. He reached out and rested his hand on my arm, gently brushing his thumb over my skin while his eyes searched my face.

I caught the flicker of amusement in his eyes, and I sat up a little straighter, wondering what he was thinking. "By the way…" he said, a small grin pulling at his mouth. "I won't tell Mom and Dad about you and Ashby."

My eyes widened instantly, heat rushing to my cheeks.

He let out a chuckle and leaned back slightly, keeping his hand on my arm. "I've always known the two of you had a special bond," he continued gently. "Since you were little, you've been inseparable, always orbiting each other without even trying. There's always been this connection between you that kept pulling you back together, no matter what was happening around you."

I lowered my gaze, feeling that familiar urge to pick at the skin on my thumbs, only this time I couldn't fall back into the habit. His smile was gentle when I looked back up at him.

He exhaled slowly, then added, "What you two have makes sense, and it's so meaningful because it has been growing between you for years. You don't owe anyone an explanation. Tell Mom and Dad when you're ready. They'll understand. But what matters is that you're happy, and that you're choosing something that feels right to you."

I pressed my lips together, nodding slowly as I soaked up his words. I felt a little weight being lifted off my shoulders, and having Wesley's support meant everything to me.

Minutes later, the room was packed with my family, friends, and even their mothers, all offering me well-wishes and praising how strong I was. It was overwhelming.

When I glanced at Ashby standing next to my bed with his arms crossed, I could practically read his mind. He wanted me to rest and to have a calm evening, but I shot him a look to let him know I was fine.

They'd soon leave when visiting hours ended, but I appreciated each of them being here. Even Scottie, who should have been resting, had come. I couldn't ask her how she was doing, but when I looked at her with a worried expression, she stepped closer and gently squeezed my shoulder.

"I'm fine, Milow," she whispered with a smile. "Don't worry about me."

I nodded, but we both knew I'd still worry.

Stan came to stand beside Scottie, studying me closely. "So, I was thinking…" he started.

"That's never good," Wesley teased as Evie hid a laugh behind her hand.

Stan ignored him. "I should quit school and become your full-time bodyguard. I can make sure nobody ever hurts you again, and I'll always be there with you."

Nobody said anything at first. We all just watched him, amused and curious to hear how far he would take this.

"It's not a bad idea, right? I have MMA training. I can take on anyone who even *thinks* about being mean to you. And it would be a real job, obviously. Gus would pay me."

Dad snorted, crossing his arms. "That's a generous offer, buddy. And completely unrealistic."

"But I'm serious!" Stan protested, pointing at himself. "I'll do it. Full-time. You can't question my loyalty and skill!"

"Oh, I'm not questioning your loyalty," Dad said flatly, and the others all chuckled when he didn't mention Stanley's skills. He was teasing him. Their bickering made me smile and, for a moment, forget about everything that happened.

"Hey, I'm skilled," Stan stated, puffing out his chest. "Tell them, Mommy."

Chelsea laughed and patted Stan's back before tugging at his sweater. "Yes, you're my super-skilled boy," Chelsea said, patting Stan's shoulder and guiding him away from my bed. "But I'm not letting you quit school."

"And Milow's got all of us to protect her. Besides… we can't cage her in," Scottie said, her hand still on my shoulder, gently caressing me.

I smiled up at her, appreciating her encouragement. I knew Stan was trying to protect me, but I didn't want him or any of them to give up their time and energy for me.

Stan sighed dramatically but pointed at me one last time. "I mean it, Milow. I'll always protect you."

I smiled, pressing my lips together tightly as I nodded.

One by one, they said their goodbyes, each of them squeezing my arm or brushing my hair back gently. Mom and Dad lingered for a moment longer, making sure my water was filled up and my phone was in reach. I wasn't sure I would be able to use it tonight, but I could move my fingers on my left hand enough to maybe type a text or two. After kissing my head and reassuring me that they'd be back first thing in the morning, they finally left the room.

Ashby stayed behind, and once the door clicked shut, he leaned in, cupping my face gently with both hands before pressing his lips to mine. That was what I'd missed the most all day, and I smiled against his lips, not wanting him to pull away. His kiss was careful, with his lips moving slowly against mine. I felt a jolt deep down inside of me, and the overwhelming feelings crowding my chest made my head lighter.

He pulled back then, but his face stayed close. "I'll be here first thing after school tomorrow," he said softly, his eyes searching mine.

I nodded, letting myself lean into his touch. The simple motion carried all I couldn't say.

"I hate leaving you here alone," he continued, a sigh escaping him as he studied my face. "But you're brave. You're strong. I know you'll be fine."

I nodded again, smiling at him.

He pressed one more kiss to my lips, then another to my forehead. "I love you, Milow," he whispered.

I closed my eyes and rested my forehead against his jaw, wanting to be as close to him as possible. One of his hands moved into my hair, while the other stayed on the side of my face. Taking a deep breath, I let him hold me for a moment longer. And while the world around us held so much chaos, between us there was serenity.

———

I only spent two more days at the hospital before they finally sent me home. The doctor had removed the splint from my left hand and told me my nose didn't need to be taped at all, since there hadn't been a fracture. The swelling and bruising were going down well, and while I still had to keep the cast on my right hand, it hadn't been as uncomfortable as I'd feared. The ache was manageable with the medication they gave me.

Since I couldn't use my right hand, I fingerspelled with my left instead, and even though it made everything slower and more tiring, everyone was patient with me, letting me take the time I needed to be understood.

I went back to school on the 10th of November, only a week after it happened. Mom and Dad kept me home for the rest of the week after I was released, insisting I needed time, even though I worried about falling behind. But in the end, I was grateful for it, because the thought of walking those halls so soon after everything had happened made me anxious. Scottie told me the atmosphere felt strange, and nothing felt normal anymore after everyone found out what had happened.

Yesterday was the most uncomfortable day I could remember. Everywhere I went, people stared. I had Ashby, Scottie, and Stan with me between classes and during breaks, which helped a lot, but every time I lifted my head, I caught someone looking at me with an expression

I couldn't quite place. Some faces held pity, others curiosity, and some just didn't know what to do with me at all. Not that they ever did. I had always been the weird girl.

I tried not to let the stares get under my skin, forcing myself to keep my focus on my classes, even when it felt like the whole building was watching me breathe.

46

Milow

Thursday, November 13th

I was sitting cross-legged on my bed, with a pencil clutched in my left hand while my right rested uselessly on my knee. Scottie had drawn on the cast during lunch one day, covering it with flowers and hearts, and every time I looked at them, I was reminded that nothing cruel or violent could ever outweigh the love I was surrounded by.

I lifted my gaze from the worksheet in my lap and studied the cast for a moment, my eyes lingering on the small "*I love you*" Ashby had written on it. Smiling, I turned my head to look at him where he sat behind me on the bed, leaning back against the headboard with a history book open in his hands. When he noticed me staring, his eyes lifted to mine.

His smile made my heart stumble in my chest, and my head went a little light. I sucked in my cheeks, trying to keep the shyness from taking over completely. The way he affected me had never faded, not once, and I didn't think I would ever be able to be casual when it came to him.

He set the book aside and shifted closer, settling behind me with his legs on either side of mine, one knee bent so he could rest his elbow on it. He pressed a soft kiss to my shoulder before glancing down at my homework. "Are you finished?" he asked quietly.

I shook my head, though the truth was that I didn't really care anymore. I set the pencil down and turned toward him between his legs, leaning back into his chest as his arms came around me without hesitation. I rested my head against his shoulder and closed my eyes, letting myself sink into the warmth of him.

He rubbed along my back and down my arm, his steady breathing keeping me calm. "How are you feeling?"

He asked me that every day now, ever since the hospital, and my answer was always the same. I felt okay and safe. And it was because of him, because of all of them, constantly making sure I was. Ashby barely left my side anymore. At school, he was always waiting right outside my classroom door, like he was afraid something might happen in the seconds he couldn't see me.

I appreciated how deeply he cared, but I could also see what it cost. His focus at school had slipped, and the nights he came home from practice, he looked drained and tense. He hadn't let himself rest at all. His mind was always somewhere else, stuck on worst-case scenarios, and on making sure I was protected at all times.

I wished I could tell him not to worry so much, to take care of himself too, but I knew it wouldn't change anything. He was already too far inside his own fear, too focused on keeping me safe. He kept pushing his own feelings aside as if they didn't matter nearly as much as mine.

Mom and Dad had noticed it too, the way he was unravelling quietly, and they had already tried to talk to him about it more than once. But Ashby wouldn't listen, brushing it off every time like it wasn't a problem. Even Wesley had stepped in, trying to explain that I really was okay, and that losing focus would only make things worse in the long run. But Ashby couldn't hear any of it. He was too focused on me, too afraid that if he let his guard down even for a second, something terrible would happen again.

I drew a slow breath and straightened my spine to look at him. I studied his face, noticing how tired he looked. He watched me just as intently, his own gaze wandering over my face, and I saw the exact second he registered the plea that was lingering inside me. His jaw clenched as a flicker of defiance flashed in his eyes, but instead of the conversation I planned on having, his hand came up to cradle my cheek. His thumb brushed my skin before he lowered his head, and his lips were on mine, not giving me a chance to sign.

Annoyingly, his plan to distract me worked.

The kiss deepened instantly as he tilted his head to the side, and his fingers came up to tangle in my hair. I arched into him instinctively, my hand fisting the fabric of his shirt to keep him right there. A low sound rumbled in his chest when I traced the seam of his lips with my tongue, and when I pulled him closer, he met my touch without hesitation. His tongue swept against mine slowly, sending a shiver through me. My toes curled, and a feeling I had tried to ignore many times before made itself noticeable again, sending small, exciting jolts from between my legs all through my body.

A wave of shyness made me want to pull away, but the

thought of not touching him right now was impossible. His grip in my hair tightened just a little, and he used it to guide me, to turn me without breaking the kiss. I went willingly as he shifted his weight, his hands moving to my waist now, and with a soft grunt of effort, he lifted me.

He settled me onto his lap as he leaned back against the headboard. My legs were on either side of his, my knees sinking into the mattress. I lifted my right hand and rested the cast on his shoulder. As useless as that hand was, I still needed to use it to touch him somehow. My other arm slid around his neck, my fingers tangling in the hair at his nape as I pressed myself closer, wanting more of that feeling between my legs, and more of him.

His hands dug into my hips, and as he pulled me forward, I felt the hardness in his sweatpants. The pressure grew against me as I moved my hips, unable to control myself. I couldn't sit still.

He met my movements, lifting his own hips in a slow rhythm that made my breath catch. His hands held me tightly, guiding me and pressing me down onto him until the friction was almost too much. Every roll of his hips sent a new wave of pleasure through me, and the kiss turned more passionate as my fingers tightened in his hair.

I was completely lost in the feeling. He pressed me harder against him, and I felt him hard right against my core, and through the thin layers of our clothes. It was so overwhelming that it made my head spin.

He broke the kiss as his breathing became more ragged, and he kept his face close to mine when he asked, "Is this okay?"

I swallowed and nodded, my own heart pounding against my ribs so hard I could hear it in my ears.

He let out a shaky breath as his forehead rested against mine before he leaned back enough to look into my eyes. "Milow…I know you want me to stop worrying, and I'm trying. I swear, I'm trying," he whispered, his voice cracking slightly. "But I can't just push this aside. I want to look out for you. I want to keep you safe. And I'm still giving my all for myself. But…please give me time."

His honesty loosened something in me that had been tight for days. He was asking me to be patient, just like he had been patient with me since we were little. The thought of that made my emotions bubble up, and my eyes started to water.

I moved my fingers through his hair, taking in his pleading face when I nodded. Through all this, I wasn't asking him to stop caring. I didn't want him to lose himself trying to protect me.

Moving my hand from his hair to his chest, I felt his heartbeat under my palm. I held his gaze and gave him another small nod, hoping he could read everything I couldn't say. That I trusted him, that I wasn't going anywhere, and that we would figure this out together.

"I love you," he whispered, his nose gently nuzzling my jaw. "And I'm not going anywhere."

I believed him. Even when I knew how hard it would be to watch him put his needs aside, I trusted he wouldn't lose himself in the process.

47

Ashby

"You can't protect her. You can't even protect yourself," my father grumbled.

His face was swallowed by shadow, but I didn't need to see it to know what was there. I knew his anger by the tenseness of his shoulders and by the tight fists at his sides. He looked the same way he always had when he was about to hurt someone.

My chest tightened as I took a step back. My instinct was to brace myself and take it, like I always had. Because I never won a fight against him.

But he didn't look at me for long.

His attention shifted, and dread crawled up my spine as he turned away from me and started walking toward the far corner of the room. The light there was weaker, the shadows heavier, and when I followed his movement, my heart dropped.

Milow was there.

She was sitting on the floor with her knees pulled tight to her chest, her arms wrapped around herself like she was trying to disappear. Her eyes were wide and glassy, fixed on my father as if she already knew she couldn't run from him. She looked so small, and I didn't understand how we all ended up in this room together.

"Leave her alone!" I screamed, my voice cracking with desperation.

I tried to move and run to her. My body leaned forward, every muscle burning with the need to get between them and shield her. I wanted to do something right for once.

But my feet wouldn't move.

The more I fought it, the heavier my body felt, and it felt like I was sinking while the room stretched farther and farther away. Every step my father took toward her felt like ten steps pulling me back.

Milow's eyes flicked to me then, fear filling her wide eyes.

She was looking at me like she believed I would save her.

And I couldn't move.

I watched him get closer. Watched her shrink in on herself. I was failing her again.

The helplessness was unbearable. It pressed into my chest until I couldn't breathe, until the only thing left was the sick certainty that no matter how hard I tried, I would always be too late.

My father's hands balled into fists again at his sides, and I cried out, begging him to stop. My voice echoed uselessly around the room, like it never had any power to begin with.

He didn't even slow down.

He kept walking toward her until his body blocked her from view. I watched him hurt her, and I stayed frozen where I was, unable to do the one thing I should've done.

Because my father was right.

No matter how hard I tried, I would never be able to protect her.

I lay awake, watching Milow sleep in my arms. She was relaxed, her body soft against mine, and her breathing slow and even. The swelling around her nose had gone down a lot, and the bruising was lighter now, fading into soft shades instead of dark ones.

She was safe. I told myself that over and over, but my mind wouldn't believe it.

I lifted my hand and brushed my thumb along her cheek carefully. I was afraid I might hurt her just by touching her, and just the thought of it made my heart ache. Tears slipped down my cheeks and dripped onto the pillow as I stared at her.

I had failed her again. Even if it had only been in my dreams, it felt real. I had stood there and watched while my father hurt her, and it made me so fucking angry. The pain in my chest stayed, and I didn't know how long it would take before I could trust myself to protect her the way I needed to. She already felt safe with me. I could see it in the way she looked at me, and in how easily she slept in my arms. I knew that should have been enough. But it wasn't.

Because feeling safe and being safe weren't the same thing to me. Not after everything. Not when I still woke up with my heart racing and my father's voice stuck in my head, telling me I wasn't enough.

So for now, I kept her close. I held her because it felt like letting her go would mean losing her. I was willing to give up everything to make sure every second of her life was safe and untouched by the things that had already taken too much from her. And until I was sure I could protect her the way she deserved, I wasn't going to stop.

48

Ashby

Saturday, November 22nd

Milow came into my room early that morning, even before I had packed my duffel for today's swim meet. She smiled the moment our eyes met, and the urge to cancel the competition and stay home with her all day hit me hard. I'd disappoint Ruben and my whole family, but being close to her was more important to me.

She lifted her left hand in a small wave, and I reached out to pull her closer. I cupped her face with both hands and leaned down to kiss her. She melted into me right away, and I held her there a second longer than necessary, then pulled back and looked at her again.

"You're up early," I said. My eyes stayed on her face. I needed to see it. It had been three weeks now, and there was almost nothing left of the injury. The bruises had vanished almost completely, but even with them, she had looked beautiful.

She smiled again as she stepped back. She reached under her left arm, and that was when I noticed the rolled piece of thick paper tucked there. She pulled it free and unrolled it with both hands. Her right hand was still in a cast, but she could use her fingertips to hold the paper.

The poster was colorful, with large black bubbly letters that read **MAKE WAVES, CHAMP!**

I smiled and took it in, admiring every single word and every scribble I knew she had made herself. "It's perfect." I looked at her again and cupped the side of her face to caress her cheek. "Thank you, Milow."

Her smile widened. She rolled the paper back up and placed it on the bed beside my bag. Then her left hand lifted, and I watched her fingerspell.

[You'll be great today. I'm proud of you.]

Her words made me feel like I could do anything. And still, I wasn't proud of myself the way she was proud of me. I hadn't been focused. I had let everything important slide. Training. School. My own standards. I had pushed them all aside, and I knew I wasn't living up to what I expected from myself.

I sighed and ran a hand through my hair as my gaze dropped to the floor. "I'm not sure it's worth even competing today."

Her hand reached out. Her fingers slid under my chin and lifted my head. When I met her eyes again, I saw the worry there. I knew exactly what she was thinking. She had been telling me for weeks not to worry about her. To focus on practice and put myself first. And I hadn't listened. Not once. Not to her or anyone.

Her hand lifted again. [You'll give your all, and I know it'll be enough. We'll be in the stands cheering you on.]

A smile pulled at my mouth, but it didn't feel real.

I even pushed her attempts to make me feel better

away, and it hurt so damn bad because she didn't deserve it. It felt like I was doing everything wrong. I wanted to be there for her, yet I kept failing in all the ways that mattered.

[You're a great swimmer, and you're an even better boyfriend. Please don't lose yourself.]

I forced myself to hold on to her words, to carry them with me into the water. Until then—until I had to focus on my strokes and my breathing—I would keep her right at the top of my mind.

———

My head spun every time I broke the surface to take a breath. My body moved, but I didn't feel like I was doing anything to make it happen. The cheers around the aquatic center blurred into a dull noise that made it hard to think. I couldn't see their faces, but I could feel the disappointment. Everyone could see I wasn't swimming like I usually did. My power was gone, my arms and legs didn't move with the strength I had spent years building.

By the time I reached the end of the lane and grabbed the starting block, I knew I had lost. I didn't have to look around me to understand, and I stayed in the water, letting the shame settle into me. The weight was one I couldn't shake, and I let it pull me under until my lungs screamed with pain.

Hands wrapped around my arms, pulling me out of the pool.

"Breathe, buddy," Jasper said, his hands firm on my back, patting me gently as I hunched over with my hands on my knees. "Come on, dude, deep breaths."

He shouldn't have been here. He should've been

celebrating, soaking in the win he'd earned. I didn't have to look up to know he won our race. The three other guys in the final hadn't stood a chance, and between us, he had dominated. And I had…I had barely moved.

I coughed, the burn in my chest relentless as I tried to expel the water and pull in air. Each breath rattled my ribs and made me feel weak. When I finally managed a long, shaky inhale, I straightened up as best I could and ripped my goggles and cap off, fisting them with my hands.

"Come on, let's get him to the back," Ruben said. I could hear the anger and disappointment in his voice. I didn't have to guess what he'd say once we were alone, and I braced myself for it. I had failed him, myself, and everyone. And the worst part of it all was, I had known that I would.

Every step toward the changing rooms felt heavy as I carried the shame in my own arms. My legs burned, my lungs screamed, and all I could see in my mind was her face: her smile, the poster, her pride. And I had thrown it all away.

Jasper helped me sit down on the bench and stayed close, his hand resting on my shoulder. Ruben paced back and forth in front of us, the tension in the room so thick it was uncomfortable. I let my head hang and rested my elbows on my knees, waiting for him to start and let me have it.

Ruben finally stopped pacing. The silence that followed was worse than his angry footsteps. I heard him take a deep breath, then he crouched down in front of me. I didn't look up. I couldn't. I just stared at the wet floor, at the water dripping from my hair and pooling around my feet.

"Ashby," Ruben's voice was low, and to my surprise, it wasn't angry anymore. "Look at me."

I slowly lifted my head. His face wasn't hard with disappointment; it was etched with a concern that felt more painful than any lecture could have been.

"That wasn't you out there," he said, his eyes searching mine. "And I need to know if you understand that what happened today had nothing to do with your training or your talent." He paused, and his gaze softened. "You've been going through something. We all see it. You've been carrying this heaviness for a while now, and you've been trying to carry it alone."

My throat went tight. I tried to swallow, but it was useless.

"Listen to me," he said, his voice firm but gentle. He placed a hand on my knee with a steadying pressure. "Being a great swimmer isn't about winning every race. It's about having the strength to get back in the water after a bad day. It's about knowing when to fight and when to rest." He squeezed my knee. "Right now, your fight isn't in that pool. Your fight is in here." He tapped his own temple. "And that's a hell of a lot harder. I get it."

He stood up, and his shadow fell over me. "I'm not disappointed in you, kid. I'm worried about you. The only person you failed today was the guy who thought he had to be perfect for everyone."

I broke then. I wasn't sure why I had expected him to tear me down even more, but he had done the opposite. He hadn't yelled. He hadn't lectured. He'd just seen me, all the way through the failure and the shame.

A choked sob escaped me, and I buried my face in my hands. The tightness I had felt inside of me for the past weeks was easing, and the shame and fear I'd been pushing down came pouring out in heavy tears. I felt so small, so stupid for thinking I had to carry it all, for letting my pride get in the way of letting anyone help, for not believing in myself enough to be strong for Milow, but also for myself.

I had been selfless when nobody, especially Milow, had expected me to be.

Ruben didn't hesitate. He moved closer again, and his hands came down firmly on my shoulders. I started to shake, and I couldn't stop it. I reached out, my hand fisting the fabric of his shirt, needing something to hold on to.

He didn't pull away. He sank back down onto his knees in front of me, then he wrapped his arms around me, pulling me into a tight hug. I crumpled against him, my forehead resting on his shoulder as I let myself cry. He just held me, one hand rubbing my back while the other cupped the back of my head.

"It's okay," he murmured. "Let it out. Just breathe. I've got you."

Jasper was still there, his hand giving my shoulder a comforting squeeze. I needed to thank them both for being here, for pulling me from the edge in my own head. They had always been there to catch me. But as much as they had propped me up, I knew the rest was on me. I had to be the one to find my footing and to make sure I could stand steady on my own and not fall back down.

But most of all, I had to stop making Milow worry about me because she deserved someone who could stand on his own, someone strong enough to let her breathe without carrying my mess on top of hers. I had to prove to myself that I could be that person for her, but also for myself.

[I'm glad you're feeling better,] Milow signed, her fingers moving carefully with just her left hand.

She was sitting in front of me on the bed that same evening, with her legs crossed and her expression soft. She was watching me patiently as if she could see every thought running through my head.

I placed my hands on her knees, letting them slide slowly up and back down along her thighs. "Me too."

[I was so scared,] she signed, her brows knitting together.

"I know." I let out a shaky sigh and drew in a deep breath. I had been scared too. My mind had shut down, and I had let my body sink into the pool without control. I was lucky that Ruben and Jasper had pulled me out in time, realizing immediately what had happened. "But I'm okay now. My mind is clearer."

She stayed quiet, watching me closely, and giving me the space to find the right words.

"I'm sorry I made you worry so much," I said. "I've caused more trouble than I meant to. I lost myself, even though I promised you this morning that I wouldn't."

Her hand came up, and her fingers brushed through my hair in a calming gesture. Then her hand cupped my cheek, and I leaned into it, closing my eyes for a moment before meeting her gaze again. "I know I can't take back what happened," I said, keeping my voice low. "But I can promise you I'll try harder. I'll keep myself together. I don't want you worrying about me ever again."

Her eyes softened, and I kept going, feeling the words spill out.

"I need to be better for you. For us. I've been letting

everything slip, and I hate that I made you scared. I just…
I don't want to lose myself again, and I don't want to make
you pay for it."

Her hand stayed on my cheek, her thumb brushing
my skin gently.

"I want to be someone you can count on. Someone
steady. Not someone who falls apart in front of you. And
I promise you, Milow, I'll be that someone from now on."

Milow's eyes filled with tears, and I wanted to curse
myself for making her feel sad again. But when she moved,
I understood that she wasn't upset. Those were happy
tears, and my body eased with relief.

She shifted forward and wrapped her arms around me,
and I instinctively wrapped mine around her too, holding
her tight. My face was buried in her shoulder, as I felt her
heartbeat against my chest.

"I love you," I whispered. "I always have, Milow, and
I forever will."

She squeezed me tighter, and I'd hold her for as long
as she wanted me to.

49

Milow

Monday, December 1st

"How does that feel?" the doctor asked as she gently placed my right hand back onto my lap. She had just removed the cast, and the air against my skin felt better than I had anticipated.

I nodded, smiling down at my hand. It was finally free.

"Oh, sweetheart," Mom said from the chair beside the bed, smiling at me. "Does it hurt?"

I looked up at her and shook my head, lifting both hands to sign without thinking. To my surprise, my fingers didn't hurt when I moved them.

[It just feels a little strange.]

The doctor looked amazed as I signed. She didn't understand me, but Mom was quick to translate.

"She says it feels a little strange."

"Hm, yes, that's normal. But it's a great sign that you can move them," she said, taking my hand carefully and studying it. "I've seen plenty of rough breaks, but fingers have always fascinated me."

I watched her, waiting for her to explain.

"You had stable fractures," she went on. "That means the bones cracked, but they stayed in place. I had a patient not long ago who slammed his hand in a car door. He said he barely felt any pain. That was probably the shock. He waited two days before coming in because his mother made him. All four knuckles were broken, yet he could still move his fingers without pain."

I smiled, intrigued, thinking it might have been similar for me. They had still put my hand in a cast, just to be safe. And it had worked. My fingers had healed quickly.

"So," she continued, placing my hand back on my lap, "you might feel some stiffness, and they may feel weak for a while. A few simple exercises will help with that."

I nodded and gave her a thumbs-up.

"And your nose has healed nicely too," she added.

I smiled.

She rested her hand on my arm and gave it a gentle squeeze. "You've been very strong through all of this, Milow. I hope you know that you handled it with courage, and that you should be proud of how far you've come."

Those were words I had heard many times before, but I always accepted them. I never pushed anyone away for trying to encourage me.

[Thank you,] I signed.

She turned and walked to the shelves on the other side of the room, picking up a small rectangular box. "Take this home and apply it to your fingers two to three times a day. It will help with the dryness the cast caused."

She handed the cream to Mom, then looked back at me. "Other than that…I'd say you're good to go."

I smiled at her. I could finally use both hands again,

and that alone made me feel lighter. I couldn't wait to show Ashby when we got home. He would be relieved, happy to see me without the cast. He had been waiting for this day even more than I had.

Before going back home, Mom had to stop at the grocery store. Before we headed inside, she made me apply the cream the doctor had given me, and after spreading it carefully all over my right hand, we got out of the car and went in. While Mom checked off her grocery list, I pushed the cart absentmindedly, thinking about all the things I could finally do again without struggling.

Signing was the first thing. Fingerspelling for a whole month had been exhausting, but at least I had still been able to communicate.

Holding a book would be easier too. I had held them with my left hand and then had to set them down just to flip the page. That would no longer be a problem.

And running both hands through Ashby's hair was another thing I was excited about. Every time he kissed me, my right hand had rested uselessly on his shoulder. I knew it had not bothered him, but it had bothered me.

I was lost in my thoughts, smiling to myself when I turned my head to see where Mom was. But in the cereal aisle, it was only Hailie and me. I jumped slightly at the sight of her, immediately snapping out of my head when her eyes locked onto mine.

It was not her presence that made me react. It was her bruised face and empty expression that shocked me. Her eyes were bloodshot, and beneath one of them was a dark-purple bruise. Makeup tried to cover it, but it didn't fully hide it. Her nostrils were red, and they looked exactly like mine had looked when she—

My jaw tightened. I refused to let my mind go back there.

I didn't know what to do. She just stood there, staring at me with a pained look in her eyes. And underneath that pain was fear. I could see it clearly. But I didn't understand what she was scared of.

Frowning, I kept studying her. It felt unreal. Like I was stuck in some strange dream, unable to wake up. But I had to be awake. I had just gotten my cast off. I was going home later to show everyone.

My heart pounded in my chest, and I still couldn't move.

"Hailie."

Her mother appeared behind her and grabbed her by the shoulder. "I told you to stay close to me. I don't want you to wander—" She stopped when she saw me, her expression shifting into regret and shame all at once.

"Gosh, sweetie," she said, stepping closer. "I'm so incredibly sorry for what Hailie has done to you. It's inexcusable. I've been meaning to come by with cookies and flowers—"

"Step away from my daughter."

Mom moved up beside me, her hand settling firmly on my shoulder.

Darla pressed a hand to her chest, looking horrified. "I'm so sorry, Iris. I was just trying to apologize."

"That's what your daughter still has to do," Mom said sharply. She was protecting me. I knew that. I just hated seeing her this upset.

I bit the inside of my cheek and looked past Darla at Hailie. She was still staring at me.

Her eyes were empty, and I could tell she wasn't

okay. Someone had hurt her. I could see that clearly too. But who? Darla? No. Darla might've been an obnoxious woman, but she wasn't violent. Then who—

"I don't have all day, Darla."

A large man rounded the corner and stopped behind Hailie. His hand came down on the back of her neck, thick fingers wrapping around it.

Hailie flinched, and tears filled her eyes.

Oh no.

"Yes, darling," Darla said quickly, her voice tight. "We're coming."

The man looked at me. His eyes moved between us, and something shifted in his expression when he understood. His grip on Hailie's neck tightened.

"This the girl you bullied?" he asked.

I flinched. So did Hailie.

"Tell me, kid," he ordered, his voice thick and raspy.

"Y-yes, Daddy."

He grunted and gave a short shake of his head, like he was disappointed in something small and unimportant. "And you've still not learned your lesson."

I didn't know what that meant, but by the look on Hailie's face, it couldn't be good. I was worried about her. No matter how much pain she had inflicted, I was scared for her safety. Her father was scary, and the way his presence made her visibly shake had to mean something was off at home.

"Come on, sweetheart," Mom whispered. I didn't have to look at her to know she was worried too. I could hear it in her voice. She saw Hailie's pain just as clearly as I did, and when I glanced up at her, I hoped she would say something.

Mom's jaw was tight. She pulled me behind her before speaking. "Are you okay, Darla?"

It sounded like a simple question, but it carried much more.

Darla swallowed hard. Her body stiffened before she forced a nod and a tight smile. "Everything is perfect," she said. "Hailie is sorry. We've just been…disciplining her."

My eyes moved back to Hailie. She was still staring at me, her eyes glossy with tears she refused to let fall. She was asking for help without saying a word, and I wanted to help her. I really did. But I didn't know how. My body felt frozen in place, and the whole moment still felt unreal.

"You have my number," Mom told Darla, her voice firm.

"I do. Thank you, Iris. We should go now." Darla gave another nod, then wrapped her hand around Hailie's arm and pulled her gently toward her, and away from her father.

Before Hailie turned, I lifted my hand in a quick wave and gave her a faint smile. I hoped it would be enough to make her feel a little less alone. To show her I wasn't mad at her, and that I didn't hate her. And that whatever was happening at home would somehow turn out okay.

———

"We're home!" Mom called as I unlocked the front door. "Come help with the groceries."

Footsteps sounded from upstairs right away. A second later, Ashby and Wesley rushed down the stairs, bumping into each other as they raced to be first.

When they reached the bottom, they stopped at the same time and looked at me. Their eyes went straight to my right hand.

"It's gone!" Wesley said with a wide grin.

"Your hand's free!" Ashby added, just as excited.

They stepped closer, and I lifted my hand to show them properly. Ashby slid one hand under mine and carefully ran his fingertips over the back of it.

"How does it feel? Can you move them?"

I nodded and pulled my hand back to sign. [It doesn't hurt, but it does feel a bit strange.]

"Damn, Milow. That healed up nicely," Wesley said, still smiling. "I'm proud of you."

"Yeah, me too." Ashby took my hand again and lifted it to his mouth, pressing a soft kiss to my fingers. "You can finally hold a book normally again."

He was teasing, but he knew how much that had bothered me.

[I'm excited. I'm glad the cast is off.]

"Me too." Ashby brushed his hand down my arm, then pressed a quick kiss to my forehead before following Wesley outside to grab the groceries.

While they carried the bags in, I went into the kitchen. Dad was sitting at the table, his phone in his hands and his expression focused and distant. When I placed a hand on his shoulder, he looked up and smiled.

"Milow, sweetheart. How was it at the doctor's?"

[Great. I got my cast off!] I signed, holding up my right hand.

His smile widened into a grin as he gently took my hand in his. "That's wonderful, Milow. I'm glad it's all better now."

I nodded. He pulled me into his side for a quick hug before I turned toward the hallway, just as Mom and the boys came back into the kitchen.

"Thank you for helping," Mom said, rubbing their backs before starting to unpack the bags. "Why don't you all head upstairs? I need to have a word with your father."

"What did you do, Dad?" Wesley teased.

"Yeah, Dad, what did you do?" Ashby added.

"Nothing, I swear," Dad said quickly, lifting his hands in defense. "Iris, honey, I swear I've been good."

I scrunched my nose at him. We all knew he had not done anything. He was just being dramatic. Mom rolled her eyes and laughed softly before giving his chest a playful shove.

"I know you've been good. You're always good. And maybe that's exactly what I need to talk to you about."

"What, you want me to be naughtier?" Dad asked with a grin, pulling Mom closer. "Just say the word, darling."

"Okay," Wesley said, patting Ashby's shoulder and gently tugging my arm. "We don't need to witness this."

I pressed my lips together as Ashby laughed, and we headed upstairs. Once we were out of earshot, Wesley muttered, "Not even Evie and I are that awkward."

"Meh." Ashby shrugged. "You two can be pretty weird sometimes."

Wesley raised a brow and punched Ashby's shoulder. "Watch it, buddy."

I looked up at them as they playfully shoved each other. When they stopped, I noticed the thoughtful look settling on Wesley's face. "I wonder what she needs to talk to him about."

[I know.]

They both turned to me.

"Yeah?" Wesley raised a brow. "What is it?"

[I think she's going to tell him about what happened at the grocery store.]

Ashby frowned. "What happened?"

I looked between them. [We saw Hailie and her parents. And Hailie didn't look good at all.]

"What do you mean, Milow?" Wesley asked. His posture stiffened. So did Ashby's. Hearing her name did that to them.

I chewed on my lip as my stomach twisted. I didn't want to say it out loud, but I couldn't keep it to myself. I could still see the pain and fear in her eyes.

[She had bruises on her face. And her father was rough with her. She was scared of him. I could tell. And so was her mother.]

They didn't say anything at first. I knew it was hard for them to feel sorry for Hailie. She had been the one hurting me for years. But I also knew that if they had seen her in that aisle, if they had seen her face the way I had, they would be worried too.

[I think her father hurt her,] I finally signed.

Ashby's gaze dropped to the floor. He shoved his hands deep into his pockets, thinking through whatever reaction was rising in him. Wesley stayed quiet as well, his eyes drifting away from mine. I gave them time. I didn't expect them to come up with a plan or suddenly know how to help her. I just needed them to understand what I had seen.

"I'm sure Mom and Dad will handle it," Wesley said after a moment, looking back at me.

Ashby glanced at him, then nodded slowly. "Yeah. If they think it's necessary to step in, they will."

I nodded too. That had to be enough for now.

Ashby stepped closer first. His hand reached for mine without hesitation, turning it gently as he checked my fingers again. "You sure you're okay?" he asked quietly.

[I'm okay,] I signed.

Wesley moved in next, his hand landing on my shoulder. "Milow…you don't have to feel obligated to help anyone. No matter how difficult it might be."

I looked up at him, knowing exactly what he meant. They had always been too worried about me worrying about others more than I ever worried about myself, but I just didn't know how to change that about me. It was rooted deep inside of me.

I looked between them, my chest tightening, but in a good way this time.

[I know.]

Ashby pulled me into his chest without another word. Wesley wrapped his arms around both of us from the side, and I let myself sink into them.

For a second, everything else faded. The grocery store. Hailie's bruises. The fear in her eyes.

All that mattered was this.

They were here. I was okay. My hand was healed. I was home.

And they were not letting go. Ever.

50

Milow

Tuesday, December 9th

"We're having dinner with his parents tonight," Scottie told me with a small but pleased smile on her face. "Honestly, it's going so much better now. I feel like the whole hospital thing really made him care about me."

I smiled and slid my books into my locker before looking back at her. [Stan has always cared about you.]

"I know, I know." She sighed and hugged her books closer to her chest. "But he's different now. Especially when we're alone. It's like he checks on me every second of the day. Before it was only every…hour or something."

I scrunched my nose and waited.

She caught herself and huffed softly. "Okay, fine. He's always cared about me. Maybe it just feels different now because it's getting serious." She shrugged like it didn't matter, but her smile gave her away.

[He's completely in love with you,] I signed, smiling. [And good things take time. He's not going anywhere.]

She watched me for a moment, then her cheeks turned

pink. "You're probably right. As always." She took a slow breath. "I just wish things could stay like this."

I frowned, unsure what she meant. Tilting my head, I signed, [Why would you say that?]

She shrugged again. "I don't know. It just feels too perfect. You know when your heart feels so full that it almost feels unreal? Yet somewhere deep down there's this awful feeling that something bad is about to happen?"

I studied her, trying to follow. I understood the feeling she described, but I didn't see how it fit her life. Things were good. There was no reason to expect something terrible to happen. At least nothing she wouldn't be strong enough to handle.

[I think that's just fear talking,] I signed. [You're doing well. And you and Stanley will turn out exactly the way you're supposed to.]

Now she was the one studying me, chewing on her bottom lip. "Hmm. I'm not sure."

For a second, she made it sound like she was waiting for something to fall apart. Like she didn't just expect it but truly wanted it. I pushed the thought away as soon as it formed.

I leaned forward and hugged her tight, holding her a little longer before I pulled back and signed, [I'm here if you need to talk. Okay?]

"I'm fine," she said quietly, her smile tight. "Always fine."

Her expression slipped for a second. Her face went blank, and then her eyes darkened as she stared past me.

"Get the fuck away from her. Now."

Scottie moved in front of me so fast I barely had time to react. Her body went rigid.

I turned. Aspen stood a few feet away, clutching her books to her chest. Her eyes were wide as she looked at Scottie.

"Didn't you hear me? Get away from her," Scottie warned again.

I touched Scottie's arm, trying to calm her, but she didn't look at me. She kept staring Aspen down.

"I just want to talk to Milow. If that's okay," Aspen said softly. Her eyes flicked to mine before dropping again.

"She doesn't want to hear anything you have to say," Scottie shot back. Her shoulders stayed tense.

I tugged at her arm again. When she still wouldn't move, I stepped around her and signed, [It's okay, Scottie. She can talk to me.]

Scottie searched my face. Her eyes burned with worry and anger, but I didn't feel that same fear.

[Really. She won't hurt me.]

That was what Scottie was afraid of. She thought Aspen wanted to start something again. But I knew better. Aspen had never really wanted to hurt me. She had just stayed close to Hailie and tried to fit into her shadow. Tried to be the kind of friend Hailie demanded. Deep down, I didn't think she was cruel.

"Fine," Scottie muttered. "But I'm staying right here."

She stepped beside me, with her arms tight around her books, and still glaring at Aspen.

I looked at her, waited for her to speak.

Her gaze moved between Scottie and me. She swallowed, then looked at me again. This time, she held my eyes.

"I want to sincerely apologize for the way I treated you."

"Well, you see…" Scottie started, unable to stay quiet. She shifted her books to one arm and planted her other hand on her hip. "Milow is the sweetest and most kind-hearted person I know. You might've tried to tear her down, but you didn't succeed. And if you ever even think about treating her like that again, you'll have me to deal with. Because I've been nicer than you deserve."

[Scottie, please,] I signed quickly, shooting her a look.

She huffed but kept going. "What? I'm just making it clear that the next time she decides to hurt you, I won't hold back."

Aspen nodded fast. "I understand. I do. I won't. I promise."

I touched Scottie's arm again. [Will you translate, please?]

Scottie scowled at me and sighed, but then she nodded. "Fine."

I turned back to Aspen and signed, then waited for Scottie to translate with a quieter voice. "She says she knows you were influenced. That doesn't excuse it, but she believes people can change. She hopes you mean what you're saying."

Aspen's eyes widened again. "I do. I really do."

I added a few more signs.

Scottie exhaled through her nose, clearly not happy about any of this. But she kept translating. "She says she doesn't hate you. She never did. She just wants things to be different from now on."

Aspen nodded fast, with her eyes wide and full of hope. "They will be. I swear. And I know I can't make excuses for Hailie, but I know she's sorry too. She's… working on herself."

"Right…" Scottie murmured.

I lifted my hands again. [Is she not back?]

Their suspension had ended already, but I had only seen Aspen in the halls. Not Hailie.

And the last time I saw Hailie was at the grocery store, where she had bruises all over her face. Aspen looked at Scottie, waiting for her to translate.

"She's asking where Hailie is."

"Oh, uh…" Aspen played with the corner of one of her textbooks. "Her parents don't want her to come to school yet. She's…I think she's okay. She texted me yesterday and said she was—ah, never mind." She knitted her brows, then added, "I know she will apologize to you when she's ready."

I nodded, because I truly believed she would.

For a moment, none of us spoke.

Then Aspen smiled gently. "Thank you. For being better than I ever was."

She adjusted her grip on her books and stepped back, and I gave a little wave to assure her that things were going to get better for her too.

Scottie watched her until she disappeared around the corner. "I still don't trust her," she muttered.

[I know,] I signed. [But this was a start.]

Scottie looked at me for a long moment. Then her expression softened. "You're too good for this place."

I knew that. But only because people had repeated it to me so many times that I had started to believe it.

"Hey, what did she want?" Ashby came up to us. Stan and Jasper were right behind him. "Are you okay?"

I looked up at him. [She apologized.]

His eyes searched mine as he placed both hands on my

shoulders, looking me over like he expected to find some sign that I had been hurt. "She apologized?"

I nodded again. [And she meant it.]

Ashby didn't look convinced. He glanced at Scottie with one brow raised.

She shrugged. "It sounded honest."

"Damn. And here I thought she didn't have a single moral left after everything she's done," Stan muttered. He slid an arm around Scottie's shoulders, and she leaned into him, her posture relaxing the second he touched her.

Ashby turned back to me. His hands moved from my shoulders to my cheeks, holding my face gently. The worry was still there, but he softened it for me. "Well, I'm glad," he said before adding, "I missed you."

I smiled and leaned into his hands. [I missed you, too.]

He leaned down and kissed me then. His lips moved slowly against mine as he pulled me closer until my body pressed against his. I slid my hands into his hair, curling my fingers into it as the kiss deepened.

Kissing him in public wasn't as uncomfortable as I once thought it would be. Still, I never wanted to make a scene. Some couples went too far in these halls, with their hands wandering to private places, and boundaries being ignored.

When we finally pulled apart, and I looked up, Scottie and Stan were both grinning at us, and Jasper leaned against the lockers with a small, satisfied smile.

He had seemed off all morning and was quieter than usual. I wanted to ask if he was okay. If he needed someone to listen. But I figured Ashby and Stan had already checked in on him. They wouldn't ignore that.

"Oh, please don't stop," Stan said, smirking. "I cleared my schedule. This is way better than algebra."

Scottie laughed. "He's right. We got all day."

Jasper shook his head, but his smile grew. "You two are unbelievable."

"You're all weird," Ashby muttered, but then laughed. He slid his hand down my arm until his fingers laced with mine.

I leaned into him, wrapping my other hand around his forearm to stay as close to him as possible.

Stan tilted his head, studying us like we were an art exhibit. "Seriously, though, if you're going to do that in the hallway, at least charge admission. We could fund prom."

"Stan," Scottie warned, though she was still laughing.

"What? I'm entrepreneurial."

Ashby rolled his eyes and squeezed my hand. "You won't make money off of my girl."

"Your girl?" Stan pressed a hand to his chest. "Last time I checked, Ace was my girl. I had her first."

"You never had her first," Ashby said, loud and clear. Then his face softened, and he looked at me with that loving expression. "Milow's always been mine. Since day one."

I felt my cheeks turn bright red, and I tried to hide it by burying my face in his chest. He chuckled and pressed a kiss to my head, murmuring, "I love you, sweet girl."

51

Ashby

Milow dropped her pencil, grinning as she threw her hands into the air before signing, [Done.]

"Goddammit! Again?" I sighed and shook my head, letting my own pencil fall onto the bed.

"How is that even possible? I swear, your brain has some superpower." I stared down at the Sudoku books in our laps. Hers was a "pro" level, mine for beginners—the one she had started years ago but had gotten bored with soon after. It had been her idea to race, and at first, we'd both solved easy ones. Of course, she'd crushed me there, and I'd been naïve enough to think I might have a chance if she moved up to a hard one. I didn't.

"Honestly, Milow, your brain needs to be studied. That wasn't even ten minutes."

She grinned proudly, clasping her hands to her chest. She glanced down at the puzzle I was failing to solve. [You were close.]

I frowned. "I managed to find all the fours and nines."

[Exactly. That's a good start.] She smiled and leaned forward, pressing a soft kiss to my cheek. [You finish that one, and I'll do another hard one.]

As fun as that sounded, I had a much better idea. I pushed our books and pencils aside, then moved toward her, easing her back to lie against the pillows. I positioned myself between her legs and braced on my elbows above her.

I looked down at her, at the way her hair was fanned out on the pillow, and at the proud, playful smirk still on her lips from her victory. My gaze dropped to her mouth, and all thoughts of numbers completely vanished. There was only her.

"You have a beautiful mind, and even more beautiful soul, Milow."

Her smirk turned into a smile, and she tilted her head slightly to the side, trying to hide her shyness.

I leaned down and kissed her cheek. "You've known me for years. There's no reason for you to get shy around me anymore."

I trailed kisses along her jaw and down her neck, and I felt her body tense just a little before her hands came up to my hair. I knew that it was still hard for her to believe any compliment thrown her way, but I needed her to understand that every word was true. That I saw all of her. The brilliant, quiet girl who dominated every class and the strong, resilient girl who had survived so much. And I loved every single part of her completely and without hesitation.

Moving up again, I captured her lips with mine. It was a soft kiss at first, but then her legs angled on my sides, pulling me closer, and a low groan rumbled in my chest. I deepened the kiss, my tongue tracing the seam of her lips until she parted them for me. I explored her mouth slowly, savoring her taste.

My body began to move on its own. I rocked my hips against hers, and the friction sent a jolt straight through me. I was already getting hard, but I forced myself to go slow. I did it again, pushing my growing erection against the soft heat between her legs, letting her feel exactly what she did to me.

Her back arched instinctively to meet me, and her grip in my hair tightened, holding me to her as she rocked her hips up to match my rhythm. I pulled back just enough to whisper against her lips, my voice thick. "God, you feel so good, Milow. I'm so crazy about you."

Then I crashed my mouth back on hers, knowing this was all we could do for now. I couldn't push her, and I didn't want to ruin something special just because I was too selfish to wait. I could control myself a while longer. For her.

Tuesday, December 16th

We sat at our usual table in the cafeteria at lunch, and the second Lacey joined us, the mood shifted. Everyone went quiet. Even Stan.

That alone said enough.

We all looked between her and Jasper, trying to figure out what had happened. They had been dating since

September, and from the outside, it had looked steady. Jasper took her on dates, walked her to class, and sometimes they moved through the halls hand in hand.

Today, he barely looked at her. His focus stayed on his food. Lacey, on the other hand, looked furious. Her jaw was tight and her shoulders stiff. She didn't try to hide it.

Stan let out a low whistle and popped another grape into his mouth. "So…are we breaking up now or after lunch? Because I got popcorn in my backpack."

Lacey glared at him, but Jasper didn't react. He kept staring down.

"Dude," Ashby muttered, shooting Stan a warning look.

"What?" Stan shrugged, glancing between them again. "There's clearly trouble in paradise. I know the signs. You two look exactly like Scottie and me when we kept fighting every other week."

They never really fought. There had been tension, but it never turned into a real fight. It never became something they couldn't fix. And I knew whatever was happening between Jasper and Lacey wouldn't explode into some loud scene in the middle of the cafeteria either.

Jasper was too calm and collected for that.

My eyes drifted to the empty seat beside Stan. He sat at the end of the table alone today. Scottie had stayed home because she felt dizzy and sick again, and none of us liked that. We had thought things were better after she fainted a few weeks ago. We had told ourselves it was a one-time thing, maybe because of stress or not drinking enough water.

But now she was tired and dizzy all the time, and I

couldn't shake the feeling that whatever had caused her to faint in the first place had never really been figured out. It didn't feel as simple as the doctors had made it sound. They had brushed it off too easily. Still, I knew Scarlett wouldn't ignore it. She would keep pushing. She would make sure Scottie got checked again and again until someone gave her a real answer.

"Do you guys want to talk about it?" Ashby asked. His hand rested on my thigh under the table, and I had placed mine over his, slowly tracing my thumb over his skin. "We're here if you need us."

Jasper shook his head, his eyes still fixed on his food. Lacey looked at him, and something in her expression snapped.

I flinched when she slammed both hands onto the table, making our drinks shake from the force. She stood, fists tight at her sides, before she grabbed her backpack. "Instead of sitting there and saying nothing, maybe you should man up and tell me what you're actually thinking."

Then she walked away, leaving all of us staring after her.

"Jesus…" Stan muttered. "What the hell did you do, dude?"

Jasper finally looked up. With Lacey gone, his shoulders dropped, and he looked relieved. "I didn't do anything."

I believed him.

I reached across the table and squeezed his hand gently, offering him a smile. When he met my eyes, I signed, [We're here for you.]

He glanced at Ashby.

"She says we're here for you," Ashby translated.

Jasper smiled tightly and nodded. "Thanks, Milow. I,

uh…" He ran a hand through his blond hair and tugged at the ends before letting out a heavy sigh. "Do you guys want to hang out tonight? I know it's a school night, and—"

"I'd hang out with you even if I had finals tomorrow," Stan cut in.

Jasper let out a quiet laugh. "I know." His gaze moved between the three of us, but the smile never reached his eyes. "I just need a distraction. We could hang out in the attic. Order pizza or something."

[I'm in,] I signed right away.

Ashby nodded. "Yeah. I'm in too."

"I'll bring ice cream," Stan said, reaching over to squeeze Jasper's shoulder. "The expensive, artisanal kind. We're not half-assing this."

"Thanks. I really appreciate you guys."

"Any time," Ashby said firmly.

His arm slid around me, and I leaned into him, resting my head against his shoulder. He kissed the top of my head and rubbed my back while I watched Jasper stand and gather his barely touched lunch.

"All right. I'll see you guys tonight. Six okay?" he asked.

"Yeah. Six is good," Ashby replied.

"Love you, dude," Stan said as he stood and pulled Jasper into a quick hug.

Jasper hugged him back just as tight. "Love you too."

I watched them, and the sight of how close they were—and always had been—made my chest warm. All the friendships we shared were so much bigger than any little inconvenience.

We showed up for each other, and we always stayed. And we never let each other sit alone with things that felt too heavy to handle alone.

But when Jasper walked away, a heavy feeling lingered in my heart. I found myself thinking about what Scottie had said last week: that strange feeling when everything looks fine on the surface, yet somewhere deep inside there is a quiet expectation that something is about to go wrong.

For a brief moment, the thought tried to settle in my mind, trying to connect everything that was happening around me into something bigger and darker.

But I forced myself not to follow it.

I didn't want to start searching for cracks before they were truly there, and I didn't want to turn normal problems into signs of something worse. And most of all, I refused to believe that just because I feared something falling apart, it meant it actually would.

———

"Have you guys heard from Bennett?" Jasper asked. He sat on one of the three couches in the attic, with a carton of pizza balanced on his lap.

I had only been to Jasper's house once before, but I remembered how big it was. The attic was not really an attic. It felt more like a small apartment built above the main house, with a kitchenette along one wall, a bathroom tucked behind a white door, and a separate bedroom at the end of a short hallway. It was quiet up here, and it was all Jasper's.

I sat next to Ashby on the couch across from Jasper, my leg pressed against his as I ate my pizza and listened.

"No. He's been avoiding me," Ashby said with a small shrug.

"Yeah, me too," Stan added from the armchair. "I don't think he'll be apologizing to Milow any time soon."

I wasn't expecting Bennett to apologize. It would be nice, sure, but I wasn't going to chase it.

The room fell quiet for a moment. The TV played in the background with some random show none of us were really watching. Then Jasper straightened, letting out a long breath as he shook his head. "It feels like we've all somehow been in a terrible accident, died, and woke back up in hell. Life feels so fucking strange lately."

He felt it too. It wasn't just Scottie. It wasn't just me. Something had shifted. I could feel it deep in my bones, like a dark cloud trailing behind us, feeling closer to some of us than others.

"Mom said something about the moon and the stars," Stan said, taking another bite of his pizza. He chewed and swallowed, then waved his slice in the air. "You know she's into astrology and all that. She told me last week that there's been some huge shift in the universe or whatever."

I pressed my lips together. I had never cared much about astrology. I liked things that made sense. Things you could explain. But with Stan's mom saying something like that, I had no choice but to believe it. It was easier to blame the stars than to accept that sometimes life just tilted without warning.

[Maybe it's just a rough phase,] I signed, and Ashby translated.

"Yeah," Jasper said quietly. "Maybe."

Stan reached for the ice cream he had brought and took a spoonful, mixing his dinner with dessert. "Either way, we survive it. We always do. We stick together and help each other out, no matter what."

"That's right," Ashby said, his smile encouraging.

Then he looked at me and squeezed my knee. "We got each other."

I smiled back at him, leaning into his side.

Whatever life was about to throw our way, we'd manage and get through it. And in the end, I knew things would always get better.

52

Milow

Thursday, December 18th

I walked downstairs with a bright smile and excitement buzzing in my chest, knowing there were only two more days of school before Christmas break.

But the second I stepped into the kitchen, something felt off.

Mom stood by the counter, and Ashby sat at the table. Both of them looked up at me, and neither of them smiled.

My heart dropped.

Oh no.

What happened?

I looked from Mom to Ashby again. His shoulders were tense. His hands rested on his thighs with his fingers curled tight as he looked away.

My pulse started racing.

I lifted my hands, even though part of me was scared to ask. [What happened?]

Ashby's hands balled into fists, and he still wouldn't look at me.

So I looked at Mom, silently begging her to answer me.

[Is everybody okay? Dad? Wesley? Evie…Scottie and Stan?]

"They're all okay, sweetheart," Mom said gently. "Come sit down."

That didn't calm me.

I frowned and glanced between them again. My legs felt stiff as I moved toward the table. I sat down in the chair next to Ashby and stared at him again, wanting to know what had him acting like this.

[What's going on?] I asked again, my movements sharper and demanding now.

Mom pulled a chair in front of me and sat down. She reached for my hands and wrapped hers around them, and I let her hold them, even though I wanted to pull away and reach for Ashby instead.

I kept my eyes locked on her face, waiting impatiently.

She opened her mouth, then closed it again, and it took her a moment to gather the words she clearly didn't want to say.

Beside me, Ashby stayed completely still. I could feel the tension coming off him, and he kept staring at the ground with his head hung low.

After a slow breath, Mom finally spoke, her voice low and careful.

"Hailie has passed away."

The words didn't register, and I just stared at Mom, waiting for her to tell me it was some sick joke, that I was still dreaming, and that none of this was real. But she didn't say another word. She didn't offer a single explanation, and the longer I looked at her face, the heavier the reality settled in my chest.

I furrowed my brows and shook my head, trying to force my mind to process what she had just said, but it wouldn't cooperate.

How did she know?

How could something like this happen?

Nothing about it made sense. Hailie was only seventeen. She was too young. She shouldn't be gone.

Tears stung the backs of my eyes as I glanced at Ashby. Finally, he was looking at me, but his expression was closed off and unreadable. I couldn't tell what he was feeling. He had never liked Hailie, not after everything she'd put me through, but now that she was gone, I couldn't tell if he was sad, relieved, or just trying not to let it show. Maybe he was sad and holding it in, I thought. Maybe he didn't want me to see him unravel the way I felt myself starting to.

My throat tightened, and a cold shiver ran through me, crawling up my spine. When I looked at Mom again, she lifted one hand to cup my face gently, but she didn't speak. I could tell she was trying to find the right words, trying to make sense of something that didn't make sense, and I didn't blame her. What could anyone say to someone who had spent years being tormented by the very person who was now…gone?

My stomach turned in a nauseating twist that made it hard to breathe, because I wasn't even sure how I was supposed to feel. Was I allowed to be sad? Was I allowed to feel scared, angry, or relieved? I wanted to cry. I wanted to let it all out, but my body felt frozen and caught somewhere between grief and disbelief.

I thought about Hailie, about all the times she had lashed out at me. Her anger had never been about me.

It had been her way of letting out her own storms, her own frustration and rage that had nothing to do with anyone else. And I had been the easiest target. The one who could absorb it without fighting back. The one she could throw all of it at without consequence. That realization didn't make me feel better; it made my stomach twist even more, because even though she had caused me pain, she was just a kid too, and now she was gone, and I didn't know what to do with all the confusing emotions rattling inside me.

My mind was racing.

What happened? Was it an accident? Did she…did she—or was it her father?

"You can stay home today if you want, Milow," Mom said quietly, her hand still resting against my cheek as if she thought I might fall apart the second she let go.

I shook my head immediately, because staying home would mean sitting with this, drowning in it, and letting every thought grow louder without distraction, and I knew that would make everything worse.

I looked at Ashby, and before I could even lift my hands to sign, he understood.

"I'm coming too," he said, offering me a tight smile that didn't quite reach his eyes.

"There will be support at school if you want to speak about it. Ashby can translate for you," Mom added gently.

I looked back at her and shook my head again. I didn't want to speak about it. I didn't want to sit in a room and dissect my feelings or explain why I felt twisted up inside over someone who had made my life miserable. I just wanted the day to pass. I wanted time to keep moving so I wouldn't have to sit here and think. It felt selfish, but there was something deep inside me that needed normalcy. I needed to pretend for a few hours that everything hadn't just turned upside down.

[Can I have warm milk and honey, please?]

The request felt out of place and childish compared to the heaviness in the room, and as soon as I signed it, shame crept up my spine. How could I ask for something so ordinary when someone had just died? What was wrong with me that part of me wanted to move on already? My thoughts tangled together as guilt and anger mingled with confusion and sadness. My heart ached so much.

[Now, please,] I added, because my body had started to shake and I needed something to hold on to to make it stop.

"Of course, sweetheart." Mom brushed her thumb under my eye and kissed my forehead before standing to get the milk from the fridge.

The second she stepped away, I dropped my gaze to my hands. My fingers found my thumb automatically, picking and digging at the already raw skin without thinking. They kept going until I bled, and until it hurt enough to distract me from the chaos in my head.

"Milow," Ashby said quietly, his hand sliding down my arm. "Hey…"

I furrowed my brows and tried to pull my hands away from him while my fingers kept moving, scratching and worrying at the skin. I couldn't stop.

"Milow, please," he said again, his voice tighter now as he turned fully toward me. He wrapped his hands around mine and held them still so I couldn't keep picking at my skin. "Look at me."

My body locked up so hard my arms started to cramp.

My shoulders pulled in as if I was bracing for impact, and I kept staring at our hands because I couldn't lift my eyes.

"Milow, I'm right here," he murmured, leaning closer. "Breathe. Come on. Breathe with me."

I tried, but my lungs felt tight and useless. They had forgotten how to work, and my throat burned as if it was closing in on itself. My vision blurred, and I could hear him speaking, but it sounded far away.

I was crying then, and my tears dropped heavily onto our hands. The pressure inside me cracked open all at once, and I leaned forward without meaning to, my forehead pressing into Ashby's shoulder as my body gave in.

He let go of my hands to pull me against him, wrapping his arms around me tightly. One hand cradled the back of my head as if he could shield me from everything, and I buried my face into his chest, crying without making a sound. My whole body trembled while he held me close.

Mom came back when I heard Ashby call out to her. Her arms came around both of us, one hand smoothing over my hair, the other resting gently on my thigh.

"It's okay," I heard her whisper. "It's okay to feel this."

I didn't know what this even was. I felt so much at once. Grief. Shock. Guilt. Fear.

I just stayed there between them, crying silently into Ashby's shirt while Mom held us both, my body shaking as everything I had tried to hold in finally spilled out without control and understanding.

———

I woke up with strong arms wrapped around me, and for a few seconds, I kept my eyes closed, letting my mind catch up with my body. I took a slow breath and then another, and as my thoughts started to line up properly, everything from earlier came rushing back in without mercy.

Hailie.

Hailie had died.

The finality of that still didn't click in my mind, but I knew it was true.

We hadn't gone to school after all, even though I had insisted at first, even though I had told myself that doing something normal would fix it, and that sitting in class would make it easier somehow. But after I broke down like that, after my body had completely given in, there had been no arguing anymore. Maybe it had been for the best. Maybe I wouldn't have made it through the day pretending to be fine.

Ashby's hand was cupping the back of my head, his fingers spread protectively against my hair, while his other hand moved slowly up and down my back in a steady rhythm. He wasn't rushing me. He wasn't asking me anything. He was just there, keeping me warm and safe.

I finally opened my eyes, and my hands tucked against his chest was the first thing I saw. My thumb was throbbing from the pain I had inflicted earlier, and there were two bandages around it now. Ashby must've put them there. When I turned my head to look up at him, I saw he had already been watching me. His eyes were soft but alert, and I knew he hadn't really slept like I had. He gave me a small smile, not moving away even an inch. He didn't loosen his hold on me either and just stayed close.

"Hey," he said quietly. "You're okay. I've got you."

I didn't answer. I just looked at him, feeling the pain still sitting in my chest.

He brushed his fingers along my hair. "You don't have to figure anything out right now."

His other hand kept moving soothingly along my back.

"I know your head is probably running in a hundred different directions," he continued softly. "But you don't have to chase every thought. Let them pass, but stay here with me."

My throat tightened again, but this time it wasn't panic. It was relief.

"You're allowed to feel whatever you're feeling," he murmured, his nose gently brushing mine. "There's no right way to react to this."

He leaned his forehead against mine before continuing.

"I'm not going anywhere. If you need to cry, you cry. If you need to sit in silence, we sit in silence. And if you need to be mad about it, be mad. You don't have to be strong all the time, Milow."

He wasn't just trying to calm me down; he was giving me permission to fall apart without fear that he would pull away.

I swallowed, my fingers slowly curling into the fabric of his shirt, and I stayed close enough that our foreheads still touched.

I lifted my hand carefully and rested it against his jaw, my thumb brushing slowly over his skin. He leaned into it without hesitation, closing his eyes for a moment before he leaned back to get a better look at me.

"I've got you," he whispered, turning his face toward my hand to press a kiss to my palm. I was mesmerized by him and everything he was saying to me, and when he kissed me, I immediately kissed him back.

His hand slid from my back to my waist, holding me closer as my breathing steadied against his mouth. Since waking up, my thoughts hadn't felt like they were spiraling out of control.

When we finally pulled apart, I buried my face into the crook of his neck, breathing him in. His arms tightened around me instantly, one hand sliding up to cradle the back of my head again, and the other wrapping firmly around my back.

"I've got you," he whispered again, his voice low in my hair. "Always and forever, Milow."

I nodded against him, my eyes closing as I let myself sink into his warmth. The ache was still there, and so was the confusion. But wrapped up in his arms, with his heartbeat steady against my ear, it didn't feel as overwhelming.

53

Ashby

Tuesday, December 23rd

The casket was being lowered into the ground, and all of us stood there in silence, watching it descend inch by inch as if time itself had slowed down just to make us feel every second of it. The only sounds breaking through the stillness were quiet sniffles and restrained sobs somewhere around us. Snow kept falling from the gray sky, settling on the dark wood of the coffin before it disappeared from view. And even though this was a funeral, even though we were standing around an open grave, there was something painfully beautiful about it. Somehow, the snow softened everything it touched.

I still couldn't sort out how I felt about any of this. I couldn't forget what Milow had endured because of Hailie. All the years of cruelty and humiliation, and the way she had come home smaller some days. That didn't just disappear because we were standing in a cemetery.

But at the same time, watching a seventeen-year-old being buried while her mother stood a few feet away, barely holding herself upright, made my stomach twist, and I couldn't ignore it. No matter what had happened between them, this was still a life cut short.

It had taken me longer than I wanted to admit to agree to come here. Every part of me had resisted the idea at first. I didn't want to stand here and honor someone who had hurt Milow. I didn't want to pretend I had forgotten. But Milow had asked me, and when she asked for something, I always said yes. So I came. For her. Only for her.

She stood beside me now, with her hand tightly holding mine. When I looked down at her face, the pain in her eyes hadn't lessened. It wasn't just simple grief she was feeling, and it made me feel sick knowing she was carrying all of that at once.

After everything Hailie had put her through, she was still standing here.

She had forgiven her. Not today, and not because she died. She had done it a long time ago, without anyone needing to witness it.

It still amazed me how quickly she forgave people, no matter how big or small the wound was. The second someone hurt her, she processed it and somehow found a way to let it go while the rest of us were still clenching our fists. I had spent years trying to convince her that she didn't always have to do that. That it was human to hold on to anger, and that anger didn't make her cruel or weak. I wanted her to defend herself more fiercely. Wanted her to stay angry sometimes.

But over time, I had to accept that Milow would never work that way. She wasn't built to carry resentment. She felt deeply, but she never clung to hatred. There was too much love in her for that. Too much compassion that stretched even toward people who never deserved it. And standing there in the falling snow, watching the grave slowly disappear, I watched her grieve in her own quiet way.

———

Tuesday, December 30th

Christmas hadn't been the same as every other year.

How could it, when a girl in this town had tragically died?

Nobody truly knew how it had happened. There was no clear explanation or final answer that settled anything. But nobody dared to make up rumors either. In a town like this, people usually talked. They guessed. They filled in the blanks. But this time, they didn't. At least not out loud. We were all left with the unknown, wondering in silence and trying to make sense of something that shouldn't have to make sense.

Of course, we had talked about it. We couldn't avoid it.

Knowing what Milow had told us a while back, about what happened at the grocery store, Wesley was sure that Hailie's father had something to do with it. Stan, Scottie, and Jasper had come to the same conclusion without much hesitation.

They were certain that the bruises and fear in Hailie's eyes had to come from her father, and maybe the morning of her death, he had gone too far.

It was a terrifying thought, one that stirred up too many complicated memories I would rather have left buried. And in a way that made me feel guilty for even admitting it to myself: it felt easier to believe her father had done it than to consider that Hailie might have chosen to end her own life.

If it had been her father, then it meant she had been living in something darker than we ever fully knew. Something that escalated beyond control. But if it hadn't been him, then she had been dealing with something so heavy and constant that no one else could see, a pain that left her feeling trapped with no way out, no relief, and no reason to go on, and it had completely consumed her.

My stomach twisted, and I forced myself to push away the heavier thoughts for a moment, to think about something else. I felt like I needed to change something in my life, to shift the narrative before it crushed me completely. There had been a weight on my chest for a while now, something I'd been ignoring because life was already overflowing with emotions.

I couldn't ignore it any longer. I needed to face it today.

I left my room and walked the few steps to Milow's bedroom across the hall. Pushing her door open slowly, I saw her sitting at her desk, music playing quietly in the background.

I knocked softly, waiting for her to notice me. She turned her head, smiled, and set her pencil down.

"We're on Christmas break, Milow," I said with a chuckle. "Studying should be illegal."

She scrunched her nose and turned in her chair. [I was just repeating some things I had trouble getting into my head.]

"Oh yeah? And what's that? Quantum physics formulas giving you trouble?" I asked teasingly.

[No, I understand those,] she signed quickly, making me chuckle.

"Of course you do." Smiling, I walked over to her. I rested one hand on the edge of her desk and the other on her thigh, leaning down so we were face-to-face. "Can I show you something?"

Her smile softened, making me melt on the spot, and she nodded. [Of course.]

I tilted my head and kissed her lips, letting the moment linger a little longer before I pulled back reluctantly.

"Come with me," I said, straightening and holding out my hand.

She placed hers in mine and rose without hesitation, letting me lead her across the hall to my bedroom. I closed the door behind us and gestured to the bed. "Sit, please."

She lowered herself onto the bed, crossing her legs comfortably beneath her, while I moved to my desk and opened a drawer, holding my breath as I looked inside.

It was time. Time to show her something I'd kept hidden, a secret I hadn't shared with anyone because until now, it hadn't felt right. Reaching for the envelope, I pulled it out and turned toward her, watching her sitting on the bed with that sweet, patient smile of hers.

Curiosity shone in her eyes, and when I sat down next to her, she moved a little closer. She noticed the tension in me and gently rested a hand on my forearm.

I tapped my fingers against the envelope nervously. I knew she'd be happy. And I was too. I just hadn't fully allowed myself to accept that this was real yet.

"Principal Madigan gave this to me one day after the accident happened."

Calling Hailie's brutal assault on Milow an accident felt wrong, but Milow wouldn't call it anything else, so I followed her lead.

She glanced up at me for a second, then dropped her gaze back to the envelope, the gentle smile still tugging at her lips. [What is it?]

I sucked in a breath, trying to steady my racing heart. Slowly, I pulled out the letter and held it out in front of her, letting her take it in.

Her eyes scanned the letter, and when it clicked, both her hands flew to cover her mouth. Pride and excitement danced in her eyes as she stared at me.

[You got in!] she signed as a wide smile broke out on her lips.

I chuckled. "Yeah, I guess..."

I hadn't just gotten into the University of British Columbia—the university of my dreams—I had also gotten a scholarship.

[Ashby, you got in! This is so exciting!] She threw herself at me, wrapping her arms around my neck.

I grinned and held her tight, still clutching the letter in one hand. Her excitement was contagious. Every time she let herself feel this much joy, it swept over me too, squeezing my chest and making my heart beat faster just from being near her. I couldn't help but revel in it, letting myself get lost in the moment with her.

When she pulled back, she glanced at the letter again, reading over it carefully. Her smile was bright as she read it again and again, then she looked at me, and I could see the tears pooling in her eyes.

[I'm so proud of you, Ashby. You deserve this so much.]

Two months ago, I wouldn't have believed her. But things had finally quieted down, and I found myself clinging to hope, wanting life to feel better.

[Are you excited?] she asked, placing her hand on my leg again.

"I am," I said, nodding. "It's just…a little surreal. Mom and Dad don't know yet. You're the first I've told."

Her smile grew at that, but when her gaze returned to the letter, a small frown pulled at her brows. I knew she was wondering why I'd kept it from them for so long.

I slid the letter back in the envelope and placed it aside, then turned fully toward her. I tucked a strand of hair behind her ear and studied her face before saying, "So much had been going on, and I just…I didn't feel like celebrating. I'd been so focused on you, on making sure you were okay, that I didn't think about my own future. I know I made you worry more with how I acted, but back then, I felt so much pain and anger, and it was overwhelming."

Milow's expression softened, and she gently squeezed my thigh, a silent encouragement to keep going.

"I know I've done more damage than good sometimes, but I couldn't go a day without fearing someone would try to hurt you again. I thought you needed me to protect you from everything. I'm sorry for making you feel like you weren't strong enough, but now I see… God, Milow, you're stronger than anyone I know. I'm so sorry…"

She lifted her hand to my cheek when she saw the tears stinging my eyes, her thumb brushing gently over my skin as she shook her head.

[You did nothing wrong. Ever. I was scared I was going to lose you, but you caught yourself in the end. You deserve to be celebrated, even if others are hurting.]

And there she went again, using her hands to speak

words so deep and honest that no one with a voice could ever match them.

"I still have no fucking idea how I deserve to call you mine," I said, letting the tears finally roll freely down my cheeks. I was tired of holding them back.

She blushed as her hands moved again. [Things will work out for you, Ashby, and I won't ever leave your side.]

"I know," I said, smiling at her as I cupped her face in my hands. "But as long as I'm close to you, nothing else matters."

BONUS CHAPTER

Milow

In all the years I'd known Scottie, I had never seen her like this. She was completely and utterly distraught. She stood in front of me, her face streaked with tears, and her body trembling as if it could shatter at any moment.

The words she had told me just seconds ago hadn't even had time to sink in, and as her sobs wracked her frame, I found myself frozen and unable to move. My body felt numb, and my head felt light, as if it were floating. As if I wasn't entirely tied to reality.

Nothing made sense.

This had to be a nightmare.

Scottie was okay.

She had to be okay.

Another sob tore through her chest, and her knees buckled beneath her. I finally moved, catching her as she sank to the floor of her bedroom, letting her weight press against me. All I could do was hold her, keep her from collapsing completely, and try to steady myself at the same time. My lips were dry, my mouth open in silent panic, and no matter how hard I drew in air, it felt like my lungs refused to fill. All I could do was stay there, holding her trembling body and praying that somehow this was just a horrible dream.

It felt like hours before her bedroom door finally opened, and Stan came storming in, his face tight with worry and determination. Ashby was right behind him, and before I could react, Stan squeezed between Scottie and me, taking my place without hesitation. I slid back until my spine pressed against the bed frame, and Ashby's arms immediately wrapped around me, holding me close as I watched.

I stared at Scottie and Stan. Her body was shaking with sobs as he whispered words I couldn't hear clearly. He rocked her back and forth, and Scottie kept crying, her voice so broken and pleading.

"It hurts," she cried over and over again, each word making us flinch.

"You'll be okay. I'll make sure of it. I'm here. I'm here, baby," he murmured, his arms holding her tight.

I glanced up at Ashby. His expression mirrored mine, but he was doing everything he could to stay calm. His eyes met mine, and he offered a comforting smile.

"Scottie's strong," he whispered to me, squeezing me tighter against his chest. "She'll fight this."

I nodded because I wanted to believe it. Because I had to. But as I watched Scottie tremble in Stan's arms, her sobs echoing through the room, I knew this wasn't going to be an easy battle.

But one thing I knew for sure: Scottie didn't have to fight this alone.

EXCLUSIVE BONUS CHAPTER

Ashby

Wednesday, October 15th

I loved spending time with our family, but today all I wanted was to be alone with Milow. It was Thanksgiving break, and we had spent the last two days eating, playing board games, and watching movies. It felt good to relax for once. To not think about the stress of swim practice and school. Being surrounded by the people I loved helped me not to constantly think about the more important things for once.

Still, this morning I woke up and decided to take Milow on a little adventure. It wasn't anything big. Nothing that would amaze her. But I knew she'd be happy to go somewhere, and I hoped she'd enjoy being alone with me too.

In the morning, I had Wesley drive us to Horseshoe Bay, where Milow and I took the ferry to Shadowbrook. It was a small island, only a forty-five-minute ride from the mainland, and we had been there once before when we were kids. I remembered it having a nice beach and an amusement park, but the park no longer operated. All the rides were still there, but they had been rusted and untouched for years.

After looking it up online, I found a cozy diner right by the beach where Milow and I could have lunch. I just knew she would love it there.

Once we got off the ferry, we walked along the beach toward the old amusement park. When she realized where we were, Milow slowed, then stopped, looking up at me with wide eyes.

I grinned. "Remember this place?"

She nodded, then glanced around as she signed, [I do. We came here a long time ago.]

"Yeah, we did. I think we were nine or ten," I said, taking in the tall trees and the old rides farther down the path. "They had to shut it down years ago. A storm came through and destroyed half of it."

My eyes drifted back to her, and I caught her smiling at me. [It still looks beautiful.]

I smiled back. "I think so too."

I watched her as her gaze moved again, taking in everything. I slipped my hands into my jacket pockets, unsure what to do with them. Even now, after everything had settled between us, after we had made things official, I still didn't know how to act around her.

She still made me nervous in a way.

I wanted to reach for her hand. Out here, with no one around who knew us, I could hold it with no second thoughts.

I wanted to pull her closer and have her at my side, with my arm around her as we walked through the park. I wanted to walk around with her like that until our legs gave out and we had to sit somewhere, and even then, I wouldn't let go.

I wanted to kiss her until it turned messy and breathless, until she blushed and pushed me away for being too needy.

But I held it all back.

I'd leave it up to her. She was the one setting the pace, and I wasn't going to rush her. She'd decide what we did, how close we got, how far we went. And I was okay with that.

Luckily, I didn't have to just stand there and long for her.

Milow stepped closer, reaching for me before sliding her hand around my wrist. We both glanced down as her fingers moved lower. I flexed my hand, then hers curled around mine.

A grin pulled at my lips when I noticed the slight frown between her brows. "Everything okay?" I asked quietly, giving her hand a gentle squeeze.

She looked up at me and nodded, the frown easing into a soft smile.

"Good," I said, my voice quiet. "I'm glad."

Her smile grew, and when her cheeks turned pink, she buried her face into my chest.

My body reacted the way it always did when she got like this. A rush of tingles started at my toes and spread through me, all the way up to my head, leaving me a little lightheaded.

I let out a chuckle and took a slow breath, trying to steady myself. The feeling was almost too much to handle, but in the best way. I needed to get it under control before my heart decided to explode like it always threatened to when it came to her.

I lifted my free hand and cupped the back of her head, holding her there as I leaned down and pressed a kiss to her forehead. "I love you," I whispered, breathing her in. "Thank you for wanting to spend time with me."

It felt almost ridiculous to say. We had spent nearly every day together since we were kids. But that didn't make it any less important to me to say out loud. I needed her to know how much it meant to me. Her time was precious, and she could've spent it with anyone. Yet she chose me every chance she got.

Milow turned her head to look up at me, her brows pulling together as if the answer was obvious. Like there was no question why she was here with me.

Her hand slipped out of mine, and she stepped back just enough to sign. [If I could, I would spend every second with you. For eternity.]

That was all it took for my heart to finally burst. Fireworks went off again, the way they so often did, and I had to focus on my body so my knees wouldn't give out. My hands curled into fists at my sides, and before I could even come up with a response that would've been good enough for what she'd just signed, Milow reached up and cupped my face with both hands.

My eyes locked with hers, and without her signing a single thing, I knew exactly what she was thinking. She didn't need me to say anything. She already knew how I felt about her. How in love with her I was, and how much I adored her and everything she was.

She smiled softly as she brushed her thumbs over my cheeks before she leaned in and pressed one gentle kiss to my lips.

That was when I finally let myself move. I wrapped my

arms around her waist and pulled her closer until her body pressed against mine. She buried her face in the crook of my neck while her arms slid around my shoulders.

"I would spend eternity with you too, Milow," I whispered into her hair. "I love you."

She squeezed me tighter, and I drew in another deep breath, reminding myself that she was right here with me. She wasn't going anywhere, and as arrogant as it sounded, I knew that wherever she would go, she'd take me with her.

After a while, our arms loosened, but I kept my hands on her waist, and hers rested on my chest, with her fingers pinching the fabric of my sweater. I let my gaze move over her face and smiled when her lips curved into one too.

"I thought we could walk around and then get lunch. There's a diner over there," I said, tipping my chin toward the small baby-blue building by the beach.

She turned her head to look toward it, and when her eyes met mine again, she signed, [Sounds perfect.]

"Good." I leaned in and kissed her forehead, then moved my hand to take hers. "Let's explore."

———

Her hand stayed in mine as we walked through the old amusement park, and after a few hours of wandering around, we made our way back to the diner. Inside, we chose a corner booth with a clear view of the ocean.

It only took us a minute or two to decide what we wanted to eat and drink, and once the waitress came and took our order, Milow turned her head to look out the window again. The view was beautiful, but all I wanted to look at was her.

She looked relaxed and happy. It showed in every part of her face. She had always been expressive, but she had to be. Her voice had been taken from her when she was very young, and without it, she had learned to show what she felt and thought through her expressions, and mostly through her eyes.

I was still so angry about everything, and I knew that feeling wouldn't go away anytime soon. But I had to remind myself that she was safe and surrounded by people who loved and admired her.

Her cheeks flushed before her eyes met mine, and a shy smile pulled at her lips. [What?]

I grinned. "Nothing."

[You're staring at me.]

"I am."

She crinkled her nose and tried to hide her face by letting her hair fall into it. [Stop it.]

"I will," I said with a chuckle, reaching under the table to rest my hand on her thigh.

Her hand slid over mine, and without hesitating, I turned my palm and laced our fingers together before lifting our hands to my lips and pressing a kiss to the back of hers. There were so many things I wanted to say, but I had already told her a lot. She knew how I felt, and because I knew she still needed time to process everything that had happened over the weekend, I didn't want to overwhelm her.

Still, there was one thing I was too proud not to say out loud. "This is our first official date."

Her eyes searched my face as they widened, and she sucked in her cheeks, trying to hide a grin.

Her other hand lifted to the side of her head. [I know.]

"And there will be many more," I told her, hoping I could keep that promise.

We both had a lot going on, and with school starting again on Monday, we'd fall back into our usual routines.

But right here and now, none of that mattered.

Her gaze drifted back to the ocean, but only for a moment before her eyes returned to mine. This time, there was no shyness in them. Instead, there was understanding.

She pulled her hand from mine and signed, [Everything is fine. I know you're worried about a lot of things, and so am I, but we have each other, and we'll conquer everything together.]

Her silent words took my breath away once again, leaving me in awe as they so often did. "Yeah," I said quietly, gently cupping the side of her head and brushing her hair with my thumb. "We will."

———

Milow

I knew how much today meant to him.

After everything that happened over the weekend, getting away from everyone was exactly what he needed. I knew how worried he was, and how his thoughts kept drifting to the darkest places.

It had always worried me, knowing how the heavy things stayed with him for so long. They didn't fade quickly. Sometimes they didn't fade at all. Ashby wasn't the kind of person who could just accept the truth and move on with life, ignoring how it affected him or anyone around him. He was the opposite.

He cared deeply, and sometimes that made it hard for him to focus on anything else, even the things that mattered more. Deep down, he knew that about himself. And I knew that, deep in his heart, he understood that coming here would help. It would take his mind off the weight pressing against his chest, even if it was only for a couple of hours.

He'd never admit it out loud, and I didn't want to pressure him to talk about it. So I didn't mention it and instead pushed my own heavy thoughts aside to focus on us.

I had enjoyed walking through the park, taking in all the broken-down rides that had turned into sculptures over the years. Some of them I remembered riding with Ashby and Wesley when we were younger, but those were the only clear memories I had of this place.

Ashby seemed to remember more. I kept catching him smiling as he looked off into the distance, letting the memories replay in his head. Every now and then, he would tell me about them. Even if I couldn't remember things the way he did, I was still glad to see him so happy.

Lunch had been as serene as our walk through the park. Ashby spoke in a quiet, soothing voice, and I only used my hands to sign when it felt necessary. Silence had never been heavy between us. We understood each other without speaking, and one simple look was enough to let the other know what we were thinking and feeling.

After finishing our lunch and lingering in the booth for a moment longer, we decided it was time to head back home. The ferry to Horseshoe Bay departed every hour, so we made our way to the terminal just in time to catch the next one.

Once we were on board, Ashby guided me to the upper deck, where we sat on one of the benches.

"If you're cold, we can go sit inside," he said, searching my face for any sign of discomfort.

[I'm not cold,] I assured him with a smile.

"Good." He leaned back and took a deep breath, and I could tell he was starting to get nervous.

Going back home meant facing the things he had managed to leave behind for a while, and it was written all over his face that he would rather stay here on this island than face the reality of all the stress and truth that was waiting for us back home.

I waited until he looked at me before signing, [We can come back here. Whenever you need to get away from everything, we can just leave town and come here. Or go anywhere you like.]

He studied me, his brown eyes holding a mix of hope and pain. His smile didn't quite reach them, but he was trying to seem okay.

"I know," he said, drawing in another heavy breath. "But I can't hide all the time."

He was right about that. Still, I wanted him to know that it was okay to be vulnerable. [No, but you're allowed to.]

His gaze stayed on mine as he slowly nodded to agree. "You're right. As always," he said, chuckling.

He shifted closer as his hand came to rest on my thigh. I leaned into him, wrapping my arms around his and placing my head on his shoulder.

As the ferry started to move, his body tensed instantly, and I knew his mind was filling with worries and questions all over again. His breathing changed too, becoming shakier with every inhale.

I lifted my hand and placed it against his chest, feeling how fast his heart was beating beneath my palm. After a moment, I felt it slow down. He rested his cheek against my head, and without another word, he let me know that he was okay as his body relaxed.

It didn't matter where we went. With Ashby close to me, I'd always be okay.

Author's Note

If you enjoyed *Close to You*, please consider leaving a review. Support from readers like you will mean the world, and reviews will help other readers find this book.

The Through the Years series will have multiple interconnected books, with each couple getting at least two books. And the way I'll be writing/publishing the books is very focused on the timeline! So, in *Close to You*, the main part of the book starts in summer and ends in winter. Milow and Ashby's story isn't over yet, and while they had a happy ending, there is still SO MUCH I have planned for them. It was impossible to fit everything into one book, which is why some things haven't been discussed yet. Ashby's past, for example.

The series follows each couple over time, with every book focusing on a (roughly) six-month period of their relationship. Each story captures a distinct phase, so you see how they grow, struggle, and change in that window. Together, the books build a longer timeline, letting you follow the couples "through the years." All the books will overlap in timelines, and there will be familiar moments from different perspectives.

So, when you feel like there are questions unanswered, know that they will definitely be answered in a future book.

Thank you for reading *Close to You*, and for loving and understanding my characters!

I can't wait to share more stories with you.

Nissa

P.S. Scottie and Stan's book is next!

Reading Group Guide

1. *Close to You* opens with Milow at six years old sneaking cereal before her father wakes up, wiping the bowl and the chair and her own face clean so he can't find evidence. She has learned surveillance, silence, and erasure before she's learned to read. How does that first scene establish what Milow believes about herself, and what does the rest of the book spend its time quietly undoing?

2. When seven-year-old Ashby learns Milow can't speak, his first question is: "Is that a secret language? Will you teach me?" Milow realizes no one has ever asked her that. How does that one moment, a kid's completely uncomplicated curiosity, become the seed of everything that follows? And how does the book keep returning to learning someone's language as an act of love?

3. Milow's father told her that obedient girls don't speak, that her silence was magical, that her voice disappeared because she was good. She carries that belief into the foster home, watches the loud girls, and feels superior to them. When does she start to understand that her silence was stolen? Is there a moment where that shift becomes clear to you?

4. The Statler household is drawn with such a strong sense of place: books stacked sideways, mismatched rugs, cookies after dinner, Iris pulling a blanket over Milow's legs without being asked. This book's emotional center is a functional family, not a broken one. What does it mean for a novel about surviving harm to anchor itself in safety and warmth? How do Gus and Iris model something for both Milow and Ashby that neither of them could have imagined before?

5. Both Milow and Ashby survived childhoods defined by harm and powerlessness. The author keeps their shared history mostly implicit, then places Ashby's flashback to his father and the cigarette burn directly before his eighteenth birthday morning with Milow. What does that juxtaposition create for you as a reader? How does surviving the same kind of darkness shape the way these characters love each other, and where does that love go wrong?

6. Food and fullness run as a quiet thread through the whole novel: the cereal Milow eats in secret, the enormous breakfasts she's finally allowed, Ashby eating at dinner "like he hadn't eaten in years," Iris teaching

Milow that spinach shrinks because the water inside it evaporates. What does it mean that a novel about voice begins with hunger? What is being fed, beyond cereal?

7.   Hailie and Aspen spend years calling Milow "the mute" and Scottie "mentally ill." When Hailie attacks Milow, she says she's going to break her fingers because she doesn't talk, as if breaking her hands would fix it. What does the novel say about how ableism and cruelty feed each other? And when Milow flips them off with both hands just before the attack, what does that gesture cost her, and what does it mean?

8.   Scottie is Milow's most active protector: the girl who tackles a bully the day they meet, throws a pie at Hailie in the diner, and is furious on Milow's behalf in ways Milow never quite lets herself be. What does Scottie give Milow that even Ashby can't? What does their friendship look like compared to what Hailie and Aspen have?

9. After the assault, Ashby stops sleeping, loses focus at practice, and waits outside every classroom. Everyone around him names it as a problem, and he still can't stop. How does his protectiveness in these chapters echo, even faintly, the controlling behaviors Milow was rescued from as a child? Does the book hold him accountable? Does it forgive him?

10. The "I love you" Ashby writes on Milow's cast is small, almost hidden inside Scottie's flowers and hearts. The embroidered initials inside the hat lining,

the striped shirt she buys because it reminds her of his sweater: affection in this book lives in objects and in hands. Why does the author reach for the tactile so consistently? What does it say about how both of them have learned, and are still learning, to receive love directly?

11. Hailie appears in the grocery store near the end of the book with a bruised face, flinching under her father's hand. Milow waves to her. Not forgiveness exactly, but something quieter and harder to explain. The novel withholds Hailie's home life until the damage is already done. Does knowing change how you read everything that came before? What do you make of Milow choosing to wave?

12. Ashby keeps his UBC acceptance letter in a drawer for weeks, tells no one, and gives it to Milow first. The novel's final line is: "As long as I'm close to you, nothing else matters." Does that land as comfort, or does it carry a weight the book has been building and hasn't fully resolved? What kind of future is the author pointing toward, and what is she leaving open on purpose?

13. The bonus chapter ends on Scottie's collapse, her body shaking, something frightening already in motion. The book spent four hundred pages building a world where Milow and Ashby found solid ground. What does it do to close on someone else's crisis beginning? Knowing Scottie and Stan's book is next, how do you read everything about them differently in retrospect?

About the Author

Nissa Renzo is a Swiss-Italian author who writes emotional romance with complex, character-driven stories. Her books focus on intense relationships and real-life struggles.

Outside of writing, she plays soccer, swims, and loves hiking.

Instagram: @authornissarenzo
TikTok: @nissarenzo